Some of this is True

Jasmine Bourke

First published in Great Britain in 2019 by Seaview House
Publishing

Cover concept and illustration, and map, by Max Taylor.

Author photograph by Jessica Dobbs

Edited and produced by Tandem Publishing
tandem-publishing.yolasite.com

ISBN: 978-1-5272-3850-3

10 9 8 7 6 5 4 3 2 1

A CIP catalogue record for this book is available from the British
Library.

Printed and bound in Great Britain by CPI Group (UK) Ltd,
Croydon CR0 4YY

For Nicky, who doubted I'd do it.

For Angie, who believed I would and helped.

For Linie, who MADE me do it and improved it.

DENMARK
to PORTSMOUTH
Leer
Hanover
THE NETHERLANDS
the EMS
Nuremberg
to PARIS
The Danube
Rege
GERMANY
SWITZERLAND

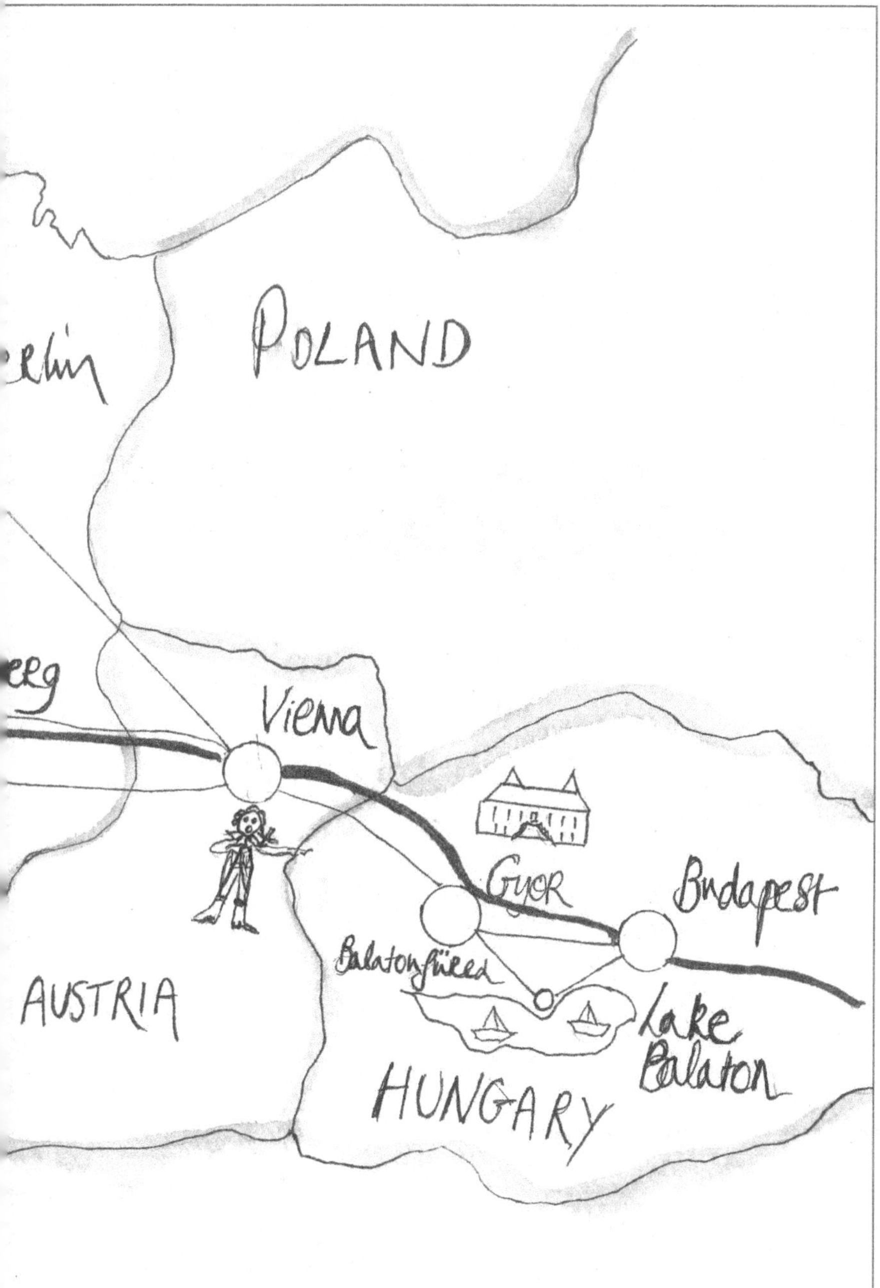

POLAND
Vienna
Gyor
Budapest
Balatonfüred
Lake Balaton
AUSTRIA
HUNGARY

1

In July 1935, the recently elected Member of Parliament for Eastbourne, in the county of Sussex, strode down Sloane Street towards his lodgings at No. 135.

The young gentleman waved cheerily to his landlady as she pottered about the deepness of her ground floor, pretending that she had not, just now, popped up from the basement at the sound of her opened front door.

"Good evening Mrs P., you look gorgeous today, as usual."

Mrs Parker, who owned the house, was not oblivious to the flattery, but replied primly: "I'm keeping well, Mr Bradley, thank you and a good evening to you I'm sure, and how is...?"

Before she could finish her sentence, or receive a reply, Mr Bradley had disappeared, two steps at a time, up to his rooms on the fourth floor.

Upon opening the door and looking around him: "Drat the man! Don't say he's gone out!" He grumbled.

"I wouldn't say as I 'ad Mr Charlie Sur," came a voice from the tiny kitchen. "And Mrs Parker wone like you raisin' your voice, nor bangin' that door neither, an neither do I," continued Albert, Mr B.'s friend and factotum, in the honeyed tones of a true "Caulkhead", a person born and bred on the Isle of Wight.

"Oh, there you are Albert."

Albert held an iron in one hand and was pulling a whiter than white shirt around an ironing board with the other. He did not look up. Vastly broad and muscular, without being tall, he had, when he wished, a palpable presence, but could with ease melt away into the scenery or the crowd. Confusingly, he had long slender fingers and dainty feet, which danced most beautifully and may partly have been the reason for his success with the ladies. And rather full lips. And oh, he was blue-eyed with blond, crisply curled hair.

Enough. Or, gentle reader, I will start to talk about the eyebrows.

"Don't be daft, Mrs P. can't possibly hear me from down there!"

"Mrs P. hears everything, she do."

"Oi think you be sweet on 'er oi do."

"Mr Charlie, oi have told you before NOT to attempt an Oisland accent. You have your qualities, but mimicry's not one of 'em.'

(At which point, gentle reader, I think you understand Albert's modus speakandi and will be relieved to hear that I shall also desist from mimicry.)

"Very well, Albert. Now you have made me lose all momentum... Where was I?"

"Drat the man! Don't say he's gone out?" Said Albert, in perfectly patrician tones.

"Did you say no mimicry?"

"None intended, Mr Charlie."

"What I was going to say was: pack the bags. We are going to Germany! We will visit cousins."

"I won't ask you why you didn't say that then. I'll just say say shall us be taking the boat?"

"Oh. Yes! No, I hadn't thought. Only I want to leave tonight."

"You can't leave tonight Mr C. You're going to drinks

at Lady Younger's, and then on to dine with Mr Aitken, which is why I'm an ironing of this shirt."

"Oh bother, Lady Younger and Aitken will understand."

"And what would Nursie say?"

"Nursie would say an accepted engagement is a tablet of stone, but Nursie is NOT here!"

"I am, and I say I say I'm shocked."*

Therefore, before we progress, a little should be told of the Hon. Member for Eastbourne, whom I have not even described, and Albert, whom I have, and might do so again if I don't keep myself firmly under control. Did I mention the tiny mole above his left eyebrow? Did I mention the eyebrows? And the clairvoyance? ENOUGH.

Mr Bradley's father, Alfred, was a man of property whose thrift was matched only by his philanthropy. His feet were firmly planted on the ground. His love and his wife was a spiritual, I almost wrote ephemeral, lady who loved literature, art and god, and god in literature and art; and whose feet barely noticed the ground, since she took off her (absurdly high) heels whenever possible. (Of course not in public, don't be silly!) Her name was Agnes. In spite of the Greenery Yallery† stuff, she managed to give birth to nine children, seven of whom survived to adulthood. Their births scarcely impinged on her consciousness, since she read Tennyson, and

---

* At this point, I fear, my clever readers, you may have formed misconceptions which I must remove. "I say I say" is an Isle of Wight expression and not be read in Bertie Wooster mode: "I say, I say, what what?" It is more of an "I ask you?" or "This is what I think" and should be read on a descending note.

1. Albert is not older than Charlie.

2. Charlie is not silly. At all. He just likes to be silly with Albert.

3. They are not lovers.

† Greenery Yallery = Grosvenor Gallery: derogative term for arts and crafts movement, people and admirers, who flocked to said gallery.

sometimes Blake or Shakespeare (only the tragedies) throughout each labour. Also Nursie was there. Agnes' husband's philanthropy manifested itself in many ways, but the idea which concerns us is this: he decided that each of his children should have a "companion" as near their own age as possible but from as different a background as possible, who would share, almost from birth, their privilege. So, in childhood, at school, at university, the companions were given every advantage. In return, the Bradley children spent time with their companion's family and discovered a world apart from their own. It is possible Agnes disapproved, but she was reading Byron at the time. Among the seven, only one failed to meet Alfred's stringent rules. The only daughter's companion, Jane, produced an out of wedlock child. Its father refused to marry her and was bought a passage to Canada with the prospect of employment. Jane, who was slightly older than Charlie, and her child, were welcomed into the family. Their story need not detain us. Albert was Charlie's companion. Albert was a success.

The Bradley family owned a house on the Isle of Wight, where they went for the summer.

A little bit about the Isle of Wight: a small lozenge-shaped island, which squats the other side of the Solent from Portsmouth and Southampton. It has a spiny ridge running across its back, like that dinosaur. Until Queen Victoria made it a popular destination (about which she was not amused) it was fairly inaccessible. Indeed the Roundheads used Carisbrooke Castle as a prison for Charles I and now there is H.M.P. Parkhurst.

However, hardy sailors have always crossed the Solent and for such people it is a veritable Paradise: tricky tides,

tricky winds and general all-round joy for those who
pride themselves on their yottie skills. It definitely moves
at a slower pace than the mainland, in fact some people
are of the opinion that it barely moves at all. If you are
born on the Island, you are a caulkhead; if not, you are
an Overner, oh, and there's never bad weather on the Isle
of Wight ... (for long). Albert was born on the Island.
He was a fisherman's son and a caulkhead. His surname
was Shieff. It should have been Schieff, but people on the
Isle of Wight like things simple: "Wot fore you need that
extra C in there, yous already got a sh sound innat?"

His grandfather, a German sailor, had been wrecked
on Bembridge Ledge, and his grandmother's father
(himself something of a wrecker) had "rescued" the
half-drowned young man (and his cargo). Will Holbrook
was not a soft-hearted man, but Albrecht was the only
man left alive, and so he piled him into his boat (along
with the more valuable bits and pieces) and once ashore
took him (with the good stuff) back to St Helens in the
donkey cart. His motherless daughter Jenny sponged
and smoothed the sick boy's brow, and soon she was the
one being smoothed, or rather rumpled. Albrecht never
returned to his country, but kept in touch with his family
and taught his children to read and write German. Little
Georg became big George, and a boatman like his father,
and when he drowned in 1912 – Isle of Wight boatmen
don't swim – his widow found employment as a seam-
stress with Mrs Bradley. Net mending is an excellent
training for fine needlework.

Her son, Albert, was to be companion to Charlie.
"Please God, the last – dear Anna." Mrs Bradley was
beginning to notice, after eight, that births were a little
difficult, also the older ones seemed almost her age.

Charlie was the ninth and last as it transpired, but as such was not to be spoiled. Therefore climbing for gull's eggs, sailing in all weathers (with Albert's uncles) and generally getting wet and muddy and escaping Nursie's attentions, was allowed and more or less approved.

Aah, how to describe Nursie. Nursie was a lady in every sense of the word. Nursie had nursied all nine Bradley children, and wept with Agnes over the poor dead ones. She was the steely backbone to Mrs Bradley's fey charm. Each child and each companion learned young: "Toujours la politesse," for of course Nursie spoke French (and German, and some Italian and Spanish). She was that particular person, the beautifully brought-up and well-educated daughter of an impecunious vicar, who loved his wife too well but not wisely, and found, like the lady in the shoe, ends couldn't meet.

So Molly became a Norland Nurse with silk evening uniforms and starched ones for daytime. She had helped shape each Bradley child and companion, which is why, dear reader, Albert has an irritating habit of quoting her maxims. These may be summed up: if you are polite, everything else will fall into place. Always scrupulously fair, it was noticed that Nursie had a certain tendresse for Albert, but then so did a number of females.

The time came for Charlie to go up to Cambridge. Albert, whose marks were rather better than his companion's, would not go. Alfred was incandescent. Albert was obdurate. Albert wanted to work on boats. Albert became a boatman. Charlie had, while still at school, decided to become a Member of Parliament. A decision heartily endorsed by his father: "You, who have received so much, owe a duty to your country, but not until you have a proper job." Agnes merely hummed the finale of

6

Iolanthe, whereupon Charlie banged out the tune on the baby grand singing "every every everyone is now a fairy" which quite ruined his father's solemn pronouncement.

Three years later, with a modest degree and articled to a firm of solicitors, while Albert was working fishing boats near Stavanger, Charlie set about finding the safest (Conservative) seat he could. Please remember, dear reader, the other main Party at this time were the Liberals. The Labour Party was a cheeky adolescent. Alfred Bradley might well have voted for them, but:

"They can't see further than their snouts. We need people who understand the world beyond us." Charlie was greatly helped by Lord Beaverbrook, the father of a friend of his at university, who owned a popular newspaper, and knew a great deal of people. (He also knew a great deal about those people, probably more than they realised.) Alfred, like many fathers, disagreed often with his son and used Charlie as a red rag to a bull, all the while extending hospitality and bonhomie. Charlie managed to remain friends with both:

"Have you seen that reprobate son of mine?"

"Yes Sir, we dined at Buck's, he's on excellent form."

"Hmm."

"Don't mean to tell me you've been toadying to my father?"

"Ribbet ribbet. I toad with the best of them. Anyway I like your father."

"Hmm."

First pointed in the direction of Basingstoke, our hero blanched at the contribution to constituency expenses of

£1,000 a year,* a huge sum for an unpaid articled clerk, who could only expect £400 towards expenses if elected.

Therefore Charlie moved on to the next available seat, about which a fellow articled clerk, whose Mama lived in Eastbourne, passed on the gossip that the previous day the Member for that town had dropped dead in the middle of a banquet. Pausing only to adjust his tie, Charles, as we shall now call him, leapt into his fiery steed (a battered 1925 Bentley) and sped south.

Arrived in Eastbourne, he sought out a Cambridge friend, who knew the daughter of – we need go no further. It suffices to say that chosen from a shortlist of three Mr Bradley was elected Member unopposed, having fielded questions about the India Bill (he was anti), and what class honours degree he had received at Cambridge. He had a Third, but managed to pull the rabbit out of the hat and say: "The same as our great leader Mr Stanley Baldwin!" (Cheers from the hall and some laughter from those in the know…) After those, questions about Canadian versus Russian timber were a doddle. The people who had daily congress with him were greatly relieved, as his usual good humour was restored. To Mr Bradley's relief he was only required to contribute £150 a year to local constituency expenses and so he took the wrong advice on what to wear and his seat on April 1st 1935.

He wore, dear reader, a short black jacket and striped trousers. Not at all the thing. His sponsors were elegant in morning coats and so should he have been. He had asked Sir Alwyn Dickinson, an ex-chairman of the Eastbourne Conservative Party, for his opinion, something which he was good at giving and he had responded

---

* Dear reader, believe and wonder.

with such authority that Charlie hadn't thought to check with anyone else. (Your author suspects that also he was unwilling to show his ignorance to some of his friends...)

But the morning newspapers decided that he was the herald of a new era, in which a Conservative Member could be introduced to the House of Commons not wearing formal dress. It gave him much publicity, not all of it welcome.

On April 2nd, Albert arrived at 135 Sloane Street, conducted heavenwards by a cross Mrs Parker, and announced to his erstwhile companion, as he opened the door: "You'll need looking after I say I say so I've come."

"You only came because you heard about *Blue Dancer*."

"Now which dancer'll that be Mr Charlie?"

"Bah! Smutty man! Second door on your left. Bathroom to the right. Then we'll dine, and see what's what."

"Very good Mr Charlie."

"If you're going to be like that, I shall take a very silly novel and a bottle of gin to my room."

"I don't think Nursie..."

"No, she probably wouldn't – I see – you've been sent here by Mother and Nursie to spy on me!"

Now this was partly true, although Albert had not been sent exactly. Those two formidable ladies had paid him a call to deliver the news (about which he knew already, natch), and had been enthusiastic about his idea of travelling to London. In passing, *Blue Dancer* had also been discussed.

Thus Albert drew himself up to his five foot seven and a bit inches, and raising his eyebrows,* "Oh so I'm a spy am I?" he made to pick up his suitcase.

"Silly arse, I don't even mind if you do – save me writing

---

* Oh bliss.

letters or picking up the telephone," which began to ring on cue.

"Go and settle in and…"

But Albert had picked up the machine. "Mr Bradley's residence," he intoned and then handing over the receiver: "Lord Beaverbrook for you Sir."

"My! Charlie you have become all smart suddenly – why didnya tell me you were a new age hero? I could use scoops like that – we could've had a photo even."

Mr Bradley had no chance to explain.

"Come and have breakfast tomorrow at eight – if your man can get you up in time harhar."

The line went dead.

Three months on and the relationship remained a contented one. Both parties did as they were told and some things were private. Albert appeared to be Mr Bradley's valet and few people looked beyond that, which entirely suited both gentlemen. Mr Bradley was courted by most of the grand hostesses in London. Albert, when not being a gentleman's gentleman, played with *Blue Dancer*, the yacht which had been one of his reasons for leaving the Isle of Wight. "Stuck in a rut, you were, and now we can sail the world or at any rate Europe" he told himself, spinning the tiller with glee as the boat lived up to her name. He didn't regret missing university; he hadn't wanted to be shoe-horned any longer. Now he felt able to take up the lines which he knew bound him to his friend on his own terms. Plus, there was also the small matter of Lucy, down in Seaview, who could hear the sort of bells ringing that Albert only heard, in the morning, after an enjoyably long night out, and often not even then, as he mostly did without hangovers.

I should now describe Mr Bradley. This is extremely difficult: he was not at all like Albert and we don't have to worry about eyebrows. Tallish, with a thatch of blue-black hair; his eyes seemed to change from green or grey to yellow like the sea. A Roman sort of nose and prominent cheekbones complete the picture. His charm was that his attention, once given, was given so completely that the recipient knew themself instantly to be the most interesting person in the room, or possibly the world. This happened with cooks or countesses, barons or barrow boys. His smile warmed like the sun or a toasty fire, but he had an evil temper, which he kept under check. Thanks be to Nursie. (Agnes was Irish with red hair and she had a father who had a rage in him, luckily that temper had skipped a generation and she knew how to defuse it.) And Mr Bradley's rage found an outlet in ambitions and enthusiasms (particularly sailing) that needed to be implemented immediately – which is why he bounded about a bit – and up stairs.

[Dear reader, this has been a long chapter. Forgive me, I couldn't stop my explanations. Those following will be shorter.]

2

Needless to say, Albert (not to mention Nursie) saw to it that Mr B. fulfilled his social obligations.

Satisfied that the boat would be ready in Portsmouth in two days' time and that Albert's nephew* would take charge of the car (a slightly less battered Bentley), Charles was at his most ebullient when he arrived at Lady Younger's party.

Lady Younger's flat in Mount Street should have been an oasis of calm, decorated as it was in shades of white reflected in countless mirrors, but this evening it was thronged with brightly dressed people all intent upon enjoying themselves at the top of their voices. Ebullience was definitely required.

"Charles dear!" said Lady Younger, "We were waiting for you."

"Surely not?" Charles dear suggested, eyeing the assembled company.

"But of course!"

Lady Younger, a woman of a certain age, shone with a diamond brilliance, which younger women tried to emulate and her contemporaries tolerated as her brittle exterior concealed a loving heart. Mr B. followed her peacock-feather-printed frock and her feather be-feathered curls to be introduced to a number of almost as elegant people. After a while of smiling and nodding

---

* Albert had a number of useful nephews. And cousins.

to his hostess' introductions our hero* found his way to where he wanted to be.

"H'haargh." It is impossible to replicate the belched greeting of Lord Beaverbrook. It emerged through a blast of cigar smoke and a simultaneous cough.

"Bradley. Glad to see ya. Sort've boring party no? Yes?"

"Not with you here Sir."

"Ghaad, you are a personable barstaaard."

"If you say so Sir, but my mother –"

"Your mother is adorable and gorgeous."

"And doesn't lie, at least about big things."

"Well, you're only a little thing so you don't count," said the Beaver staring down at his prey. "But hey, I'll revise that: not personable and definitely not a barstaard. Dining with the midget later?" Lord Beaverbrook's son was almost as tall as his father but very slim.

"Sir, Max may lack your stature, which is good for you, but he also lacks your girth, which is good for him."

As Lord B. exploded into his drink, a gravelly voice came from behind him. "Girth? Did I hear girth? Do you know, Charles, how he keeps modesty intact when in his swimming trunks?"

"No, Lady Younger."

"Who is Modesty? And what is she doing in my trunks?" The Beaver strained to achieve a loftier height while attempting to control said girth.

"Be quiet, Beaverbrook! He hitches them to his wart!" Charlie had reason to believe Lady Younger to be rather more than friendly with the Beaver, which accounted for her intimate knowledge. Although he had heard the wart story before.

He tried not to look, but was mesmerised as his

* The time has come to recognise him as such.

13

lordship's tummy first fell alarmingly but then rose magnificently to its customary position either side of his waistband and more or less between his beautifully paisley-ed braces.

"Well done my dear, I'm sure you could join the circus as a strongman. Meanwhile I should attend to my other guests before they find this party TOO boring! If you find it so you could always leave."

Smiling seraphically, Lady Younger wandered away.

Lord Beaverbrook gave another snortbelchcough. "Dreadful woman" he scowl-smiled "but a good friend. Tell the boy to come and see me. And I hear you're going to Germany?"

"Yes Sir."

Mr Bradley wondered how he knew but refused to inquire.

"Waarl, keep your eyes open. Don't send me anything – write me stuff and bring it back. Don't trust their postal service. And don't trust them. You wonder why I know about your summer trip? You didn't aaask so I'll tell you. Winston told me, and if you're keeping your eyes open for him, you can do so for me."

"I don't see why the commissions should exclude each other, Lord B." said Charlie with aplomb, and with a smile and a wave he was on his way. His progress was impeded, however, by a young lady whose cap of auburn curls glittered and snapped in the mirrors as though it were alive. The emeralds at her throat and on her ears behaved rather better. Miss Amy Tarrant spoke directly:

"Mr Bradley! I want to play on your boat this summer. Will you be at Cowes?"

"Good evening, Miss Tarrant, how well you look! But I'm not sure about Cowes, I'm off tomorrow on an extended trip to Germany, and I may not be back in time…" Charlie was hoping to nip any further plans in the bud but…

"Excellent! I should adore to visit Germany, when do you leave? I shall come too!"

"No no Miss Tarrant – not at all suitable – no room – no other females only chauffeur," babbled our hero.

"What do I care for what's suitable?" Amy lit a small cigar and inhaled mightily. For once at a loss, Charlie had opened his mouth in the hope that something useful might emerge, when fortunately Lady Younger swanned by. She gathered her most recently arrived guest by the arm and took her away.

"Amy dear, just the person I needed! Don't let yourself be bored by Mr Bradley. He's just leaving, and the people over here are much more fun!"

Unseen by Miss Tarrant, she tossed a wink in Mr Bradley's direction and with a motion of her hand shooed him away.

Breathing several sighs of relief, and savouring the shimmer of summer sky in the Serpentine, our hero walked across Hyde Park to Max Aitken's small house in Trevor Place. As he walked he wondered at the jungle drums that seemed to operate all about him. Everyone, and not just Albert, seemed to know more about his business than he did: telephones! A devilish invention. Of course, Albert had no truck with them, he could find out whatever he needed to know if he chose.

Charlie's mother, the seventh daughter of a seventh daughter, was another matter. Nonsense of course, but how many years now had they won on Derby Day and the Grand National? A good many. Dating back to when they were eight or nine and Albert had placed the bets via one of his uncles. Even he deferred to Mrs Bradley's choice.

As for Mr Churchill and his lordship, they were thick as thieves. A pair of magpies finding a use for any bright object their beady eyes discovered. Charlie had no objection to being such an object: Mr Churchill was our hero's hero, and the Beaver a slightly decadent alternative to his own altruistic, sensible Papa.

It had been both pleasant and highly gratifying to be invited to Chartwell the weekend before. The only reason he could find for his so being singled out was his continued support for Winston by voting against the India Bill, as it ground its way through Parliament. Part of Charlie's charm, dear reader, was that he was unaware of it.

(N.B. The India Bill, initiated by Ramsay MacDonald in 1929, was finally passed in April 1935, with India gaining independence in 1947.)

What a weekend for an aspiring politician of only twenty-five years! To see Mr Churchill in large sombrero and swimming trunks, moving like a "stately Spanish galleon" towards the pool; to be offered ripe peaches from trees espaliered on the famous wall (built by W. C. during his "wilderness years"), shlurped then and there, chins running with juice; to play tennis with the Misses Churchill, and throughout to enjoy Clementine's legendary hospitality: Charlie shook his head to return to normality as he mounted the steps of No. 26.

Led upstairs by his friend's gentleman ("Dreadful man! Sent to spy on me by my father" Max hissed), once said gentleman was out of sight, Charlie enjoyed a comfortable all-male supper. He remembered to convey Lord Beaverbrook's "invitation" which was not well received.

Otherwise, a veil can sensibly be drawn over the evening, except for a reply from Max, who had been in Germany in 1934, to Charlie, who had asked about Adolf Hitler.

"Hitler represents the young people in Germany. He is leading them against the old stuffy regime of Hindenburg* and co. Most Germans want to see change, and they think this is the man to produce it for them. I imagine if you and I, Charlie, were Germans we might support Hitler."

---

* Field Marshal von Hindenburg, elderly president of the Weimar Republic 1925–1934, was a staunch monarchist, but he nevertheless appointed Hitler Chancellor in 1933.

3

We will not inquire how Mr Bradley returned to his rooms in Sloane Street early the following morning. (I expect he found a cab, or the cab found him.) The fact is: he managed somehow.

It will be enough to say that when Albert entered and opened the curtains, letting in shiny daggers of July sunshine, he was greeted by a groan and an under-pillowed head.

"I'll be driving then, Mr Charlie?" inquired Albert, allowing himself a distinct smirk.

"Anything! Anything you say, only please close those curtains!"

Albert exited leaving the curtains open, "From someone who wanted to leave yesterday! It's nearly ten o'clock."

Albert returned bearing a cup of Lapsang Souchong which only palely coloured the inside of a hand-painted Royal Copenhagen teacup. He set it beside the bed upon its hand-painted saucer. In his other hand he held a small glass of turgid-looking liquid, a brew of his own devising. Imagine the nastiest medicine you were ever given as a child: well, it tasted like that. Imagine the "medicine" Captain Hook made for Peter Pan: well, it looked like that. It changed colour slightly, and glinted malevolently as Albert swirled it about, lifting the glass to the light with a satisfied air. A steamy miasma, as from a New Orleans bayou, rose from the liquid's surface.

"Aagh, all ready now I say I say Mr Charlie, drink it up or it'll not work proper."

"There's nothing proper about that pong. You're trying to poison me again. And it's only 9.35" said a muffled voice.*

"9.35's nearer to ten than nine they do say, and I say I say you do need to feel better."

Very slowly, tightly closed eyes and even more firmly shut lips emerged as the pillow was pushed aside. A naked torso and naked arms appeared, and pushed our hero into a semi-seated position.

"Couldn't find our pyjamas then" said Albert in a neutral sort of way. The eyes opposite flashed open. They resembled the colour of the contents of the glass, but without the steam. They also felt like the bottom of a budgie's cage.

"I chose not to wear pyjamas last night and before you mention the N word… She, who has more compassion in her little finger than you have in your entire be-muscled body, would be proud that I found my bed, never mind pyjamas – now get thee gone and stay not upon the order of your going! You'd've done well administering to compulsory suicides in Rome."

Albert withdrew with dignity to the sound of his friend quoting:

Finger of birth-strangled babe
Ditch-delivered by a drab…"†

---

* Did I say what Albert's pick-me-up SMELT like? Have you ever been near a glue factory? No? Lucky you. Just think of one of those smells which gets inside your nose and remains there for weeks.

† Macbeth, Act IV Scene I.

The excellent delivery was ruined by a series of groans between each line.

The Bentley's boot remained not quite shut, in spite of three different dispositions for the bags (previously packed by Albert). So it was that our gents motored out of London shortly before eleven.

Mr Bradley fell asleep before they reached Battersea. Albert began to sing German lieder rather loudly. He interspersed these with Neapolitan love songs, which he sang rather better. Were you, dear reader, to inquire whether he was trying to drown the snores of his companion, I would reply that Albert had a fine tenor singing voice, and was enjoying the glorious weather.*

The sun shone in Portsmouth, where they were met by young Albert, Albert's Uncle Will's boy. He watched, with small envy, as his cousin and his boss readied the *Blue Dancer*, waved goodbye, and then with huge satisfaction sank into the Bentley's driving seat. Savouring the leathery smell, he purred away with the wonderful toy, his for several weeks. He was not fond of the sea.

Meanwhile, on the yacht, Mr Bradley took charge. He soared and plunged out of Portsmouth harbour like a gull after the first mackerel of the season, and hit the wind as though to cut right through it.† Albert contented

---

* I am also biased. Pay attention.

† Dear readers, who are not English, unless you are reading, please god, in translation, this is an excellent sentence to analyse. You might try and find how many are the silly spellings of my mother tongue. For anyone else it is perfectly possible to have a glorious day AND strong winds in the Solent.

himself with a tightening of the ropes, accompanied by the occasional cough.*

After an hour or so there came a croak:

"Coffee Albert."

At the helm's hand stood Albert with steaming coffee laced with a little bracing something.

"Take it down, Mr Charlie, let it go a bit, we ain't in any hurry, is we?"

Charlie gulped gratefully.

"Damned sight better than the rotgut you dealt me this morning! But thank you for both. In fact, thank you for everything: you are egg-like in your goodness."

"Salt of the earth," murmured Albert.

"So good with eggs," and they exchanged Cheshire cat smiles.

"I'll take the helm then shall I?"

"Not just yet, I've a few more cobwebs, not to mention the spiders inside them, to blow away. Give me another hour or so, and you shall have her and I'll have a zizz, but I'll be jealous as hell, so behave yourself with my darling!"

"No regrets then?"

Mr B. had somewhat overextended himself with the purchase of *Blue Dancer*. Members of Parliament in 1935 received a salary of £400 a year, with a small contribution to expenses (Miss Blamey, who typed and answered a telephone – sometimes. Travel: petrol or rail fares – 1st Class).† Mr B.'s father, however, was quite pleased with his youngest, and reckoned he needed to get

---

* Another one for people who are learning English, please also try Slough, Chough, Hiccough, and Rough (please ladies, not you).

† Please don't laugh in a negative way, dear dear reader, such WAS the case.

out and about, away from the stews of London and so had helped him towards the *Blue Dancer*.

He had lied to Miss Tarrant about Cowes Week. He fully intended to be there and win as many races as he could, not only for the glory. He had made an arrangement with the shipbuilder, whose boats might just sell better after one of them had won a good race or two. He didn't need anyone coming to play on board, least of all bossy Miss Tarrant.*

"Pah! What's money? She flies like an angel!"

"If she's an angel, I'll have no difficulty behaving then will I?"

"Go to your bunk man, and leave me with my one true love!"

"Oooh, never let Miss Tarrant (how does he do it thought Mr B.) hear you say that I say I say she'd be ever so cross."

"I shan't ask how you know I'm being pursued. I shall just say – Lucy."

"You are a cruel man."

"Lucy, Lucy, Lucy, bed Albert."

"Now you've put me in mind of 'ER, how'm I to get any sleep I say?"

"I say: I can't help your filthy mind, but am I to get any peace? I say."

Thus, bickering and grinning, the *Blue Dancer* took the pair across the North Sea to Germany where at Leer, at the mouth of the Ems, they were met by Albrecht, a cousinly contemporary of our Albert.

Great grandpapa might never have returned, but there

---

* We shall see, however, dear patient reader person, how his race plots will fail in the face of several INFINITELY bossier women.

had been a constant to-ing and fro-ing between German Schieffs, who were mostly sailors, and Isle of Wight Shieffs, who mostly weren't.

Except for Albert.

Dear reader, I hear you ask: how this meeting was affected? Well, there were telephones, the swift mail packet and, had you been paying attention, you will remember Albert's clairvoyance. Yer pays yer money, and yer takes yer choice.

While I have been attending to the minor problems of my readers, Albert and Albrecht have been heartily wringing hands and talking vast quantities of German. Mr B. did not speak this language (in spite of Nursie's efforts) so he lit a Players, and tidied his *Dancer*, lovingly coiling ropes and checking fenders, hatches and portholes, smoothing sails and cushions and generally wishing his boat a well deserved rest. All totally pointless as he and Albert had already ship-shaped her half an hour before.

Family news and boat details exchanged, Albrecht led the way to a brightly noisy bar.* Owned, natch, by another cousin, all the beer, schnapps, and excellent Wiener Schnitzel were on the house, and I regret to say that Mr B. enjoyed himself hugely. So much so that he was heard to say:

"Come on you two girls – back to the boat with me!"

Fortunately Albert was the one to hear him say it. Apart from the (solitary) lady in question (another cousin).

Once mumbled outside past the merry throng, and before Albert could even deliver a 'Nursie' homily, a

---

* No, I didn't say raucous, and I didn't say gay either (although it was in the proper sense of the word). I said brightly noisy – do pay attention.

transformation took place. Our hero stood straight, cricked his neck about (a nasty habit, worse than cracking knuckles!), pushed his hair back and,

"Phew! A lucky escape! She would've eaten me for breakfast."

"My gently nurtured cousin?!"

"Gently nurtured, my giddy aunt!* She did something to me under the table with her foot that made my eyes pop."

"You don't know how lucky you are – she doesn't do that to all the boys…"

"You Shieffs are disgraceful, all you think about is sex."

"Cousin Ilsa is a sweet innocent young Thing."

"Really? If she's sweet and innocent, never mind my giddy aunt, I'm my maiden aunt!"†

"Never let it be said that you are a maiden anything Mr Charlie."

"Not even a maiden over?"

"Bed, I think. My cousin's house is just round the corner."

"What? The Good Lord save me from all Shieffs. I think I'll sleep aboard."

"She's an elderly lady, Mr Charlie."

"So I'll be safe, I say I say?"

And so, as Mr Pepys might say, our friends to bed.

---

* Most unfair as none of Mr B.'s aunts was in the least bit giddy: their idea of an excitement was to have the vicar to tea. Oh. And there was Joan who went to live with a sheikh in a tent, but that's another story.

† What is it with Mr B. and his aunts? But I do have to say that his Aunt Joyce WAS a most proper person: she wouldn't even have the vicar to tea in case he made advances. She was beautiful as well as proper, so maybe she was right.

4

A most delicious smell of coffee, warm bread and sausage awoke our hero from deeply duveted comfort.* Pushing back Hansel and Gretel shutters, he smiled: it was a glorious day! The open road beckoned, but first he padded, nose twitching, down the stairs in slippers (velvet; embroidered with small chough – his crest) and dressing gown (silk, paisley, a present from his Mama).

Albert, fully dressed, which he either was or wasn't, not choosing to wear clothes in bed, and Ursula, who wore her steel-grey hair in old-fashioned braids high upon her head, were seated at the large kitchen table. They were sorting the problems of the world, or possibly talking about gardening, or boats, or family, or telling each other jokes: who could tell? Mr Bradley certainly couldn't, but on his greeting they turned and spoke in English.

"Good morning, dear Albert's friend." Ursula beamed, "Some breakfast? What would you like?"

"Everything please, Mrs Berger. It smells delicious and after such a comfortable night, I am SO hungry!"

"Ursula, Ursula, please!"

Albert, who was nursing† a small cup of treacly coffee, raised his eyes heavenwards: "When you've finished

---

* You must remember, dear reader, such quilts were NOT in use in England at that time. Slippery linen was the order of the day – which I for one infinitely prefer.

† No, he is not fixated. My choice of word not his. OK, holding, cupping his hands around? No, nursing, so there. Grrrr dear, or not so dear, reader!

eating my cousin out of house and home, you might care to look outside."

Deliberately obtuse: "I have! Sun and blue skies and perfect."

"And the open road."

"And the open road."

"On foot?"

"Well why not? I'm sure we'll manage to hitch a lift." Determined not to rise, Mr B. munched his way through several platefuls, much to Ursula's delight.

"And now, dear Mrs Berger, I mean Cousin Ursula, might I have a bath?"

Albert frowned, and hastened to diffuse the situation.

"It's late and we should be away."

"We're on holiday."

"I'll bring you up some hot water."

"Yes, yes," said Ursula, slightly pink and fussing with saucepans at the stove – "hot water."

"Ursula's bath is here in the kitchen and you may NOT use it," hissed Albert in Mr B.'s ear, and then more loudly "While the water's heating FOR YOUR SHAVE, you might like to take a stroll outside."

"Whoops" said Mr B. "Sorry, you might've warned me though."

Outside he went, knowing more or less what he might find. Pausing to puff on a Players, he examined the shiny red monster parked in front of him. He looked at the dashboard, he checked the drop-head roof, kicked the tires and looked inside the bonnet.

"And you open it up, and in spring: it's a mass of daffodils" he said to no one in particular.

Albert, who had followed him outside, only just resisted

the temptation to throw the jug of hot water over his friend. Mr B. smiled seraphically:

"It's not a Bentley, but I suppose it will do."

He watched as Albert's ears grew quite pink, and noted the hot water threat.

"Of course it's not a Bentley, IDIOT – it's a Mercedes. We are now in GERMANY, in case you'd forgotten."

At this, Mr B. burst with laughter.

"I'd better take that" he said, swiftly relieving Albert of the jug.

"You're the idiot, of course it's perfect, but I couldn't let it go to your head, could I? Well done that cousin." Adding as he went off to his ablutions, "except it'll guzzle petrol." Which rather ruined the compliment.

Cleaner, and carefree, Charlie and Albert, enthusiastic farewells once said to Cousin Ursula, meandered further and further from the coast, enjoying the sun, the countryside, and the beer in the village kneipes. The car purred and our companions wound each other up in the warm sun. Cowes Week came and went as they found hills to walk in, birds to look at, and fish to catch (courtesy of a Schieff cousin). They also found dirndl girls to dance with, and even attended a concert where audience and orchestra were afloat. Albert forbore to join in, with some difficulty.

Mostly, they avoided towns, and certainly skirted big cities, until reading an English newspaper, bought at one of their (many) refuelling stops for the car and its occupants, Mr B. announced:

"Think we'll go to Nuremberg."

"Very good Sir" said Albert in his poshest tones.

"No – look here –"

"Can't Sir, seeing as I'm driving."

"Hmph, very droll – well, the Nazi Party is holding a rally there, and I think we should take a look."

"Then I think so too Mr Charlie, there's a few things in my head which need sorting."

"If you're going to be gnomic, I shall drive."

"Thass not fair, you know I can't help my head." (Pay attention dear readers, Albert is clairvoyant!)

"You can't help that ugly mug of yours either, so let's get to Nuremberg, before we're stopped on the way for infringing the beauty code."

The harvest was under way: on every side farms and fields seemed fat and fruitful, smiling children waved as the Mercedes motored past.

"Those children are very clean Albert."

"They do look well scrubbed."

"Too clean Albert." And later "it all seems a bit too clean, don't you think? Unnaturally so."

"Too good to be true?"

"Hmmm."

5

Our friends proceeded to the Grand Hotel, which a friend of a cousin of Albert's had assured him was the best in the city.

There they were greeted with consternation:

"Two rooms? With bathrooms?"

The concierge's voice rose to a squeak of irritation.

"The hotel is fully booked for members of the Party and their official guests."

"Oh dear" said Mr Bradley, opening his eyes wide and fixing them upon the uniformed person in front of him.

"We were so looking forward to staying in your elegant establishment, and seeing some of the celebrations. Perhaps you would consult your manager. Tell him that an English Member of Parliament would be most grateful if accommodation could be found for him and his chauffeur."

Albert, who always wore uniform on these occasions, remained mutely in the background. He held his peaked cap at an appropriate angle, and did not display his linguistic skills.

In a little while, someone in a Nazi uniform came to find the English people. He saluted, and wondered if they would allow him to escort them to their rooms. The concierge raised his eyes to heaven but managed to lower his voice for the next person requiring his services.

Mr Bradley professed himself to be extremely satisfied with his rooms, particularly the bathroom which, leaving the two uniforms to find Albert's accommodation, he prepared to enjoy to the utmost.

Twenty minutes later, having exhausted both his repertoire of songs and the hotel's generous supply of unguents, our hero sat, wrapped in a towelling robe smoking a contemplative cigarette, when there came a knock at the door. A different, diffident, Nazi officer stood without and, clicking his heels:

"May I present Prince von Hessen's compliments and would you care to join him in the bar at six o'clock for a glass of German wine?"

"That's very civil of His Highness, please thank him, and I should be delighted." Though surprised, Mr B. remembered his manners.

He was further surprised when, as he dressed, a written invitation to dinner later that evening arrived from a Herr von Ribbentrop. "Well, well, what a popular bunny I have become" thought Mr B., as he changed into white tie, praising Albert for his prescient packing. "I wonder if they think I'm a B.U.F. man?[*] At least I shall have things to tell Mr C. and the Beaver," and he wrote a brief note of acceptance for the redoubtable concierge to dispatch.

Joachim von Ribbentrop had a penchant for the British aristocracy and was later made Ambassador to England at the end of 1936. A job he was spectacularly bad at. He was a former champagne salesman, who had joined the Party in 1932. He had Hitler's ear and became Commissioner for Disarmament in 1934 and concluded the Anglo-German Naval Agreement in 1935, enabling Germany to construct a navy of 35 per cent that of Britain's and a submarine fleet the same size. Charlie had

---

[*] British Union of Fascists.

heard him described as "Vain, arrogant and pompous." This would be a very interesting evening indeed.

Just before he left for the bar, Albert appeared.

"Well you're obviously engaged for the evening" he opined looking his friend up and down, "I shall just have to tuck myself up in bed with a good book."

"Not a silly novel?"

"NOT a silly novel and I say I say I'll not be waking the young master too early tomorrow then. Bonne nuit. Sois sage."

"No. You be good, I'll be careful."

"Better 'ad be" said Albert and was gone.

The party in the bar was a male-only affair, and most of the company was in uniform, except for the Prince, who it seemed was invited to the same dinner as our hero, for he too was in white tie.

The German wine was surprisingly light and dry and very delicious. Mr Bradley complimented his host on its excellence.

"Aagh, we prefer to drink our home wine! Of course, the Führer does not drink alcohol, and finds this habit of American 'cocktails' particularly barbarous, and bad for the brain do you say?"

Charlie, who was slightly yearning for a large dry martini, or a huge gin and tonic, murmured:

"Barbaric and degenerate?" And was rewarded with a hearty clap on the back, which nearly lost him the drink he did have.

"That is it! Just so. Mr Bradley do you read German?"

Before that person could zip his lip, out popped:

"Yes, but I do not understand a word of it."

"Oh dear, silly me," he thought as a thunderous look crossed the Prince's face: it was truly spectacular. The ruddy bull-necked visage greyed almost to black, then white, at last regaining its hearty pink.

"Ha ha ha" said the Prince (and this time Mr B. was ready for the celebratory slap).

"An English joke I think! Ahaha! Come and see a compatriot of yours: another member of your Parliament, and meet a member of our Bundestag."

Mr Bradley realised as he was being guided across the room, that there was present a very militant member of the B.U.F. Fortunately he managed to avoid shaking its hand by making a small bow (he didn't click his heels). Unfortunately, the Prince seemed to think this a mark of respect, rather than the distanced hauteur our friend had meant to convey. To complete the effect, his compatriot replied with "Bradley old chap! Good to see you here – Excellent stuff." Before any further contact occurred, however, old chap Bradley managed to move away and enquire of the Bundestag person, who was also wearing white tie:

"Charles Bradley, Sir, are you perhaps going to Herr von Ribbentrop's party?"

"Johannes Uber, no, I am invited elsewhere. I think all over Nuremberg there are parties tonight! Is not so? But von Ribbentrop has an excellent chef, you will dine good!"

Some conversation followed about their respective constituencies (both by the sea, but Herr Uber's was a fishing port as opposed to a holiday town). Herr Uber had been sitting for a number of years but could well remember what it was like to be a 'new boy'. "Most scary, do you say?"

Mr B. nodded and told the story of his first day in the Palace of Westminster wearing the wrong clothes. Herr

Uber laughed but said: "It is surely true that many things are changing...

"Sometimes I prefer the old ways." He sighed. "It is bad for a government to be slavishly adulated. We who do not wish to be slaves must keep our bottoms and our heads."

Mr B. smiled.

"I think I mean seats not bottoms? Excuse me! But I do like very much your song about never being slaves. A good sentiment."

"Mr Thomson also wrote our National Anthem..."

"Aah, yes: 'confound their politicks, frustrate their knavish tricks!'"

And so they parted exchanging cards, smiles and handshakes.

Then two or three uniforms buttonholed our hero to try out their English, some with more success than others. Embarrassed by his poor German, Mr B. made his way to his host to say goodbye. Positioning himself so that he might avoid further claps on the back, he presented his hand at the full extremity of his arm.

"But no, my dear Mr Bradley, it is not goodbye! We shall go together to my friend von Ribbentrop, more comfortable and also you will not get lost yes? We can leave now. These guests..." the Prince eyed those remaining with disdain, "can continue without me."

Relieved that he didn't have to find his way across the city, Mr Bradley was unconvinced about the comfort, as the conversation was as prickly as the limousine, which conveyed them, was smooth.

"Now, now my friend we shall have a very special evening: good food, pretty ladies yes?" A firm nudge was given to our hero's un-upholstered ribs. And immediately: "Mr Gordon Canning is a good friend of yours yes?"

"Mr Gordon Canning is barely an acquaintance."

"But you like him?"

"I'm afraid I don't know him."

"We, in the Party, we like him very much. And we look after our friends."

"Bully for you," thought Mr Bradley, but what he said was, "That was a most enjoyable party, your highness, for which many thanks. All your guests spoke such excellent English, I was ashamed to have so little German."

"Perhaps you should learn…" said the Prince, and then they were at their destination.

6

Mr Bradley was accustomed to grand hospitality in England, but he was somewhat awestruck by the lavish festivity which confronted him that evening.

"Foie gras, caviar AND smoked salmon" he inwardly exclaimed, feeling a little like Mole at Ratty's picnic, "and all before the soup."

The Prince introduced him to his host and hostess and then moved away.

Johanne, Frau von Ribbentrop, exuded money from the tips of her peepy sandals to the top of her glossy head. The jewels about the rest of her person shone like the bubbles in her Papa's *Sekt*. Joachim was immaculately starched with a razored hair cut and an equally razored face. His eyes gleamed like oily black olives, through heavily fringed eyelashes. "Are you wearing mascara?" wondered Mr B., as he was taken across a rather modern saloon which featured a surprising quantity of Venetian glass.

"Your Highness, may I present Mr Bradley, a Member of Parliament from England."

"Mr Bradley, Her Highness the Duchess of Brunswick (whose father was our Kaiser), and her daughter, the Princess Frederika."

Mr Bradley bowed over the proffered hands. The Duchess had a smile which crinkled her face up towards her high cheekbones, and deep-set eyes.

"I so love England! We have so many connections from there, and now my daughter is at school in Broadstairs!"

"I will be leaving soon Mama," interrupted the young lady, whose eagerness suggested she did not wish to be thought a schoolgirl, although one or two eruptions about her face gave the game away.

"Of course, my darling. But first you will be head girl and we are so proud."

Frederika's blush almost concealed her spots, and Mr B. leaped in with: "Goodness! I shall have to mind my Ps and Qs, Your Highness; I was terrified of our head boy! But Broadstairs? Excellent sailing around there, or at least just around the corner, so to speak, have you tried?"

With a grateful smile all her own, Frederika returned: "Yes, we have a sailing club on Saturdays. It is such fun!"

"What do you sail?"

"Oh only dinghies – nothing smart."

"Nothing wrong with dinghies."

"You obviously sail."

"Sailed over to Germany's matter of fact, left the boat at Leer."

"How jolly! What kind is she?"

"A six-metre" our hero replied with pride, a bit disguised.

"Oh! I saw one once – such beautiful lines – but big scary sails, I couldn't helm one."

"I'm sure you could." It was quite a sturdy Princess... And to the Duchess:

"Your Highness will allow me to take your daughter out on my boat one day? In a party of course."

"An excellent plan, how charming of you. I do not feel that Frederika meets as many young people as she should, apart of course from her school friends. But now for the moment, perhaps we may entertain you? Do you speak German Mr Bradley?"

"If I had a pound for each time I've been asked that question," grumbled Mr B. internally, but smiling sweetly "I'm afraid not – just restaurant stuff: Wiener Schnitzel, sauerkraut und kartoffeln."

Frederika giggled: "but your accent is ser gut!"

"Perhaps then you, with your good accent will accompany us to the meetings of the party and I will translate what isn't to do with restaurants?"

Laughing, our hero accepted.

"Perhaps also Your Highness would accompany me to a restaurant of your choice."

"Where I might introduce you to food other than kartoffeln and sauerkraut!"

And so, much pleased with each other they went in to dine. While her Mama was whisked away to sit beside her host, Princess Fred (that's what they call me) sat on Mr B.'s right and became less bashful. Quite forgetting she was no longer a schoolgirl, she regaled him with needle-sketches of her mistresses and classmates. Amusing as these "tales out of school" were, our hero became increasingly, and uncomfortably, aware of the lady on his left, who was talking in German in what seemed to him seductive tones to the gentleman on her left. Out of the corner of his eye he could see that she wore a dress of violet silk draped to reveal a slash of ivory back to – well – to where the chair got in the way, and she smelled, not of violets but, "Lily of the Valley actually" she said, as finally Frederika turned to the gent on her right and Mr Bradley swivelled to his left. "You shouldn't snuffle so, it's very impolite. I think it's rather good on me. So sorry if it upsets you."

Would it surprise you, readers mine, if I wrote, "Our

hero nearly blushed"? All right then: our hero did blush. His neighbour continued:

"Unlike the young person on your other side, I didn't go to school. We had governesses, lots of governesses, because we were beastly to them, and most of them left before teaching us anything at all, which leaves me pretty uneducated, I suppose."

"Certainly pretty" thought Mr B., but what he said was: "Obviously no one taught you not to eavesdrop! And I wasn't snuffling."

Staring across the table, fork halfway to mouth, "You sniffed, definitely, several times, and I call that snuffling. And I don't think you can eavesdrop at a dinner party... Surely everyone's conversation is for general consumption, like the food? And oh do look! There is Herr General Consumption over there." The fork popped between rosy lips. Mr B. forced his gaze away across the table, where sat a large, many-jowelled person with many silver stars on his black-clad shoulders. He was, in Isle of Wight vernacular, "punishing his eats", but stopped briefly to smile and raise his glass in the direction of the Lady of the Pun. As she smiled and toasted him back, Mr B. thought he must laugh, but just then he encountered for the first time the full force of two widely spaced and unblinking blue eyes, and found that he couldn't breathe or talk, never mind laugh.

"Laughter would not have been appropriate. You don't say very much though, do you? Is it because we have not been introduced? How do you do? My name is Constance Bennett."

Mr Bradley found his mouth was open, oh dear oh dear, shut it, swallowed, conjured his best smile and "My name is Charlie Bradley, how do you do."

"I'm sure we shall chatter away like starlings now! Have you come to admire how the Party works?"

"I came to Germany on holiday, but I admit I am interested in the goings on, and as a Member of Parliament naturally." Oh blast it, blast it, what am I saying, what is the matter with me? Thought our usually modest hero.

"Gracious! Are you really an M.P.? I thought they were all whiskery silver-haired gentlemen? I don't see any whiskers; in fact you look as though you should still be in school. No wonder you were put next to Fredka, you're obviously frightfully suitable."

The way in which Miss Bennett intoned "suitable" turned the word into a veritable insult. "I'm afraid I'm not suitable at all, in fact I verge on the raffish. I have a sister who is an actress! And I haven't a father." This was said with pride and a certain defiance.

"But you are young too Miss Bennett!"

"Only in years, Mr Bradley, and maybe not even in those." She sighed, sweeping her eyes to the ceiling.

"Recently I have realised that I might be the reincarnation of Queen Hatshepsut,* which would make me very old indeed."

Now Mr Bradley did laugh: "Do you always talk such tosh, Miss Bennett?"

"Only when absolutely necessary, I assure you!" and smiling seraphically, she once more presented our hero with the glimmer of her back and a waft of Lily of the Valley, or was it Narcissus? Turning briefly: "Don't snuffle" she mouthed, and then was once more a back.

Feeling the situation to be totally out of his control, and as though he had been beaten about the head by

---

* For my less knowledgeable readers, Queen of Egypt of the 18th Dynasty (c.1478–1458 B.C.) She has a beautiful temple near the Nile.

several hundred angry butterflies, Mr Bradley winced as the Princess on his right clapped her hands:

"Tomorrow we shall see Udet! He is so wonderful, you will love him!"

Noticing his muddled face, she continued: "Aagh – you do not know Udet? He is a sturzflug bomber, a dive bomber – so brave, so exact, and also very handsome!" She opened her eyes wide and raised her schoolgirl eyebrows:

"So many girlfriends also..." The Duchess' hand on her shoulder stopped Frederika in mid flight:

"Mein liebling, the ladies are retiring now, and the gentlemen will follow shortly if they too wish to see your hero. It will be an early start. Mr Bradley: we will collect you at 8.30. Be ready please!"

"I thank Your Highness, and good night."

As he bowed goodbye, Mr B. caught the violet silk leaving in company with a glamorous peach number.

"Bother," which B word (or possibly another less-suited to my gentle readers) was repeated inwardly, when he found that the Prince von Hessen was enjoying himself immensely, and would under no circumstances allow Mr B. to call a taxi. Therefore, too many rounds of schnapps later, a note was taken by a different concierge, all smiles and bows ("the word's out" thought Charlie) to Albert's room.

It was in telegraph format: VITAL BE UP AND ALIVE AT 8.15 A.M. STOP PLEASE PRODUCE CARING REMEDY AT 7 A.M. STOP TEA AND TOAST AT 7.30 STOP POSSIBLY FOLLOWED BY COFFEE AT 8 A.M. STOP ON NO ACCOUNT MENTION EGGS OR BACON OR INDEED SPEAK STOP HOPE YOU AMUSED YOURSELF STOP CB.

And at 4 a.m. our hero found his bed and stumbled onto it.

Gentle reader, he did not clean his teeth.

I can assure those sensible readers, who are also wondering about Albert's activities, that he was not tucked up with a (or even The) good book. He bathed, changed into "mufti" and presented himself at one of the hotel's bars where he ordered a Löwenbräu and retreated to a small lamp-lit table to read the evening newspaper. He did not initially notice who was serving his drink, but upon lowering his paper his eyes bumped into two yellow-pebbled almond-shaped ones.

"Guten abend."

"Guten abend." And "Oh bother, oh drat!" he thought, clairvoyance does this to you: he knew. And he hadn't thought the party over. Leonora, for that was the name of the nemesis in front of him, knew too. Which was odd, as she did not have the sight. "Quelques temps" as the French say, "Ça arrive." (So much better than "Stuff happens," don't you think?)

Le coup de foudre.

They returned to their positions behind newspaper and bar. Another Löwenbräu was ordered and delivered. Fate marched in with a tipsy German soldier who assumed that Leonora came free with his beer. The bulk of Albert loomed; a few quiet German words were spoken; Hauptmann Fritz flounced off fulminating. "Too Jewish-looking for me anyway!"

Leonora joined Albert in the Gastätte around the corner when she had finished work. There they learned about as much as any two people can about each other in as many hours. (Albert learnt the most, natch.) This included the fact that Nellie had a brother, who had tormented her as a child. Apart from 'hanging' her best beloved elephant teddy, he had later blinded (with lighted matchsticks) and then drowned her beautiful Burmese cat. Nor, when their parents had died, was she allowed to keep more than a few keepsakes. "And no photographs, too Jewish." Returned to the hotel, they decided more might be learned in Leonora's bedroom. Please, gentle reader, be not shocked, Destiny is sometimes pretty disgraceful.

7

Charlie did clean his teeth the next morning though, immediately after downing Albert's potion.

"If only I could as easily get the stench out of my nostrils"* grumbled the ungrateful, still-not-quite-sober M.P. for Eastbourne.

Albert smiled serenely.

"A good evening then, Mr B.?"

"An excellent one, thank you, and now I'm off with a Royal Highness or two to watch someone called Udet?"

"I was relieved,† since my cousin has only one spare ticket, and I would like to be there too."

"I wouldn't have robbed you of your umpteenth cousin's ticket! You can wave at me in the Royal Box!"

"I'll wave, Mr B., but he'll be marching I'm afraid; the only wave you'll get from him will be a heil. Quite besotted is our Fritz."

"You move in National Socialist circles then?"

"As, it seems, do you!"

Huge black limousines drove the party, which included Mr B. (in the front with the chauffeur, who didn't drive nearly as well as Albert,‡ or indeed Mr B.), the Duchess and her daughter, who was wearing the uniform of Hitler Youth, in the back. As they purred towards the Zeppelinfeld, Albert Speer's grandiloquent but unfinished campus, every building was covered with flags

---

* See back for how Albert's potion smells.
† Pay attention, Albert is clairvoyant, OK?
‡ Of course not.

bearing the swastika. The streets swayed with thousands of swastika-waving people.

"Your Highness? What are these flags?"

"They depict the emblem of the National Socialist Party." The Duchess gave a little tsk as her tongue hissed back from her teeth.

"And I am afraid that soon…" She hesitated and then in a different voice:

"But we are here!"

And in a moment there they were: ushered into balcony seats with velvet cushions.

It was warm. It became hotter. There was no sign of the libidinous Mr Udet, but Mr Hitler arrived to great applause. He spoke to the vast crowd and as one the people roared approval, leaping to their feet to give a standing ovation lasting several minutes. Once reasonable calm resumed, Mr B. wondered what had caused all the excitement.

"As I had suspected," said the Duchess "Mr Hitler has made the swastika emblem our national flag."*

"No more boring stripes – much more fun" said Frederika. Our M.P. reflected on the desultory patter of clapping as at a school prize-giving which might greet him or even the Prime Minister in England. Other considerations soon crowded comparisons from his brain. Breakfast had been a while ago and Mr B. eyed with yearning the vendors of ice cream and soda pop. Unfortunately, in the confusion of an early start he had left behind his Reichsmarks. He betted to himself that it was a plot of Albert's. Just then, the Duchess spoke.

---

* Dear clever reader, I know this was done in the Reichstag. I have moved the scene to Zeppelinfeld, as I am sure Hitler would have preferred. If it offends you, tant pis.

(She reminded Charlie more and more of the Queen of Hearts in *Alice in Wonderland*.) He rubbed his neck gingerly, but she didn't say "Off with his head!" merely "I suppose you might be hungry? All men are so!" And opening her capacious handbag, she offered our hero an assortment of broken biscuits. Noticing a crestfallen Fredka, Mr B. grasped a handful, muttering:

"Suggestives! My favourite."

"No, no, Mr Bradley, these are Digestives!" Laughed his hostess. He hadn't the heart or the saliva to explain, as with a dry mouth and his most charming smile he munched and swallowed as best he could.

His mouth became drier still as Udet suddenly flew out of the clear blue sky and seemed to drop like a bird of prey, no, faster, like a stone, directly upon the top of their balcony, spinning away at the last minute into the stadium and up into the air, only to dive again and spin again until our hero's hazy eyes and hungry stomach made a dizzy pact to let him down entirely. Nudged by the Duchess, he took a deep quiet breath as she hooted in his ear: "See! Here come the army and here the Uhlans!! When my father the Kaiser took the salute in 1913, I rode in front of them on a white horse as Colonel-in-Chief. The same music played" and she hummed a little snatch, tapping fingers to handbag.

"You must miss those days, Your Highness?"

He was given a very sharp look.

"Those days," the Duchess spoke in quotes, "are long gone, and these days are here and now and we must live in THEM." She looked carefully at Mr B. and seemingly coming to a decision, she whispered:

"Would you take Fredka back to England with you? I should not say it, should not ask it, it's hard ... but I am not happy with some changes here, and I am not happy with some friends who advise her not to return."

"Your Highness, I can understand, I would be happy to take care of Fredka. But what of you?"

"Me?" There was nothing so unladylike as a snort, a subtle intake of breath perhaps.

"I am the Kaiser's daughter. Nothing will happen to me, but my child is being corrupted – what can I do? All her friends wear the uniform – they find it exciting, and God forbid, they find him exciting." She indicated the small man a little beyond them who was taking the salute. "A waxy moustache and a waxy face," thought Charlie, "like a pockmarked waxing moon." But he had to admire the way the diminutive figure stood hour after hour as the regiments marched past, mostly armed with spades or picks at the slope because the Versailles Treaty forbade German military rearmament.

Huge cheers completed the day's entertainment, and eventually the Duchess' party found its car and its way home. Goodbyes, bows and firm handshakes were exchanged and a blushing cheek was kissed.

"A cup of tea, Mr B.?"

"No Albert! A bloody stiff whisky!"

8

There was yet another grand dinner that evening, and both the Vons* hinted that something important was being arranged for the next day.

"Busy, busy, busy," thought Mr B., wondering what Albert was up to and with whom. In less of a daze than he had been since taking a large glass of whisky and a ham sandwich, he found himself in conversation with an extraordinarily beautiful woman.

"Don't know what I am doink here," she said, "I would much rather be at home in Hungary. What are you doing here darlink? So young, so handsome – you should be somewhere more funny." (I think our hero blushed, but he may have been too tired/tipsy/trance-like.) In a voice that belonged on the stage she continued. "I can't bear this nasty little man, but my husband thinks we must see what is going on – Aaa! Here is Sandor – See! It was an excellent idea to come to this party! I have found an English gentleman to talk with."

A huge dark-visaged person, his nose like a bird of prey's, looked over Mr B., gripped his hand with a crack, and smiled, "my wife is excellent at finding kindred spirits!"

"Oh no," thought our hero, "another smack on the back!" But it was worse: a triple kiss. Inwardly he shook himself, like a dog in from the rain, meanwhile returning the courtesies.

---

* Ribbentrop and Hessen – do pay attention readers mine.

"I am sure he loves to shoot small birds just as you do, so he will come and stay with us at Gyor."

"We will travel home in two or three days' time and would be so happy if you would accompany us."

"But my dear Sir! You don't know me from Adam."

"I am your dear Count de Hedevar, and you are?"

"Charles Bradley, M. le Comte."

"Sandor, please. And I can tell that I shall know you, my wife has decided it."

"Who's Adam?" wondered the Countess, "We shall sit together at dinner and so discover everything about ourselves."

"But M. le Comte…?"

"Sandor – but me no buts, I shall say but to the butler, and it will all be arranged. Your host tonight is a cousin of mine." This in reply to Mr B.'s raised eyebrows.[*] "If I had a pound for every cousinly encounter," thought he, as Magdalena enfolded his arm in hers and moved him gently towards an alcoved seat.

"Is nowhere safe? Really I might have to go back to Munich." Charlie found that he was the focus of Miss Constance Bennett's narrowed eyes.

"Dahlink," Mme la Comtesse and Miss Bennett treble kissed.

"You know Mr Bradley? I thought I had found him for me, now typically you are there first. It's too bad, are you madly in love?"

"No!" Togetherly said Miss B. and Mr B.

"Well, you should be. I have definitely scented it."

Mr Bradley, having been battered by butterflies was now finding himself exterminated by exclamation marks.

"Now, Mr Bradley is coming to Gyor to shoot small

---

[*] Oh dear – they weren't Albert's, gentle reader, never mind.

birds with Sandor. You must come too dear Constance; we haven't seen you for so long. It will be perfect."

Mr B. thought it might be just that, but "No" said Miss Bennett, "Thank you, I promised to stay with Unity until the end of next week."

"Pah! Unity, she look after herself."

"I'm not sure she can, Magdalena, and I've had a long letter from her Mama to tell me so."

"But she is in comfortable circumstance?"

"Of course, but emotionally she is well away with the fairies."

"Away with the?"

"Fairies, she lives on another planet – in the stars, and she's starry-eyed about, um, strange people."

"Oh, you mean the nasty little man! I cannot dog him."

"Bear," our hero murmured.

"Magdalena, lower your voice for goodness' sake. You've no idea how dangerous things are…"

"Pah! For some poor gypsies and Jews possibly, but for Magdalena Hedevar, I do not think so!"

"Darling M., remember your Mama."

"So, she was Jewish AND a gypsy. AND she danced on the stage… So?"

Mme la Comtesse flashed sparks from her eyes and her cheekbones indicated, if not red for alert, certainly the warm glow of a semi-dormant volcano. Constance hugged her.

"Be careful, that's all."

Mr B. thought best to intervene purposefully this time.

"Dear Mme de Hedevar, please tell me about Hungary and your family."

"I don't need to tell you, you shall see for yourself my

darlink, you will adore it. You will fall in Love!' She smiled slyly, but nobody blushed.

The food that evening was not as richly saucy as Mme de Hedevar's gossip but every bit as delicious. She had quietly moved place cards and sat next to Mr B. Her husband's reliance upon the butler was a mistake. "Oh dear, Sandor is not happy; look he has old Mme Strelitz, and plain Isabella von Eckdorf. How good for him it will be." A fleeting Cheshire cat grin possessed her face.

"He always gets his own way you know, so sometimes…"

Mr B. thought, "Perhaps the butler butted the Count?"

Then enquiring vaguely how the Countess knew Miss Bennett, he learnt that her father, Peter, had been an actor (not good darlink, not good, but oh so handsome, violet eyes, lashed like a hussar's epaulettes) "Hmm," thought our hero, "pretty apt description really."

"You think I exaggerate? I nevair exaggerate! Just maybe emphasise…"

"And embroider."

"Oh yes, my petit point is something so delicate, I will show you when we are at Gyor, but that is beside the point—" Mme la Comtesse widened her totally innocent eyes in Mr B.'s direction:

"Oh, ha, ha ha, I have made an English joke, no?" And reaching for her handbag, a rectangle of black enamel clasped by a fan of diamante (just thought, dear reader, you should know, Mme de H. wore a black draped Crepe de Chine with beadery under the bos. Constance was in pale yellow. Sorry I didn't tell you sooner.) She produced a tiny gilt notepad and pencil.

"My husband will not believe I made an English joke," she confided, "so I must write it down and you must sign it."

There was some difficulty in recalling exact words, but eventually the joke was immortalised in lead.

"Now you must sign and say it made you laugh." Mr B. wrote, "I laughed like a drain."

The Countess wrinkled her nose:

"But this drain, this is not nice no? Do you mean train perhaps?"

"No, Drain; gurgle gurgle gurgle."

Mr B. did his best impression and smiled impressively.

"And now," said his ever-excited companion, almost bouncing in her seat.* "I am going to make second English joke. I see now why you are a success with all the girgls."

The second joke inscribed and signed –

"Of course," said Mme, "his mother was Hungarian which explains his beauty because we Hungarians are all Ravenous!"

Since the Countess was at the moment tucking with gusto into her Tournedos Rossini aux champignons sauvages avec ces petites pommes de terre château, Mr B. had no difficulty in agreeing wholeheartedly.

"I'm beginning to find out," he said, hoping the malapropism would pass un-remarked. He wanted to know more about Constance, and "English Jokes" were impeding progress.

"So. Peter's father Edward came to Hungary to look at our big farm, how do you say?"

"Estates?"

"Absolutely – because his father, like Edward, was also a youngest son, and a church person."

"A vicar?"

---

* Small, gilt, red silk upholstery, not suited to bouncing so just as well.

"Yes, a holy man but with the thing you put beside fearful horses' eyes?"

"Blinkered?"

"Perfectly, but he was not so blinkered that he couldn't see that his son needed to earn a living and he thought Ystaty management would be the thing. Edward would meet and marry the daughter of the Ystaty and all up the ladders again. No?"

"Yes."

"No. Unfortunately, or fortunately he meet and marry Matilda who is distant cousin of my husband and so should be suitable. Yes?"

"No?"

"No! She is a foreigner! With too few pennies, and she likes to dance and sing and give poetries and dressing up?"

"Charades."

"Yes. And they – the vicar and his wife – do not understand. But then is born Peter, and they worship him. He is like God, and they know how to treat God. Good for God maybe, very bad for young boy. So Special. Nothing could be wrong. Meanwhile, what does he learn? He learns dressing up gets you clappings and sweet-smelling ladies cuddle you up and so maybe you are up and away. Ystaty Management get you grumpy Uberlord and grumpy Ystaty people –"

"Tenants?"

"Yes, yes. And smelly pigs and things. No choice there for his mother's son. Although I understand the vicar's speeches –"

"Sermons?"

"Were quite theatrical, so maybe he too has these genes."[*]

"Did he do anything good?"

"The vicar?"

"No, Peter."

"He did this – he did that, he did Ivor Novello I think, nothing so special, but everyone adored him. His girls adored him of course. A father who flirts is the best kind – and their mother." Mme looked sadly at her plate, now empty, and took two sips of wine.

"This is really delicious; I must compliment Sonia, or is it Isabella? I cannot remember. Ah so, I think Isabella." She sipped again and plates were removed.

"Aah – now a surprise, but I shall cheat and un-surprise you. We are to have a Rare Buck Bit. Me – I do not like all that chocolate pastry and cream. But I love the Jesus!"

Mr B. avoided another English Joke by concentrating on his own (delicious) Rare Buck for a bit. As the chair on his left was still conspicuously empty, he had no need to turn, so after a companionable munch or six, he enquired, "And Miss Bennett's Mama?"

"You are definitely in love; can you not talk of anything other than Constance?"

"Forgive me Mme, but you forbad me to ask about Hungary. Shall we talk about the English Parliament?"

"No."

"The State of the world?"

"No."

"At least then 'justice for Hungary'."[†]

---

[*] Dear reader, jeans weren't much worn in Europe in 1935 otherwise Mme de H. might have bagged another joke. Genes were known though.

[†] A campaign trying to return to Hungary territories that were lost under the Treaty of Trianon.

"No and no and no! I would rather return to Miss Bennett."

"No! Enough, I would rather hear about Mme de Hedevar and her life."

Mr B. and the Countess exchanged grins.

"Bah! My life has already been long – I will instead introduce you to Constance's mother – a formidable* lady."

Our hero swallowed an un-chewed Buck Bit and tried to see in which direction the Countess was looking.

"Silly boy – she is not here! Hmmmm." She found a smidgeon of Rarebit and conveyed it with pleasure to her lips.

"Now we will get beastly pastries and after that I'll be sent away with the 'girglies', so I will tell you quick, because if you are not now in love, I predict you will be. Lalage was the much loved only daughter of French Aristocrats, who still talked of times before the revolution."

"1789?"

"1789 – can you imagine? Well I suppose when she was born the family had lived in England only a hundred years or so – where in France Charlemagne or maybe Henri IV probably were close relative. Also people lived more slow then I think. No pennies but always pretending, so the dressings up came naturally and there (because they lived near to Edward and Matilda) Peter and Lalage meet. And so five exquisite girls and one son later Peter joins the Painters Guns –"

"Artists' Rifles?"

"Quite so, and is killed in 1918. Just before the Armistice. No money, no nothink." But Surprise,

---

* Dear reader, pronounce in French please.

Lalage's best friend is the oh-so-grand Unity's mother and so they could share governess. (I nevair had governess, pah! I taught myself to read and to play the piano.)"

"That explains the unusual English," thought Mr B.

"Did you teach yourself to dance too?" Is what he said.

"That not", Magdalena laughed, "that is partly blood and mmmm – partly who I dance with. When the music plays in Gyor I will demonstrate."

Staring beyond Mr B., Mme lowered her voice.

"Watch out, for here comes Miss Unity Trouble. You will have to turn, but I shall re-turn to rescue you. Another Joke, yes?"

Mr Bradley signalled, yes.

"Unity darlink! Here, I present my friend Mr Bradley who is a member of your English Parliament and an excellent companion for dinner."

Mr B. rose, "Miss Unity."

The lady had sat down and was posting a pastry into her mouth. Her dress clung to all the right places and the candles shimmered off its oyster satin. Wine was offered and refused.

"Wasser bitte."

Somewhat mesmerised by the glimmer, Charlie took a fortifying swig from his grateful glass and tried to marshal his thoughts.

"Have you met the Führer?" asked his companion.

"No, Miss Unity, but I have watched him."

"I have just come from his presence." Unity trembled. "His vision, his wit! Incomparable. He is magnificent, when I see him, I glow in his light. He is divine." Unity turned towards our hero, and inspected him for the first time.

"I can see you are the kind of person from England who puts his head in the sand like an ostrich."

"It's tricky, I think," Mr B. said, "to call anyone divine. There are a few occasions when people have had unhappy experiences after such an accolade."*

"Yes? And who, and where? You are talking about a veritable God! And he is here and now."

Mr B. looked at Unity. She did indeed glow – her skin gleamed, but disdain curdled her beautiful face.

Mr B. thought briefly, but – person who reads this book – he probably didn't think for long enough. You may remember that he was brought up reading the Bible and the classics.

"There's Semele, of course, who having been loved by Jupiter asked to see him in his true form. Big mistake. When confronted by his divine glory, she burst into flames."

Miss Mitford failed to find an analogy.

"And Herod is a case in point, I believe."

"Herod?"

"Yes, Herod the Great, appointed to rule in Judea by the Roman Senate. Not to be confused with the Herod Antipas."

"And?"

"His people acclaimed him as divine, which he rather enjoyed, but not for long. An angel smote him (I do like that smiting bit, don't you?) and he was eaten up with worms. Then, and I think† I quote correctly, 'Gave up the ghost'."

"What?"

---

* A Royal Accolade: drink with bubbles in a bottle – oh never mind dear reader – lighten up. (Peter Cook and Dudley Moore.)

† Acts Ch. 12 v. 23.

"Yes. Nasty business really. My Nursie always says a few parasites are a good thing. Obviously Herod had two or twenty too many."

Miss Mitford snaked her eyes and hissed, "With your stupid talk of Nursie and your frivolous chatter you, Mr Bradley, embody all that is rotten in England at the moment. But, you will not see England again. You will be smitten! I shall arrange for the Führer to have you beheaded."

"Not shot then?" said Mr B. But the space on his left was already empty. Indeed, its chair was lying on the floor. Not for long, however, as the Prince von Hessen neatly picked it up and sat upon it, flapping his hand at our hero to remain seated.

"A good party, yes?"

"An excellent party. What generous hosts you have introduced me to. My sincere thanks."

"It has been my pleasure." The Prince inclined his head, "And now I have a truly fantastic invitation for you!" He paused, eyeballing Mr B.

"The Führer WILL SEE YOU tomorrow!"

"Oh will he," thought our hero, "is my execution already arranged?" But he said "What an honour."

"It is so. I will collect you and bring you to him at 13.00 hours!!" The Prince left with two exclamation marks, and a small bow.

Mr B. thought, "Only two punctuation marks, to underline this solemn occasion? How restrained. But I must not get into this habit – it is catching!!"

In his place arrived M. de Hedevar, who complained mildly about modern butlers not knowing their places from their placements, repeated his invitation and gathered up his wife. They went away, but left their smiles behind.

"And so," Mr B. said to himself, on his way to find a taxi, "To bed."

***

Meanwhile, Constance, descending from a cab with Unity, noticed a commotion opposite the house where they stayed with the Grafin von Friedland: three blond soldiers had a growling dog by the tail and the ears. Two others were using cigarettes upon its back, which changed the growls to yelps. She confided Unity into the butler's care and "I'll only be a minute," she said, "I want to see…"

"Fräulein!"

But Constance was across the street and already stamping her yellow satined foot: "What are you doing, you odious creeps? Stop at once and give the dog to me. Who are you exactly and have you a Captain or someone to command you?" She withdrew a notebook and pencil from her yellow silk handbag. "I think he should be told exactly what you are doing in the watches of the night, when you probably should be watching something or even be in bed before your arduous duties tomorrow."

"Dear lady," said a blond bullet-head, "we are sorry to upset you, but this, you see, is a Jewish dog, and so—"

"It is not a Jewish dog, you TOAD, it is a Dog. Dogs do not have a religion and even if they did it would not be one that you would recognise. In fact, I doubt if you would know a religion if you fell over one early in the morning, never mind late at night. Now, Give me your officer's name and that of your company and give me the dog. You may use this..." pulling her belt through its loops.

The young men around her had begun to shuffle their feet. One of them said, "We are with Hauptmann Hiller of the 11th Brigade." Another bent down to the dog and assayed a pat. He got bitten.

"Surely that doesn't surprise you?" said Constance, putting away her notebook and accepting the belt which now did duty as lead and collar. Blood welled on the Aryan hand.

"I do not wish to keep you from the important things you have to do, but that bite needs a plaster and possibly an anti-tetanus injection. And so goodnight. Perhaps you should remember that your Führer is particularly fond of dogs."

Constance strode across the road, dog in tow. The young men dithered, uncertain. Until one said, "Well, we had to be polite to the young mädchen."

"Klaus, it was a good thing you gave the wrong Hauptmann and Brigade."

Therefore, they all laughed and went on their way looking for more amusements.

The butler, who had watched the confrontation, almost saluted as Constance returned.

"But, the Grafin will not allow dogs..."

"That's fine Wilhelm, please call me a taxi, and ask Anna to pack my things. We," she patted the dog, "will wait here."

By the time the luggage and taxi had arrived she had a note ready for Unity, one for the Grafin and several crisp ones for Anna.

"Thank you so much and sorry to be a bore at this time

of night. Please give this to Miss Unity and this to the Grafin and this is for you."

Anna pinked with pleasure.

"I have been happy to help you, Fräulein. I was not sure exactly which clothes were yours and which Miss Unity's... I have packed nearly all the ones you have been wearing, but there were some which wouldn't fit into the suitcases."

"Wunderbar, Anna! But did you pack that hat?"

"No, I have it here." Constance crammed the violet creation upon her head, and beamed.

"Anna, you are a star, thank you. And Wilhelm, maybe you could parcel and post whatever is left? VERY slow post to London?"

She squeezed his hand, leaving behind yet more notes, "You have both looked after me perfectly! Auf wiedersehen."

On her way to the Grand Hotel, Constance momentarily wavered and wondered what on earth she was doing. Out came the notebook:

"A list calms anxieties." She thought.

I've had enough of Germany.

Ditto of Unity. (Though she is sweet mostly, or should that be Mosley?)

I have acquired a dog who is currently loving my ankles and ponging poor taxi man's cab.

The de Hedevars like dogs. I like the de Hedevars. Fun.

Mr Bradley surely likes dogs. I like Mr Bradley (a bit).

No, probably more than a bit. Might be fun.

So: all in all sensible course of action.

Niggle? Wouldn't it be more sensible to go home to England?

No definitely not. Fun first.

9

The silly person who had thought he would soon be in bed was contentedly puffing on a Players, whilst nursing a small digestive* (or was the digestive nursing him?) when there was a knock on the door.

"Mein Herr?"

Tightening his dressing gown† about his person.

"Ooof – too many smart dinners," thought he, "or maybe it's the exclamation marks that increase the girth." He opened the door.

Two people stood beyond it.

"Mein Herr," said the No. 2 concierge. "I tried to prevent…"

"I've had enough," said Miss Bennett, "and I will come to Hungary."

Mr B. avoided the young man's agitated visage, preferring to gaze at the vision of loveliness conjured up by the second voice.

Unfortunately, the person who sounded like Miss B. was anything but lovely, hidden as it was in a greige mackintosh from head to soggy toe.

Upon the former was a most fetching violet hat, but its feather had given up any attempt to caress its owner's cheek. Instead it dripped violet teardrops upon her shoulder in damp protest.

There was also a truly terrible smell: very old unwashed

---

* Not the Biccy dears!

† It was the most beautiful paisley patterned silk, dear reader, Noël Coward, if you like.

flannels mixed with rotten apples and finished with a fine farmyard aroma of faeces. Mr B. sniffed. Plodding forward on the end of the inglorious vision's belt came the ugliest and certainly the pong-iest thing Mr B. had ever encountered. (And some of his shooting cronies' dogs were pretty* pong-y.) He supposed it to be a dog, but it could have been anything, including a mangy bath mat. Mr B. shifted once more. The mat growled. Probably a dog then thought our hero.

"Don't snuffle or we won't come to Hungary with you," said Miss Bennett, following the stench into his room. "I had to walk in the pouring rain, from the top of the road, as it was clogged with horrid great cars, so I'm afraid we are rather damp."

"Mein Herr, the lady insisted."

The stooge stuttered on, in spite of the witherer he received from the lady in question.

"We do not allow…" he failed to finish the phrase.

"This is not anstandig?"† he tried to continue, failing again with flapping fingers.

"I quite agree" said our dressing-gowned hero, "you are absolutely right. Miss Bennett should not be standing – she seems damp and upset. Come and sit by the fire, Miss Bennett and I will leave the door open in case you, or – I'm sorry, Mein Herr I have forgotten your name?"

"Franz, Sir."

"In case you or Franz should be worried. And dear Franz, will you bring," he turned to his dogged guest, "Brandy? Schnapps?"

---

* Some of them weren't at all pretty either, dear reader, but much loved.

† Anstandig = Respectable.

"Schnapps please und caffe bitte schön, Franz," Miss B. smiled sweetly, "Oh, and a small bowl."

She had shed the unfortunate waterproof in the bathroom and was revealed in most of her former glory: tightly encased in a greenish something with small buttons here and there and mostly down her back, and a neckline that didn't come very close to her neck, Mr B. noted happily (Constance had managed quickly to change out of the long Yellow in the Grafin's library while Wilhelm held the dog). Like a rabbit caught in the beam of a poacher's lantern, the unfortunate Franz found it difficult to move. Mr B. coughed, "and brandy for me, thank you Franz."

Franz fled from further confrontation, tails and hands a-flapping.

Miss Bennett was, from our hero's point of view, being overly friendly to the dog in front of the fire. The warmth had increased the pong by about a hundredfold* and when he came closer it growled and bared its teeth.

"He doesn't like your dressing gown" said his less soggy guest. "And I'm not surprised."

She had removed the hat and her hair seemed to be curling around her head as if the tendrils knew where to go.

"Look what they have done to him."

The dog had a six-pronged star burnt into its back; hair, shaggy about the rest of its body, had been crudely snipped so that the emblem could be burned deep into its skin.

"There were five of them. They did it with cigarettes."

Mr B. looked at his, and hastily put it out.

"Who did?"

"A bunch of nasty young men who think their uniforms

---

* Remember Mr B.'s biblical background, dear reader.

entitle them to behave as they wish! They blame Jewish people for everything that goes wrong and if they can't find a human to bully, they torment their animals. It's disgusting."

"And you? How did you, uhm, gain possession of the animal?"

"I told them to stop of course. And then I used my belt for a lead."

Mr B. stared with incredulity at the slightly built person whose hand was being gently mauled by the mat/mutt in front of the fire.

"I speak German. That's why I've been in Germany. To learn German. I told them to stop and they did. I said they should be ashamed of themselves. They were. What is odd?"

Mr B.'s mind boggled at the thought of his guest confronting five thuggish young men, and I'm afraid his face showed it.

"Do you think I am feek and weable?" thundered said guest, rising to her full five foot three inches in stocking-ed toes.

Were the drying feet and shoes contributing to the general stench? Wondered Mr B.

Herr General Stench! Guden Abend!

"Why are you smiling?" Stamp of stocking-ed foot. "It's not funny."

"Fräulein? Schnapps and caffè? And Mr Bradley, some brandy."

"Perfect timing Albert."

"I was rather afraid they would fall from Franz's flailing hands, and the bowl is for…"

"Miss Bennett's dog. Miss Bennett might like to join us on our visit to Hungary."

"To stay with M. de Hedevar, Sir?"

Albert filled the bowl with water and gave it to the smell, which didn't growl, but lapped amiably, wagging its tail. From a pocket, a twist of greaseproof paper proved to contain some minced veal, which looked as if it should be part of a person's elegant repast. It too was graciously accepted.

"Do we leave tomorrow, Sir?"

"Yes, that's if Miss Bennett agrees? Miss Bennett, this is Albert, my absolutely best friend in all the world."

"How do you do, Albert, best friend in all the world."

"How do you do Miss Bennett?"

"Oh no!" said Mr Bradley, not really wanting this mutual admiration society to continue. "We can't leave tomorrow, I have a meeting with Mr Hitler tomorrow, or possibly today." He inspected his watch, "definitely today, but fortunately not until much later, so we could leave after that."

Albert had been collecting clothes and ashtrays and generally being busy, but he paused and "Are you? I say I say."

Miss B. glared, "I'm not sure I shall join you after all!"

"For Heaven's sake! How could I refuse? The Prince presented me with the meeting like the finest caviar on a Lalique plate, which was nearly shattered by his multiple exclamation marks.

"Anyway, I might discover something useful, and I'm likely to be granted only a few seconds of the great leader person's time."

"Well heigh ho for that, I am all in favour of useful things." Miss B. drained her schnapps and looked about her expectantly. "Now, where shall I sleep?"

Albert bowed slightly, between the eyebrows* and the dimples, his blue eyes almost disappeared.

"We must avoid anything anstandig I say I say. So if Mr Bradley would condescend to sleep in my room, I think as Miss Bennett might be quite comfortable in this one."

"Perfectly† comfortable I am sure Albert."

"But what about you? I could sleep on the sofa look," said Mr B., leaping tidily onto the overstuffed mentioned article. He closed his eyes and snored hopefully.

A small crease between the eyebrows indicated that Miss Bennett didn't favour this idea.

"Madam, I have a friend –"

"Not a cousin?' This from a somnambulant Mr B.

"Who would be happy to share her room with me, so that Mr Bradley could have mine."

"Albert! You lascivious beast! What would Nursie say?" Our hero tried to pull the ultimate punch – it didn't work.

"Nursie," Albert intoned as though invoking the Delphic Oracle, "would have said, 'well done that Albert for rescuing someone who would like to leave this city.' Miss Leonora will also provide Miss Bennett with female company on our trip to Hungary."

"Albert, you are definitely best friend in all the world." Miss Bennett rose. So did the dog with its multitudinous smells.

"Goodnight," she extended her hand. The dog wagged.

"Albert, you are a conniver, an evil fornicating 'scuse me Miss Bennett, so and so and you'll come to a sad end, but mostly you're a good egg."

---

* Sorry to mention the eyebrows again, but they are beautiful.

† Our hero's glance indicated that Miss Bennett would be practically perfect in any situation.

The dog growled.

"Most like Sir, most like. Now, I'll show you where's my room and I think I'll get the dog bathed, if you're agreeable Miss Bennett?"

"Dear Albert, you are full of excellent ideas."

Mr B. coughed and cried "Hem".[*]

"Am I allowed to say sleep well and probably lock the door? We don't want Franz flapping around. And may I have my toothbrush?"

"I certainly shan't need it."

"I shall need to dress in the morning."

"I should hope so. Don't worry, I'll be up early and take," she paused, eyeing Mr B., "Snuffles for a walk."

"Good night." And she shut the door firmly.

Mr B. followed Albert and Snuffles towards his new room. On their way he noticed a large amount of luggage in the corridor. "Miss Bennett's essentials," said Albert. "But don't worry, my friend has only one suitcase and our fine car has a large boot."

"You forget it's full of daffodil bulbs," said Mr B.

---

[*] This is reference to *She Stoops to Conquer*. I hesitate to mention to my well-read readers.

10

Mr B. settled with a small sigh into Albert's shoe-box-like room and almost immediately there was a knock on the door.

"It's half past seven and I'm off to walk Snuffles. Up you get and bathe and dress while I'm out. I might have breakfast with you."

This offer induced our hero to leave his bed with more alacrity than usual and within half an hour he was shaved, besuited and tied.

Miss Bennett returned with a different dog.

"Not another one! Where's Snuffles?"

"This is Snuffles, foolish person."

"But this is rather an appealing dog…"

"He is clean, and Nellie has brushed him. Nellie likes dogs."

"Nellie?"

"Albert's friend, Leonora."

"And this is she," Albert said, following his friend into the room. They each carried a heavenly smelling tray and wore Cherubic smiles.

"How do you do, Mr Bradley, I am Leonora Hirsch."

Charlie, who had been simultaneously admiring the breakfast smells (Don't Snuffle) and his friend's taste, pulled himself together, "Miss Hirsch, I'm so pleased you are able to join our Hungarian trip."

"As am I" said the self-contained girl, accepting his offer of a seat. Small and pale with dark hair folded into a chignon, she took coffee and a small piece of gingerbread. Constance was surrounding an omelette mit käse und Schinken, with some help from a well-buttered slice of toast. Mr Bradley wondered silently where she put it, and Snuffles, sensing his mistress was unlikely to leave even the tiniest morsel for him, went and lay at Nellie's feet in appealing mode. She stroked his tummy, "Poor boy, you are Jewish only by association. Whoever heard of a Jewish dog? It would be funny if it weren't so sad, because we are all 'Jewish Dogs' in Germany, so I am glad to go, glad that my parents are dead, not to see this, and glad to go with Albert too."

Albert didn't blush. He finished his apfelstrudel.

Constance clapped her hands, and said "Perfectly put. Keep the man till last."

"I do find it odd, this hatred of a section of the human race. I expect some Jewish people are horrid, but some English people are horrid, and for that matter some English people are Jewish. My father has a problem with Roman Catholics, but even he admits that Dr Spencer, who worships God that way, is an excellent person." Charlie finished his omelette (it was, or had been, quite delicious). "Perhaps I shall ask the leader person when I meet him."

"I say Mr Charlie, you should be very careful with that mouth of yours when you meet Mr Hitler."

"Don't worry Albert, I'm not a complete idiot!" Albert's face indicated that sometimes he did wonder. "Anyway my appointment isn't until 13.00 hours, as we say, and meanwhile I would love to see something of this city which has nothing to do with march pasts or shouty speeches. Miss Bennett, could you suggest a gentle walk with perhaps something pretty to stare at from a café, when we've had enough exercise?"

A raised eyebrow caused him to review his sentence. "Of course, if you agree to accompany me, I shall have something pretty stare at whichever way we walk."

Miss Bennett had the grace to smile.*

"Flattery will get you anywhere, and on this occasion it and I will get you to the church of St Laurence, where we could have a drink in the square and I expect you'll enjoy the fountain."

"Excellent. Albert?"

"I'll see to packing up the car, Mr B., and" he winked at Mr B.'s discomfort, "to Snuffles."

"That will be an undertaking and a half! Please Miss Bennett could you not leave some things behind?"

"Oh, I already have! The Graf's dear Major D. is sending some things to England for me. But I won't leave Unity's cast-off French frocks behind; she might decide she wants them back."

Mr B. looked at the fitted little number she wore, Navy Blue: it had white bits here and there; pockets and a collar and cuffs, and those bits had big navy buttons on. He decided to lose the argument.

"Leonora?"

"I have to finish my job here in the bar before I may leave."

Albert said, "So if we aim for 4.30ish, even if we don't travel too far this afternoon. I say I say I have a cousin in Regensburg."

"I knew you would say that," said Mr B.

"Will I wire him then will I?"

"Please do, dear Albert, till later then."

Miss Bennett found her hat and gloves. Mr Bradley

---

* No, dear reader, she did not blush. You should realise Miss Bennett, to use a modern phrase, doesn't do blushing.

found her arm. Goodbyes said, and good mornings bid to a redly blushing Franz, out they went into the September sunshine, walking between half-timbered houses potted with geraniums. It has to be said that Mr Bradley's idea of fun was not visiting churches (remember his upbringing, oh best beloveds) but the sun was in the sky, his arm was still in that of Constance as she named for him the statues on the Church's façade, and once inside, "There" she said. The light from a stained glass window fell upon and illuminated the plain wooden sculpture of an annunciation. "Yes," he said. She wandered off to light a candle, leaving him to work out who was which apostle along the nave.

The square was full of light and people talking, walking, sitting, eating, drinking. Charlie and Constance sat near the fountain and drank *Sekt*.

"Why should I admire the fountain?"

"Because it depicts the seven virtues."

"Aah," said Mr B., who had noted fourteen cascades of water – "natch."

"Can you do them?"

"Can I do what?"

"The seven virtues?"

"Personally, hardly any, or even none at all."*

"Well, try at least to name them. Everyone always forgets one."†

"Faith, hope and charity."

---

* Please don't dislike my/our hero for this disingenuous observation. As Albert has said, he needs to watch his mouth.

† Like the actors who played the magnificent seven in the film, here are six: Steve McQueen, Yul Brynner, James Coburn, Robert Vaughn, Charles Bronson, Horst Buchholz (oh yum) and I will take a small bet, readers mine, that you do not remember No. 7. Or like the twelve countries spelt with four letters, answers on the next page.

"The Christian ones, good."

"And then the Aristotelian ones, fortitude, justice and wisdom."

"And?"

"And," said our tarnished hero, swirling the *Sekt* around his glass and smiling,* "the one which should have been left out, Temperance."

"It means moderation in all things, not just drink, you toad!"

"I believe in moderation in all things, especially moderation."

"You should go to your appointment."

"Won't you come too?"

"No, I've just seen someone I would like to talk to."

"I'll get lost."

"No you won't! Off you pop!"

So off he did, tail slightly between legs and muttering to himself, "too clever by half."† ‡

---

* No reader, he smirked, disgraceful.

† Whether this applied to himself, dear reader, or to some other, who can tell.

‡ Brad Dexter. Iran, Iraq, Fiji, Laos, Mali, Chad, Cuba, Guam, Niue, Oman, Peru, Togo.

11

With only one wrong turning made, Mr B. arrived at the Grand Hotel at ten minutes to one, to be greeted by Franz, flapping and tapping his watch. "The Prince has been already here funfzenn minuten!"

"Oh dear," said Charlie, "then the Prince was early. He probably wanted a nice cold glass of something at the bar."

"Mr Bradley!" exclaimed the Prince from exactly that place, "a small glass of beer before we leave?"

"Yes please, Your Highness, I have been walking about this lovely city and it is thirsty work!"

"Thirsty work? Aha, another joke yes? Most amusing! But do not tell the Führer jokes! He is a serious person. He likes to discuss."

It was one thirty before they left the bar.

"The Führer prefers no early meetings. He is always talking late into the night – or writing speeches – and so he, how do you say – pulls himself out in the mornings."

"Unwinds?" Suggested Mr B., feeling the need after two steins to pull himself, "into the little boys' room if I may?"

"Of course, of course! Together we will go."

"Hi ho hi ho," thought Mr B., but he managed not to hum.

They sat, wreathed in bonhomie, as a Mercedes purred them through the streets of Nuremberg. Mr B. ruminated that although they had found the best hotel, they had not found the most ostentatious. Marble steps and a great deal of gilt greeted them. Not guilt then, thought our cross hero.

Immediately, they were surrounded by people. "Ah, Schaub," said the Prince, making his way up the curved staircase without pausing. Mr B. was imagining a Busby Berkley set piece descending towards them with Constance Bennett at the front waving her revealed pins.

"Guten Morgen, Herr Hoffmann," said the Prince and, nodding, "Dietrich."

Wrapped around by this trio, they came to ornate double doors. With a brief tap and a "Mein Führer?" the man called Schaub pushed the doors open. Mr B.'s companions made the Heil Salute, while he contented himself with a bow of the head and an outstretched hand, which was taken in a surprisingly gentle grip by the man who rose neatly from the largest desk Mr B. had ever seen. It was also the emptiest. The man named Hoffmann proceeded to snap away from a camera mounted on a well-positioned tripod.

"May I present Mr Bradley, a British Member of Parliament who has been most interested in our proceedings."

"And who has upset my friend, Miss Mitford."

"We had a biblical discussion, Sir. My intention was not to cause offence."

"Von Hessen, please sit, and you Sir. Sometimes my friends are overprotective." The interpreter's voice clattered away.

Small, close-set eyes bored upwards at Charlie from beneath eyebrows which closely matched the moustache. They didn't exactly bristle, but almost.

"I want to talk to you about the milk and fats, I hear you know about these things?"

Charlie wondered where the knowledge came from, but replied, "a small family company only. Cow and Gate."

"Milk and fats are very important for the Volk. I would like to improve production, and so, I would like you to speak to Carl Goerdeler. I want you to visit bottling plants and factories and I want you to send me pictures and statements from England about how your bottling works."

Mr Bradley began, "Alas, Sir, I am leaving..."

The murmur of conversation, which had continued behind him, was suddenly interrupted by joyful barks, and a large Alsatian landed on Charlie's lap. It proceeded to give his face a thorough washing, whilst pawing remorselessly at his shirt.*

This trip has been dogged by canines, thought Mr B., who could not resist a pun, even without an audience.

After a while, "Blondi! Kommen sie hier!"

You really enjoyed that, didn't you thought Mr B. as he mopped ineffectively with his hanky† at the paw and slobber marks on his shirt.

"Ah you like dogs, this is good. She is only a puppy – vi sitzen!" Blondi wandered over and sat. "She is only a puppy and not yet quite obedient. Dogs and countries need strong masters. What do you think of Mr Baldwin?"

"Mr Baldwin is my Prime Minister and a good man."

"But not perhaps a strong one?"

"In England, I think we prefer gentle‡ men to lead us:

---

* Pale blue silk, dears, with a little monogram on the pocket. Please remember no expenses in those days.

† Also pale blue silk.

‡ Mindful of Albert's admonishment he held the pause, thinking the insult to himself.

'In peace, there's nothing so becomes a man as modest stillness and humility.'"*

The eyebrows and, it seemed, even the moustaches were raised and the man stood.

"A leader should be strong, strong, strong! All else leads to decadence." Applause from around the room startled Mr B., but he managed not to jump. Now, "set the teeth," he thought but probably not just now, fair nature lost out to hard favoured rage a while back.† Herr Hitler paused, lifted his head, bristled again at our hero, and said definitively:

"Goodbye! Herr Goerdeler will call on you and later I will expect information."

"I wonder if Miss Bennett would enjoy touring a bottling plant," thought our hero as he bowed his farewells. He followed von Hessen down the swirly staircase. (This time he was in a top hat and tails with a shiny stick and Miss Bennett on his arm.) Meanwhile he nodded sagely at whatever words emerged from the man in front. Finally, the man said "I must stay with our leader, but the doorman, a taxi will you find."

"So kind, but I think I would like a little walk through your lovely city, may I repeat my thanks for all your hospitality… If ever you are in England?"

Cards and handshakes were exchanged.

The Prince might have been surprised when around the corner a very laden Mercedes pulled up beside Mr Bradley. Mr Bradley was not.‡

There appeared to be one suitcase which had not fitted into the boot. It was wedged between the two young

---

* *Henry V*, Act III, Scene I.

† Harry the Fifth once more (sorry), Act III, Scene II.

‡ You do remember about Albert? If not see p. 44 etc. And pay attention!

ladies and sat upon by a tail-thumping dog. "Ah, he's pleased to see you," said Miss Bennett.

"I'm not sure I share his enthusiasm. Does he have to come with us?"

"Of course, where else is he to go? The de Hedevars love dogs."

"And where did you stash the daffodil bulbs, or was it tulips?"

"If the young master will get in? We seem to be in the way of a rather large tank."

"A tank? Where's the camera!" Mr B. hopped in beside Albert.

"The camera is under your seat, but I took several snaps while you were enjoying the Führer's favour. I don't think anyone noticed."

"We posed and simpered," Miss Bennett giggled.

"In that case, no one in their right mind was watching Albert, well done you lot!"

"Snuffles helped too."

"Oh, yes? And what did Snuffles do?"

"He leapt from the car and pretended to run away and most of the contents of the tank followed him."

"How do you know that he was pretending?"

"Because he whizzed left, left and left again and hopped back into the car. The soldiers were exhausted. It was very funny," said Leonora.

"I thought you were going to explode!" Constance was reproving.

"You had tears running down your cheeks," accused her newfound friend.

"I was of course, upset by the loss of my Snuffles. Anyway, they were sweet, they are dog lovers!" And

Constance smiled and waved as they drew away from the curb.

"The leader likes dogs too, I shan't need a bath for a week, I've been thoroughly washed by an Alsatian."

"I don't wish to hear tales of depravity," Miss Bennett briefly put her hands over her ears, only to ask with a sly wink, "did she give you a massage too?"

Amid the levity Albert hoped that no one had taken down the Mercedes' number plate. He had muddied it earlier, but some people's eyes could make six out of one plus one.

"Now, what's been happening while I've been playing statesman – oh, and anyone want to visit a bottling plant?"

"Why? Does it have pretty flowers?" Constance kept a poker face.

"I thought you probably wouldn't, fortunately I'm hoping we'll have a previous engagement with Albert's relatives in Regensburg."

"I say I say as 'e's found us rooms above his cousin's restaurant in Watmarket."

"What Market's that then?" This came from Miss Bennett in a reasonable rendering of Albert's accent, to stifled giggles from her neighbour.

"I feel there's a certain amount of unnecessary laughter in this car. Any minute now those bulbs will burst forth before their time. They'll think it Spring with all this hot air around!"

"Well why not? No more Unity. Discord. Now I'm on holiday – yipppeeee!" and Miss B. flung her hat in the air. As it whipped away in the wind of their passing, Albert enquired, "Shall us stop to fetch that Miss?"

"No thank you Albert, I say I say it were a horrid hat!"

"I rather liked it."

"Anyone who wears paisley dressing gowns can have no opinion of a person's hat." Mr B. hoped that if he ever gave that person a hat she would not be so profligate with it.

"Anyway, it belonged to Unity, she didn't want it. Tant Pis."

"Oh goody, can we throw out a couple of, no several, suitcases as well?"

"So long as one of them belongs to you?"

"But I have only one."

"Ha!"

"I say I say if I may, hush up small change or I'll spend ya!* M. de Hedevar's sent you directions to his place, or we can meet him in Vienna, and this also arrived from the Duchess of Brunswick."

"For heaven's sake! Frederika. I had forgot. Excuse me?" He smiled to the back of the car, and opening the letter read, "Dear Mr Bradley, I have enjoyed your company blah blah most charming etc..." Albert raised his eyes heavenwards.† "I meant what I said, do you please visit us at Schloss Marienberg before you leave Germany. Frederika would also enjoy this and might welcome a lift to England. Yours, Viktoria Luise Brunswick."

Mr B. sighed, a hand on his shoulder and a question, "Is something wrong?" His covered hers, hers withdrew slowly.

"The Duchess asked me to ensure that Frederika returned safely and definitely to England. I said yes.

---

* Nursie had antipodean cousins and little birds in their nests should agree.

† Don't worry dear PC Person, his driving didn't falter. In any case there were no other cars on the straight(ish) road.

She's calling in my promise and we haven't much room in the car."

"Frederika is at a dreary stage. Don't let's worry about her now. We can always dump the bulbs." Constance winked at Albert in the mirror. "Let's enjoy our hols."

The occupants of the car were certainly in holiday mode when they crossed the medieval Steinerne Bridge to their destination.

"See, the beautiful Danube IS blue." And Constance, followed by Nellie, began to sing.

12

"It's so peaceful" Miss Bennett breathed in deeply, and lay back in her chair, eyes closed to the sun, glass of *Sekt* in hand. Mr Bradley was scribbling a letter.

"You are destroying the peace, please say you are not writing to the Duchess."

"All right, I am not writing to the Duchess."

"Liar!"

"True!"

"You adopt too many strays."

"Are you straying?"

"Certainly not, nor shall I be! I am – voyaging and WAS enjoying the sunlit peace. I didn't realise how tired I was of those endless parties. The frocks were nice though."

"The frocks are better than nice."

Mr B. eyed the little aquamarine number opposite and wondered how it undid. It seemed glove-like.

"I wouldn't have thought that you and Unity could be –"

"Friends."

"No, the same size."

"Hah – you think I'm fatter."

"No but –"

Constance sat up eyes akimbo.* "You do! You think I am huge."

"No, no, not at all," floundered our hero, "but you have more, I mean better shape... Oh dear, let me get

_____
* I know eyes can't be akimbo, dear person reading this, but I wasn't going to say eyes flashing. And actually I think it's a good picture.

you some *Sekt*, yours must be warm or gone or some-thing. Look at the cathedral and think of higher things."

"It's you who should think of higher things."

"I'll consider your eyes then." Those, no longer akimbo, narrowed at him.

"I think I might be sick."

"No more *Sekt* then."

"Yes, more *Sekt*."

"What do you say?"

"I say I say now!"

"Did I hear someone with a woigh-tish accent?"

"Dear Albert … and Nellie and Snuffles, your friend is being tiresome. He will get the *Sekt*. You sit down and rescue me."

Said friend strolled away, singing fairly quietly.

"Figaro su, Figaro giù, uno alla volta per carità."

"Stop! I almost prefer the snuffling to the singing." At this moment the dog joined in with some mews and moans all his own.

"Clever Snuffles. How well you accompany your master," cooed Constance, rubbing the tummy offered to her.

"What?" said Charlie, returning with a bottle and some pretzels and tiny sausages.

"It's YOUR dog."

"No no, you took him in."

"I took you in, not the animal."

"I have never been taken in by anyone."

"Not even by the three-card trick? I must show you."

"I say I say children, children, Regensburg was a peace-ful place before your arrival and you're making the dog feel insecure." The combatants subsided, each taking a shlurp of *Sekt*.

"I have found my cousin's restaurant, just the other side of St Peter's. It smells delicious, but we have rooms above which don't smell at all."

"Hmm, let's go then – a snooze before dinner'd be good. But let's finish these dear little wurstli, are there any more? And these pretzels are good too. Nellie?" Nellie and Constance prepared to leave. As they reached the car, another smart Mercedes sidled up to theirs.

"Mr Bradley? Carl Goerdeler at your service." Said the man who stepped from it.

"Bottling Plants?" Said our hero.

"A new variety with beautiful smelly flowers."

Constance clapped her hands and smiled seraphically.

"I say I say a good expletive: bottling plants, bluebells, and bother your aunt Betty." Nellie held quite tightly to Albert's arm. Herr Goerdeler seemed somewhat fazed by the laughter which greeted him. (His face was quite moon-like.) He cleared his throat and adjusted his spectacles.

"Yes, the leader is most insistent that you should come and see our innovations and comment on our plans for the future. He was upset when you left so suddenly."

"Herr Goerdeler, how do you do. So sorry for being so shy, but we are on holiday, you see. May I present Miss Constance Bennett, Miss Leonora. I did try to explain to Herr Hitler that we had been invited to stay with friends and were leaving immediately, perhaps he had other things on his mind."

"Herr Hitler has many things on his mind, but he does not mislay any of them. He wishes you to visit factories and I am here to escort you."

"We are expected in Vienna tomorrow," said Mr Bradley gently, "we cannot retrace our steps."

His charming smile detracted from the force of his "cannot".

"Fortunately, my dear Sir, there is a plant very near Regensburg. I will bother you for maybe two hours of your time."

"Then I shall look forward to our visit, but we were just going to our rooms. Perhaps you would like to join us later for dinner?" Mr B. trod not too heavily on Miss Bennett's toe.

"WHAT a good idea," her voice was pitched a little high, "about eight o'clock then? At the restaurant in the Watmarket."

"Thank you Fräulein, with pleasure I accept."

"Bye-bye then," Constance smiled and hopped (I use the word advisedly) into the car.

"May we perhaps meet beforehand to discuss matters, Mr Bradley?"

"There is a bar across the square," Albert said.

"Wat bar?" hissed Constance.

A meeting at 7.15 was agreed and then the Mercedes went their separate ways.

Constance lit a cigarette.

"How did he know we were here? And who is he anyway with his magical bottle growers."

"I know who he is." Nellie was in the front with Albert, and she held on to a piece of his jacket as though to a rabbit's foot. "And he knows who I am. He was Mayor of Leipzig, and he was my father's patient."

"I say I say don't get the oars out yet." Albert smiled, "he can't interfere."

"But I have no passport."

"Soon you will, soon you will. My cousin has a friend."

"For crying out loud," Mr B. also lit up. "Enough of

your relatives. Might it be one of them who told the Boeterleterler where we were going?"

"The hotel will have known," said Albert, un-grumpily. "I imagine they opened M. de Hedevar's note and probably listened to any telephone conversations."

"Intolerable."

"Fact. Naturally, we have been watched since we arrived."

"Why didn't you tell me?"

"You were having too much fun."

"Sometimes Albert Shieff…"

"But what's this about a passport or the lack of one?" Constance's gloved hand squeezed Nellie's shoulder.

"It is difficult for a Jew to acquire a passport."

"It's virtually impossible" agreed Albert.

"But there are ways … and here is our way."

Jolly geraniums, cheerful green shutters and a rubicund Schieff wearing a green apron presented themselves.

"Wilkommen, wilkommen! Herauf Kommen!"

Up they went into the eaves, where were crisp white sheets, flowers and flasks of water, wine and beer, and little bowls of biscuits, nuts and fruit.

"How lovely," Constance smiled, "no Albert, just those two. Thank you!"

"Two?" enquired our hero.

"Certainly two, how do I know what I want to wear tonight, what with your smart pal comin' an all." Constance observed Mr Bradley's crossness.

"But if you don't tread on my toes again, I will be on my best behaviour at eight."

"I say I say me and Nellie are off to see a man about a dog, so could you be on your best as well, 'cos we don't need no dog fights."

85

"I'll take Snuffles," Mr B. turned into his room and hung up his jacket. Looking around he found a happy hairy person panting upon his pillow.

"No, No! Not there." The tail wagged.

"To the bottom," a stern command. The dog considered then plodded to the bottom of the bed, leaving delicate footprints on the pristine linen.

"Good boy!" And our hero zizzed. After about four minutes the dog cuddled into his master's shoulder and buried its head around his neck. Mr B. pretended not to notice. He sniffed and sighed; over and above the dog niff, Snuffles smelled faintly of lilies of the valley.

13

In another four minutes, or so it seemed:

"I say I say you spoil that dog you do."

"Good Grief, urgh, seven o'clock."

"And time for Snuffle's din-dins, isn't it Snufflekin?"

The wagging tail and conjoined bottom wagged all over Mr B.'s face.

"Urgh, ugh, urgh. Go away, get down! Is the passport sorted?"

"Yes Mr Charlie, my cousin's sister-in-law has a daughter who…"

"I don't need to know the details, but is Nellie still Nellie?"

"Fortunately my cousin's sister-in-law's daughter is also Leonora."

"So she is Leonora what?"

"Leonora Jager. She has gone from being the deer to being the hunter."

"And you are her prey?"

"My name is not Beute,* but still Shieff."

"Rescue boat then, I say I say good old Nursie." Charlie exited quickly to wash away the dog hairs and escape the eyebrows.

Carl Goerdeler awaited him in the weinstube.

"Not, wot bar, but witch bar!" thought Charlie peering into the gloom.

---

* Schiff: boat in German; Beute: booty or prey. Albert's surname is an Isle of Wight corruption.

"Mr Bradley! Some Riesling? Or would you prefer *Sekt*? Or a glass of beer?"

"Riesling please," he sat. "I fear I have been rude, making you chase me across Germany. I had not understood that Mr Hitler so valued my not-very-informed opinion. I do wonder though, how you found us?"

"When you are working for the Führer, it is not difficult to find whatever you need.

"But I should tell you the reason for requesting this meeting. It is I, more than the Führer, who seeks your advice."

Mr B. stared.

"You may not know, but I am Reich Commissar of Price surveillance."

Mr B. shook his head and waited.

"I have asked twice for this committee to be wound up. It is an elephant without tusks."

"A white elephant? A toothless tiger?"

"Just so."

"Maybe an armadillo then, or a rhino?"*

Mr Goerdeler frowned.

"The Führer wishes to be seen to take care about food."

"Milk and fatstuffs."

"Precisely, but he doesn't want to spend money in that direction. He wants to buy arms. And he wants to stretch out Germany to beyond her old borders. I would like to see people fed, and we wish to have wonderful exportation of cheeses and wursts."

"I understand, sausages."

"Indeed, what are weapons for? Another war we need not."

---

* I fear our hero is talking too clever by 'alf again. See the *Just So Stories* by Rudyard Kipling.

Mr B. nodded and waited.

"There will be starvation. Money will be in wheelbarrows again." Mr Goerdeler shook out a rather crumpled handkerchief and blew his nose firmly.

"It is difficult to convince the Führer," he said sadly. "But you could help. You could persuade your company to import our cheeses. It would be a beginning? And maybe you could send someone big to help us with our fat?"

Mr Goerdeler was not a small person but our hero kept a straight face.

"Mr Goerdeler – how many people think as you do? It will be difficult to arrange these things with unsympathetic customs."

"I know it will not be easy, but please will you try. You must see it would be better to spend money this way than…"

"That," Mr B. thought of Udet and the march past.

"Good! Sehr gut. Here is my card. I shall hope to hear from you soon."

"And the bottling plant?"

"Do you really wish to see one? I do not think it is necessary."

"Oh, but I think it will be a vital part of Miss Bennett's education. We should love to visit."

"May I say two things?"

"Of course."

"The de Hedevars are not friendly to the Führer."

"Nor are you it seems."

"Only on this one issue – THEY laugh at everything."

"Yes, it is rather endearing."

"They are watched."

"Just as we are," our hero bared his teeth. It was not a smile.[*]

"And the second thing?"

"Leonora Hirsh is in your party?"

"Leonora Jager is in our party."

"Leonora's father treated me in Leipzig. He was an excellent doctor; unfortunately he was married to a Jewess. Leonora was an excellent nurse. Of course she couldn't train to be a doctor. She is married now?"

"Leonora Jager is not married." Yet, thought Mr B.

"I shall be pleased then, to make the acquaintance of your friend who was once a deer and is now the hunter."

"Grrr," thought Mr B., "why does everyone want to educate me?"

---

[*] But he had brushed them m'dears.

14

Albert's cousin's restaurant was wreathed in smoke and other fumes of a more nutritious nature. Albert was alone at their table. He stood.

"Mr Shieff, my friend Mr Goerdeler, is looking forward to seeing Miss Bennett and Miss Jager. Perhaps you would tell the young ladies that he is here?"

Albert's eyebrows* signalled a minor panic.

"My cousin Wilhelm has chosen for us, but I would like to be certain that our guest approves of the menu."

Betting to himself that there was indecision on the frock front, Mr B. strode upstairs to find two totally dressed persons: one pale and mulish, the other inhaling deeply.

"Nellie won't come down."

"I'm sorry Mr Bradley, but he knows me and yes, I am afraid. I am a coward."

"Leonora," Mr B. sat beside her on the bed, "you are not a coward, you are understandably wary. But Mr Goerdeler has made me a business proposition, which he will not want to jeopardise. He will accept you as Miss Jager. It will look odd if you don't join us, and in that outfit it would be a crying shame."

"Humph, I suppose you think Nellie fits Unity's frocks better than I do?"

Miss Bennett is in green-eyed monster mode, thought Charlie, eyeing the jade-coloured shimmer before him. He refused to rise, however, merely saying:

---

* Swoon.

91

"We shall, I hope, be honoured by the company of both beautiful ladies. But be warned, Albert's cousin has ordered our food. We may never need to eat again. I give you two and a half minutes. Then I shall invite Snuffles to the table instead. Where is the damn – sorry darling – dog anyway?"

Constance laughed, "your dog finds your pillow his preferred place of rest."

Charlie bowed, hand on heart.

"If only others felt the same," and removed himself smartly, in the face of an about-to-be thrown, beautifully green, shoe.

About three minutes later, the Misses Bennett and Jager entered the packed dining room to a great many male swivelled heads and not a few Fräulein frowns. Constance sat herself between Mr Goerdeler and Albert and proceeded to engage the former with such a flood of conversation that he was unable to speak to Nellie on his left.

The blinis with smoked fish came and went, the spicy soup was schlurped. The Schnitzel of veal with potato dumplings and apple-y red cabbage vanished. Wilhelm then arrived with gingerbread and almond biscuits, vanilla ice cream and,

"Oh heaven," cried Constance, "Welsh Rabbit."

"A Regensburg Rabbit, Meine Dame."

"An even more heavenly rabbit then, thank you Wilhelm, thank you Albert!" And wolf-like she proceeded to devour the Rabbit. Charlie, still impressed by the quantities of food Miss Bennett consumed, recited to himself, "The Assyrian came down like the wolf on the fold, and his cohorts were gleaming in purple and gold."* Then he changed it to: "Miss Bennett came down like a wolf she was seen, and her dress it was gleaming in silver and green."

Waking from a pleasurable reverie, he saw that Mr Goerdeler had finally fixed on Nellie. "Tant Pis," he thought.

Constance shrugged too and they both turned to Albert with praise for Wilhelm, supper, the ambience, next day's plans, this plus that plus the other.

Meanwhile, "Fräulein Jager, it is good to make your acquaintance." Herr Goerdeler spoke in German.

"And yours, Sir," Nellie replied.

"Have you ever lived in Leipzig? Your face seems so familiar?"

Nellie wondered whether to lie.

"Yes, I used to live there, but now for some time I have lived in Nuremberg."

"I too am from Leipzig."

"It is a beautiful city."

"It is and I had a great friend there, A Dr Hirsh. Do you perhaps know him?"

What to do, what to do? Nellie glanced at Albert but he was in deep conversation with Constance, while Mr B. was conferring with the wine waiter.

"My dear," Mr Goerdeler's hand encompassed hers upon the table. "He was a good friend, a great doctor. I would like to hear from him."

"Impossible."

"Impossible?" Nellie retrieved her hand. She looked at her dinner companion.

"He's dead."

"He was not old?"

---

* Byron.

"No. He was sad. After 1933, fewer and fewer people visited his surgery, and no one came to my mother's concerts."

The ultimate word came as a whisper as Nellie realised what she had said.

"My dear, I knew. You are so like him."

Goerdeler gently pulled away the hand which covered her mouth.

"The Jewish thing doesn't bother me – what is it, you have two Jewish grandparents?"

"Three. More than enough."

"Well, I am concerned with food production, not ancestry. Please tell me what happened. I saw your father, what, eighteen months ago?"

Nellie badly needed to tell the story that she had boxed and put away. Words jostled their way out of her mouth.

"My mother was stopped from performing. She practised and practised. She practised until her fingers were raw. For what? My father had no patients and no patience.* They quarrelled. She took alcohol and pills and soon she was dead. We were not allowed to bury her in the cemetery near my parents' home. She was carted off to some unknown place. My father wouldn't go there. He died within the month."

Goerdeler's hand again reached for hers.

"Please believe that I am so sorry."

Leonora looked at him. "I believe you, but are you doing anything to stop more and worse things happening?"

"Leonora!!!"

"The exclamation marks tell me everything. No you are NOT. Tell me, Herr Goerdeler, are you a perfect Aryan? Do you know the stories of Mary Poppins who

---

* Auch no geduldijand no nicht geduld – it works in German too!

94

was practically perfect in every way? That is how we must be now in Germany. Practically perfect. But only in an Aryan way. And people who should know better stand back and do nothing, as though deaf and blind."

Mr Bradley's hand was on her shoulder.

"Miss Jager," his voice was as firm as his hand. "Some coffee?"

"Please," she smiled but her voice let her down with a squawk.

"Mr Goerdeler, for you?"

Dinner concluded with coffee and schnapps and pursed eyebrows from Constance.

"Herr Goerdeler. I understood we were to visit an exotic garden with wonderful plants. Silly me."[*] She said with composure.

"I did not imagine clanking machinery of jangling bottles. I really do not think my nerves could stand it. Will you forgive me if I forgo the pleasure?"

"Of course, Fräulein. It was your friend who thought you might be interested."

"My friend? Oh, you mean Mr Bradley – how very sweet of him, but he doesn't know me very well, and he is certainly NOT my friend.[†] Goodnight, it has been most charming. Come Nellie."

Constance's smile encompassed the room and mesmerised most males therein.

Left behind, the gentlemen slowly finished their drinks. It was decided that Mr B. would visit the factory with Herr G., leaving the ladies a lazy morning. Albert felt the car needed some attention before proceeding to Vienna;

---

[*] Q: Do you think Miss Bennett means this? Answers on one side of A4.

[†] Only a joke, hoped Mr Bradley.

"Do be careful of those bulbs," said Mr Bradley, to the mystification of Mr Goerdeler. Then they walked him and the dog to his hotel.

Herr Goerdeler professed to love dogs and bent to stroke Snuffles, but was nearly bitten for his pains. Mr Bradley walloped the dog, but said: "Sorry, he's had a hard time and is somewhat nervous. Miss Bennett rescued him from being beaten up by uniformed thugs."

"No matter, no matter," said Mr Goerdeler.

"We thought it did, actually," bowed Mr B. "Goodnight."

Dearest readers, the next chapter will not open with a description of bottling plants, see how well I look after you. But you should know that a bottling plant is a place where people guide bottles along a track so that they may be filled and stoppered. It is noisy and smelly. We may prefer a place where bottles are emptied which is also noisy and maybe smelly, but a lot more fun. What I will tell you is that our hero, on previous bottling plants visits, had to stop himself from knocking a bottle into a domino fall. This occasion was no different. He was very proud of himself therefore, as without knocking anything over and smiling sweetly, he bade adieu to Mr Goerdeler.

15

What can anyone say about Vienna that has not been said before? You, dear reader, I am sure, know Vienna better than I and certainly better than Mr B. and Albert, neither of whom had visited the city. There was a small argument in the back of the car. The ladies had both been to Vienna on numerous occasions and could not decide where to go first. It was settled that Sacher's was the immediate necessity, where tickets for the opera and the Lipizzaners could be further discussed. Albert thought he might have a cousin, but Miss Bennett with great sweetness insisted that they stay with her mother's friend, Lydia von Liebenstein.

"She will be devastated if she hears that I have come to Vienna and not stayed, besides I sent her a wire."

"You are an ad-or-a-ble bossy boots," said Mr Bradley. Albert still thought he and Leonora should stay with the cousin.

So Sacher's was visited and Sachertorte munched and in some cases hot chocolate drunk as well. Charlie and Albert confined themselves to tea, looking forward to something stronger later.

Constance's mother's friend lived alone and was definitely delighted to receive visitors. Even Snuffles, who growled, but "dear little dog!" said his hostess, who mostly thought the best of everyone. Her husband, whom she had met when he was a dashing attaché to the Viennese Embassy in London, was prematurely dead and her children grown-up.

"But my dear, I am still here and I still enjoy company. I miss Josef, but what could I do? Not leap into the poor dear man's coffin! So I have organised a little dinner party tonight, and then tomorrow we are invited just outside Vienna to my great friends the von Beckburgs and then –"

"And then cara, we have tickets for the Lipizzaners – we bought one for you too."

"Oh wonderful – sorry to rabbit away and organise you so, but I want to show you off. Also I am afraid because I live on my own, I gush at guests." Taking Mr B.'s arm, she confided this last truth sotto voce into his ear. "I shall say no more until we have a glass of champagne. Fritz? Friiitz?" She shrieked forgetting to move her mouth away. An elegant old man seemed to materialise at her elbow, carrying a tray full of champagne glasses.

"Madame?"

"Fritz, there you are. Sometimes I think you are becoming deaf."

"Yes Madame." His soothing tones were unmatched by the smile and the wink he gave as he turned to Mr B.

"My name is Fred, Sir; I came from London with Miss Colvin, that is Mme von Liebenstein after she was married. She thought Fritz better suited to Vienna. Let me know if I can be of assistance and," he whispered, "speak into her left ear."

"Thank you Fred," said our hero, who rather thought his left ear might never hear again.

"And Karl has taken up your bags."

"Charlie?"

"No, he really is Karl."

Albert resisted every invitation to stay with Mme von Liebenstein and after arranging a meeting place for the following evening he and Leonora departed to stay with the cousin. Snuffles, his family split in two, sighed deeply and occupying as much of the Aubusson as he could, offered his tummy for inspection/tickling/compliment. Preferably all three.

"What a shame," said Lydia, "that they wouldn't stay. Such a handsome man and those eyebrows…"

Mr B. wondered inwardly how rich he'd be if he had £1 for every time the eyebrows* were mentioned by a lady, but he said, "Albert has an extended family and coming from the Isle of Wight and living in London, doesn't see his relations often."

"Interesting looking girl too… Isle of Wight? Oh, how I remember Bembridge† in the 20s. What fun we had. Do you know Bembridge?"

"My father has a house in Sandown, on the South Coast."

"Oh well, you're bound to know the Medways? No? Well then the Reddingtons? No? Island life is so – insular. Now – thank you Fritz."

Lydia allowed her glass to be filled.

"Tonight my darlings, if I may say darlings, I've heard so much about you Mr Bradley. I feel I may say darling, if you don't mind? You don't? Excellent."

"My wire was quite succinct, I thought." Constance interrupted the cascade.

"Dearest, you wire that you are bringing an unknown (to me) gentleman friend to visit, and you don't SUPPOSE that I will make enquiries? Really! I know I am a sad lonely old bore, who will have almost ANYONE to stay, but there are LIMITS. Of course I telephoned Lalage."

* Here actually he used a very shocking adjective but I do like to protect my dear readers from unnecessary vulgarity.

† Some people who visit the Isle of Wight do not admire Bembridge, or even acknowledge its existence. Sandown was once rather grand.

"You telephoned my mother? In that case, Mr Bradley, I'm afraid we are probably engaged to be married."

"Delighted, of course," bowed our hero. "Was that a proposal?"

"No."

"Good, because that wasn't an acceptance."

Lydia stared at each of them in turn, momentarily silent.

"Are you engaged or not?"

"No!" Came the jointly firm reply.

"Oh well. I dare say… Anyway, your Mama was useless, but I spoke to Antonia Plunkett…"

Through gritted teeth, Mr Bradley interrupted:

"Dear Mme von Liebenstein."

"Lydia, please."

"Dear Lydia, you do know she is the most indiscreet woman in London?"

"Is she dear?"

"The announcement is probably already posted in *The Times*, or at any rate set abroad in the gossip columns."

"Now dear, don't confuse me. I thought you said you were not engaged."

"We're not!" Came the simultaneous response.

"Well. So Antonia was very helpful. I shan't repeat what she said, you might blush."

"Oh no he wouldn't," hissed Constance.

"But every hostess in London is after you for her table."

"Only for her table? That's a shame. I don't want to be a table."

"Hush up small change or I'll spend ya." Constance found good use for Albert's phrase.

"And then I spoke to Clemmie Churchill." Mr Bradley bent his head towards his knees.

"Oh, you needn't be worried, Clemmie is charmed by you too, and she's not your only female admirer in that family. So you see I know all about you. And I was able to reassure dear Lalage as well."

It was Constance's turn to look at her shoes. Nice blue ones today, thought Mr B.

"You have not telephoned your Mama for a while, Constance, would you like to use mine? Fritz will place a call for you."

"I think I'd better," Miss Bennett said grimly.

"Now my surprise, you remember dear Unity from your schooldays? Well, she is here in Vienna, isn't that grand! So I have asked her for dinner tonight, won't that be fun? Such a pretty girl and so clever. When did you last see her, I don't suppose for ages?"

"Last week," muttered Constance. "She was in Nuremberg."

"Oh dear, you don't sound too pleased, you two are still friends?"

"Oh yes, we're friends, in fact these are her shoes. I've just seen rather a lot of her lately."

"And you – you will love her Mr Bradley."

"Charlie, please."

"She is so beautiful and witty."

"I have met Miss Mitford."

"There, how clever of me: people who know each other and people who don't. The perfect party mix. Of course, no one who has met Unity forgets her."

"No indeed," our hero remembered that his days were numbered. Constance enquired, "Unity is not the only guest?"

"Oh now, I think we will be twenty or so. Some Italian friends of mine, with a very handsome son, by the way.

Italian men are so charming, but they do not make good husbands." Lydia's blue eyes became a more piercing blue as she looked with what she thought was nonchalance around the room.

"Also that man who used to be Ambassador in London, who is a sweetie but whose name escapes me, and his wife who is rather dull and frumpy, but a dear, a complete brick, franchement carrément. And my neighbours, the Fredricks. And the Walderdorfs from Salzburg who are staying with them and dear Josef's cousin, Wilhelm. We will be a little family party."

Fritz was refilling their glasses.

"Thank you Fritz dear. Now who else is coming tonight? My memory."

"Mr and Mrs Cunningham, Madame."

"Oh so charming. And on their honeymoon."

Lydia stared beadily at her guests.

"And M. and Mme Serurrier."

"Of course, from Paris but currently in the French Embassy here."

"Luncheon is served whenever Mme is ready."

"Thank you Fritz, and please book a call through to Mrs Bennett in London, Regent 214."

"If you will excuse me, I think I must take Snuffles outside briefly," said Mr Bradley, hoping for a peaceful five minutes. Snuffles, upon hearing his name, spun from prone to attention and danced over to Mr B., giving tongue to his, "what a good idea, what a good idea" song.

"Your dog" mouthed Constance.

"No no no, Charles, I will not be parted from you. Karl can take the dear boy walkies."

At this word, Snuffles ratcheted up his song a decibel or two.

"Or Johann."

Johnny? Wondered Mr B. to himself, and abandoning all thoughts of peace, offered up Snuffles' lead to Fred, who said:

"Certainly, my young nephew Jonathan will happily oblige."

Mr B. asked himself why he was surrounded by people who read his thoughts, as he sat down to an aromatic omelette with salads of tomato and onion and cucumber, and – oh joy! Sautéed potatoes all crunchy and golden.

Constance whispered, "because your face is sooo open."

"Just a little light smackerel of something." Said Lydia.

"Afterwards we can have cheese and appfelstrudel or wild strawberries."

Which they did, our hero allowing the waterfall of words to wash over him; but he went for a long walk with Snuffles afterwards. Constance spoke to her mother.

16

"It's quite all right!" said Constance.

"What's quite all right? I see very little in store for me this evening which even approaches all right."

Constance flapped a hanky either side of Mr B.'s face.*

"Gracious, you have little puffs of steam coming out of your ears! How peculiar!"

She walked around him.

"What? What are you doing?"

"What, what? Just making sure steam is not escaping from anywhere else. Once can't be too careful!"

"As well as being infuriating you are also vulgar. Now, how exactly is this going to be all right?"

"Oh my Mama has published a denial of any engagement between us, so it's all right."

"What?"

"What What?" She mocked again.

"That's worse than anything."

"So you would like to marry me?"

"No – No, well not until I've asked you anyway."

"What?"

"What what!"

They were waiting in the drawing room, an elegant confection of pale-ish green with touches of apricot, for Lydia and her guests to arrive, and "what is all this whatting?" enquired their hostess, swishing into the drawing room draped in eau de nil silk; closely followed by Fritz/Fred with fizzing glasses.

---

* It was quite clean, dears.

"Oh we were just wotting away while waiting for you, how lovely you look, dear Lydia, in that beautiful dress."

"This is a venerable old frock. I am pleased you dignify it with a compliment. Whereas yours, my dear, is obviously bang up to the minute. Is that what they call Shocking Pink?"

"I suppose it is. It was certainly a shocking price. Fortunately, Unity paid for it. I wonder if she'll remember it. She doesn't usually wear things more than twice."

To Mr B.'s mind, the dress covered a little too much of Miss Bennett's body, but on the other hand, it did seem to emphasise the bits it covered and all in all it rather suited her.

"Dear Lydia, how lovely, Constance! What fun! Thank you Fritz."

A patrician voice peppered with exclamation marks intruded upon his reverie.

"I say, you look sweet in that old frock, so glad I gave it to you! But – have you got that hat with the feather? The purply one?"

Constance stared blankly, "NO."

"Lying toad," thought Mr B.

"And there's another I'm missing – a rather fetching navy trilby?"

"Dear Unity – so lovely to see you. But I NEVER wear trilbies, most unbecoming."

Mr Bradley didn't say "So that's why you threw it out of the car." He had not long to wonder how good Constance was at poker, before…

"You! What are you doing here?"

Miss Mitford's eyebrows raised themselves almost to her immaculately curled hairline.

"You should be dead."

"Sorry to disappoint you…"

"The Führer."

"Aah, well you see, I was invited to meet your friend and…"

"Impossible!"

"Well, I think you made me out to be such a creep, he thought I might be quite fun. His dog liked me anyway. So maybe that was in my favour."

"I don't believe you! In any case, Blondi only likes me!"

"Perhaps she might have more than one friend!" Mr B. declared – that exclamationism was definitely catching, as he wondered whatever to say next. Just then an exuberant Snuffles pranced into the room. He had had another good walk, but he looked at his pack and seeing one of them was not at all happy with the person he was barking at, he carefully lifted his leg over her trailing, beaded handbag. His master noticed, but failed to make mention of the misdemeanour, since he had been scooped up by Lydia.

"Dear Unity, you must not monopolise our nice Mr Bradley. You will be able to talk to him when we dine. Come and meet the Serruriers, Charlie, and do bring Snuffles. They love dogs."

"Actually I think it's time our baby went to bed."

"Your baby," hissed Constance.

"My nephew has taken a great fancy to the dog and would be happy to look after him." Murmured Fritz, omniscient and omnipresent.

"Maybe that would be best," said Lydia. Charles quietly signalled gratitude. Snuffles exited, bowing right and left; a long piece of Bugle beadery trailing from his mouth to be enjoyed later. Unity appeared not to have noticed as she greeted the Cunninghams.

"He'll have an upset tummy and he's sleeping with you," Constance hardly moved her lips.

"Could you have an upset tum too?"

"What?"

"What, what?"

"I do not ingest beads!"

"Bet you put them up your nose when you were little…"

"As a child, Constance was Mary Poppins-like in her perfection," said Lydia, "Now do come on, Mme Serrurier, may I present Mr Bradley? Charles, Mme Serrurier, whose English is perfect."

"Aussi, mon Francais n'est pas trop mal."

"Alors! Nous allons nous amuser." Mme Serrurier was a lady of a certain age, but being Parisienne, très soignée chic et aimable. Mr Bradley smiled his best smile. "What do you most enjoy in Vienna?"

"Voilà Monsieur, je suis ici pour le travail de mon mari, mais j'adore les Lipizzaners."

"I have not seen them, but we have tickets for tomorrow night. Miss Bennett is full of admiration for them."

"And you are full of admiration for Miss Bennett, n'est ce pas?" Bottling plants to Lydia, thought our hero and managed, in a strangulated English way, "She's a most amusing travelling companion."

"Ah non! C'est bien plus que ça! Moi, je suis Parisienne et perspicace. En plus, evidemment, elle vous aime aussi."

"Qui est-ce que j'aime?" enquired the travelling companion, joining them with, from Mr Bradley's point of view an un-admirable sense of timing.

"That little chienne of course." The words tripped off Mme Serrurier's tongue sans blague, sans blush.

"It's a boy."

"Vraiment? But so pretty, I should say handsome, who

would have known? I have a Vendéene qui m'aime aus-siment. She is so clever but – she thinks she is a lapdog* which is vachement agaçant. So the lovely Lipizzaners – and maybe the opera?"

"*Die Entführung aus dem Serail*, and we have eaten cake at Sacher's, so we have our hat-trick."

"But here is Countess Walderdorf, who will want you to see much more of Austria."

"Of course, I would recommend Salzburg," smiled Harriet von Walderdorf. "We have our own lovely opera house and so many lovely churches and castles."

Mr Bradley reckoned his ration of opera to be one a year.

"Sadly we are off in the opposite direction to stay in Hungary with the de Hedevars, but I should love to return."

"I insist that you do."

The evening might have proceeded with more charming chitchat, but Fritz appeared, sans bottle, and coughed.

"Excuse me Mesdames, but there is a gentleman down-stairs to see Mr Bradley. The Gentleman who was here the morning, Sir."

"My apologies," bowed our hero, thinking how unlike Albert to interrupt.

It was also unlike Albert to be pacing up and down, but that is what he was doing.

"I say I say as I'm sorry," he said. Oh dear, eyebrows down thought Charlie, who didn't share the ladies' admi-ration for Albert's eyebrows, but noted them, rather as one would a dog's tail.

"Nellie has walked out."

---

* Vendéenes, reader mine (probably only one left now) are huge hairy basset hound types.

"Albert you foul toad, what have you said – or done?"

"Not funny Mr C. – my vile cousin, not to mention his wretch of a wife, took it upon themselves to deliver some cosy Nazi rhetoric while I was out seeing to the car. Nellie left me a note saying she didn't want to 'embarrass' me in front of my cousin. Hah! I should've known when he hinted earlier that he was involved in the president's murder last year."

"Dolfuss" (Engelbert Dolfuss, Chancellor of Austria). "That's him."

"I thought all those brutes were in Jug?"

"Obviously not this one! I expect he's all mouth and kept safely to the sidelines, but his claptrap obviously upset Nellie. She told Dietrich she had to leave to visit a sick cousin."

"Now that is funny," Charlie said, hastily continuing – "no no obviously not!"

"You must take," "May I take…" "The car." They spoke together.

And, "good" they said.

"She might come here?"

"I did keep a look-out on the way."

"Don't be too worried. I'm sure Leonora can look after herself: she managed before we arrived in Nuremberg – maybe she's re-thought her slightly impetuous decision to join us?"

"As for impetuous, there's a lot of that about, as for the looking after, I'd decided to take charge of that; and I may have a sick cousin in this city, but she certainly hasn't. On another matter – may I stay tonight? I am persona non grata with my reptiles, having ventured an opinion about Mr Hitler and his silly ideas which wasn't to their liking."

"I'm sure that'll be fine, I'll speak to Fritz/Fred. Tell me, have you, um, tried seeing where Nellie might be?"

"I'm like a blind man."

"Oh well, go and search and good luck."

The friends shook hands.

Mr Bradley returned to the party as it was about to settle down to supper and received a frown from his hostess as he had failed to take his assigned lady into dinner. Since this was Unity, he smiled sweetly, but, speedily casting his eye about the room, slotted himself into a seat next to Mme Serrurier. As he hastily overturned the placement card, a blushing young Austrian appeared:

"I think I am to sit here?"

"No no, Mein Herr, Miss Mitford has particularly requested your company over there," with one hand he indicated the empty space beside Unity while with the other he summoned Fritz/Fred to give him the offending card. Fritz's frown was more intimidating than his hostess' but it didn't last that long and our hero even received a wink as he escorted the Austrian across the room.

"Now I see you ARE the politician." Bluebells to Lydia – lots of them Charlie sighed.

"And I for one will never trust you again. On the other hand I am most flattered that you seek my company – or is it that I can be of assistance?"

"Madame, you are, in this roomful of beautiful women, one of the most beautiful and perhaps the cleverest. Therefore I am delighted to sit next to you."

"But also you and cette jeune femme – how do you say: you do not sit knee to knee?"

"Most certainly not! How shocking would that be?"

"Silly boy, I think I mean eye to eye?"

"She has some rather alarming friends."

"So the diplomat as well as the politician: formidable. But it is well to be alarmed; my husband has many worries about Germany and also Austria. He does not trust the people who are in charge, however much they seek to charm us and put sheep over our eyes."

"Sheep is good Madame – I think some people have become like sheep. In Nuremberg, I met Mr Hitler: he and his dog were eager to be friends. He asked me to write a report on England's milk production for him, aren't I the honoured one?"

"And will it be written?"

"It might be written, but I fear the post can be very unreliable, n'est ce pas?"

Once they were in the drawing room, Lydia pounced upon our hero, saying, "such bad manners! I cannot approve! And nor will Lalage. And now Constance has removed herself. What has become of society?"

"We have had a few hiccups this evening Lydia, I am so sorry if they disrupted your lovely party."

"You were not sitting where you should have been."

"But I am so in love with Mme Serrurier. I couldn't sit anywhere but beside her."

Constance overheard the last sentence.

"Now who are you pestering?" She rolled her eyes, "you are like some awful dog which wants to be loved by everyone."

"Speaking of which?"

"Speaking of witches, no not really, dear Unity has left, she had a tiresome headache, so Fritz found her a cab. She sent you apologies and thanks. Then I went to see the other awful dog."

"You love him really."

"Snuffles possibly, but not every awful dog. Anyway he is fine. Unity isn't and nor is her bag."

"No."

"No what."

"No you know well what."

"If you are going to what away at each other again I think I shall have a tiresome headache too. If you had sat next to Unity, I am sure she would be feeling quite well."

"Or a lot worse."

"Bah! Constance, please go and save Harriet Walderdorf, she has been stuck for aeons with that boring young man. I wonder why I invited him. And you Charles, leave Rosalie alone and you may briefly entertain your hostess."

17

The evening finished with no further hiccups, but with no sign of Albert or Nellie, even when Charlie walked Snuffles roundabout before bedtime. Returned to Lydia's house, the dog seemed undecided about where to sleep, but since the door to Constance's room was firmly closed, he made several circles around Charlie's pillow and plumped himself upon it with a sigh.

"Don't even think of remaining there, you're not the only disappointed male around here. Please stick to the bottom of the bed."

Snuffles half-opened one eye, and closing it, settled more deeply into the feather. So our soppy hero carefully lifted him, pillow and all to the bed's bottom. Fortunately there was a further uncontaminated pillow. Later on, however, a hairy something curled itself into the curve of Charlie's back with another sigh. Throughout the night any attempted move by the human was greeted with a growl from the dog.

"Good grief! You are about as tiresome as that one who wears hats." Said Mr Bradley, as he rose unrested from their bed. "I suppose you wish to go outside now?"

Snuffles' tail indicated that he did. Pulling on uncomfortable clothes our hero prepared to take the, by now singing, dog out and about.

"Mr Bradley?" The knock on the door sent Snuffles into rapturous snufflings.

"May I take the dog out of for you? Such a good boy

aren't you?" Said Johann/Jonathan, as he took the grate-fully proffered lead.

With relief Mr Bradley took himself down to the dining room and breakfast. Lydia and Constance were already seated and delicious smells interested his nose. "Don't sniff," mouthed the younger lady.

"Ah, dear Charles, I ordered a proper Englishman's breakfast especially, but Constance has eaten most of it. Why she isn't the size of an elephant I do not know!"

"I've left you some bacon," smiled the not elephant.

"Sweet of you, but I'm a tea and toast sort of person," Charles lied through his teeth. "Lydia, thank you for a wonderful party, much enjoyed by everyone I think."

"Well, Mr M.P. I don't think. Constance has been telling me about this and that."

"Wot about what."

"No, silly what person! About Leonora and Albert."

Constance answered his raised eyebrow. "Albert was here briefly early this morning. We spoke. There's no further news."

"And I have had a telephone call from Unity about her handbag."

Just then the handbag eater entered, accompanied by Johann, who was unsure whom to ask:

"Shall I feed him Madame, Miss Constance, Mr Bradley?"

"I think he's had enough to eat," said Lydia.

"But yes, please do and let's hope he's not sick."*

"Sorry about the bag."

---

* Dear dog-loving reader, if I haven't made mention of Snuffles' repasts before, it was because they didn't seem important. He has been fed, I assure you, regularly.

"So you should be, it's your dog. No, don't worry, she has others." Constance, I have to say, giggled.

"Apparently, Snuffles caused a domino reaction. The bag is now beadless."

"Which bag?"

"What?"

"The bag is now bead-less but not bagless!"

"What?"

"Oh, no more what-ting." Lydia folded her napkin crossly. "But what shall we do tonight."

"What?" said the other two, unable to resist.

"Shall we cancel the Lipizzaners?"

"No!"

"There's an echo in this room. Very well, but I shall cancel the von Beckburgs and leave you the day to sort out your friends. Shall we meet here at six o'clock?"

"Dear Lydia, sorry to upset your plans, but yes please, and thank you."

"I find modern manners most perplexing," said their hostess.

That evening they joined the glittery crowd as it flooded into the Hofburg Palace. Smells around them of sawdust, sweaty horse and scented Viennese.

"However often I come here, it is never often enough." Lydia settled into her seat with pleasure. "It is truly a ballroom for horses."

"I agree," Constance nodded.

Mr Bradley (having been kicked by a horse at an early age, and who, as you may remember, preferred boats, on the whole, to animals*) kept his counsel. Looking around the still-lit hippodrome, he saw Nellie's face. She was

---

* Snuffles excepted.

sitting between Herr Goerdeler and another gent whose monocle sparkled and flashed across the sandy floor. Constance had spotted Nellie too and they exchanged alarm signals.

"Gracious…"

"Good grief" and,

"What?" they said together, causing Lydia to frown.

Albert appeared and bowed.

"How lovely," she said. "Please sit here. I'm so sorry your friend is missing, but at least you won't be missing the horses."

Albert folded himself into the seat beside her. From beyond him, the others said, "we've seen her, and she's sitting –"

In loud tones Lydia interrupted, "is that not your friend, Leonora? She is with that ghastly man von Papen and somebody else who looks equally creepish. What is she doing there? Why is she not here with us?"

"Lydia dearest, shush. I didn't tell you everything," and Constance whispered into the ear that heard.

"Oh but poor little thing – what shall we do?"

"Dear Madame, we shall do nothing for the moment." Albert was calm, as (mostly) ever. The lights went out, the spots came on, and so did the beautiful horses. Lydia's party hardly watched as they gracefully trod their hooves about the ring. When the lights went up for the interval, Constance stared across the arena and receiving an eyeful from Nellie, she rose.

"I think I will powder my nose, excuse me Lydia." Albert stopped Lydia from joining the expedition by immediately wondering how many times she had seen the Lipizzaners, and which were her favourites. Distracted and entranced by Albert, she stayed put.

Constance, nose un-powdered noted Charles, a little out of breath but still elegant, slid past the other people in their row and into her seat just as the lights dimmed. "Speak later," was all she said. The horses made more magical patterns and pranced and danced. Similarly, round and round cantered at least five, if not seven, people's thoughts.

They walked around the corner for supper. The restaurant was full of people poring over menus of vast size and no doubt delectability, but:

"Georg, bring us whatever is best please." Called Lydia to the maître d, "and *Sekt* – whichever is good and cold – and?" questioning Charles and Albert.

"Löwenbräu," they answered together, "please."

"So! Now! Don't even think of trying to keep me out of this!"

Exclamationitis, thought Mr B. Albert, unusually, just looked worried.

"Of course not, darling Lydia! I am sorry to involve you, but we may need your help now. Here's what's what. Oh, stop it – I didn't mean to joke. When Nellie left Albert's horrid cousin's house (sorry Albert – you can't choose your rellies) she thought of coming to find us chez Lydia, but she couldn't find a taxi and she had her bag. So she got on a bus, not knowing exactly which way to go and she ended up in completely the wrong place, and then a car stopped and it was Herr Goerdeler. Well, as we know he knew her father when he was a doctor in Leipzig, and he was kind to Nellie in Regensburg, so she accepted his offer of a lift. But he didn't take to her Lydia's, but to where he's staying with Herr von Papen."

"Ghastly man," said Lydia.

"So he virtually kidnapped her and won't let her come

and see us, although Herr von Papen," "horrible person," interjected Lydia, "keeps asking her questions about us. So she cosied up to Herr G. and said if she couldn't get out of the house she would go mad, and she'd always wanted to see the Lipizzaners and could they go tonight, and he agreed."

"Bet they knew we'd be there," said Mr Bradley.

"Nellie says not."

"Well, we saw her, they must've seen us?"

"Apparently not by the interval. Surely Herr Goerdeler would have come and said hello?"

"Maybe he thought we would go to the bar."

"Enough maybes. The point is: we are going to the opera tomorrow night."

"Oh joy!" thought our hero.

Their food arrived, but Constance hardly glanced at it.

Mr Bradley considered this and decided that bossing people about was, to Miss Bennett, an even greater pleasure than eating. "Nellie will get them to take her and we will leave our seats to do girly things during the interval, as we did today. But Albert will have the car ready and off they pop to England. Oh my goodness! These are absolutely delicious." And the rognons de veau a la crème stopped her mouth for several minutes.

"What about the rest of us?" asked Charles.

"I have a suggestion," Lydia sipped *Sekt*, "Albert should take my old car which is less conspicuous."

"Excellent suggestion, but we can't leave you carless?"

"Oh, I have my new car, the one we were in tonight."

"Which is very conspicuous."

"So that we" Constance tried the word out, with hesitation, deciding she quite liked it, and continued firmly, "we can go to Hungary as planned and the Goerdelers will think Nellie is with us, but meanwhile she will be with Albert and all the cousins and all will be tickety-boo."

"But, does Nellie approve this plan?" Albert's eyebrows knitted themselves, with military precision, into a perfect row.

"She may not want my company or that of my cousins come to think of it?"

"If you think that then you are a goose, and deserve to be force-fed and turned into paté."

Albert was silent,* watching mesmerised as Constance mopped up the last vestiges of sauce on her plate with a piece of bread, scooping it into her mouth without ruining her perfectly painted lips, or a single drop falling onto her frock.

"So, we are agreed."

"Just a couple of maybes."

"Well, I suppose those are better than 'whats' but could we have something to eat first."

"Constance – you are a pig – you've just had something to eat."

"Sorting out problems makes me hungry."

Remarkably, Georg was just then bringing perfect little biscuits with pots of melted cheese, and also some fraise des bois surrounding small dishes of soured cream.

"Oh decisions, decisions."

"Fräulein," said Georg, "I hesitate to offer advice, but some berries with your champagne, and then I will bring you some very special red wine for the cheese. Yes?" Constance could only nod in blissful agreement.

"You have become very bossy, Constance, I shall have

---

* He probably knew a thing or two about Nellie's preferences. You have been paying attention readers mine... Unreliable in emergencies, Albert's antennae are attuned to trivia – think Mel Gibson in *What Women Want*.

to inform your Mama. You used to be such a gentle little girl..."

"Dearest, always to you I hope. I have been in some very bossy company recently and I have to be careful not to be reduced to a nithing."

"A nithing?" said everyone.

"A person without any status in early Scandinavia. Don't show your ignorances."

"Nobody would ever think you are a Nithing, my darl..." Mr B. stopped at the frowned face opposite. "My daddy always told me people with violet eyes could never be Nithings."

Peering, Lydia said, "How ridiculous, nobody has violet eyes. Oh well, perhaps some people do, but was your father a Scandinavian scholar to know about Nithings? How interesting. We were posted to Stockholm in '28, I wonder if he knows the..."

Albert said, "Mr Bradley senior is not exactly a scholar, he just knows everything about everything, and there isn't anything about which he doesn't have an opinion, in spite of never having travelled further from England than the Isle of Wight."

"Now Albert, that's unfair – he's been to Paris, and um, Edinburgh, and I think Hull."

"Hull is in England," said Lydia.

"But it's not at all English."

"I say I say you're not contradicting me on his opinions then?"

"Oh, I never contradict those who are better informed than I," said the junior Mr Bradley, primly.

"I think we should have that in writing." Constance felt she had been out of the conversation long enough. "Meanwhile, are we agreed?"

Since the wine for the cheese and the dunk-able things had arrived, the others proceeded to sort out their maybes and what ifs with hardly an interruption.

"I said it was tickety boo."

"And I said you are exceedingly bossy."

"I say I say home, and until tomorrow."

18

The trouble with tomorrow was that there was an awful lot of it to get through before the exciting/ scary bit. At breakfast Lydia, with all the what ifs and do you thinks, went off to make a telephone call and came back wreathed in smiles.

"Tant pis, tant mieux," murmured Mr Bradley.

"Lydia is not your tante.' Constance knew her 'captions courageous'.

"Darlings, our hosts of yesterday are away today, but we may visit and use their pool which I think will be excellent for all of us."

So they took the conspicuous car and a conspicuous picnic with some completely inconspicuous bottles of champagne all shrouded in newspaper. Fritz drove and Johnny, Albert and Snuffles rode in the other car.

Some people played tennis.

"Oh! how I dislike tennis," said Constance but she ploughed up and down the pool, and Lydia, neatly diving, swam a length or two. The sun shone, the picnic was delicious and plots were forgotten, or at least not mentioned.

That evening, changed (aah, the blue one, thought Mr B.) and surrounding a morsel of foie gras on toast, Constance worried whether there would be time to eat a little something in the interval.

"Don't be absurd, you've eaten enough for twenty already today."

"Feeling nervous makes me hungry."

"Anything and Everything makes you hungry."

Albert looked up from his watch: "Perhaps we should get this show on the road."

"My feelings entirely," said Charlie who was wondering what *Die Entführung aus dem Serail* might possibly be about. "But when shall we three meet again?"

"In two weeks? At my cousin's? If I'm delayed by bad weather…"

"What, Albert Shieff delayed by bad weather?!"

"I say I say I shouldn't like to put that *Blue Dancer* in a spin, and you can always –"

"Swim?" suggested Constance.

"No, enjoy the cooking, at the cousin's pub."

"Well then, I hope there's a wonderful storm." Constance licked her lips.*

As they passed conspicuously through Vienna's sunny streets, our hero tried to educate himself. "Mozart – fine, but what's this *Entführung* business?" Constance giggled and Lydia did too.

"It's quite perfect! It's an escape – and I'm the heroine and it's got nasty foreign baddies – you'll love it. There's a drinking song."

"Is there a banqueting scene?"

"No."

"That's a surprise, if you're the heroine! What about the hero?"

"He's just a soppy tenor with a beautiful handkerchief."

"So no Snuffles."

"No, but there is a Eunuch."

"He's the baddy."

"He's that too; but he's a bit of a sweetie as well."

---

* Of course, she only pretended, the rose-pink colour remained intact.

123

This silly conversation helped Mr Bradley not at all, but he was beguiled as soon as the curtain rose to reveal a sunlit street with a tenor singing about his beloved Constance. Unfortunately Lydia was sitting between him and his Constance, so he couldn't put the aria to any good use. There was a very jolly march and suddenly the interval was upon them.

Constance's blue frock rustled down the dress circle but there was a queue for the ladies and she could not see Nellie. Down to the foyer – no Nellie.

"They can't be in the Gods."

Into the Stalls – wrong side, Gents. Back to the foyer and around and nearly bumped into fussed friend exiting from the downstairs facilities.

"Oh!"

"Oh, thank goodness!" A brief hug, and "come, let's not waste time."

Out they went, beyond the grand doors, where Albert stood, in chauffeur mode.

Constance waved as Albert and Leonora sped off in the not exactly shoddy Volkswagen. Constance returned in time to hear Constance sing how even the breeze couldn't carry her bitter pain away (since she had lost Belmont).

"All's well," she whispered. And in a different part of the opera house someone said, "Alles Gut."

On the way out of the Opera house, Herr Goerdeler intercepted Mr Bradley.

"Both milk and music in common, we have now yes? A beautiful evening, which your friends enjoyed as well I hope?"

"Yes," said Mr Bradley, "they did. Thank you." As he bowed goodbye, he noticed Herr Goerdeler's companion smirking in the background.

Constance and Lydia had collected their cloaks.

"Perfectly done," said one, "Absolutely," said the other.

Mr Bradley was not feeling so sure: what are that lot so pleased about? He wondered, and why no mention of Nellie? In fact why didn't I mention Nellie? All this skulduggery is pathetic. I should've just gone over to them, demanded to know what they were doing with her, and brought her back with me. Is Albert keeping quiet about something?

"You're looking mulish," Constance said.

"It was the only way, otherwise Nellie might've bolted again – or didn't you like the opera?"

"I loved the opera; the tenor was particularly fine I thought. I admired his sentiments entirely."

"And the heroine?"

"She was a bit wet, all that pining stuff – I thought Blonde was much more fun."

"What?"

The car had arrived and Lydia settled into it.

"Yes, do you know what? I think I will come with you," Lydia had not been following this exchange. "I suddenly feel quite claustrophobic. Vienna is wonderful, but our day in the country has reminded me of other pleasures."

"Fritz?"

"Madame, you would like a little drive to Hungary?"

"I really think I would, please. Johnny can look after Snuffles till we return."

"Oh," said Constance.

"She so likes something to cuddle at night."

"The dog sleeps with you!"

"What?" asked Lydia.

"What what?" Miss B. and Mr Bradley repeated together.

"There will be plenty of room for Snuffles in our car," said Mr Bradley, "Miss Bennett need not worry."

"I wasn't."

"Liar," mouthed our hero.

"But so much more fun to be altogether."

"What about Herr Goerdeler and what about Albert?"

"Supposing we need to rush away?"

"Then we will all rush together." Lydia was firm. "I shall telephone Magdalena tomorrow."

Fritz ahem-med, "And Madame's maid?"

"Oh I shan't need Edwina. She can have a well deserved rest. There will be village girls to help us. After all Constance hasn't a maid."

"I seldom have."

Fritz directed a "what more can I say?" glance at Mr Bradley.

"We shall love travelling with you in this lovely car." Constance was positive.

Strangely the lovely car was sadly out of sorts the next morning. No dose of oil, no tweak and no massage of the clutch, nothing Fritz could do, would cajole its engine to stir. "I am afraid I should telephone the garage Madame."

Lydia was livid and tried fiddling with the starter buttons herself.

"I think we must go on ahead," said Mr Bradley, "I have to be back in England before the end of the month."

Constance nodded, "but we'll see you really soon and, you can bring Edwina and we'll take Snuffles."

"This is a conspiracy! I have been well and truly stitched up. What about the lack of chaperone for Constance?"

"Lydia, angel, the need for chaperones n'existe plus."

"All men are now safe in taxis?" said Charles.

"What do you know about NSITS?"

"From the point of view of NSITS, practically everything."

"Well, we won't be in a taxi, so I shall be entirely safe." With a kiss and a wave they made their way to the Mercedes.

"Do you think we should have a bundle?" asked Constance, looking at all the bags.

"Oh definitely. In fact five bundles would be good, but probably not until after the wedding."

"What?"

"What What? Just these two for the moment then." Our hero backed away from an enraged Miss Bennett. Once en route, however, she sighed and said, "This is nice," and promptly fell asleep. Snuffles, who had been comfortably sprawled on the back seat, climbed cautiously into the (today white-linen-trousered) lap.

"Don't fancy your chances when she wakes up, you lucky brute." Muttered Charlie, and drove. I'm afraid dear reader, he also sang.

Miss Bennett did not appear to notice, even when Snuffles decided to join in with falsetto howls and the occasional low groan when his master was in Bing Crosby mode.

19

Fortunately the conspicuous car only needed a slight tweak (Lydia's disbelief fell upon the stony ground of Fritz's composed sangfroid) and was soon on its way after the Mercedes, indeed, to the satisfaction of its occupants, it swiftly overtook the advance party. Thereafter, for those in the cars heading for Hungary, the major entertainment was: who was in the van? Apart, of course from the Bradley/Snuffles duet: I do not know if Fritz sang, quite possibly he accompanied his mistress in a little light Lieder, or some Offenbach.*

Then Constance awoke in the midst of a lengthy countertenor yowl. She shoved the dog on to the back seat and declared, as she removed several unwanted hairs from her white lap, that if the noise continued she'd really rather walk. Then there was a small and somewhat stony silence; but afterwards, dear reader, I am afraid that some distinctly silly games were played such as "I packed my bag and in it I put," and "I spy" and "Splotto".† Snuffles enjoyed this last game, squeaking enthusiastically from the back each time someone splotted.

Then Constance decided to sing, "Un éléphant qui

---

* Which Snuffles might've enjoyed – sorry.

† You don't know about Splotto? Reader mine, you obviously had an underprivileged childhood. You choose a colour and the first person to say Splotto when the car in that colour is seen earns a point/sweetie. Obviously in 1935 Germany you do not choose a black car…

se balançait sur une assiette de faience"*until Charles begged her to stop, whereupon she turned her voice to French songs with less innocent content. The music was seductive and our hero was soon humming the choruses, but it was a good thing that his French didn't stretch to the argot employed in some of the rhymes. Nursie would not have approved though she would have chuckled inwardly.

At Magyorovar, the car slowed and Constance's repertoire faltered. "Don't say a word, we can't stop yet, Fritz is right behind me and I want him to overtake me, before we stop at an excellent little gasthof."

"An excellent little csárda, with rosti."

"Very well, but a private little czárda and I'm sure there will be potatoes."

"On our own?"

"On our own."

Since there was no more singing, the canine countertenor decided to inform anyone within a five-mile radius that while his mistress might requite rosti, he required a tree, or a lamppost, or even a small stone and he required it now.

"I think we can stop here," said a promising voice. "There doesn't seem to be a conspicuous car." Said another.

"Maybe they went the scenic route? That Fritz is worse than Albert, he's full of tricks."

"Do hurry up," sang Snuffles. Parked around the side

---

* For those of you fortunate enough to never have heard this song, it can continue for as long as however many elephants get on to the pottery plate before everyone goes screaming mad. I suppose Constance was feeling kind, otherwise she may have segued into "un kilomètre à pied". Which is truly awful in its similarity.

of the chosen czárda, Charles liberated Snuffles and brought him back a relieved dog.

Meanwhile, Constance had powdered her nose, ordered herself a glass of Torley fizz and some Kobaaya beer for Mr Bradley. She had also discovered lángos.

"Just as good as rosti – in fact, better! They don't mind your dog and are bringing it water."

"Are those for you or can anyone?"

"Well, we might have to order another plate."

Constance offered the remaining potato cake. And dear reader, I must tell you it was crispy outside and slightly soggy in the middle, and it got dunked in sour cream with chives, or spicy tomatoes and it was absolutely delicious, and really, they might have stopped there only there were slivers of foie gras, followed by beef 'modra budapest', with white asparagus and peppery sauce, all too delicious to deny.

"But no cakes," said Constance.

"I'm driving, I need energy, I shall have a cake. Those chestnut thingies look most appealing."

"I could drive?"

"No."

"Oh well then I shall have a glass of wine and watch you getting fatter."

Mr Bradley M.P. drew himself in and up, "Not 'er'," he said.

"You vain thing! Yes, definitely 'er'. Perhaps I shall have some cheese," Constance looked dreamily in the direction of the kitchen.

"I think I agree with Lydia – why are you not the size of an elephant?"

"I have the soul of an elephant and the countenance of an elephant and probably the ears and wrinkles of an elephant, but those last two are hopefully in the picture in the attic."

"What picture?"

"What what? Don't you know your Oscar?"

"So as you become more of a flibbertigibbet, some poor old Ellie feels the brunt upstairs?"

"I object to flibbertigibbet! And I bet you spelt it incorrectly."

"I spoke it for heaven's sake."

"Hmm, you can't be too careful when you are such an important person. I bet if a reporter from the *Daily Express* had been listening he'd have written in his note pad, 'M.P. for Eastbourne can't spell flibbertigibbet.'

"NB: ask him next time if he can say/spell anti-disestablishmentarianism or Llanfairpwllgwyngyllgogerychwyrndrobwllllantysiliogogogoch."

"I'll be careful with *Express* reporters then, but fortunately I'm rather friendly with the Beaver, so he might be quite kind about my spelling, and even look after the elephant, wherever it might be."

"Goodness, or rather badness, that old lech? He's more likely to turn you into a dead elephant."

"Maybe he's a man's man."

"He's a woman's man as well, and he hitches his trunks to his wart."

"You've been speaking to Lady Younger. There's nothing wrong with his hitched trunks. Let them remain hitched, say I, by what ever means."

"At any rate, don't sell your soul to him."

"There's only one person I'd sell my soul to and I wouldn't want any money."

"That's ridiculous, it doesn't work like that!" Constance put down her napkin. "If you've quite finished eating I shall take your soul into St Gothard's church and Snuffles for a walk which will be good for both of you."

The bill paid and a reluctant Snuffles retrieved from the cook, they walked to St Gothard's church which didn't entirely fulfil their expectation: it was busily baroque and no one could tell them anything about its saint.

"Perhaps he was a lonely goat herd? I know a pass…"

"I'm sure you do, but don't dare to try it. It means strong for God, silly and has nothing to do with goats or their minders. Speaking of which, I wonder how Albert and Nellie are."

"Albert is not my minder, and it's very rude of you to call Nellie a goat. And I am sure they are fine."

"I don't think you've had enough culture, we shall have to visit the Gyurkovitch collection."

"I do beg your pardon."

"Why?"

"I was accepting responsibility for your Gyurkovitch, too many lángos I think."

"Vulgar person, you definitely need more culture."

But the exhibition was as gloomy as the church had been over-exuberant, and the castle, although sitting prettily on an island, was no longer really a castle. Even Snuffles was happy to be ensconced once more in the car.

"Stay in the back though!" Constance ordered.

"You'd better stay awake then."

"I shall be awake and please may I drive?"

"No."

"Then I shall sing."

"Fine but no elephants on dishes."

So Constance sang, this time disgraceful English songs, some of which Charlie knew and her robust handling of them nearly swerved them into the ditch upon a couple of occasions. He joined in, however, when modesty would allow.* Snuffles snored throughout whether in disapproval or because of an overfull tum, who knows, but I reckon the latter since the French songs hadn't fazed him; at any rate he stayed in the back.† Soon they were in the plains around Gyor, and lost.

"Never mind," said Constance, "if you'll stop – I'll get out and shout."

"What?"

"Oh, what what! Just stop."

Mr Bradley stopped the car. Constance stepped (verb used advisedly) out. She made some sort of wolf-like noise, not unlike a yodel. Snuffles woke up and obviously was very helpful, for after the second go there was an answering yowl. Quite soon, two young men who seemed to be dressed in frocks appeared, bowed and sat upon the bonnet waving their arms.

These shouts/yodels were pretty common in the days before telephones. They are most common in mountainous regions where the sound carries better, but in the vast steppes they were used as well. You just had to shout/scream louder/higher. A bit like a silent dog whistle. Constance has been to stay with the Hedevars often and is always anxious to learn new skills.

"I suppose I'll get used to this," said Mr Bradley, "I think we're going round in circles. I do hope they're not denting the bonnet."

"They are pretty skinny."

"Skinny! I suppose so, pretty? No, I'd prefer to see you in one of those things they are wearing."

---

* Modesty was of course sitting in a grump and in the back of the car with Snuffles. (Having removed herself from the Beaver's trunks.)

† All dogs are multilingual. It is possible of course that he was snuggled up with Modesty.

"I do own one actually."

"Oh, bliss!"

"Just feast your eyes on those boys – seeing me in mine is unlikely!"

"Hmmm – unlikely – not a complete negative then?" Thought Mr Bradley. They travelled to slightly higher ground – following a river busily making its way to the Danube and there on an absurd hill, its park set before and about it like the skirts of some nineteenth-century dowager, stood the castle of Mosoni – except it wasn't really a castle.

"Isn't it a lovely bungalow?" Said Constance. Mr Bradley attempted to look unimpressed as light bounced off the egg-yolk walls and terracotta roof. White sash windows and twin round towers completed the symmetry.

"Symmetry is such a cliché, don't you think?"

Mr Bradley thought again that he wished people wouldn't read his mind.

And then they were round the drive and in front of curly wrought-iron balustrades and staircases. A person bowed. (He reminded Charles of the butler from the Addams family cartoons in the *New Yorker*.)

"Mademoiselle."

"Imre, so lovely to be here – this is Mr Bradley."

"I was informed Mademoiselle," Imre did not look over-pleased.

"And this is Snuffles."

"Madame let me know of him too. I love the dogs." The statement was unconvincing.

"M. Mme and the other guests are shooting the duck, please enter and I will bring tea."

"Should I tip the frocks?" asked Mr Bradley. "Too late, they're gone."

And so they had, now mere flashes of white embroidered linen in the distance. The glittered leaves shone with sun, so that they hardly wished to be inside, but it was distinctly cheery to sip tea by the hall's fire. Imre, who perhaps liked dogs after all, had removed Snuffles to be fed, and, "what are those? I think I see chestnut-ty things!"

"Now you see them, now you don't," said Constance. "You can't eat them all."

"No, but I have eaten one, and I shall eat some more, but you shouldn't have any on account of your piggery at lunch."

"What piggery? Which piggery?" Our hero's oratory foreshadowed future success in the House of Commons.

Constance blew out her cheeks, making a distinctly unladylike noise when deflating them.

"Ahhh, darling girl, I thought it might be you. So bien élevée – it gives me wonder great as my content to see you here before me."

"Oh my soul's joy, dear Lydia," said Mr B. who knew his Shakespeare.[*]

"If after every tempest come such calms," they said together.

"You are such show offs!" Constance grumbled, "we haven't had any tempests, and if we're doing recitation I shall give you my 'lays of ancient Rome'."

"All of them? And probably 'the boy stood on the burning deck' as well."

"It's not a competition darlings. Aah, Imre, tea, how lovely. Thank you."

"Have a chestnut-ty thing before Constance scoffs the lot."

---

[*] *Othello*, Act II, Scene I.

"Well, do you know, I think I will, I've had a great deal of culture today and feel fairly frazzled.

"Fritz thought it necessary to go via Csorna – to see the Church of St Helen. I am Lydia Helen you see." (St Helena: daughter of Coel, King of Colchester, c.250–530, married Roman General Contantine Chlorus, who divorced her in 294, when he became Emperor. Her son greatly revered her, however, and when she became a Christian, he did too. On a pilgrimage to the Holy Land she is supposed to have found the true cross. Bithyria and Frier also claim to be her birthplace – but we know better, gentle reader. Old King Cole is much more fun. She is buried in Rome and her feast day is August 18th. Shortly after Cowes Week. The true cross has fetched up in many places: Santo Croce in Florence and Rome and Saint Cross in Winchester. There is also a St Cross Street off Hatton Garden, must find out why.) "Well done that Fritz," thought Charlie, but he said:

"I love St Helen: an all-round good egg. We'd probably all be worshipping Wotan if it weren't for her. She's much better at finding things than St Anthony."

"And she was married to the Emperor Constantine and brought the true cross to…"

"And she was the daughter of Old King Cole, that merry old soul."

"I see we are at one with hagiography, nursery rhymes and Shakespeare."

"Un Elephant!" threatened Constance.

"We certainly got lost," said our hero, changing the subject as he detected irritation in his beloved's eye.*

---

* Dear acute persons, please pay attention, I think by now I may say beloved. Onwards and upwards.

"But Constance found us, and she found us the most elegantly frocked guides, which she howled for."

"Angel, I didn't know you could do that! Could you teach me?"

"Of course, let's start now."

"I think you should go outside and practise, I might get indigestion."

"Who will get indigestion – no one in my house I hope?" The duck shooting party had returned, Magdalena Hedevar to the fore.

20

Certainly no one felt unwell after that night's sumptuous* dinner although a few found it difficult to stir from their slumbers the following morning, in spite of – or maybe because of – the almost tropical sunshine.

Not so Snuffles who, banned from bedrooms, had spent the night in front of the kitchen range with his new best friends, Fluellen, a Welsh springer spaniel, and a Weimaraner bitch named Flossie. Very pleased to see his humans, he was raring to go.

"We can't take him."

"But he wants to come."

"You can't always get what you want."†

"Certainly but –"

"He'll bark at the guns and gobble the grounded game."‡

"I'll find a long lead for him."

So Snuffles came.

And behaved beautifully, even retrieving a few partridges (on his long lead) once he noticed this was the done thing. Time flew high and by with the birds as they walked on crumbly soil, through sunlit Indian corn.

---

* I think unmentionable orgies should be mentioned (and annotated in detail) and so should sumptuous dinners. Therefore dear remaining reader(s), you may salivate with precision over: cold spinach soup (with crispy bacon bits and crème fraiche on top), roast saddle of lamb, pink inside and charred on the out (with petits pois à la Française and castled potatoes) and finally raspberries and cream and asparagus to dunk in melted cheese. One guest was heard to say "Oh bliss."

† Autres moeurs, autres temps: but our song remains the same.

‡ Note again our hero's talent, this time for alliteration.

So it was only when lunch arrived in horse-drawn shooting brakes that the company realised how very hungry and thirsty they were. Tents were erected and ice-cold white wine and water were consumed together with salads too complicated to name and sandwiches of egg, cucumber and rare roast beef. There were also blackcurrants, which had been dipped in egg white and caster sugar, and funny little bits of goat's cheese rolled in herbs to jerk the taste buds awake. But maybe not the rest of the system. Some of the party lay contentedly upon shady rugs. For others the Danube beckoned.

Constance emerged from a tent, her hair turbaned and wearing a rather startling green number just as Mr Bradley ducked out from another labelled "changing for gentlemens".

"Oops! I'd better find a fish net."

"What?"

"What what? To catch all the frightened fish."

"Are you frightened? I thought I looked quite nice." Nice wasn't how our hero would have described the emerald hour glass in front of him – partially veiled by a towel.

"Well, I'm not a fish – so..."

"Aren't you? I'd never have guessed."

"In that case I need to give you biology lessons."

"Hmm – I laid myself open to that one."

Mr Bradley assumed a puzzled expression – "That one? Couldn't you lay yourself open to this one?" And I am afraid he winked[*] lasciviously.

"Disgusting person. Go away and swim very far in the wrong direction." They had reached the Danube by now and Constance, entering the water without so much as a

---

[*] No, he did nothing with his eyebrows – he leaves that to Albert.

"brr you leave" swam off upstream and was soon out of sight. Snuffles leapt in and followed. Charlie, who knew a bit about ebbs and flows but nothing about the Danube ones, contented himself with a few brisk stokes and then lay on this back contentedly watching his wiggling toes.

"Hah! Pas un elephant, c'est un hippopotame!" said a voice and he was pulled to the muddy depths and rolled over by sharp-nailed hands.

Surfacing, he found a hairy face and lolling tongue before him and laughter from the bank behind. Constance was rubbing her hair, the turban removed. Why does it curl so beautifully after it's wet? Wondered our muddy hero, and "Oh!" he said, "Oh, oh," and he crinkled his brow and bent his lip in pain.* "I think I am caught in a trap."† He made as though to reach for his foot, and shuddered, "Oh bother, ow, that really hurts."

Constance flung the towel aside and plunged into the water. Snuffles, on the other hand, got out, shook himself and settled down to await events.

"Where oh, where?"

"I think it's this leg." Constance dove down again and felt about. Mr Bradley smiled bravely, no he smiled happily. (He did not smirk!) Constance surfaced. Bits of mud dripped off her shoulders and something that matched her costume twined in her hair...

"I can't find anything," she panted.

"I'll have another go when I've got my breath back," her open mouth gave our hero his cue and he took it. After several moments:

"You're a lying toad. That was quite horrid."

"Was it? Sorry, I'll do it better this time."

---

* He did he did and he did not use his eyebrows.

† Les mots du passé sont les chançons de nos jours.

A bit later…

"I didn't mean that, I meant your beastly trap trick."

"I'm glad you meant only that, but speaking of traps and tricks – I would say that you and that Venus fly plant have a lot in common."

At this point, fortunately for the susceptibilities of my gentle readers, Snuffles, sick of the soppy stuff, began to bark.

"Be quiet you horror!"

"I was entirely silent, but I am a little cold."

"Don't seem cold to me," but Constance climbed the bank and, avoiding Snuffles' tongue, found her towel. They sat awhile on the bank. Charles traced with a finger the tiny knots dotting Constance's spine.

"Hmmmm," other eminently traceable parts showed as Constance lay back, her face towards the sun.

"It's probably tea time," she said with a sigh. Snuffles sighed too and back they went to magnificent samovars steaming with tea strong enough to trot a horse on.

The men went for the duck again, but the ladies returned to the château, riding in the shooting brakes. Constance found herself beside her hostess.

"Dear Magdalena, such a lovely day, thank you."

"It has certainly agreed with you, my darlink!" Magdalena made a silent inventory. 1. Eyes sparkling; 2. Cheeks pinky; 3. Lips which have been put to their proper use.

"Did you enjoy your swim?"

"Oh yes, it was most invigorating."

I bet it was, thought Magda, who had considered swimming herself, but found the Danube a trifle crowded.

"But now you can rest a little time and Krystina will draw you a bath."

"Oh! Thank you for Krystina. Such a treat to be looked after. She's a real sweetie-pie. What present could I leave to say thank you?"

"Tomorrow, or the next day – throw her a lump of ice. Those village girls, it is like chocolate for them. They love it."

Although not wanting to queer the pitch, Constance thought she might leave one or two of Unity's lace hankies.

"I can see you think this is rubbish present, but darlink: this is Hungary. Thinks are different here – the people in the village are well looked after."

"It does seem a trifle feudal."

"Not so long ago it was the same in England."

"Not anymore."

"No, your people have changed so much. But after that last war, I think, our people were happy to go back to what they knew before, most of them. Yours not – all that industry towns and smoke! Here is so – rural – that is it. People feel still comfortable in the old ways. Hah – except for some who are angry that the Czechs stole Hungarian land at Trianon, and some believe that horrid little man will help them to bring it back."

"Will he?"

"I doubt it! We lost land you know, but the families there seem content. Sandor sees them because he is 'important' but it is difficult for them if they have relatives over here – papers and this and that. The same for the ones here, why do people who know nothing of history interfere?"

"Because they can?"

"You have it right! But I would add that it is generally

people who live in towns and do not understand the countryside who want to fiddle with our existence."*

The fiddle word made Constance sigh and briefly close her eyes, but aware of Magdalena's stare, she smiled, stretched and repeated:

"Such a lovely day, I can only believe sense will prevail."

"Hah! Darlink, with men in charge, when has it ever! But tonight we shall have fun and dancink and tomorrow you throw some ice to Krystina."

Snuffles, exhausted, yawned.

"You are quite right, ugly dog, a boring conversation – aaagh! Don't lick me."

Magdalena recoiled as, given an inch, Snuffle's mile-long tongue sped forth in her direction.

---

* Hmm, any resonance in today's England?

21

Those who had had a zizz were pretty pleased with themselves as the entertainments continued until the sky lightened.

There were prizes for the guns that had shot the most (which were given to the beaters), gypsy music, a huge dinner,* more gypsy music and toasts. Then Constance's yodelling friends unloosed their tonsils. Constance was persuaded to join in, a vulgarity which caused some consternation amongst the older guests, but even they laughed when Imre brought in Snuffles who had been irritating the chef by howling in the kitchen. The dog proceeded to wag his tail over to the small ululators and accompany them pitch perfectly.

The dancing, which followed, began rather sedately and Mr Bradley stood up with Mme de Hedevar for a waltz. Unfortunately, at her signal the music changed to a Czardas, and our hero found himself whirling or rather whirled about like a dervish. There also seemed to be a lot of clapping and stamping of feet.

Mr de Hedevar, who had been dancing with Constance, bowed and swapped.

"Now my friend, you will see how it is done."

Gradually everyone made way as the two de Hedevars took over the floor as a sinuous, clattery, one. Constance

---

* Oh very well, I don't wish to upset my curious readers: foie gras with little toasts and quince jelly, smoked trout with horseradish sauce, lángos to accompany sliced filet of beef in paprika sauce with chestnuts, appfelstrudel or, in Constance's case, melted goat's cheese with biscuits to dunk.

and Charles were happy to watch for a while, but they were not to be seen when the band changed tempo.

Some time later, Imre had cause to disturb them on the terrace, where the cool night had obviously caused them to huddle together: various arms and indeed two heads needed unwinding, before he could deliver his messages. SO GLAD YOU CAN GIVE FREDERIKA A LIFT AND STAY STOP VIKTORIA LUISE STOP THE DE HEDEVARS CAN EXPLAIN HOW TO GET HERE STOP.

The other was from Albert and was equally succinct, if more puzzling: ALL'S WELL HERE STOP VIENNA IN 5 DAYS TO RETURN CAR IF OK STOP HOPE YOU ENJOYED THE DANUBE STOP.

"Well at least he didn't say bring gum boots." Said Constance.

"What?"

"Hah, what, what! You may know your Shakespeare but obviously not your Stella Gibbons." (*Cold Comfort Farm*, best telegram ever.)*

"Will there be replies Sir? The young man is waiting."

"Yes please – to Viktoria Luise. In say, a week's time?"

"I suppose so, I won't say what a wheeze, but I do hope Frederika hasn't too much luggage. And say to Albert, the Danube was very muddy and he should not be looking into it."

"That's far too long – how about: the Danube is full of frightened fish. Stop. See you in Vienna Saturday. Stop. Bradley."

"Mr Bradley loves to joke Imre, but he is not always funny."

"Yes Mme, his dog though, is very amusing I am told."

---

* WORST FEARS REALISED DARLING SETH AND REUBEN TOO SEND GUM BOOTS.

"Your dog."

"*Your* dog."

"Whoever owns the dog, the chef would prefer it to be out of the kitchen tonight as it has been a little overenthusiastic with the birds."

"What?"[*]

"He does not seem to understand not to chase them when they are dead, Sir, and has been discovered pursuing them on the top of the oven."

"Oh no, his poor paws!" Constance was off in the direction of the kitchens.

Mr B. thought of Solomon and the women with the baby, and smiled.

"Thanks Imre, I hope this will ease any difficulties arising from Miss Bennett's dog."

And he gave Imre some notes which made that person revise his opinion of Englishmen.

Snuffles, whose paws[†] had not suffered, was banished to sleep in the car, in its warm stable. After several rotations, and one forward extension, he slept on his back, paws flopping in the air, awaiting his humans to take him somewhere jolly.

The humans had returned to the party to find that the band had taken a rest and a fellow guest was playing the piano and giving a fair Noël Coward impression.

"A room with a view, and you." Lydia, in cream silk and lace "this old thing?" was turning the pages. She raised a hand and waggled fingers at Constance and Charlie. Returning immediately to concentrate on her silver-haired companion.

---

[*] Oh no – not again! Sorry.

[†] I wanted to say that they were pawfect but I didn't – I am very restrained.

"Hmmm" and "well" said the Bennett Bradley Brigade, viewing Lydia's behaviour from their own standpoint.

"No bad news, I hope?" their hostess had joined them. "And as you see, there is more than one charming couple in the room."

"No bad news, thank you," said Mr Bradley, "and certainly you and M. de Hedevar are a glorious dancing pair."

"Certainement, we love to dance my little ones, but that is not…"

"M. Jamet plays so well," Constance interrupted.

"Noël Coward, with a French accent – lovely!"

"Wait till you hear his Maurice Chevalier, that is truly magnifique."

"Have M. Jamet and his page-turner met before? Not to be impertinent," added Mr Bradley hastily.

"Well, here and there obviously, as one does 'en passant' but for a while I have been wanting them to meet in a situation 'plus intime'. And I think I have been right!"

"Is there, was there, a Mme Jamet?"

"Dear Jacqueline – what a character! She drove her little car into a tree to avoid some ducks on the road. Pierre survived. Terrible. His guilt at being alive, with his love dead. But…" Magdalena gave herself a little shake, "it is ten or so years now and who knows…"

"Lydia looks so happy – perhaps she too is ready?"

"I shall try and keep them here for a week or so and we shall see … you too darlinks, I hope?"

"Ahhh – Mme."

"Magdalena."

"Magdalena, so sorry – I suppose one telegram did contain bad news, for we really must be back in Vienna by Saturday."

"So soon? Are you not enjoying? I haven't shown you anything. All you have seen is birds."

"And the Danube." Constance's face was straight.

"But no culture." Mr Bradley wasn't sure he'd missed it much, but he said, "of course we'd…" – Constance tried to ignore the 'we' but failed because of an insistent small glow inside her – "love to stay longer, but the House sits again shortly and…"

"Well, Constance you at least can stay and go back with Lydia." Magdalena smiled like a vampire at her trapped prey.[*] The prey, however, answered serenely.

"Darling, of course I could, and I would love to, but I've[†] been asked to take Frederika Brunswick back to school and Mr Bradley has kindly agreed to drive me."

Mr Bradley quietly seethed at this usurpation of his role, but smiled sweetly and:

"I'm to make sure no fish are frightened on the way."

"Is that an English joke?"

"No. It's very unfunny."

"But then why is he saying it? And why is he laughing?"

"Oh, you know men – sometimes they have to open their mouths for no reason whatever."

"True darlink, very well. We shall see what we can do in three days. You can leave early on Saturday." Disagreement was not an option.

"Bring swimsuits."

Decisions made, their hostess returned to her metier.

"And now, the Zigeiner have returned and we shall do a few more dancings." Which they did and so to bed, with Charlie unconvinced of the appeal of three days' concentrated culture.

---

[*] Or like the Cheshire cat if you prefer.

[†] She nearly said we.

22

He had worried needlessly: Magdalena was not the sort of person to hit three galleries and six churches in a day with every picture and statue viewed and ticked.

"Darlinks!" she said on the first day, "I do not stuff you."

"Force feed," suggested Constance.

"We will see two or three pretty things that we can watch with a cup of coffee or a glass of wine and then we will walk a little and so we will have a good memories and so when we return to Hungary," she eyed them beadily, "we will want to find out more n'est-ce-pas? And the hotel where we stay you shall want to stay in for your Sweetie Moon."

"Magdalena! I can't afford smart hotels." Constance was as direct as ever, "I've given away my last ice cube."

Mme de Hedevar's tongue clicked.

"This is my fun and games, away from shootings and husband. Showing my country is my pleasure."

"We will let you treat us, if when you visit England we can entertain you." Said Mr Bradley.

"Oh dear," Constance thought, "two more plural personal pronouns." *

Over the Chain bridge and into Budapest they went, Imre driving and coffee gratefully schlurped while considering the Gresham palace.

---

* No she didn't, that was your author being alliterative – she thought, "uh oh, 'we' again."

"Secession?* You either love it or it makes you want to be sick." Said Magdalena.

"I do like peacocks," Constance smiled at Mr Bradley who was wearing what he considered to be a particularly fetching tie of that bird's blue, "If only they'd shut up."

"Don't say 'shut up' it's rude," he replied piously.

Then on to look at the parliament house.

"Pat the lion and look at the Dome."

"Home from home and back home soon – bother," thought our M.P.

Next stop was a metro stop. The Oktagon, where Imre left them to enjoy the little trains clattering up to elegant stations of iron and wood.

"More Secession."

Imre took Snuffles for a walk.

Magdalena, Constance and Charles got out at Varostiget and walked a little way too, enjoying more home from home, through the 'English Park', until they reached Gurkels' restaurant which was entirely Hungarian and entirely to Constance's taste.

"Here we eat pancake." Replete, they wandered in the afternoon to look at Vajdahunyad Castle and "my favourite statue. See how elegant it is. A grande dame, Except – look at her hands and her shoes… She is a man. A writer of the twelfth century who refused to say his name. Touch his plume."

"Quill?" queried Mr Bradley.

"And you too will write well."†

"Nothing ventured nothing gained," Charlie stepped up to the touch, Constance following more slowly. Her

---

* Secession = Hungary's answer to Art Deco.

† Obviously your author has, dear reader, which is why you read on.

tapered fingers stroked the pen but her eyes gazed at our hero. Who may have blushed.

Snuffles and Imre were waiting to take them back to Buda.

"Go by the Millennium monument please Imre. You must see the God of War. No one now could want I think to celebrate him, but he is beautiful."

"I bet he doesn't wear paisley dressing gowns," said Constance. Charles intoned,

> The God of War went forth
> To ride, upon his favourite filly
> I'm Thor!, he cried,
> The horse replied,
> You forgot your thaddle thilly.

"Is this English Joke? His name is Rydwan, not Thor, and it is not a saddle and silly?"

"The God of War Rydwan, is difficult to scan, or rhyme," muttered our hero.* But he thought for a moment and declaimed,

> Rydwan the God,
> Ruled war with his rod,
> But his horse disliked it
> When he bare-back rided it!

"This must be an English joke!" Magdalena reached for her notebook.

"It is appalling!"

"Well, it's the best I can manage in two minutes – you try!"

---

* Not a god.

Constance (who had been thinking) offered:

> When the warring is over
> Rydwan thinks he's in clover,
> But no one felt dutiful
> To his body beautiful
> And nobody heeded
> A deity not needed.

"That was just as bad and rather sanctimonious."

"This poetry –"

"Doggerel…"

"Oh! It is for Snuffles! I see, well it is not so fun as English jokes. Rydwan is meant to be a symbol of '96. So much changed then. Many many buildings, all with beautiful decorations. I was quite little, but I remember shoutings and flag wavings."

"I'm sure you only remember photographs," said Charlie.

"Sweetie Pie! But I remember the ice cream and that was not in a picture. But here is my other favourite. Well done Imre! Elizabeth married to Franz Joseph: she loved Hungary and we loved her back. Our independence was finished in her boudoir."

"Completed?" suggested Constance.

"Yes, and such beautiful clothes too! And now we are completed and will find our hotel."

Which was, envious reader, maybe not the most glorious hotel in all the world but certainly one of them. The Géllert sits comfortably underneath the hill from which the poor saint was thrown in his barrel. He probably would not approve of its lavish stained glass, miraculous mosaics, sumptuous statues and suites, first-century monks tending to the ascetic, but he would have been amazed, as were even our worldly heroes.[*]

"I have decided I love Secession," said Constance.

"This is a playground for grown-ups! And so, go and play – you have…" Magdalena consulted the vast clock above them, "about three hours before we meet for some champagne. Then we will go and watch Mr Strauss' bat."

"Oh oh oh," Constance clutched Mr Bradley's arm – "there's a wave pool!"

"For saying hello to friends?"

"Bah! You're wasting time – go and find out, unless you want tea?"

After a gentle whizz up to their rooms, in a wrought-iron peacocked lift, Constance and Charlie changed into bathers, found fluffy robes and found wave pools, hot pools, steam baths and saunas. They even found a pool in which to swim up and down. I'm ashamed to say that Charles pretended that he had cramp. Fortunately our heroine,[†] wise to his wiles, swam swiftly away. Unfortunately, a blonde Valkyrie believed him and, wrapping her arms about the Bradley body, swam him to the pool's edge. She seemed about to administer the kiss of life when Constance intervened, encased in green and arms akimbo. (How I love that word. It should be set to song.)

"I should try tickling him first, if you can be bothered that is."

"Einezest? [Sorry?]" said the beauty.

"Bless you," said Constance and began to fiddle with the Bradley feet.

---

[*] I think we have two now.

[†] For she is.

"What? Oh What! That's horrid – desist."

"I think he'll be all right now," Constance smiled at Miss Hungary and returned to her lengths.

"You have pretended? You are a beast," the vision disappeared huffily.

"Hello, still alive?" enquired Constance after a little while. "Hope I didn't ruin your fun?"

"Well yes you did. She was gorgeous and I didn't even discover her name."

"She'd have eaten you for breakfast."

"I'd like to be eaten for breakfast. You haven't offered."

"I'm sure Snuffles would oblige."

"If you would prefer me dead I shall incontinently drown myself."*

"But the lifeguards are all male – I shouldn't if I were you."

"What would you do if you were me?"

"I should take me back to the wave pool and behave apologetically."

Peace, or at any rate a ceasefire was negotiated in the wave pool, and they were on time for the champagne and the Bat. Constance wore a slithery blue number finished with what Charles considered to be a very silly, unnecessary long bit at the back which had to be picked up and draped across in cars. He saw its point, however, as Constance and Magdalena sashayed up the opera house's grand staircase, trains lingering behind them.

***

"A perfect day… Thank you Magdalena. Oooh, but I feel sleepy." Constance stretched a little and almost yawned,

---

*   Othello Roderigo to Iago, Act I, Scene III.

like a cat, thought Charlie. They had finished supper* on the terrace of the Gellért and the lights of Budapest were spread below them.

"It's time for sleep and for more excitements tomorrow. Lydia and Pierre will join us."

"What fun! But where are we going?"

"We are going to bed!" Magdalena led the way without answering the question.

---

* All right, all right, eggs benedict and white peaches in brandy. And our hero managed secretly to pay the bill – clever boy!

23

Constance devoured eggs, bacon, tomatoes and just one pancake for breakfast, having slept "divinely, thank you Magdalena", and been for a swim, she also accepted a glass of *Sekt*.* Charles, who had passed a restless night,† managed some coffee and a cigarette. Magdalena, nibbling on toast, shook her head, "you will be sick in the car and we have a few ways to go to Lake Balaton."

"Aha! So that's where we are going!" said the other two. (Not that the name meant much to Mr Bradley. Didn't sound too much like culture though.)

"Bother, now surprise gone!" Said their hostess, "but one more piece of culture first."

They walked, with Snuffles, to the Rock Church.

"I wanted to be married here, but the monks you know? It seems marriage is a woman thing and not to be done here. But I shall light a candle all the same."

They stood their flickering candles beneath the Madonna, high and white in her night-black grotto, with the day-gold glow of the Rock all about her.

Snuffles had made several new friends when they emerged, but he was relieved to have his proper humans back and also to see Imre and his car. Imre, frowning severely at the assaults on his trousers, gave the dog's chin a quick tickle. The others pretended not to notice.

Two small extra parcels had been squeezed into the

---

* What else can you do to *Sekt*, except, accept.
† Don't ask why, dear reader, pay attention.

car, and as they motored south, Magdalena offered them to those seated behind her. Beautifully wrapped in tissue were ashtrays, each decorated with Secession peacocks in blue and gold. "Now you will remember Hungary," said a satisfied Magdalena.

"We weren't going to forget anyway," came a chorus from the back. Magdalena smiled to herself and said:

"I was going to buy one turquoise one and one blue, but thought a pair preferable."

"Thank you," said the pair, "they are lovely."

"But you haven't been smoking?"

"I ran out."

"You ran out? Why did you run? You could see no shops? Surely the Gellért had a tobacconist?"

The backseat pair had started to laugh.

"What? Is this a joke? What have I said?"

"What what?" I am afraid to say laughter stopped further conversation until Charles said, "I suppose I was thinking of other things."

"Hmmm," said Magdalena, "I think I saw that."

The lake of Balaton sparkled at them as they came towards it. It was ridiculously blue and surrounded by frivolous golden reeds. The turquoise water clashed slightly with the blue of the sky in which stupid puffy clouds hung about hoping for a wind.

"There," said Magdalena, "beautiful, beautiful, beautiful, No?"

"Beautiful."

"Beautiful, yes."

"And what about this?" Magdalena pointed, "this is your reward for smiling at culture."

"This" was a sleek sailing ship waiting gently for them with Lydia and Pierre waving from the deck.

"Oh," said Mr B.

"Now," Constance smiled, "we shall see how grand a sailor you are!"

"Just keep to the north side of the lake," Imre whispered as he handed over Snuffles, "the South is sandy and shallow."

Lydia was wearing a blue and white striped matelot jersey with pearly buttons across the shoulders with white trews cropped to reveal elegant calves.

"I had nothing suitable to wear my dears, but we found a darling little shop and Pierre thought I looked nice in these, so I bought him a cap."

"Pierre! You look perfectly naughty!" Magdalena kissed him.

"We have been perfectly good, I assure you, although there is a lovely cabin downstairs…"

"Below," murmured Pierre.

"And a delicious hamper on deck."

"Oh do let us get started, although I think I have made another joke which I should write."

"I am hoping that you are more nautical than naughty." Charles had sidled up to Pierre.

"This is quite big to sail alone."

"We shall be a team, n'est ce pas?"

"Phew," thought our hero, as the dear little clouds began to breeze about and the good ship *Feher Hal* flew off her mooring.

"Is a good name no? You are from White Island? Here you shall sail a White Fish."

"Magdalena, you are so sharp you'll cut yourself, and yes that is another joke."

Dear reader, I would like to tell you that there was a storm, a shipwreck, wet shirts stretched over pecs, wet knickers, a dead somebody – a dead dog maybe, but no, disappointingly, everyone was entirely safe and had an exhilarating time, especially Snuffles, who we know[*] loved swimming. Jumping in to join the humans' fun in the quiet cove where they anchored, he had to be helped out. When he dove in for the umpteenth time like a Newfoundland rescue dog, it was decided regretfully that he should be tied up by his lead while the humans ate. But whoever had packed the hamper had included a juicy bone, so he was not too downhearted.[†]

Later, comfortably full, they sailed a little further down the lake, sipping wine and munching the occasional strawberry before retuning to Balatonfüred, Imre and the cars. Snuffles was allowed one last swim since his chops reeked of barbecued dead animal. Then he was bundled in a rug: "We'll take him," said Lydia, "we've got a boot with a grille so he won't be able to jump over and love us!"

Snuffles grumbled all the way back to Gyor – unnoticed by Lydia and Pierre who were enjoying each other to the exclusion of all else.

In the other car, Magdalena said nothing with a smile.

"I am remembering my Anna ball – so many years ago! So grand you know, a bit like your Queen Charlotte's

---

[*] Pay attention dearest reader.

[†] For those of my readers who are sailors (and I hope there will be lots) don't worry: a piece of old tarpaulin was found to protect the deck. For those who would like to hear more about the picnic hamper please see Ratty's picnic, Ch. 1 in *The Wind in the Willows*. "'What is in there?' asked Mole. 'There's cold chicken in here,' said the Rat, 'Cold ham, cold tongue, cold beef, pickled gherkins, potted meat, cress sandwiches, salad, lemonade ginger beer soda –' 'Oh, stop stop stop stop,' cried Mole." I think we may delete the lemonade or at least the ginger beer.

and we all had to wear the same frock – well not to share but the same…"

"Design."

"Yes, you are right and I should not have been there because my Mama was so unsuitable.* But my Papa was a column of dignity –"

"A pillar of the establishment?"

"Yes, yes, just so and so no one could say no, and then one girl is chosen out of all…"

"And it was you?"

"Yes, it was, and Sandor was there and saw me."

"I now see the reason for the smile."

"I have two other reasons to be content."

"What?"

"What what? No more what-ting! I have sorted problems and am content."

"Problems? You don't have problems, you have a beautiful house and a husband I am almost in love with…"

"Well now I have found for friends."

"Have you found me a house?" Mr Bradley wilfully misunderstood, "so kind, I'd love to live in Hungary, but unfortunately…"

"Unfortunately, you are foolish – of course no house in Hungary! Sweety moon in Hungary yes! No need of house! Hotel is best, later you stay at Gyor. I have found people for people and that is my best and why I am content."

"Well, I found a dog," said Constance, "and he's practically the best."

The other occupant of the car saw fit to sniff – "he is, don't sniff!"

---

* See p. 49 if you have not paid attention!

That night, after dinner,* mellow and soppy, Charlie said "Magdalena didn't find us."

"No, we found us," said Constance, "but Magdalena helped."

"I suppose she did. It doesn't really matter who or what or why. I like the comfortable feeling."

"Actually, I prefer the less comfortable feelings – Oh!" The dog had found his humans and was on a mission to lick them to death.

"No no no, this is an uncomfortable feeling I can do without!"

"At least someone has washed him."

"Very well – you can take him to bed."

"Couldn't we share?"

"No," the dog looked between humans and chose the man again as the least fussy.

---

* Poached eggs en gelée, truite au bleu, pommes de terre nouvelles à la menthe, haricots verts, millefeuilles aux chocolat and hard sheep's cheese.

24

In the morning, goodbyes and thank yous said and peacock ashtrays packed, our heroes motored forth without once getting lost. As they reached Vienna, Charlie suggested, "Just as well – I don't think anyone would answer your howls around here!"

"That's what you think," and Constance prepared to exercise her tonsils.

"No, no, I believe you, I'm sure everywhere you go there are boys in smocks just waiting to succour you."

"As many as there are waiting to take you for a sucker."

"Not many then."

"Enough."

"Enough is as good as a feast."

"Not for you it isn't – you'd probably want one more Welsh rarebit."

"Or I might want six."

"Six, even for you, would be an exaggeration."

"Or an embroidery?"

"What?"

"What what? Indeed."

Snuffles, who was irritated by this banter, began to sing his song of six pennies to spend so it was fortuitous that just then they reached Lydia's front door, opened by Johann, into whose arms jumped Snuffles, a dog with more friends than your average sixteen.*

---

* Why? You ask, dear reader, with his revolting habits of jumping up and eating people's handbags. I shall find you a photograph and of course he was no longer smelly, which helped. I wonder what might have happened if he had met Blondi – another time, another book.

Albert bowed to Constance and shook hands with Charlie. Snuffles, who knew an alpha male when he smelt one, rolled on his back and presented his tummy in a most obsequious way. Albert rubbed said tum absent-mindedly with his foot.

"How is Nellie? We missed your company in Gyor, but I'm glad she's safely in England – yes please Johann, Snuffles would love a walk," and Constance relinquished lead, hat, gloves and a smile.

They moved to the salon, where Karl offered refreshing glasses, "Dinner will be served in an hour, if that is convenient, Mlle?"

"Wonderful," said Constance, and to Albert, "Now tell all."

"Nellie is, I hope, learning to love Nursie."

"You left her with Nursie?"

"Couldn't think of anywhere better."

"Nursie?" Constance eyed two grown men with a raised eyebrow.

"You'll meet her and love her and understand."

"Hmmm, I never feel comfortable about people I am bound to love. I rarely do."

"What did Nursie think?"

"Nursie reminded me that I hadn't been to visit her for nearly a year and wondered why Nellie had no luggage."

"For heaven's sake! Didn't you buy her any stuff on the way?"

"Nellie is very proud."

"Not too proud to come with us at the drop of a hat!"

Mr Bradley intervened, "speaking of dropped hats –"

"That hat was thrown."

"And impetuous journeys."

"I was saving a dog, don't distract me, I want to know about Nellie."

"The unfortunate thing about Nellie, is that she has a brother."

"Good grief, I've got seven, why would one be unfortunate?"

"And I have four sisters which is much worse."

"Your brothers, I say I say and your sisters, Miss Constance are not under pressure from people who think they might be Jewish and would prefer them to discontinue their studies."

"You've met him?" Charlie, realising the implications, ceased to be facetious.

"Briefly only, but I have spoken at length to Mr von Papen's valet, or rather his put-upon servant."

Constance interrupted, "I hesitate to say, what? But please explain in short sentences. Which do not contain too many polysyllabic words."

"We were able too easily to extricate Nellie from her captors."

"Yes, I think we worked it rather well."

"Because we were allowed to."

"Allowed to?"

"Nellie is now in a position to spy upon people who know a few things about what's going on in England."

"But she is a kindred spirit? I thought she was a kindred. She should be sent back to Germany immediately. Or possibly shot!"

"She is still a kindred, dear Miss Constance, but I say I say she has a brother and is being blackmailed on two fronts."

"Why didn't she say? I say I say!"

"She hardly had time and what time she had was scary!"

"When did she tell you?"

"She didn't exactly tell me..."

Albert stopped. "Um, Constance you should know that Albert sees things sometimes – that other people can't," said Charles.

"Uh oh, like the Danube I suppose!"

Albert blushed with grace.*

"Hmm, fortunately I behaved perfectly on that occasion, the same can not be said of your – what shall I call him – confrère perhaps. He behaved in a dastardly manner and I have not forgiven him. And he tried it again in Budapest."

"We were speaking of Nellie."

Albert said, "as we drove to the coast, I became aware of things she wasn't saying – discrepancies, a certain reticence, although she was eager to be in England, she was nervous. I can't pinpoint the moments. I was nervous too, that we might be followed. Surprised when I could see we weren't. Anyway, Nursie took charge, Nellie wasn't too happy, she thought we would be in London ... she wanted to meet people."

"So she could start spying! Definitely she should be shot."

"Constance."

"A cyanide capsule then – I don't like being taken for a sap."

"What if one of your sisters were in danger?"

"Pah! I've two or three to spare!"

"Don't make yourself out to be a heartless hussy – I know you aren't."

"Anyway, Nursie found out stuff."

---

* You spot the difference dear reader? Albert can blush. Mr Bradley does not blush. He is after all a Member of Parliament!

"As well she would," said Charlie, in Nursie tones, "Now, Leonora, you have a lovely clever brother, tell me all about him…"

"Exactly, well, Nellie sobbed on Nursie's shoulder."

"Poor darling, a lifetime of soggy shoulders."

"And this is the histoire: before we extricated Nellie, her brother Alexander turned up in her bedroom one night; he began tenderly, but ended by saying that if she didn't agree to everything his patrons suggested, he would bring some friends of his to visit her: they are gentlemen of an amorous nature who enjoy having fun together. Those may be Nursie's euphemisms, but I think we understand what he meant."

There was a silence.

"And then he smashed what few precious things she had left."

"That story is disgusting, thank goodness I haven't a brother."

Albert spoke into the no-man's-land between hostile warriors, "when I returned to Vienna, I discovered Mr von Papen's servant's favoured hostelry and we drank a tankard or three together. He told me about the young man that his master had befriended and whose studies he was funding. His name is Alexander Hirsh. Apparently the boy's father was a doctor who successfully treated our friend Herr Goerdeler."

"But," said Charlie, "Why didn't Herr Goerdeler tell Nellie about her brother? And he must've known the parents were dead…"

"So many secrets in Germany and Austria – I think he was working out how he could use Nellie to his advantage."

"And surely it is dangerous for those two gents to be helping a Jew?"

"Mr von Papen's servant was of the opinion that he wouldn't be able to continue helping him, he said, 'he's obviously a Jew and stuck up. He thinks he's God's chosen all right.' I watched for Alexander the next morning – he and Nellie are dead spits."

"We must kidnap him and take him to England."

"The young man disapproves of his sister. Imagine working in a bar! And wishes to stay in Vienna. He trusts his benefactor and is an ostrich about events in Österreich. We would have to take him kicking and screaming."

"Hang on," the Bradley brain had got its spinnaker up, "if Nellie wants to learn stuff from us – why don't we let her learn stuff, but the wrong stuff. Then maybe later we can extricate the bro?"

"They both sound pretty ghastly to me!"

"Constance, you've never been blackmailed."

"Maybe not, but I'm sure I would've biffed that man one, had he suggested that I –"

"Which would probably have achieved nothing."

"It would have been deeply satisfying though. Tell, Albert, how bad do you think this Jewish thing is getting? Ghastly Hitler Youth being beastly to dogs, people not allowed to work, what'll happen next? Some people in England dislike Jews but no Jewish person is afraid for their life."

"Here they have been made scapegoats for all sorts of nonsense. The same as in Germany. Herr Hitler is incarcerating anyone who doesn't agree with him. The next step may well be anyone whose race he chooses to dislike."

"Where I was staying, near Munich, crowds of people were marched away. No one paid any notice."

"But Alexander should be all right for the time being and if necessary..."

"I know," said Constance, "you have a cousin."

"È anche vero," smiled Albert, "and he could contain said kicker and screamer better than we could."

"I wish said kicker and screamer could be well kicked and screamed at, and I still do not see why he should be rescued at all?"

"Alexander is Nellie's last relative. She cannot like him, but she does still love him."

"And you love her."

"È ancora vero."

"Oh well then, but please don't expect me to be polite and with some good luck Snuffles will bite. Oooh, I think that's a poem."

"A good plan, then, especially as he might have got in the way of your luggage, my d –"

"Pah – Frederika's luggage more likely. I shall powder my nose and consider the situation," said Constance, all haughty with a sniff.

"Don't sniff!"

"I shall sniff if I whiff," said his beloved, whereupon she ruined her exit with hooted laughter.

25

The difference between staying at Gyor, and at the castle near Hanover, cannot be imagined. Fortunately the travellers knew how to behave. Albert put on his chauffeur's hat and drove away with a moaning Snuffles, while Constance and Charlie were escorted with baggage but without beverage to their separate apartments. There was no sign of their hosts.

"Oops" whispered Constance, "best behaviour here."

"Toujours la politesse," said Charlie.

"Toujours prends toujours un S," sibilated Constance for no particular reason.

"What's that supposed to mean?"

"It's just grammar silly."

"You're nervous," Charlie was incredulous.

"So should you be. Just you wait…"

He didn't have to wait long. Changed and downstairs he was directed to the library.

There sat the Duke,[*] behind an imposing desk. He stood. They shook hands.

"I must thank you for returning my daughter to England and for being so kind to her in Nuremberg."

"My pleasure on both counts. And it was your wife who was kindness itself to a lonely Englishman."

His host raised an eyebrow, "Not so alone now though? Excuse me, I have some papers to sign. You will read the newspaper perhaps."

---

[*] He had abandoned the title in 1918, but did this make a blind bit of difference? It did NOT.

Here I am, back at school, thought Mr B., as he sat and reached for the day before yesterday's copy of *The Times*. He had looked through it twice, with particular attention to the engagements, marriages, births and deaths, hoping to find a name to conjure with, when the Duchess entered, followed by Frederika and Constance. Frederika had been crying which did not improve her complexion.

"My dear, you are ignoring our guest?"

"Perfectly happy, I assure you – good to catch up on English News."

"Come come, we will go to the drawing room. I am sure refreshments are needed."

Dear reader, do you remember the broken biscuits? It wasn't quite that bad. There was salty smoked carp ("from our lake") on dry pumpernickel and some slightly sweet Moselle. Later, in the draughty dining room, they ate ruined roast beef accompanied by apple sauce and potato dumplings. Then there was a cake. "The sort of cake," Constance said later, "that Captain Hook would have been proud of."

Frederika looked miserable throughout and the conversation trickled only because Constance produced her flopsy bunny act, "Oh, silly me, I can't get anything right."

Charlie was interested to learn about her fall into the Danube and her near loss of an eye from standing in the wrong place during the shoot. He did recognise their lost route on the way to Gyor, but even this was embroidered into a web, glistening with raindrops. He only just managed to continue discussing Budapest and its treasures with the Duchess when in his mind Constance was dealing with Councillor Wormworthy on her right and Mrs Digby from the W.I. on her left.*

Probably everyone was relieved when Snuffles made an appearance.†

"My apologies Your Grace, but," said Albert as the dog bounced onto Constance's palest pink chiffon.

"I am so sorry! You bad boy." Snuffles, who knew better, wagged and wagged. "He wants me to walk him. So delicious but may we go and enjoy the evening in your beautiful garden? Frederika, will you come too?"

"You may accompany our guests," said the Duke, frowning at the dog, who would have growled, only his mistress had him, as they say, by the short and curly ones!

"Breakfast will be at nine." Their host continued, and with good nights and bows and two filial kisses our heroes and their sulky appendage retired.

In the September evening light they wandered down steps into a formal (natch) baroque garden. The only sound was the perfectly raked gravel crunching underfoot and the flit of moths above. Charles lit them all cigarettes, which he had slowly walked out and bought in Vienna… Snuffles hunted off into the gloom.

"I can't think why you aren't champing at the bit to get to England."

"But Constance! All my friends are here! I am German! We have such exciting times at the moment – I don't want to miss a day, let alone a year! England is so boring! And so so pompous!"

The gravel crunched under a stamped foot. Thoughts flitted about with the moths.

"Poor darling, you'd be an expert on pomposity. If

---

* A total fantasy dear reader – this won't happen.

† You see? A divine dog.

fewer exclamation marks means boring, I'm all for boring," thought Constance.

Aloud, she soothed, "We* will come and take you out, or perhaps you could come on the train to London?"

"I don't want to come to England, let alone London."

"London is more fun than Broadstairs, you know" said Charles gently.

"If I'd known you were shut up down there I would've got Mummy or even one of the Aunts to take you out, but as you know, I've been in Germany, missing my friends…" Constance added.

"So you know what it's like! And I've done FOUR years to your one!" The gravel crunched mercy again.

"Your true friends will still be here in a year's time."

"I've never had friends before! It was impossible. Sometimes being here, sometimes being there, only meeting the children of my parents' friends. And in England," Frederika began to cry again, stamping on her fag end. The gravel winced. Mr Bradley put a brotherly arm around her shoulders:

"Frederika, don't cry, you will make your lovely face all blotchy and it won't solve a thing."

"But I am so frustrated and CROSS."

Another moth thought fluttered past: frustrated being the operative word. A boyfriend, a lover even?

"Frederika," said Constance, "Give this term a go, after all you are to be head girl. So special!"

Moth thought to H.Q.: "I'd've died, had I been so honoured! Not that the opportunity arose. And delete the

---

* Oh dear! Another first person plural, dear reader, what is Constance becoming! Not a soppy miss – she'll not be that. Nor a soppy Mrs either – oh very clever you at the back!

exclamation marks!!" (Constance would not have liked to be head girl.)

"Hah! It just means you do the Headmistress' dirty work."

"We'll," – another Moth thought – "this We-ing must stop" – Constance managed not to giggle.

"We'll come and see you, and get you to London as often as we can before Christmas, after all, your Mama has asked me to introduce you here and there. That's not long!" Charles took up the burden.

"Then if you are still hating Broadstairs, we can get Constance's Mama to form ranks with various other Mamas."

"She's good at that."

"And explain to yours, that you'd be happier at home. I don't think even the Duchess could resist such a formidable crew!"

"Suffragettes and the daughters of Suffragettes, they are in constant need to form ranks about something," interpolated Constance. Frederika had hid her face in Charlie's jacket (blue Alpaca, very soft). Our heroine decided enough was enough and offered a hanky before he could.

"So, please let's enjoy your lovely house for tomorrow with no more tears, and then we'll take you back to Broadstairs and promise we'll have lots of fun."

Frederika appeared to nod and they wandered, with lit cigarettes, back to the castle, where Constance refused the sodden ball which once had been a handkerchief. A moth thought flew – "Unity's, tant pis!"

Snuffles, whistled for, skidded up the path very pleased with himself. He needed a few feathers removed from his chops before Charlie walked him, reluctantly, to Albert's room.*

---

* Query: which male left with most reluctance? Mr Bradley had given both cheeks a chaste kiss – if he had had a tail it would've flopped as low as Snuffles'.

26

The next day passed without event: breakfast, lunch and dinner followed each other with varying degrees of disgusting-ness. Constance hissed occasionally at unlistened times, "I am faint from hunger." Charles didn't bother to reply, since he reckoned that, camel-like, Constance had some reserves stashed away.

It was with huge relief that our heroine found herself in Albert's cousin's kneipe. The very same where Charles and Albert had eaten their first night in Germany.

"Oh, heaven, proper food. Sorry Fredka but your parents are so perfectly ascetic – I don't think they enjoy food. They eat it to stay alive, like a car needs petrol, whereas I – Oh oh oh, Kartoffelklosse! Here Fredka, have one, or two! And then we will powder our noses before more delicious things."

The evening passed pleasurably with a plethora of good things, and 'no carp!' Constance positively purred and even Frederika was seduced into enjoying what was put before her. On a merry note, they were walking Snuffles (also fed F to B[*]), when a group of shadows approached. Frederika stopped. One shadow emerged from the crowd of black. Constance held Frederika's hand tightly. Snuffles growled.[†] Fortunately he was on a lead. Mr Bradley and Albert moved in front of their

---

[*] Oh dear, "full to bursting". They not only do things differently in that other country the Past, they say things differently as well.

[†] Excellent boy!

ladies, and Albert, in perfect German (natch), enquired what was the matter?

A beautifully coiffed, bronzed blue-eyed person confronted them.[*]

"I think," he said in perfect English, "you have a friend of mine with you. And perhaps she would rather be with me?"

The hand that was not tightly held made a dash to cover Frederika's mouth, "Wilfried?" was whispered.[†]

Wilfried's friends sauntered forwards. One or two were quite handsome, and some of them had eyebrows, but dressed as they were in Hitler Youth uniform, they were not the sort of people one would wish to meet in the dark of an unfamiliar street. For a moment there was a communal snarl. Then Constance said firmly:

"The Princess Frederika is going back to school in England. I am sure she will be happy to give you her address. In fact – better still..." And she passed the clasped hand to Charles, "why don't you give me your address?"

Violet eyes to the fore, she marched up to the "Wilf". "I'm sure you have a card? No? Oh dear, I thought all gentlemen had cards about their persons. Well, never mind. All ladies have a pencil and a notebook. And I shall write your address in mine."

Constance smiled sweetly into the beetling non-brows of the Wilf. Pencil poised, she paused: "I see," She continued in German. "I suppose that is, 'of no fixed abode'. Very well, Mr Bradley will give you his card, and you may contact the Princess via him."

---

* But he had no eyebrows, dear reader, and therefore not to be trusted.

† Well, there you have it, readers mine – no eyebrows and a Wilfried, the extra E does not make it better.

Constance retook Frederika's hand while Mr B. searched here, yes, and here and there and could it be inside here? for his calling card.* While he was finding the useful object, the shadows assumed a more menacing aspect, but Wilfried probably realised that he had been outwitted† by a flibbertigiberty lady in a hat. (IT was cream and rose today, readers, and sat just so, towards the left ear.)

"You think you are funny?" The curled lip was not as attractive as Snuffles'.

"Come Frederika – leave these ridiculous decadent people!" Hand extended – growls emitted. Hissed and whispered words while hands still tightly held.

"You promised."

"I love him."

"He loves your status."

"You don't understand."

"Yes, I do."

"For heaven's sake, you can't love a Wilfried."

"Charles?"

"Charles is fine, it may not be Ernest, but it's fine, let's go back."

"No, no – I want to..."

"He will be here when you come back at Christmas. For now leave him! What sort of lover needs a gang behind him?"

"We will go now I think. Frederika."

"Yes, oh yes."

"Sorry, absolument pas." Constance's jaw, always a formidable part of her anatomy, jutted. The band of

---

* He is a Man, dear reader person.

† He had been out whatted too – but he probably wouldn't have understood.

shadows, jutted too. Mr Bradley and Albert seemed out-numbered, but just then some cousins emerged from the cousinly pub.

"Ooh," they said, probably in German, "has our English cousin found a problem? Poor little 'un, shouldn't be let out alone."

Miraculously, at that moment, Mr Bradley found his card and presented it with a small bow, no, a nod to the Wilf.

Somehow the cousins were suddenly between the shadows* and their prey and our heroes gently led a forlorn Frederika back to her room. She was not only forlorn but in a filthy temper.

"You are old," she accused Constance, "you and your pompous English boyfriend, I am young and I will be free."

Constance considered, and she decided she was quite old, Charles did wear pyjamas, and that dressing gown. Oh dear.

"I'm afraid you are probably right. But at the moment, we are also probably right, because nobody who aspires to love another person behaves in this manner." Constance bathed Frederika's face and gently hugged her.

"A lover is someone who may tease you, but who always looks out for you and he certainly does not bring his bully boys when he comes calling."

"They are his friends."

"We are your friends. Please Fredka, however ancient we may we seem, come to England with us, you may find your perspective changes."

"It will not."

---

* No one, I repeat no one is to start singing "The Young Ones". All right?

"Well then, angel face, we will drive you back to your parents in the morning."

"I don't want to go back to them, I want…"

"If you think we're going to hand you over to some unknown person in a dirty-coloured shirt you've got another think coming." A clatter of pebbles on the window put a stop to the increasingly acrimonious conversation.

"Frederika?"

"Wilfried."

"Come down, there will be a fire. Be quick."

The Duke's daughter pulled open the door and pounded down the stairs, followed by a despairing Constance. Standing formidably at five foot, ten inches in her stockinged feet, Frederika shot the Wilf Gang with words like machine-gun fire.

"Fire? What fire? Why is there to be a fire? 'Come down quickly.' To whom do you think you speak?"

"But darling…"

"Don't darling me," Constance noticed with admiration that the stockinged foot did not stamp.

There were six men outside with flaming brands of wood. Two carried jerry cans. Of petrol, worried Constance.

"I will burn the English dogs who try to come between us, and any traitors who abet them."

The two with the petrol started towards the back of the pub, one was laughing.

"Bring with you their animal and I will myself, set it alight."

"You are threatening my friends? How dare you? You are a nasty little TOAD."

"At least an inch shorter," applauded Constance silently.

"And I do not wish to see you or your cronies again. There will not be a fire, and you will go away, NOW." Our heroine, the old one, watched the foot and nearly cheered. Several cousins, not to mention Charles and Albert, had now crept from the woodwork, and there was in fact, a round of applause, not to mention barkings.

The Wilf Gang went and Constance escorted a some-what stunned Frederika inside.

"You were marvellous! Well done that Fred!" Whereupon said Fred burst into tears.

"Oh, oh, oh, I loved him," she looked at Constance, "how could I be so stupid?"

"Join the club my liebling, if you only knew how stupid I've been here and there. The world is full of toadish men and we women must beware."

"I'm sorry to have been rude."

"I expect I deserved it – being bossy as usual."

"You were right to be bossy." And thus the night dissolved into utter soppiness.

27

An uneventful crossing and a purring Bentley saw Frederika back at Broadstairs. Albert's nephew having delivered Mr Bradley's pride and joy (the mechanical one that is) to Portsmouth. Albert had pottered around it and concluded, "I say I say you couldn't grow neeps in this'n."*

"Fred, Fred, dear old thing – how are you? What did you do in the hols?"

The Duke's daughter was enveloped by a girly crowd. She was barely able to say her goodbyes, although some friends would have liked to linger near Mr Bradley and his car. It has to be said that looks also lingered on Miss Bennett's hat.† No one looked at Albert, of course, because although he too wore a hat, he was in chauffeur mode and therefore invisible.‡

And so to London.

"I can't remember what London looks like," sighed Constance, "and I'm not sure I wish to be reminded." She sat beside Charlie who drove and who offered her a cheering smile. "We've promised Frederika some fun, I don't see why we shouldn't have some too."

"You'll be all pompous and M.P.-like, and I shall have to find a job and then there are my sisters … oh dear. I shall start to sob like Fredka, or at any rate snuffle like you!"

---

* Dear reader, please see p. 67 if you have not been paying attention – daffodils.
† Neatly navy with a white button or two.
‡ Silly them!

The dog wagged his tail.

"Oh," they both said.

"I can't –"

"I can't either. There is a garden, but we're not supposed to have dogs."

Snuffles, who was not stupid and had had a long and boring time in the car, began to wail.

"I say I say as I'll be taking Mr Snuffles down to Nursie's. Don't fuss boys and Miss." Snuffles desisted and offered his tum for a rub.

"Nursie dislikes dogs."

"You leave Nursie to me. We won't be there long. I say I say as you'll be needing me in London."

"What then? And what about Nellie?"

"Aah, well, you know Old Lady Methuen, your father's cousin?"

"You have cousins too?"

"Don't you?"

"I try very hard not to. Sisters are quite sufficient."

"I say I say as her companion upped and offed to get married, and what is more, her dog it was that died."*

"Oh, very well read, and excellent person. This seems like a good wheeze."

"I shall miss you all," said Constance, as they came to the outer circle of Regent's Park. "But most especially you, Snuffles. Be a very good boy and on no account growl at Nursie. Albert please be kind and help me with the luggage, as Mr Bradley should stay in the car. My sisters are probably watching from the window upstairs and I do not propose for them to get a grandstand view.

---

* Oliver Goldsmith,1728–1744: "Elegy for a Mad Dog". The man recovered from the bite, the dog it was that died.

Or to see anything which might fuel fanciful thoughts in their nasty, I mean dear little minds."

"What about fanciful thoughts in my dear little mind?"

"We will shake hands, and I might quite like to see you again." They shook and smiled and with the piled luggage beside her, Constance turned her key in the lock, pushed and vanished inside. Snuffles flopped down with a groan.

Constance was squashed by sisters.

"You're back!"

"Who is he?"

"Who are they?"

"What a car!"

"That's a nice hat, but your hair is terrible and you are positively stout."

"That's five goes, and I know Winifred is in Hollywood, so that's two too many!"

"Girls!" from upstairs came a gentle voice which, however, did not allow contradiction.

"Please allow Constance to return home without too much NOISE. Bridget, I think there may be bags to bring up."

"S'all right, mummy darling, I've got most of them." Constance hauled luggage up the stairs and hugged.

"Oooh, what larks, what tales!"

"And what males?" said Barbara.

"Barbara, take your uncontrolled tongue down the stairs and help Bridget. Constance, it would have been polite to let me know of your impending arrival, but it is wonderful to see you. I expect you would like to wash your hands and remove that fetching hat. Put it somewhere safe, or Eva will make off with it. Then, I think, Bridget, some sherry, in the drawing room? Please."

Bridget, eyes like saucers, bobbed.

"Margaret, would you help Bridget with the glasses? Eva dear, please discreetly discover whether Bridget has prepared enough supper."

"Constance doesn't need any supper – so there'll be plenty."

"Barbara: are you sure there is no more luggage? In which case you will want to wash your hands. Possibly you could chew a bit of soap as well?"

Lalage settled into her drawing room and watched with sangfroid as Bridget wobbled into the room carrying tray, plus decanter – so far so good. Margaret had the glasses and Barbara was not around to say 'booh!"

"Beautifully done," Lalage smiled as Bridget set the tray down upon the right table.

"Thank you Mum, I do try my best."

"You certainly do."

"And Miss Constance – she looks so lovely – just like Miss Winifred only –"

"All my daughters look alike, Bridget, but some are better behaved than others."

"Yes 'M'."

"Please try and practise 'Madam', Bridget. It will give you a certain cachet, don't you think?"

Bridget had no idea what a cachet was, but she definitely wanted one. She had only been in service with Mrs Bennett for one week, but the orphanage was now a blurred memory. She could speak French and knew how to cook!

Well, she knew ever so many French words and could make five or maybe six dishes if the girls helped her. And they were so sweet – even Miss Barbara who was, well, quite rude sometimes – she only meant it as a joke. And jokes were a new and jolly thing to understand. Margaret interrupted Bridget's précis of life chez Bennett: "would you come and help me? I can't find those napkins with the swans."

Lalage was left for a peaceful moment. Her drawing room was small, not really a drawing room at all, but it gave her huge satisfaction and strength. The few precious Louis XV and XVI pieces glittered amongst the more austere Art Deco furniture. Tall windows (which fortunately had shutters) were draped only in muslin, but the muslin was lined and edged in a deep sea green and it rippled and glowed against the eau-de-nil of the walls.

"Oooh, it's nice to be home," Constance sat and stretched. "I seem to have been in a car for several years."

"Darling girl – so lovely to have you home – you look, mmmm, quite polished."

"I'm positively shiny! Unity sends her love, as does Lydia. Also Mme de Hedevar, Countess M. and all of the others who sweetly put up with me."

"I hope you kept a diary."

"With pictures. But I'm afraid just recently…"

"You've been busy."

"We have been about a bit and I must tell you about Nellie."

"I'd rather hear about Mr Bradley – might he – I assume it was he – not have introduced himself? Most of my friends seem to know him. I feel at a disadvantage."

"Mummy, you blessed me with sisters and –"

"I understand."

"I intend to see him again and of course I will introduce you, preferably when we are on our own." To illustrate the point, in came the sisters. Kept away for as long as possible by Margaret, they were now rabid with curiosity.

You, dear reader, know already about Nellie and some of the larks. I do not propose to tell you about Constance's earlier sojourn in Germany. You are aware that she speaks its language fluently and so may suppose that she studied hard, behaved charmingly to her hosts, and never got into mischief. Or, you can imagine what really happened. You can also decide which version she related to her mother and assembled siblings. Do not write in the margin and only on one side of your paper.

28

Meanwhile, not back at the ranch,* but in Sloane Street, Mr Bradley bounded up the stairs past Mrs Parker. We've been here before haven't we reader(s) mine? And he gave his landlady a big hug and a beautiful china beer mug.

"Now what will I use that for Mr Bradley?"

"Flowers of course, Mrs Parker," and Albert produced a bunch exactly the right size. So Mrs Parker hugged him.

"It has been very quiet all summer I must say. I suppose I shall just have to get used to the noise again."

"Noise? What noise? Do we sing? Do we dance?"

"NO, but you do pound up and down those stairs and it rattles my chandeliers," which is where we came in and what they did, showing huge disrespect to Mrs Parker's lighting, only to pound down again as she squawked: "There is a lot of post for you here Mr Bradley."

"Bills, I expect."

"No, there are postcards mostly from young ladies, but one very disgusting one from your friend Donald, it seems to be drawn by a Mr McGill, of whom I cannot

---

* Dear reader, I know we are not near a ranch, the expression comes from a (probably) B-movie. Cowboys in black and white are dashing away on their horses, MEANWHILE, insidious Indians are creeping towards the homestead, OR maybe the dastardly baron of the plains is knocking on the door. Mom is making apple pie and securing the shutters over the windows. Once we are in glorious Technicolor, these will have red and white gingham curtains and any minute Doris Day will enter, singing, "I just blew in from the windy City, The windy city is mighty purrty." Bliss.

approve. Please ask him not to send such missives through my letter box."

"You needn't have looked."

"I needed to see to whom it was sent."

"It was probably for Miss Vincent on the first floor."

"Mr Bradley!"

"Mr Bradley," descending the stairs, a lady of a certain age and certainly years ahead of our hero, formed her painted lips into a smile.

"Welcome home."

"Miss Vincent. I hope you have had an excellent summer, you look quite blooming."

"Thank you Mr Bradley, I am well and would like to invite you for a glass of sherry and to see my photographs of Rome," Miss Vincent drew on her gloves, "tomorrow evening?"

"Aah, oh, yes, please. How delightful." Our hero was caught in a trap (again, but this time for real). Miss Vincent left.

"Mrs Parker," Charlie produced a handkerchief in consternation, "I must say your lodgers leave something to be desired."

"I say I say what bit to be desired might that be?"

"Albert, don't put your oar in."

Their landlady drew up her formidable bosom: "I do not like the tone of this conversation, desires and whores have no place in polite society. I bid you good day."

"Good day Mrs Parker." Tails between legs, our gentlemen plodded up the stairs. No they didn't, they pounded and bounded, and their laughter, though muted, increased the noise of their progress.

There were bills, also some invitations and two

notes to telephone respectively Mr Churchill and Lord Beaverbrook.

Please telephone when you return to London. Regards
PPS. I guess you will need to write me a few articles to finance your long vacation. Call me. Max B.

Bills pushed to one side, postcards appreciated.

"I say I say you got one from that Miss Tarrant, her that likes to play on boats."

"I say I say I don't see one from Lucy."

"Hmmm."

"Hmmm... You are off to the Isle of Wight. Give my love to Nursie."

"You should be telephoning your grand friends and I will walk Snuffles."

"Oh!"

"You'd forgotten him. I shall tell Miss Constance!"

"Mr Bradleeeee," came another squawk from the nether regions of No. 135. "There is a dog that is interrupting my peace of mind and it appears to be sitting in your car. I hope you are not about to bring an animal into my house?"

"She allows Miss Vincent to stay," said Charlie.

"Shhh." They pounded down again. Out of the car came Snuffles, wagging like mad and moaning for a lamppost. A quick trip down the street sufficed and then he was ready to ingratiate himself with Mrs Parker.

"I do not like dogs at all, as you very well know, but this one seems remarkably polite." Snuffles, perceiving an alpha female, had sat crouched with nose on paws, tail a-wag and finally rolled over for tummy inspection.

"I do suppose I might allow..."

"Sweet of you Mrs Parker, but Snuffles is off to the Isle of Wight with Albert, so we needn't trouble you. I will bear that in mind though, a kind thought."

Albert, piling stuff into the Bentley, said, "I say I say as I'd get that in writing."

The friends grinned and shook.

Charles telephoned, a secretary answered.

"Mrs Churchill would like to speak to you, Mr Bradley, please hold the line."

"Charlie dear, so glad you're back safe and sound – did you have fun? Good. Will you be able to stay at Chartwell the weekend after this one? Good. I hear you met one of the beauteous Miss Bennetts on your travels? Might she be persuaded to visit us do you think? Good. I will telephone her. Tea time on Friday? Good. Violet would like to speak to you now. Goodbye."

"Mr Churchill has asked me to say: Lord Beaverbrook will be at Chartwell the day after you arrive. Please desist from giving him any information before then. Mr Churchill has gone to the Riviera for a few days. If anything is very urgent, you may contact him there."

Mr Bradley said that nothing he had to tell was of great urgency and replaced the receiver. He felt a trifle breathless, but inhaling deeply, he rang the Beaver. Getting through to him took rather longer than his first call. Eventually, "Charlie boy – welcome back! Hear you bin breaking hearts all over the Continong."

"Only those you haven't already broken, Sir."

"Har Har – wodaryagonna write for my noosepaper?"

"I thought young Max was in charge these days?"

"He thinks he is. Wadayagot?"

"Um, what fashionable ladies are wearing in

Nuremberg? The Lipizzaners of Vienna? Tales of a shoot near the Danube?"

"Nah nah Charlie boy, don't get me cross."

"An interview with Princess Frederika of Prussia?"

"Now yar talking… What's the goss?"

"She's a virginal seventeen-year-old?"

"Charlie Boy yar disappointing me. Winston's got to you hasn't he?"

"I'm told we will both be at Chartwell, the weekend after this one."

"You might just be off my payroll, boy."

"How is young Max?"

"He's a pain too," and the conversation was severed. Our hero expelled air. "Ho hum."

Constance.

He hadn't even got the dog to encourage her. Never mind. He had his constituency and other animals to deal with, in fact he would go to Eastbourne tomorrow, which had the advantage of excusing him from Miss Vincent's invitation. A soothing train journey, while he reminded himself of other people's problems would be just the ticket. He definitely would NOT telephone Constance for a bit. Not just now anyway. In bed he missed Snuffles.

29

When our hero returned from waving himself around Eastbourne.

Our M.P. meets Adolf Hitler were the headlines in the *Eastbourne Herald* that week. There was a note from Lord Beaverbrook simply saying, "Bastard."

Charles decided he definitely needed to telephone Constance.

"Soreeee, can't connect you."

Ten minutes later.

"Soreee, can't connect you."

Mr Bradley pounded down again and found a cab. Once inside, he realised he had no idea in which house of the outer circle dwelt his beloved. Fortunately the cab driver did.

"I suppose you don't know a house where five beautiful sisters live?" Silly question really.

"I'm a cabby ain't I? And the eldest one's gawn to Hollywood – she's been in the back of my cab 'fore now, and she's a right knockout an all. Bit highfalutin if yer asks me – I reckon the younger ones'r more fun."

Charlie noted this accolade for later use, and delivered to the right door, one he now remembered, administered a large tip.

"Good luck to yer Guv."

He rang the bell. The door was opened by a small round person in a maid's uniform.

"May I call upon Miss Constance Bennett?"

"Bridget? Bridget!" A redhead with impossibly long legs came galloping down the stairs.

"Miss Constance is indisposed."

"I know what you told me to say Miss Barbara, there's no need for you to –"

"Perhaps I might call on Mrs Bennett?"

"If you would come this way, Sir?"

And up they went past the huffy legs, where they were greeted by our heroine, face painted white and swathed in white wraps.

"Oh dear, I'm so sorry, I'm afraid I feel too ill to go out tonight," she said with cast-down eyes, "the telephone is broken otherwise I would have…" From behind, a sister commented:

"I think you are playing to the wrong audience."

"Ha hah," from Barbara.

"Hello," said Mr Bradley.

"Oh, what?" said Constance.

"What, what" arms outstretched reached and clasped hands. Then there was smiling and laughter.

"Mr Bradley, I think you may join me in the drawing room. Constance, go and remove that ridiculous paint." Charles found himself in Lalage's drawing room. He shook hands. She watched him.

"Would you like some tea? Or perhaps whisky? I dare say you need to be revived after that unnecessary performance. It was intended for another follower. Bridget, please bring the whisky decanter, that is the square-shaped one with the brown liquid. And a tumbler, some ice* and?"

"Soda, please, if possible."

---

* The theatrical tend to American habits.

"And the soda siphon. I will have a glass of champagne, thank you. Miss Barbara will help you with the cork."

"Are we celebrating something?"

"Yes, your imminent departure for school."

"You'll miss me really."

"I will. Now go."

Mr Bradley had watched in his turn during these exchanges. Mrs Bennett's hair was entirely white, but it curled around her head in the same way as Constance's. She wore a biscuit-coloured blouse and skirt with white lace here and there, which on another might have been dowdy: upon Lalage's elegant person it was the epitome of chic. They drank a few sips in silence.

"My friends seem to like you."

"I rather like your friends."

"Constance is not an easy person."

"I like that."

"Are you an easy person?"

"I am probably the best-natured person in the world." Our hero was the recipient of what was known, en famille, as a 'Lalage Look'.

"Oh well, maybe not…"

"So, then?"

"We'll fight I suppose, and make up. It'll be fun."

"It will NOT be forever fun and it is foolish to think so."

"We are friends, and are having fun and I see forever, but I haven't asked…"

"What haven't you asked?" enquired Constance, entering sans white paint or white wraps, but with red lips, mascara'd eyes and a bright blue frock which Charlie seemed to remember, "buttons," he thought, but he said, "Whether you might be able to come out this evening,

194

that is, if you are feeling better, and your Mama doesn't mind?"

"Mummy, I will help tomorrow – promise. And you've got Bridget, she seems like a good find."

"Off you go. I will deal with the girls."

"I'm sure you will." A kiss and a handshake, and they were down the stairs.

"Don't eat too much," said Barbara.

Once in the street, Charlie looked about for a cab, but at least two drove past without him noticing, because there were more important things to look at.

"Would you like to go to Quags?"

"Oooh – that would be a treat! What fun, only," Constance threaded her arm through his.

"Only what?"

"Only you'll be sure to know hundreds of people there – if not everyone, and I might know some too, and I'd quite like not to have to chat to all not to mention sundry."

"He's always there on Tuesdays."

"When it might be more fun…"

"To talk to each other…"

"Exactly. If we walk around the corner, I'm sure we'll find somewhere." Knowing his companion's fondness for food, it did not surprise Charlie that only the third hostelry met with approval. A chop house was dismissed, our hero wistful at the thought of steak and kidney pud. A trattoria?

"Italian food should be eaten in Italy."

A tiny French café beckoned from across the road.

"Oooh, Steak Diane and yes! Pommes croquettes and petit pois à la française and you can have rognons flambés, since I denied you your steak and kidney pud."

Snuffles was the first topic of conversation, followed swiftly by Nellie and Albert. The visit to Chartwell was discussed, then there was a sweet remembrance of times past, whilst Constance dreamily polished off our hero's kidneys* and pommes purée and wondered about sorbets. She refused profiteroles, but then asked if she might take some home with her "for the girls".

"I was supposed to help tonight you see, after all, I have been gallivanting all over Europe and they have been stuck here, although Wini is going to pay for Eva to go to the R.A.D.A. and maybe Margaret in a year or so, which is ridiculous – Barbara is the one who should act."

"What about you?"

"Me? Didn't I tell you? I made a couple of films here (one was rather good actually) but Mummy thought I was 'attracting the wrong sort of follower', which is why she sent me to Germany."

"Doesn't Winifred attract 'the wrong kind of follower' in Hollywood?"

"Wini is much stronger than I."

"Wow," thought our hero.

"And Hollywood is different – she has a chaperone and a secretary and an assistant and goodness knows how many people fossiking about her. I don't think she has any time to misbehave. Also not the inclination."

"But you had both?" Was it the rognons, why did Mr Bradley's gut feel Gordian and who was the other follower?

"It is flattering to be followed, especially when you have always been in your older sister's shadow and places like Quaglino's are seductive when you have been brought up

---

* Really, dear reader, those remaining on his plate! This is not a vampire story.

without much – in a frugal way." Our hero listened while suppressing a shudder.

"But I am very old and wise now, and I go only to delicious cafés with high-minded Members of Parliament."* Constance's smile cut the knot in Charles' stomach. It was only then that they noticed chairs on tables and a solitary waiter, eyes semi-closed, leaning against the wall. A large tip seemed necessary, then carrying the profiteroles, they meandered back to the outer circle. Where Eva had fobbed off the other follower who had left flowers. "I love my sisters," said Constance. "Now I know I am home."

---

* Dear reader, if you laugh cynically this book will snap shut upon your fingers. Most of them were then, some are now...

30

Mr Bradley arranged to visit his cousin.
"Now, which one are you?"

"This is Charles," said Nellie.

"Charles? I remember a Charlie, are you Harold's boy?"

"No, Alfred and Agnes' boy."

"Did they have a Charles? I suppose they did, if you say so." In came Snuffles, singing and launched himself into Alfred's son's arms.

"So it's you who found me lovely Leonora and dear George?* Come here and have a treaty, gorgeous boy!" For a brief moment Charles thought he might be offered some little trinket, such as one of the Fabergé eggs sitting prettily beside Lady Methuen, but Nellie had opened a tin and was producing digestive biscuits clearly meant for the dog, which had now landed on a tweedy lap.

"WHAT a good boy!" Leonora, please find the other gorgeous boy a glass of beer, he looks quite put out at not being the only one around. And will you join me in a glass of sherry?" Once the biscuit supply had dried up, Snuffles/George wagged his way back to our hero, who was having ungenerous thoughts about traitors and cupboard love while enquiring about his relative's health and children. Half a glass of beer later:

"The thing is, cousin Betty, I was wondering if we – I, could borrow Snuff – George for the weekend. We – I

---

* Lady Methuen's dogs were all named for her late unlamented husband.

– am going to the country, and I think he might enjoy a change from London life."

"I expect you miss him too?"

"I do rather."

"You are a soppy old dear, and so am I, but actually it couldn't be better timing. I shall be visiting chums this weekend who do not welcome strange dogs and I so wanted to take Leonora. Show her a bit more of England, nothing more English than Houghton don't you know? And now I can." Betty Methuen beamed.

"And don't worry – your man did say that George and Leonora were only on loan. A shame, because I love them both, but truthfully, George is a little large for me and Leonora certainly has more entertaining things to do with her life than to look after old Lady M.! Awfully attractive your man, by the way, wonderful eyebrows."

Charles raised his poor imitations in salute and sighed inwardly.

"Now, where are you gorgeous boys going? Is it George that makes the We, or someone other?"

"Doesn't miss a trick," thought Charles.

"George and I will be going to Chartwell," he said.

"Oh? Give Clementine my love – knew her when she was a girl. Her mother and I came out together. I think she rather wanted to marry George, wish to God she had!"

So everyone was content. Except for Nellie, who embarrassed Charlie as he said goodbye by asking whether she too couldn't go to Chartwell.

"Houghton Hall is beautiful, you'll love it."

"Wonderfully English, but not like being at the centre of English politics. Couldn't I be Constance's lady's maid?"

"It's not that sort of house. I won't be taking Albert." He thought, "Careful Miss Hirsh your camouflaged petticoat is showing."

"Are you not taking Albert?" said Lady Methuen, popping into the hall like a jack-in-the-box. "Can I borrow him? Fair exchange." An impressed Charlie registered another trick un-missed.

"I'll see what I can do to persuade him. He's very fussy about the cars he drives and I'd promised him a free weekend."

"It's a Roller."

"That'll probably do."

At least that's cheered Nellie up, thought our hero as he walked Snuffles back to Sloane Street. Snuffles probably agreed. They bought flowers for Mrs Parker.

"You're a very expensive dog." Snuffles, probably agreeing again, preened. He earned his keep, however, by cosying up to the landlady, "in a sickening manner," as Charles told him on their (quiet) way upstairs.

"Don't you let Miss Vincent see that dog! She wants cats." Mrs Parker hissed to their backs. "I don't know, I really don't, I must be getting soft in the head," she confided to the photograph of her dear, dead Ernest.

Strangely enough Albert was quite happy to be seconded to Lady Methuen for the weekend.

"Thass a marvellous house they're going to."

"House?"

"An I might get a sail or two – there's a…"

"Don't tell me – a cousin…"

"Who works at the Hall and her husband's a fisherman, but he has a tidy little craft he lets out in the summer to the trippers."

"Nothing to do with Nellie then?"

"No, no course not," Albert winked.* "She'll be busy anyway. I say I say just you say to your cousin that I'm happy to drive them down and back, but I'll need to be off duty in the day."

"And at night?"

"I say I say you leave the night time to me Mr Charlie Sir."

"Very well, that's settled."

But Mr B. did ponder, in the watches of the night, about true love's path and how it wiggled from the straight and narrow.

---

* I cannot condone this disgraceful lack of sensibility, I may have his eyebrows singed later. Watch this space.

31

In the outer circle, however, all was not sweetness and light. Constance, on the prowl for something new to wear, found Winifred's door locked. The trunks from Nuremberg had not arrived and:

"Oh for heaven's sake! Who locks their door when they go away?"

"Wini does," said Barbara.

"You can borrow anything of mine," said Margaret.

"Or mine," said Eva.

"Darlings, you are so sweet but..."

"You are too fat to fit into their clothes," said Barbara.

"Barbara, you are a person of no consequence who should be seen and NOT heard, and the sooner you go back to school the better!"

Lalage, emerging from the kitchen, said, "Constance – that was unkind. Say sorry."

"Sorry Barbara."

"You don't mean it."

"Oh yes, I do darling," hug hug, "but I MUST find some clothes to wear!"

"Constance, you have cupboards full of clothes."

"But the smart few he's seen before, and the rest are OLD."

"I would like to think it is your character that is admired, not your clothes."

"Who's admiring, anyway?" said Barbara.

"No one in particular, you silly little girl, but I am going away for a smart weekend and I need to look – smart."

On this second use of the same adjective in one sentence I am afraid our heroine stamped her foot AND
growled.* She removed herself to her room, where she
put a great many articles of clothing into a suitcase for
the Salvation Army.

Informed by a tap on the door that her Mama and
sisters intended to take a turn about the park, Constance
put Plan A in motion. Winifred's bedroom being directly
above hers, all she needed were a quantity of ruined
stockings and a high-heeled shoe. Flung to the balcony
above, and wedged, the stockings became her handrail,
while the drainpipe provided a place for feet. Up she
went and in she tumbled.†

"Hah! Wini always believed in leaving windows open.
'Ventilation is SO important my darlings, in California.'"
Pah! Now, here she was in Aladdin's cave: what to choose?

Item:

Little blue and grey linen suit.

Creamy chiffon not-quite-long evening frock.

Ooh! Nifty little navy divided skirt and sort of a sailory
top. Fetching navy cloche too.

Ooh, ooh! Two swimsuits, one with matching robe and
turban.

Spose I'd better take sensible flannel trews and pale
pink cashmere top. And brogues. No! Blast, they don't
fit.

Take white linen trews as well. Got top for them.

Very elegant emerald draped silk short number.

Satisfied with her hoard, Constance tied all her booty
into Winifred's counterpane and lowered it carefully out

---

* Dear reader, I think we may gather that Constance is not always
as confident as she seems. Rather endearing don't you feel?

† At a later date Constance's resourcefulness will win her medals.

of the window towards her balcony, but as she swung the bundle in, it unravelled and all the beautiful clothes landed upon Bridget who was tidying the terrace below.

"Ooh, Ow! Wh, What?" Bridget was enveloped in chiffon and linen (not to mention camberwick).

"So sorry! I'll be down directly!"

Constance waved at a bewildered Bridget, clambered out of the window on to the balcony, grasped the stockings, found the drainpipe with her toes, and it didn't hold. Slowly and gracefully it slipped away from its anchorage. Constance managed to slide, until – smack – she met a fixing which held. The pipe snapped, hurling her into a raised flower bed below.

She woke surrounded by her loving family, some members of which suppressed giggles. Also there were Dr James and Bridget who had a plaster above her left eye.

"Oh, Bridget, I'm so sorry, did I land on you?"

"No, no Miss Constance, we think it may have been one of them…"

"One of those," said Lalage.

"Those big buttons, only it wouldn't stop bleeding."

"Connie," said Dr James. Our heroine winced at the diminutive, and winced again as she tried to sit up.

"Your concern would do you credit, where it not for your previous reckless and STUPID behaviour. Even Barbara would have more sense." Behind Dr James' back Barbara's tongue stuck out. She didn't like "even".

"You've had an unbelievably lucky escape. Why I am not taking you to hospital or the mortuary, I don't know. You have mild concussion and some bruising. Can you stand for me?" Constance stood. There was mud in her hair and grime on her torn frock.

"I gather this exercise was in aid of some kind of party? I do not think, Mrs Bennett, that Connie," Dr James enunciated the two syllables with care, "that Connie," he repeated, "is in a fit state to attend any jollification whatever. She certainly would not be allowed to do so were she my daughter. Good day to you Mrs Bennett. Should she be sick, let me know immediately."

Further mortification arrived as a cheery voice enquired,

"Oh dear, who is going to be sick? I hope I won't be in the way." And Charlie, preceded by Snuffles, passed the exiting doctor on the terrace steps. The dog, unbothered, in fact enthused, by mud and torn things, leapt arm-wards. Constance's sangfroid liquefied like that of a Neapolitan saint, "Oh! you darling dog! I have missed you so." She sobbed, and her mother said, "You are not at all in the way Mr Bradley. In fact you have come at a time when Constance needs some support."

"Actually, she needed support earlier," giggled Barbara. Lalage looked, "I think I'll help Bridget make some tea," and the youngest Bennett removed herself.

"Constance had a nasty fall in the park and is a little upset, but Dr James has said there is nothing to worry about. Whether she will be well enough to go to Chartwell this weekend is another matter."

Mr Bradley (who isn't stupid, dear reader, do pay attention) saw a torn-off drainpipe and articles of clothing on the ground, and made five out of two plus two.

"Here's a shawl," said Margaret, hissing, "You're scarcely decent."

"Thank you MOST awe-fully," Constance had not lost her power to wither. "It's only Wednesday, I shall be fine." She locked witherers with her Mama.

"We shall see," said Lalage.

Bridget brought tea and cucumber sandwiches, "made by me!" said Barbara. Bridget whispered, "I've got them – those – clothes safe in your room – don't you worry." Constance smiled her thanks.

Charlie thought that this was the third time he'd seen his beloved in disarray and on the whole it was rather enjoyable. A cup of tea and two cucumber sandwiches later he took Snuffles away. He worried that Constance had eaten nothing.

32

The doorbell of Mrs Bennett's house rang at ten o'clock on Thursday morning. Bridget, eyes saucering, came to say that two gentlemen had called to mend the drainpipe and could they make a start? Constance saw Mr Bradley's Bentley from the window and was rapidly down the stairs and up again.

"It's Albert! Mr Bradley's gentleman, Mummy, and a cousin and they seem to have all the right stuff with them. May they go ahead?" Lalage descended with less haste.

"Mrs Bennett? Albert Shieff." He bowed. "Mr Bradley has told me of a drainpipe problem and asked me to address it, if I may?"

"This is unexpectedly kind of Mr Bradley. Please, it's through this door."

"This is Thomas, Mrs Bennett, here to help me."

Albert beckoned to a brawny lad in the street behind him who was carrying a satchel and assorted pipes. He bowed too. "Good morning Mistress," he said.

Assisted by copious cups of tea brought by Bridget, who became pinker with pleasure every time Thomas said "thank you", the drainpipe men were finished by lunchtime. They refused payment and sandwiches, but Thomas smiled at Bridget, and Albert said, "I say I say Mr Bradley hoped his reward might be to drive Miss Constance to Chartwell – if she's entirely well that is?"

Lalage laughed, "I see I have been out manoeuvred and cannot refuse. At what time should she be ready?"

"Would twelve o'clock suit, Madam? Mr B. thought they might stop on the way…"

"To let Snuffles have a walk."

"Madam, I say I say natch." Which piece of slang mildly surprised Lalage, although she continued calmly (natch) with her goodbyes and thank yous.

"A very attractive man," she thought as she went upstairs, "I wonder what is the history? Bridget? The terrace will not need sweeping for a week, possibly two – come upstairs now please." Fortunately, she did not enter her drawing room, where her number two daughter was blowing kisses to Albert from the window, or she might have been greatly surprised.

* * *

Bridget packed for Constance on Friday morning, "no, no Miss Constance – I love to do it – Mrs Bennett's showed me how. Look – I got all this tissue paper see? Because Mrs Bennett says you might be unpacked for and you're to use this suitcase." In admiration she held out a battered but beautiful valise, "and this matching boxy dressing case, and I'm to put all your lotions and creams into these." Glass, enamel and silver gilt bottles and tubs.

Constance, who had managed most of Germany, together with Austria and Hungary, with nasty but sturdy canvas bags and no tissue even in grand houses, was moved to run downstairs and hug her Mama.

"Oooh, you are so kind! And after I've been so stupid… Thank you."

Lalage would have grinned had it been in her nature to do so. Instead, she smiled, "Don't lose or abuse them and treat Wini's clothes with deference, and I want a complete account of the weekend upon your return. Including the dog's P for relief on the way down."*

"Q for fish," said her daughter.

"R for Mo."

"S for U."

"T for two."

"U for me."

"V for La France."

"V for L'Italia, all right all right! W for two bob."

"Cheapskate – W for a quid."

"X for breakfast."

"Y for heaven's sake."

"Z for breezes."

After which exchange, dear reader, both women were tearful jellies of laughter. It takes all sorts.

"Shall we go from the top? A is for..."†

"No! Go. You will not be ready."

But she was, the sun shone and so did Constance in Winifred's navy divided skirt, blue and white top, not to mention the cloche. She had found navy peep toe wedges of her own.

"We're not sailing you know," said Charlie, "but have you brought a tennis racket?"

"Oh dear me (eek), no! I'm afraid me and tennis don't agree – in fact – I will not play it. But look I have the perfect excuse!" Constance pushed up her sleeve to reveal a purpled swollen arm. "Tennis elbow look. You

---

* Lalage can be surprisingly vulgar on occasion.

† Just in case you don't know the cockney alphabet... A is for Orses, B for Mutton, C for the Highlanders, D for Ential, E for Gabor, F for vescence, G for Police, H for Respect, I for Novello, J for Oranges, K for Rancis, L for Leather, M for Sis, O for the garden wall.

can say that I'm a brilliant player and they're all lucky I'm off games!"

"It's a beautiful colour, but are you sure you're all right? Perhaps a laying on of hands?"*

"Certainly not. Well, not here anyway. Look upwards." Constance waved at three faces peering from the drawing room. Charlie waved too and drove.

They found a pub and stopped. "For a pint and a piddle." Which remark earned our hero a small frown.

"You may powder your nose, visit the ladies room or even use the facilities if you choose. I shall have a piddle."

After drinking her gin and tonic Constance chose one of the preceding options. Leaving the car in the car park with some nasty smells from the pub's kitchen, they walked with their picnic up a little hill towards a wood. The late September sun shone, but there were no wasps. They ate hard boiled eggs and bread and cheese with chutney. There were also russet apples and a bottle of Menetou-Salon and a bone for Snuffles. Constance removed her cloche and Charlie his jacket. Snuffles yawned.

They only just made it in time for tea at Chartwell, which was a slightly grander picnic on the lawn with chairs and tables and the tiniest little sandwiches, "Memo to Barbara," thought Constance, eyeing the very soggy rich fruitcake.

Winston had bought Chartwell for £5,000 in 1922 and taken up residence in 1924. It was a grey, dilapidated, unprepossessing Victorian mansion, but it stood on a hill above a lake: the Chart Well, beyond which the land rose towards groves of beeches. Glorious views of the

---

* Those of you who have paid attention will remember our hero's religious roots.

Weald of Kent were what sold it to him, and stripped of the ivy and Victorian frills and furbelows, it became a comfortable and elegant house. Clementine was never in love with her house in the same way as her husband, but she did love her dining room.

As they approached, Winston who had been painting and wore a becoming smock, stood up, arms outstretched. Mary had been swimming and was in a towelling robe – "No smart turban though," Constance noted – and Clementine came from further down the garden in stout boots and gloves.

The only formality was the large silver teapot, which sat in front of her. The cloche was definitely de trop, but our heroine was definitely NOT going to remove it.

(Even if it makes me look like a stuck-up London piglet.)

Charles was glad to see that his friend had regained her appetite, but TWO slices of cake? Mary, in irritation, was thinking more or less the same. They talked of Mummies and mutual friends and cousin Isabel, "What a trooper!"

They talked of dogs (though not of black ones) and Snuffles' adoption and good points were admired. Snuffles had found Mary's pug to play with and so was not around to be embarrassed. As they went in to change,

"We're just en famille tonight," said Clementine.

"Oh lawks!" thought Constance, "Thank you Wini for white linen trews."

"But tomorrow will be fun," said Mary, "Mlle Chanel is coming for lunch – she is so smart and witty!"

"One of my heroines – how exciting!" Our heroine inwardly lawks-ed again about what to wear.

"The Beaver isn't invited until tomorrow," said Winston

to Charlie, "so I shall hope to have some undivided attention after supper. I am hoping you have more to tell me than you told the *Eastbourne Herald Chronicle*. Has Max been in contact?"

"Yes, I offered him what smart young ladies are wearing in Nuremberg."

"Huh, huh, and?"

"I was sacked."

"Huh, huh – Good boy."

33

Had he not seen it in action before, Charlie would have been overwhelmed by the charm machine that was Constance: gardening (of which she knew nothing) became a major interest when she talked to Clementine, but skiing (of which she knew a great deal) took a back seat while she listened to Mary. With Winston, she discussed Art and which picture they'd like to own, money no object. Eventually, they agreed upon Delacroix, although they both wanted a Turner as well and Constance wished for a "teensy" Blake, which Winston allowed.

"I shall have my Cézanne then." It was time for port* and Winston and Charles, reversing the usual pattern, removed to the library, leaving the ladies behind.

"I think we'll stay in here. I like my dining room and it's pleasing to sit in it without cigar smoke." Said Clementine. They drank coffee and a little Poire Williams and discussed why Germany was so belligerent again – and why Italy, so beautiful and so entrancing, was led by such an ugly bull-necked bully boy?

They decided that English men probably made the best husbands, but for flirting?

---

* My greedy readers would like a menu – sorry. Vichyssoise, poached salmon trout (caught by the host), peas and new potatoes (from the garden), white peaches (from the greenhouse) in Armagnac syrup, cheddar cheese (from Fortnum and Mason) and apples (from the orchard).

"Italian," Constance asserted.[*]

"Swiss," suggested Mary, and immediately blushed.

Constance asked about Mlle Chanel.

"I shall feel peculiar whatever I wear."

"Silly girl," said Clementine, "when she is here she doesn't think about fashion. In fact, I don't think she bothers about it most of the time."

"She always looks just perfect," said Mary, "effortless."

"That makes it worse, not better. Peculiar it shall be."

Meanwhile, once more not back at the ranch, but in the library, Charles and Winston were enjoying port and Charles was telling his host about the summer. Whilst describing Hitler and his dog, he became rather over-excited and knocked the port glass into his host's lap. Winston mopped with a handkerchief and went to fetch the decanter.

Pouring, he said, "you'd better drink that up quickly, before you do it again. I only have two more bottles of the 1912, and only one more pair of these trousers."

Charles didn't know whether to laugh or cry,[†] well, he probably wouldn't have cried, but he felt very silly.

"Deep breath and continue," he thought.

They talked again about Hitler's dog and his dilemma to spend money on arms or food.

"Munitions factories and soldiers mean employment, importing 'Milk and fats' doesn't."

They talked of Herr Goerdeler, of Udet and of Youths in uniform. They talked of Snuffles, Constance and Nellie.

"Your Constance?"

---

[*] Dear reader, I have been remiss. During her year abroad Constance spent six weeks in Venice. And a few weekends in Florence and Rome. Disgraziata, or fortunata as you wish!

[†] Sometimes clichés are the best way forward.

"Not mine Sir!"

"Well, get on with it boy – or someone with more sense will snap her up. Constance, then, is a brave if foolhardy woman. I may have a job for her."

"She does need a job, but I don't know if…"

"The acting still beckons?"

"I think it does, even after her unfortunate experience."

"We shall see. The job I have in mind will need the qualities of an actress. I need solitary thought. And so I thank you for an informative evening – let us find the ladies, and so to bed."

* * *

Beaverbrook bustled in brightly while Chartwell's hosts and guests were still at breakfast.

"Max, you have no manners."

"So they keep telling me, my darling Clementine."

He placed a small orchid upon the table beside her toast. This was followed by violet creams for Mary and a large tin of Sevruga for his host. There was a dog biscuit for Mr Bradley:

"Har Haaar, Charlie boy, hear ya like dawgs."

And for Constance, a lacy handkerchief embroidered with a C.

"You might need this my dear, come and sob on my shoulder any time when the b –"

"Max!"

"When the boy lets you down."

"How sweet," said Constance, "I'll bear that in mind."

"Coffee'd be nice," said the Beaver. "Thank you." He beamed at the assembled company. "And then I thought you and me'd go for a walk Charlie Boy, I expect Winston's told you what we can talk about?"

Charles, who had in fact been handed an early memo note of two lists, with 'yes' and 'no' at the top, was abashed.

"What, hasn't he left me anything?"

"I'm sure, Sir, that we could have a very interesting conversation."

"But we were going to play tennis," said Mary. "You'd like a game Constance, wouldn't you?"

"Oh whoops, didn't I say? I've got a horrid elbow and can't play." Constance, who was in the navy divided skirt again but with a top that didn't shout 'Ahoy!'* pushed back her sleeve and was rewarded by horrified gasps.

"Oh no don't! It looks far worse than it feels, only I probably shouldn't lift a racquet, which is a shame really because…"

"Constance adores tennis!" said Charlie.

"What rotten luck!" Mary was sympathetic.

"Not rotten luck. Pure stupidity, I tripped and fell."

"In the park" put in her beloved.

"So it's my own silly fault."

"I'm sure tennis could take place after the walk, Clemmie, isn't the Prof.† arriving soon? He would make up a foursome? I shall bathe."

"Could I perhaps join you?" Constance was determined to put the turbaned robe to good use. "I could just flop around on my back?"

The Beaver choked on his coffee.

"Max."

---

*   It shouted acid yellow instead.

†   Professor F. A. Lindemann, scientist with a special interest in aircraft.

"I promise not to get in the way?"

"I would be delighted to have your company. Shall we meet in forty minutes?* Max, let us finish our coffee in the library."

* Do you suppose, dear readers, that Mr C. had not planned exactly this? Those of you who didn't spot it coming, close the book tidily and give up.

34

While the walkers decided what articles Charlie might write and which gobbets of information might be fed to leader writers, Winston and Constance swam. And talked.

"Your swimming costume is most elegant.* I'm afraid my trunks have seen better days."

"I think this is a glorious day and I'm glad to be seeing it with you and your trunks. Thank you for inviting us, I mean, me."

"It's our pleasure!" Constance may have been pink from her exertions, but I don't think so. They swam for a bit.

"Your friend Nellie…"

"I'm not sure she is my friend anymore."

"I think you have a bigger heart than that."

"To spy on us?"

"Because she loved someone."

"I couldn't do that."

"Well that's a bore, because I was hoping you would."

"What?" Constance waggling her toes on her back in the deep end, nearly drowned. There was no one to say "What, what". Instead, Mr Churchill, rising like Neptune from the water, called, "come and sit for a while in your pretty robe and listen to what I have to say. Sitting on this bench I feel I could be by the Mediterranean Sea."

Constance swam to the shallow end.

"Your arm seems better. Good."

---

* The emerald one, dears, remember the Danube.

Our heroine also rose from the water, and above this comment. She put on the robe and turban and felt prepared for just about anything.

"My dear, it seems to me that we can help each other. You speak German, and I think, French?"

"And Italian. Also gibberish and rubbish."

"We might definitely need the last two – huhuh."

"A bit of Spanish too."

"Is there no end to your talents?"

"I can't cope with spiders or tennis."

"Two very serious faults, which we will, however, disregard. You know a number of people on the continent?"

"I suppose I do."

"Here's my thought. Could you travel to Germany and Austria with Nellie and do some pretending? I would like you to see Herr Goerdeler again and his colleague von Papen. I would like you to see your friend Miss Unity and I would like you to meet with Mr Hitler. Then I would like you to return to England and tell me about it."

"Surely this is something Mr Bradley could do better?"

"No. I think neither Mr Bradley's (not inconsiderable) charm nor his opinions are appreciated in Germany. Also Parliament will sit next week. I need Charlie here. You, on the other hand, have I think, no commitments and you have kept your opinions mostly to yourself. You would be back in London by December at the latest, by which time your friend will be feeling suitably bereft."

"You mean the dog?" Snuffles had come to lay his nose upon Constance's feet. "He is so special and loving, and undoubtedly he will miss me."

"Will you think about my plan?"

"No."

"What?"*

"I am at your service. But I still wonder exactly what I'm to do."

"We can discuss that later. I'm not entirely sure either. Irons in the fire my dear, I do like to have several irons in the fire. Then when I need one of them, it or he, or she, is hot and ready for me. Meanwhile you are on the payroll, so please don't apply for any stage roles or any other roles."

They walked back to the house arm in arm, turban and Panama bent towards each other in accord.

"I shall take a gin and tonic to my room to drink while I change, can I offer?"

"Delicious – yes please."

"Oh dear," thought the turbaned one, "another decision."

Not the navy divided: Crumpled.

Linen suit: Too formal.

Grey bags: Too hot.

It has to be the white trews with the sailor top, but not the cloche. Which proved an initially embarrassing choice, as when Mlle Chanel arrived an hour or so later, she was dressed almost identically: white linen trousers and a blue top, but instead of a sailor collar, her neckline was swathed in a stupendous string of baroque pearls. Slung over a shoulder was a white tweedy jacket, flecked with navy and gold, secured by the chain of a little navy handbag. On the other side her hand held the lead belonging to a small dachshund. Somehow she blended perfectly into the surrounding chintzed tweediness.

---

* Phew, once more no echo.

"Whereas I," thought Constance, "look as though I'm auditioning to tap dance in a second-rate pantomime."*

"Clementine cherie, please excuse the dog – Bendor has given her to me to cheer me up."

"Don't worry Coco, there seem to be more dogs here this weekend than humans," said Winston, "and here is the owner of one of 'em – Miss Constance Bennett – Mary you know, of course, and Max Beaverbrook. And here are the Cazalets and Charles Bradley. Charles, I believe, has a part interest in Miss Bennett's dog, a bit like sharing a racehorse, only you own a paw instead of a hoof."

Said dog then entered, having smelt the sweet aroma of female dog from a long way off. He advanced, lay down upon his tummy, paws foremost and sang a little. The dachshund echoed his moves, wriggling forwards until Snuffles was able to bathe her face with his tongue. The (mostly) dog-besotted company clapped with delight.

"My dear," said Winston, "we seem to be running a bordello for beasts."

"Or possibly a beastly bordello."

"Max!"

"I'll take them out, I think," said Constance.

"Well done that girl," encouraged her host.

"Merci, Mademoiselle, magnifique. Il faudra que je vous parles."

"Avec grand plaisir."

Constance took Snuffles and Baguette, "she is called Baguette because she looks like one with legs, no? Also she is a young little bag, while I am the old bag, hein?"

---

* She didn't, dear reader, she looked as though she had stepped off a film set. Not quite the same thing.

for a short walk and found, or was found by, the gardener's boy.

"Is this your dog, Miss? He's a funny one – very friendly – but I might lose my job if he brings me any more things to throw."

"Oh, I do hope he hasn't been a bore? Um?"

"Ben, Miss."

"Ben. Now he has a girlfriend."

"I'm going for my dinner now, Miss. I could take them if you'd like?"

"I would like, Ben. Thank you very much. This is Snuffles. And this is Baguette."

"Bagits a funny name – she a good shooting dog is she?"

"Probably not, but watch Snuffles, he's partial to partridges." Constance handed over the leads.

"It's my afternoon off – so I'll keep an eye on them till four, mebbe?"

"Ben you are a hero," Constance smiled.

Ben looked into the violet eyes and all his newfound socialist principles melted away, but he couldn't, even had he wished to, tug his forelock, on account of dog leads in either hand. "See you at four." Constance waved and was gone.

35

There was steak and kidney pudding for lunch.

"I didn't think you skinny young'uns ate this kind of food," said the Beaver, as Constance used a spoon to scoop up the last delectable drop of gravy.

"Mmm, yum. Well, I'm not skinny and I do."

"Say,* have you a sister called Winifred?"

"Must we talk about her?"

"She's noose!"

"For a small fee, I'll dish the dirt."

"Go ahead."

"I'm wearing her clothes."

"And?"

"That's it."

"That's it?"

"I didn't say I would dish the dirt on Wini I meant on me. I'm a mean, beastly thief, and I have the scars to prove it." Constance waved her elbow once more.†

"Tell what happened."

"I climbed the drainpipe to rob my sister's room, but on the way down it dumped me in the garden."

"Harh, harh, ya tell a good story."

"It's true."

"What's true? Who cares? Will ya write me a fashion column, weekly?"

---

* Not to be confused with I say I say, although the Beaver's eyebrows were pretty splendid.

† Dear readers, Constance is becoming tiresomely proud of her war wound, don't we think? She should get her comeuppance, but I don't suppose she will.

Constance thought, "Golly, I have been offered two jobs in one day. What have I done right?"

"I can't think of anything I'd like more, but I will be travelling again quite soon."

"That's fine, I don't mind your thoughts on what smart ladies are wearing in Vienna."

"How does he know where I'm going," Constance wondered.

"I just don't need Charlie boy's opinion on the subject. So Winston's got you spying has he? I would've liked to have been a fly on the paving round the swimming pool."

"You might've been trodden on."

"Maybe a wasp then, and I'd've stung ya!"

"I'm careful where I put my feet, far too careful than to take up spying. I am accompanying a friend back to her family."

"You've already got the lies off pat."

"It's true, to repeat myself: è anche vero. The spy thing does not appeal. I like the idea of me as hard-bitten female journalist. I shall wear outrageous hats and talk very fast."

"Katharine Hepburn."

"Exactly."

After lemony syllabubs with thin tuile biscuits and some Roquefort brought by Mlle, the ladies took coffee in the drawing room. Mlle Chanel indicated the sofa beside her.

"Come, Mlle, you who are clever with dogs and who shares my taste in clothes, come and talk – since I also definitely share your taste in men."

"Coco, you must join the queue! Now that he's out of earshot, I may say we're all in love with Charlie, but I think Constance has him tidily sewn up." With admirable aplomb the stitcher said:

"Mrs Churchill, you make me sound like a spider and I can't abide spiders. It's just that he loves that dog. I do agree that he can be an amusing companion." Mrs Churchill, who had noted a few wisps of grass under yesterday's elegant cloche, kept further thoughts to herself.

"I need," said Mlle Chanel, "more English women to dress like you, or rather like me. I would like to enlist you, Mary and you, Constance to encourage your friends."

"We'll do our best, of course."

"I'm not sure country people –"

"Bah! I am in the country, non? Am I de trop? I do not think so. Maybe, next time you need something special you will come to my shop. Clementine, you are so chic always you do not need my shop!"

"But we do?" asked Constance giving as good as.

"Definitely," she got.

"But where is my dog? I must find Baguette."

"Fraid she's called Bagit around here and she and Snuffles are with Ben."

"Ben with the socialist principles, specially selected by Winston in order to be observed?"

"I suppose he must be the one, but he was entirely charming and volunteered to dog watch on his afternoon off."

"Shall we go and find this beau garçon? And the dogs, naturellement. Merci Clementine for a delicious luncheon. We will reassemble, when?"

"There will be a cup of tea at 4.30 if you would like one and then eight o'clock."

Constance said thank yous too and was firmly escorted out by Mlle Chanel in search of dogs.

"Cherie, I think I have seen you in cinema? I was so cross. Bendor he was entranced by you. For the love of – ah – Dick?"

"Scuse me, 'Mike', it's a joke. It's like saying 'for heaven's sake' or 'Goodness Gracious.'"

"Pourvus que le ciel ne nous tombe pas sur la tête?"

"Not quite, my character was called Mike, short for Michaela, so –"

"It's saying you are heavenly?"

"No, not at all, it's saying I am silly."

"You 'ad a silly swimsuit."

"But I had a pretty frock."

"So even more I should love for you to show off my clothes."

"A third job," thought Constance, in whose veiled eyes lots of pounds swam.

"I would love to show off your clothes too, but…"

"But it is not 'comme il faut' to be a mannequin?"

"Heavens! IT is not 'comme il faut' to be an actress, some people equate actress to prostitute. Anyway I am good at not caring what people think but…"

"You would like to marry Charlie and for that il faut que vous soyez convenable."

"Plutôt bonne bourgeoise."

"Vous ne serez jamais ça, j'en suis sure."

"Merci, but I must try."

"You could model for a charity evening and we can get some of Bendor's cousins or whatevers and so it will be tout a fait bon chic bon gout."

"That sounds like fun – yes please, and may I keep a dress?"* Coco pretended to look shocked,

"Constance, vraiment! Mais tu es ma sosie."† Two bisous were smacked upon the Bennett cheeks.

Dogs found and Ben tipped (he managed to overcome further socialist scruples), Coco and Constance meandered back towards tea.

"What will you wear tonight, ma petite?"

"I have borrowed emerald silk from my sister."

"Parfait, I shall be in black with pearls. Toujours les perles. We shall complement each other."

---

* You must remember dear readers, that Constance has been brought up in straitened circumstances. Mlle Chanel's girlhood was a good deal worse.

† A sosie is a kindred spirit which is why Coco gives Constance the Tu.

36

Dinner proved to be a fairly riotous affair. Neighbours called Sidney arrived, prepared to enjoy themselves and every other aspect of the evening.

Egg mousse was consumed followed by rack of lamb, with runner beans and parsnip mash.[*] There was a crème brûlée and some Stilton with the port, the ladies did not withdraw and around this time Winston gave:

"The boy stood on the burning deck" to much acclaim.[†]

Constance, asked to contribute, did Titania's "Out of this wood do not desire to go…" directed at Winston as her "Bottom".[‡]

Charles was once more clichéd with laughing or crying, or retreating to the lavatory or under the table, but his host loved every minute and stood to bow with his newest employee when she had finished.

"Encore" was cried, so Constance in similar vein produced Ruth's: "Entreat me not to leave thee,"[§] which she gave sitting next to the Prof. Charles felt like Mr Bennett.[¶]

---

[*]   A lifelong vegetarian, the Prof. had the egg and the veg. Winston as usual shook his head sadly.

[†]   'Casabianca' by Felicia Hemans. The boy was the son of an officer on the French ship *L'Orient* at the Battle of the Nile. (It is a most affecting story and anche vero.)

Constance and her sisters knew another version:
>   The boy stood on the burning deck and picked his nose like mad.
>   He rolled it into little balls and flicked it at his Dad.

[‡]   Midsummer Night's Dream, Act III, Scene I.

[§]   Book of Ruth, Ch. I, v. 16.

[¶]   *Pride and Prejudice*, Ch. 18, dear reader, not a relation of Constance.

"That will do extremely well Child. You have delighted us long enough, let the other young ladies have time to exhibit."

He need not have worried: Mary, who was as accustomed to post-prandial recitations as Constance, embarked upon an excellent, if less flirtatious, rendition of:

> The Assyrian came down like the wolf on the fold,
> And his cohorts were gleaming in purple and gold;

Coco sibilated Racine's *Andromache*:

> Pour qui sont ces serpents qui siffle sur vos têtes.

Our hero managed to produce as his contribution:

> Moses supposes his toeses are roses,
> But Moses supposes erroneously,
> Cos nobody's toeses are posies of roses,
> As Moses supposes his toeses to be.*

Bed was a relief.

* * *

There was time for a quick swim before lunch on another glorious September day, after kedgeree (for some) and toast (for the more fainthearted) and church.

When Constance came downstairs (in the blue and grey

---

* Which is harder to say than you might think, readers mine. Try it after champagne, Chablis, Châteauneuf-du-Pape and Cockburn's. Charles was word perfect and deserved his applause.

linen suit), two new guests had arrived: an elegant lady and a saturnine gentleman whose crinkly eyes and tufted eyebrows* and baby lips made him resemble a wise owl. "Or Squirrel Nutkin's nemesis" thought Constance. The owl and Mr Bradley were positively chortling together. Winston introduced, "Mrs Herbert m'dear and Alan[†] whose 'Maiden' speech was more of a brazen hussy and who has been entertaining us in the House ever since! Miss Constance Bennett."

Gwen Herbert's serenity was warmed by her smile.

"I am deeply in love," said A. P. H. bowing over Constance's hand, "with my wife, otherwise I would ask you to meet me behind the pavilion," he consulted his watch, "at three twenty-five p.m."

"We haven't a pavilion," said Clementine.

"No pavilion? Then Winston must build you one. We shall start immediately after luncheon. I must have somewhere to take adorable young ladies."

"You could try the potting shed," giggled Mary.

"Tsk. Tsk. Miss Mary. Would that be a romantic setting? Please promise me to set your mind on higher things and more beautiful words: pavilion trips and rolls around the tongue. Potting shed is pedestrian and shoddy, but useful I suppose."

"Fortunately you are deeply in love with your wife," Gwen suggested, "and need not exert yourself in either direction."

"Am I, ho hum. How about a poem then?"

"A poem would be perfect."

"I also would like a poem M. Herbert."

---

* Dear reader, start looking at eyebrows. You will be illuminated.

† Alan Patrick and Gwen Herbert, he a poet, M.P. and prankster – 1890–1971.

Coco had entered in demanding mode, and in blue and grey.

"Whoops," went Constance.

"Bain – c'est tout a fait rigolo!" said Mlle. "We shall do a dance together later – ma sosie!" A. P. H. interpolated:

> Mamzelle Coco Chanel
> Gracieuse comme gazelle
> Delicieuse comme quenelle
> De toutes la plus belle
> Notre propre Arc en ciel
> Mamzelle*

He bowed.

"Comme c'est jolie. Merci Monsieur, write it for me and sign it s'il vous plaît?"

They didn't eat quenelles, but roast beef, Yorkshire pudding, roast potatoes and cabbage. (So the Prof. was well catered for – cook had even saved him the cabbage water which he savoured like the finest Marc de Bourgogne.)

"Dear oh dear," said Winston.

Apple pie and clotted cream tidied up the lunch. Coco and Constance did not dance. Nor was a pavilion built, before it was time for goodbyes.

---

* I don't think A. P. H. would mind me giving him these rhymes. We loved each other dearly, which is why I called my daughter Taffeta. (Because Gwen wouldn't let him use it for one of their daughters – who were called Lavender, Jocelyn and Christabel.)

37

Our heroes drove back mostly in silence, especially after Constance said:

"Winston would like to meet Nellie, so I shall organise that for next week."

"I'm not sure which days I might be free." A hand went out to his.

"I'm not sure, my darling,* that you are invited."

Charles, torn between the endearment and the dismissal, was shut up.

They were quiet too, outside the house in the outer circle, not knowing quite what to say. At least, they were silent, until shards of crystal syllables fell upon them from the top of the steps:

"I hear, and now I see, that you are enjoying my clothes."

"Win!" Constance was out of the car in a second. "How lovely to see you!" she hugged and kissed her eldest sister, who said:

"Yes dear, and that little outfit does suit you. I would worry that you've stretched it – except that I returned via Paris and so…"

"And so it doesn't matter that your fat little sister stole it. Darling Wini, I shall keep it then if I may? I admit to a few other bits and bobs as well."

---

* What is this? I fear, gentle readers, our heroine has let us down. I thought she was made of sterner stuff. Which she is, as you shall see.

"I have noticed." Winifred's icy tones fizzled off the glow of Constance's happiness.

"Charles Bradley," said himself, extending a hand, "how d'ye do? The only sister I haven't met." He beamed.

"I suppose you've – heard a lot about me, and probably only to my detriment if the account came from Constance."

"No not really, just that you were older." Charlie hadn't enjoyed his beloved's sister's unwelcome wounding. Words failed Winifred:

"I'm sure you have a busy evening – goodbye," was all she could manage.

"I'll just take these bags up and say hello to Mrs Bennett."

"Our mother is out for the evening."

"That's strange," said Constance, "I thought…"

But Charles had the bags up the stairs and was greeting various other sisters and Bridget.

"Mrs Bennett is in the drawing room," she said, "and may I bring you a drink Sir? Mrs Bennett asked me to say."

"Thank you Bridget, whisky please."

"Didn't she do well?" said Eva.

"Quick," said Charles and he whizzed Eva into Lalage's room and was seated, having greeted, by the time Winifred and Constance arrived.

"Mama, I had the most wonderful time, and thank you for the beautiful suitcases. I WAS unpacked! So thank you for the tissue too. And I have three jobs!"

Winifred did not wrinkle her brow, nor purse her lips: actions which might have strained her perfect skin. Had her eyes not been veiled, however, there might have been lighting flashes.* Constance looked at her.

"Darling, how did the film go? Are you egg sauced? Poor angel."

"I am totally exhausted. And I am home to have a complete rest, which has been somewhat interrupted."

"Winifred," her mother had no objection to frowning, "we have heard about your time in Hollywood. I should now like to hear about Charles'" she smiled in his direction, "and Constance's time at Chartwell. But first I must thank you for my new drainpipe. So very thoughtful."

"My pleasure, Mrs Bennett, need to keep the boys busy. And they asked me to say thank you to Bridget for the excellent brew." That young person nearly dropped the drinks tray she was carrying, in her delight.

"So tell us," said Lalage, as Bridget exited, once more pink with pleasure.

"Constance swam with Winston."

"And Charlie walked with the Beaver – ooh and Mlle Chanel was there and she asked me to model her frocks. She has a sweet dog called Baguette – whoops, Snuffles! I'll go and get him."

"A dog? In this house?" Winifred did her ice maiden bit.

"You'll love him," said Barbara. Snuffles charged up the stairs and into Bridget's arms. She nearly said, "Lawks a mussy me," but managed, "goodness gracious" instead.

Constance removed the dog.

"That's a great compliment Bridget, he doesn't go to everybody, you know."

---

* Winifred is not horrid. Just a little worried about her beautiful younger sister. Not easy. Plus back from being the one and only, to one of many in the hurly burly family.

Bridget smiled, uncertain about how the muddy paw marks complemented her pinny, which was now certainly mussy.

"This is Snuffles, everyone, the one the oafs were torturing, look, you can still see the swastika under his fur. Didn't I tell you about it? Quick tail of a wag, then we'll listen to Wini for the rest of the evening."

Cast as hero, Mr Bradley was happy to sip his whisky while regarding the sisters and hearing a bowdlerised version of Snuffles' rescue.

Later: "The telephone is mended," said Constance after she had kissed him goodbye.

"On the whole," he said, "I prefer physical contact," and proved it.

"You are entirely disgusting," she lied.

"May I hear the result of the Winston meeting?"

"Of course and I may be going away, so…"

"So?"

"Actually I would like you to be entirely faithful, if you don't mind?"

"I suppose you can't not go away?"

"No, it will be fun and exciting and I definitely want to do it."

"Does this involve Nellie?"

"Yes."

"And Winston?"

"Yes."

"I want to say the B word."

"Oh? Well say it."

"Bother."

"Only bother? I think you could be more cross."

"Balls, bang me arse and brick dust."

Constance retreated upstairs. Charlie took Snuffles

back to his cousin, from whence he managed to escape after a mere forty minutes.

38

Nellie, wearing the softest grey, piped here and there with scarlet, was excited and prepared when Constance arrived to collect her.

"You've been shopping" accused our heroine. Before a reply or a question as to where they might be going, Lady Methuen, who was not to be deprived of gossip, called from the drawing room:

"Leonora, please introduce your friend."

"It would be rude for me not to say hello," whispered Constance.

"Bennett? Bennett? Was your father an actor?"

"I'm afraid he was."

"Saw him once – handsome man – fine leg for a boot I recall."

"But he couldn't act."

"Didn't need to. Now: you are a friend of Alfred and Agnes' boy?"

"Charles," supplied Nellie.

"Yes," said Constance.

"Have you time for a little sherry wine?"

"How very kind, b…"

"Good. Leonora knows where everything is, such a good girl."

There was a scuffling down the corridor and in danced Snuffles, filthily pawed. Lady Methuen pulled a disgusting blanket over her lap and up he flew.

"And here's my good boy. What a good Georgy Porgy! Albert? Albert! Thank you Albert." Albert appeared with a towel and bowed to the ladies, managing to throw it at Constance just before Snuffles, smelling his favourite,[*] launched himself in her direction. She was wearing[†] pale lemon silk with a white jacket, lemon silk collared and pocketed.[‡] Bibbed and tuckered with towelling Constance received muddy love.

"I'm back to Mr Charlie's now Miss Constance, might I drive you anywhere on my way?"[§]

"Albert, that would be lovely, I was going to get a cab."

"Don't rush the girl! Here is our sherry."

"I'll wait in the car then your ladyship."

"Thank you Albert."

Then Lady Methuen wondered had Constance been at Chartwell?

"Knew Clementine's Mama – tempestuous but splendid. Charles is always in such a rush – tell me all!"

And then told of their trip to Houghton, whereupon even yearning-to-go Nellie enthused about the Stone Hall and the pictures and the gardens.

"Thank heavens for Albert!" said Constance as they made their escape, "we would still be up there gossiping and mightn't have found a cab for ages." (Actually, three empty ones passed as they were getting into the Bentley.)

"Where can I take you Miss Constance?"

"Morpeth Mansions please, and I'm afraid we're a bit late."

---

[*] Snuffles is fond of several humans, in fact he is positively gregarious, but Constance is the love of his life. Natch.

[†] Dear reader, prepare to be horrified.

[‡] No it wasn't Wini's. Constance had submitted and been paid for her first article: "An interview with Mlle Chanel". Our heroine is another one who doesn't miss a trick. Oh there were also lemon shoes and a clutch.

[§] Albert is a star, if not a deus ex machina. He is certainly clairvoyant.

"I say I say we'll be there in a jiffy," and they were. Which was just as well as Constance was finding it difficult to talk to Nellie who noticed and found it equally difficult, especially since their destination remained a surprise.

"Champagne, I think," said Winston opening his own door. Constance enjoyed the consternation beside her.

"Miss Hirsh? How d'ye do. A very basic luncheon, I'm afraid, but Mrs Pearman has done wonders – and here she is with the glasses – excellent work Mrs P."

"Forgive us for being so late, Lady Methuen rather likes to talk."

"No matter, no matter, often late m'self! I heard you wanted to meet me, Miss Hirsh and I always pander to pretty women's whims – so now, is there anything you'd like to ask me?"

"Mr Churchill, I had no idea I was to meet you," Nellie daggered at Constance, but continued with calm assurance, "I am very pleased, but questions elude me."

"Perhaps there is something you would like to tell me then? Mrs P.?"

Mrs Pearman held a glass of champagne, which she placed untouched beside her, instead she took up a notepad and pencil.

"What is this?"

"Nellie – we know…"

"What do you know?"

"Albert…"

"You know he is my lover – and?"

"We know you have been – persuaded – to send information back to Germany."

Constance was pleased to say it.

"But I have told nothing to him or to anybody."

"Albert doesn't need to be told things, he can see them. I'm not sure how to say clairvoyant in German."

"I understand," Nellie stood, "I should go now."

"Not at all, my dear, here we are and here you are and maybe we can help you and you can help us. It's all very simple." Said Winston.

Nellie stood straight and small, her face grey as her frock. Bitterness bled from Constance.

"Dear Nellie," she put an arm around a resistant shoulder, "you were in an impossible position. We understand."

"We shall extract your brother from Vienna," Winston rumbled.

"He will refuse to be extracted."

"I'll bet he won't, if offered a place at one of our universities."

"But what about his sponsors, Herr Goerdeler and Herr von Papen?"

"Herr Goerdeler will be pleased to hear from Mr Bradley about the milk business and may also be pleased to be relieved of his responsibilities towards your brother. You may leave von Papen to me. I may be unpopular in Germany at the present time, but he and I understand each other. Now, sit down and drink your champagne. You have a good friend in Constance."

"I know it," watered eyes wavered in her direction.

"And you both have one in me. So now we shall lunch and you may put away the notebook, Mrs P."

They had more champagne and smoked salmon with very thin slices of brown bread and butter, cold chicken pie –

"My compliments Mrs P."

"Your compliments should go to Mr Fortnum, Mr Churchill."

– And tomato salad and crème brûlée.

"This time your compliments might go to Mr Mason."

"They deserve my compliments, because the inestimable Mrs P. granted them our patronage."

Amongst the compliments and the delicious food, a plan was formed and Nellie's anxiety subsided.

"Supposing my brother were to send information to Germany?"

"What hold would anyone have over him?"

"He might choose to. He admires the Führer."

"He shall be shown Mr Hitler's true colours and he will change his opinion."

They had coffee and "Brandy? Which I will have, or perhaps a little Poire Williams?"

"My favourite! What a treat!" said Constance.

"I had an idea that you were amusing yourselves without me!" said Mlle Chanel, entering with Baguette under one arm and an elegant bag over the other.

"Yes please, Mme Pearman, café and Poire, delicieux!"

"My friend, Leonora Hirsch, Mlle – Nellie – Mlle Chanel."

"Another belle jeune fille. Winston! you are a bad boy so to surround yourself. In this, of course, I include you Mme Pearman."

Violet Pearman had worked for Winston for a number of years. She did not blush: "Merci, Mlle."

She said, "et maintenant au revoir, j'ai des lettres a finir."

"Toujours, si travailleuse!"

"Vous aussi, je pense, Mlle."

"Absolument! Mais il faut aussi jouer – and Baguette

wished to play with Mr Snuffles – where is ce brave chien?"

"He's on loan to Charlie's cousin, who is dogless at the moment."

"So you are bereft. This is not at all good. I think Bendor has a brother of Baguette's left, I will see…"

"Coco, you really mustn't organise everyone all the time."

"Not everyone – those who need it."

"Mlle, I will be travelling, sans chien is better."

"Mais non! Travelling with dog is far more entertaining, although I concede parfois plus difficile."

"Constance will be working for me so no dog, but if Bendor has a pup…"

"He could be Lady M.'s new George when I get back!"

"Lady M.'s new George? Qu-est-ce que sait que ça?"

"Charles' cousin, who has Snuffles, calls all her dogs George, after her late husband whom she disliked."

"But she likes the dogs?"

"She adores the dogs. But commands such as 'sit George', 'beg George', 'roll over George', and possibly even 'naughty George, bad boy' give her much merriment." Baguette gave a little moan at Constance's severe tone and pushed her nose under the Chanel jacket.

"Ça va, ça va petite – mais – elles sont folles ces Anglaises."

"Folles, mais amusantes."

"C'est vrai, but where are you sending this poor child? Really Winston, if anyone is bossy it is you."

"We are going to Vienna. I need to see my brother there, so it is not really Mr Churchill being bossy."

"Hein? Well, me I might need to go to Vienna too. We

can rendezvous and you can return to England via Paris. Nous nous amuserons!"

"We might have my..." puffed smoke and a frown from across the room changed this to... "we will have my brother with us."

"If he's as good looking as you, he will be most welcome."

"You are organising again Coco. Let us see. The telephone can be used. It is not as if we are trying to encounter some person on their grand tour in 1700. Now as we discussed, I cannot allow Charlie to escort you with the election looming. And he will need Albert. Mrs P. will book your train tickets."

"Trains are lovely. It will be an adventure. And we can stay with Lydia."

Mrs Pearman entered: "Mr Bradley's Albert is here Sir."

In came Albert, much to Mlle Chanel's delight.

"Quel beau garçon, a lalalala!" She hissed in Constance's ear. "Ma cherie, you are worse than Winston with his girls."

Albert pretended 1. that he couldn't hear and 2. that he couldn't speak French.* He bowed: "Mr Churchill, Sir, I say I say I understand as these ladies may be travelling while we'll be campaigning and so will need to take the train." Face to face with another frown and puff of smoke, Constance squeaked, "Not me! I haven't said a word to a soul. Albert just knows things."†

"Does he indeed."

Albert bowed again, "Sir, I say I say if the ladies were

---

* He also understood it. Nursie. Pay attention readers mine.

† We know that don't we my preciouses?

to take the boat train to Dunkirk, I have a cousin who could meet them there and drive them to Vienna."

"Albert, you and your cast of a thousand cousins are quite brilliant." Constance clapped, Leonora smiled with love in her eyes. Mlle Chanel rose. "Très bien. I shall definitely go to Vienna. Winston, please ask Mrs Pearman to post me their itinerary and I will send them mine. Also telephone numbers of where they stay. Definitely telephone number of cousin." She winked at Albert.

"Merci beaucoup, mon cher. Allons Baguette! Au revoir tout le monde! À bientôt, À Vienne."

Once everyone had left, Winston had a zizz.

39

The ladies were in fact reunited before Vienna. Clementine persuaded her friend Lady Dacre to hold a tea party at which Coco's designs would be modelled. Lady Dacre's town house was at No. 35 Cheyne Walk. As luck would have it, two days ago, its ballroom had relished the reception, following the marriage of Lady D.'s daughter Deirdre and was totally covered in flowers.

"Come along Joan, think of all those lovely flowers going to waste."

"They were not going to waste, they were going to St George's Hospital."

"They still can! And we'll charge a small entrance fee which can be going there too, or wherever you choose. And you can invite all the chums you've upset because you couldn't squeeze them into the wedding." At this dig, Lady Dacre gave in. Invitations were rushed out. So many people accepted that two sittings were arranged – 3 till 5 and 6 till 8.

"But we'll need champagne," wailed Lady D. Bendor organised champagne. Lady Dacre's cook, Margaret, gave notice. Albert's aunt, Heidi, had a restaurant in Soho. She closed it for the day. Lady Dacre's cook withdrew her notice and graciously accepted help.*

Now le tout Londres was in a bicker about who was

---

* Margaret and Heidi became firm friends. In fact Margaret would visit Heidi and her husband when they were unfortunately interned in 1939.

going when. "We are going at three – so lovely to be invited first."

"So much more fun to go at six, I really dislike tea!"*

Then the gentlemen wanted to buy tickets too.

"Ah, ça. Main non mais non mais non!"

"You did say you wanted some champagne?"

There was time for little else for Constance and Leonora who, joined by Iris, Grace, Rose, Honor and Helen, fled from fittings to pen placement cards, where they were joined by Mary, livid at not modelling.

"Bientôt, ma cherie, you will see, all these ones will be vieilles soon and then you will outshine them all."

Constance was also summoned more than once to Morpeth Mansions. Albert was ubiquitous.

In the middle of the muddle, Frederika telephoned and was somehow put through to Mlle. "You are bored of Broadstairs hein? And you are a friend of Constance Bennett. Eh, bien, come here avec toute vitesse and we will blast away your boredom. What? Headmistress? Mais non, mais non." Coco eyed Bendor, "you will say, his Grace the Duke of Westminster's chauffeur will collect you in two hours' time and will bring you back?"

Bendor took the telephone.

"Tomorrow, do I understand you are at a school in Broadstairs, whoever you are?"

"Princess Frederika of Brunswick and yes, I am."

"Well give my love to Phippsy† and we'll see you anon."

"Merci, mon petit chou," Mlle purred.

"Pas de quoi, Mlle Bossyboots."

There was no place for Mr Bradley at either sitting.

---

* Actually champagne was served at both sittings but the six o'clockers weren't bothered by tea.

† Miss Phipps, innumerable years before, had taught His Grace French. They remained in touch and firm friends.

Mrs Bennett and Constance's siblings were there, Barbara came up from school. Clementine and Winston were there. A breathless Frederika and Mary helped the mannequins in and out of their frocks, and loved every minute. The audience did too. The show was not over by eight o'clock, and various stage door johnnies were allowed in, ostensibly to "help clear up". They did help a bit, but mostly Mr Bradley sat drinking champagne with Miss Bennett and occasionally holding her hand. Albert and Nellie were very busy in the kitchen with Lady Dacre's cook, Margaret (who had actually gone to bed) and Heidi who talked too much to notice what was going on in the pantry.

"Oof, vous voilà mes amis," Coco collapsed beside our heroes, "you have been wonderful, so many thank yous Constance."

"It was fun, and it wasn't just me – everyone helped and we all enjoyed it and it was the frocks which were the succès fou!"*

"You must each choose something as my present to you."

"I want them all," said Constance.

"Ça, pas! Ma petite. A glass of champagne I think, and then – au lit."

Frederika came to join them, "Mlle, I've not had so much fun since, well since I can't remember. Thank you so much."

"Well, there you are, Mlle La Princesse, or whoever you are – you see – London is fun. And bien plus amusant than Germany at the moment."

---

* The day was a grand success, except there are at least two ladies who are now non-speaks to this day because of which sittings they attended.

"Vous avez raison. I have been silly."

"I do not know about your silliness. But you should always know who are your friends. Ahh – Bendor, merci pour le champagne et maintenant le chauffeur. Vous mes enfants?"

"I think Albert will drive us Mlle."

"Fredka, you can stay with me. It will be squashed but jolly" said Barbara.

"I would love to."

"Alors, on y va. But first Lady Dacre needs to be thanked profusely and awarded a particularly fetching hat."

"I really think I WILL wear this," said her ladyship.

40

The following day, after Barbara and Fredka had shared a squashed, but jolly, night, at breakfast even Winifred was quite proud of her sister. "No more borrowings needed then?" "More travellings?" said Lalage.

"Only till Christmas and I shall be paid! Think of that."

"Some of us know all about being paid."

"Wini, don't be such a prune." This from Barbara.

Eva said, "Wini the Prune. Excellent name."

"Connie the Cow." (A cartoon of the time, quite apposite, as the cow had huge eyes and long eyelashes.)

"Children! I wonder sometimes…"

A chorus chimed, "Where we were dragged up."

Frederika found the frankness alarming. Bridget opened the door to Mr Bradley.

"Am I disturbing a family feud?" he enquired. "If so, I'll take my leave."

"Oh no," said Barbara, "do join in!"

"I wouldn't dare," said Charlie, "but I would like to take you all to lunch, since I probably won't be seeing you for a while."

Various ohs and aahs were heard. Winifred said, "where exactly would you take us?"

"We found rather a jolly French restaurant round the corner the other day, I thought we might go there?"

"Yum! It was delicious – let's," said Constance.

So they went, and Mr B. paid and even Winifred enjoyed herself. (Well actually, Wini always enjoyed HERSELF.)

Frederika returned to Broadstairs with the promise of more fun in London anon.

Constance and Leonora left for Vienna the following day. Albert drove them to the station. On the platform waited Mr B. and Snuffles, who were kissed goodbye. Albert bowed.* Snuffles was not happy and showed it: tail down and moaning, he was led away by Charlie who was unhappy too, but naturally did not show it.

Constance and Leonora settled into their adventure with smiles and books.

---

* He's good at that.

41

At Dunkirk, Albert's cousin Pierre waited wreathed in smiles beside a shiny Citroën.

"Mesdemoiselles!" he said.

"How did you know who we are?" enquired Constance. (In French, natch.)

"Look around! I was told to meet two beautiful ladies. There is no competition!"

As he put their bags in the boot, Constance muttered, "I think that might almost be rude."

She had looked around and the only females were dressed in black and somewhat portly.

"We shall motor jusqu'a Bruxelles and then stay the night."

"Avec les cousins," said the Demoiselles ensemble.

"Tiens! Vous parlez si bien le Français, magnifique!"

Then, Pierre's verbosity sped the miles away as he informed them of his life and pleasures. After a while the beautiful ladies found they only had to add a 'oui' or a 'vraiment' or even a 'magnifique' every so often and so could nod off now and again without seeming too rude.

Pierre was not really a chauffeur, he was training to be an airplane pilot, but Maman and Papa did not approve and so he was trying to make enough money to continue his course.

Had the Mademoiselles been in the air? Yes, one of them had. Wasn't it wonderful? Well, yes.

"But you know, I really prefer trains or cars." Said Constance. (Nellie being asleep.)

"But the thrill!" Said Pierre, eyeing Constance in his rear view mirror, "the thrill is the thing!"

"Dear Pierre, I am sure it is and I envy you, mais a ce moment j'ai tout a fait besoin de m'endormir pour quelques minutes. Excusez moi."

"Bien sure, Mademoiselle." Had Constance seen the curled lip which accompanied this assurance she might have been better prepared for the things that went bump in that night.

Eventually they stopped at a small pension. "You will see – nous allons bien manger!"

When Constance and Nellie returned downstairs, having settled their things and themselves, Pierre swaggered into the dining room as the man in charge and proceeded to boss the waitress about and horror of horrors: to order for them.

Three courses, and beer. Constance did not need to look at Nellie as she said firmly: "Dear Pierre, you have sweetly driven us all this way, and are no doubt, tired and hungry. We are tired too, but we do not want to eat huge quantities of food." (You, dear readers, who know our Constance, may be somewhat surprised by this last, but even she had her limits and she might be missing somebody … or a dog.)

"We would love you to eat whatever you would like, but for me: une omelette aux fines herbes, s'il vous plaît. Nellie?"

"The same please, perhaps we could partager une salade de tomates?"

"Good thinking – est-ce possible?"

"Mais oui Mesdames."

"Peut-etre des frites?"

"Nous n'avons pas de frites."

"WHAT!" Said the Mesdames.

"Mais un pichet de vin blanc sec, s'il vous plaît." Concluded Constance.

Pierre was still munching Tarte aux Pommes when the ladies eyed each other and agreed to retire. The evening had not been a success. The combined charms of two very different ladies had failed to stop Pierre from becoming monosyllabic and maudlin as he munched and swigged and belched.

"Goodnight, Pierre! What time tomorrow?"

"What's wrong with tonight?" said Pierre. "I will see you to your bedrooms."

"Oh, there's no need – truly," Constance began, but Pierre had already pushed through the restaurant and started up the stairs.

"Vous voici Mamzelle," he said, opening Leonora's door.

"Merci Monsieur."

"Et maintenant, Mamzelle – here is for you," and he sidled past Constance, taking possession of her hand on the way. "Un grand baiser et puis une grande bite, that is what you need, n'est ce pas?"

His wet lips found hers as he shoved her to the wall with his groin, moving his hands upwards and downwards towards the interesting portions of Miss Bennett's body.

Dear readers, he stank of garlic, which could not mask the fact that his overall personal hygiene left much to be desired. In fact he was probably the least desirable male ever to cross our heroine's path. She had met a few. Bertie Garton sprung to mind. But back to the current ugly mug: she might have been brought up in an all-female household, but Constance knew where her knee might hurt worst and she followed the knee-ing with a punch to the ear. She was wearing two quite large rings, Pierre was poll-axed.*

"Disgraziato!" she spat as she lugged him by the legs into the corridor.

"Nellie? Nellie!"

"Yes?" Leonora's door opened.

"Could you whiz downstairs and ask Mme for Pierre's key? Just say he had too much to drink. Oh, and you might see if he has paid."

Madame returned with Nellie.

"What is this? I cannot have this in my house, je suis horrifier!"

"Madame, our chauffeur, after a long day, took too much to drink. That is all, now if we can put him into his room, he can sleep it off."

"He took his key... Voyons, let me look in his poches, otherwise I will bring the master one."

---

* Here I must quote A. P. Herbert: "Lines on a Book Borrowed from the Ship's Doctor". (A. P. must have run out of more inspiring literature!):

> The portions of a woman which appeal to man's depravity, are constructed with considerable care:
>
> And what appears to you, to be a simple little cavity, is really an elaborate affair.
>
> And doctors who have troubled to examine the phenomenon, in numbers of experimental dames,
>
> Have made a list of all the things in feminine abdomen and given them delightful Latin names.
>
> There's the Vulva, the vagina and the jolly perineum, the Hymen (in the case of certain brides)
>
> And a hundred little gadgets you would like if you could se'em, the Clitoris and Lord knows what besides.
>
> What a pity then it is, that when we common fellows chatter, of the mysteries to which I have referred,
>
> We should use for such a delicate and complicated matter, such a very short and unattractive word!

Madame was obviously more used to this behaviour in her house than her horrified outburst suggested. She searched efficiently through pockets and found the key.

"Eh bien, allons-y."

They shifted the dead weight into Pierre's room, which was situated between those occupied by Constance and Nellie. "Hmmm," thought the former. Madame turned the key on the outside and pocketed it. She also pocketed several notes from Constance.

"Pour notre souper et pour vous Madame, pour vôtre patience."

"Merci a vous, Mesdemoiselles – les hommes – hein!"

Madame shook her head, her late unlamented husband had come to mind as a result of which she probably would not sleep that night.

Neither did the Mesdemoiselles, who were wakened by terrific bangings and shoutings during the watches of the night.

"Rich rutting bitches – you think you are too good for me – just you wait! You vile sows – you chamelles!"

Eventually the rantings ceased. The travellers were dressed and downstairs packed and early.

"I will deal with the cretin when he wakes, have no doubt." Said Madame, who had also heard the ravings. To make her point she produced a sturdy rolling pin.

"That's the way to do it,"* thought Constance.

Declining breakfast, the pair accepted coffee while Madame found a taxi to take them to the station.

"Au revoir, Madame." Probably not.

"Au revoir, Mesdemoiselles." Ah ça certainement pas.

They bought tickets to Cologne, there to reconsider.

---

* Punch, dear readers, Punch: Punchinello – he of the nose, sausages, crocodile, baby AND Mrs Punch, she of the rolling pin.

Constance suggested, "A person cannot guarantee every cousin to be charming."

"A person cannot even guarantee a brother."

"Or a sister."

"I am glad he didn't wait till the middle of the night. Then it would have been harder to stop him."

"Me too."

At Cologne, they found a porter and were walking towards the taxi rank when a blond young man accosted them.

"Entschuldigung, Meine Damen, but do you perhaps have a friend named Albert Shieff?"

"Oh," said the ladies, looking at each other, "we do."

"Ser guht! I think you met my cousin Albrecht at Leer? I am Wolfgang and your friend, Mr English Albert, has told us of a problem you have found.* It seems that French cars are unreliable."

"As unreliable as their drivers certainly."

"Well, I have an excellent Mercedes in which almost to Vienna I will convey."

"Hmmmm," said the damen, "how do we know that you are more reliable than Albert's French cousin? Indeed, how do we know you are who you say you are?"

"Ahh," said Wolfgang, tapping his nose.

"I am to send love from Shnuffles ... is guht?"

"Is guht."

"And I am to say that with these you may hit me if I am bad." He handed over two tennis rackets which made Constance laugh.

"At last a use for those horrid things!"

"Tonight, in Regensburg, I driving finish. Tomorrow Frau von Liebenstein's gentleman, Fritz, will to Vienna

---

* Altogether now ... Albert has the sight!

drive you." Wolfgang produced a card from his pocket and beamed.

"I think I said everything well, yes? And I did not read it!"

"You said it very well, Wolfgang, thank you. But you could have said it in German which we both speak."

Wolfgang worriedly looked at his card. "But then you me might not believe."

"Albert thinks of everything," smiled Constance, "we would love to be driven to Regensburg, thank you."

"Danke Wolfgang."

Bags and ladies comfortably settled, the journey continued.

42

Wolfgang drove quite fast, but he thoughtfully stopped at a petrol station which had a café and a 'Damen'. Somewhere after Frankfurt he stopped the Mercedes a little way off the main road. The sun was still warm at midday and he produced a picnic which was very much to the damens' taste. There was a grassy meadow and a stream and they munched on sausage, hard cheese and rye bread, with glasses of white wine.

"Is guht?" anxious Wolfgang enquired.

"Is serr guht, dankeschön."

Wolfgang did not talk about himself, rather he sought to improve his English by questioning his travellers. Since he had driven them in silence thus far, the damen were happy to further his education (only linguistically, dear readers, although anything to do with tongues does sound rather rude).

Thence they motored to Regensburg, where various cousins waved hello and goodbye and once more they were in comfortable bedrooms with the prospect of an excellent supper.[*]

In the morning, Fritz was outside with the conspicuous car.

"How lovely to see you Fritz, we have had a bit of a bumpy ride!"

---

[*] I know you want to savour it, dear ones… Little cheesy crispy things, finely sliced venison with rosti and red cabbage. Gingerbread tuilles and yes a little more cheese for Constance and still she is not an elephant.

258

"I am relieved to see you in good health, Mesdemoiselles. There was word of an unfortunate occurrence."

"We see off 'unfortunate occurrences', don't we Nellie?"

"We do."

"So – a smooth ride to Vienna – but no Snuffles."

"No Snuffles – we are on holiday!"

"Johnny will be sad."

"Dear Johnny! He was marvellous, but how is Madame?"

"Madame is well and looking forward to your visit. But I think, if I may say, that she is finding Vienna increasingly irksome."

"But Madame loves Vienna."

"I expressed myself incorrectly: it is not Vienna, but the people in it, that are tiresome."

"Tiresome – such a Madame word – if she broke an arm it would be 'tiresome!' What can the Viennese possibly have done to upset her?"

"It is not the Viennese – or mostly not, it is the proliferation of uniforms. They are in Madame's favourite café. They are in the restaurants she prefers to frequent and," Fritz added with feeling, "their cars clog the roads and they drive like – they drive exceedingly badly."

"Poor Fritz, I see they have upset you too! To be clear, these are German uniforms?"

"Yes, Mademoiselle."

"Hmmm." Nellie had been monosyllabic since Regensburg and now Constance too stayed silent and thoughtful.

In Vienna, Johnny opened the door hugely grinning, but his crest definitely crashed when no wagging Snuffles appeared.

"Dear Johnny, we will bring him next time."

"Next time? NEXT time? You have visited twice this year, are you to invade me a third time?"

"Dear Lydia, so sorry to trespass upon your hospitality again, but…"

"Darling, only teasing – it is my pleasure to have you to stay, please come as often as you care to, but remember, we do also like to see the gentlemen. Now, here is Johnny with the champagne. Come and sit and tell about the awful Frenchman."

"Well, the worst thing was his halitosis," began Constance accepting a glass, "although the rest of him was pretty pongy. Otherwise he was quite drunk and no match for my knee or my knuckles, equipped as they were with Great Aunt Sophy's rings." She surveyed her filigreed fingers with approval. Transferring her gaze, "Nellie was a brick, as was the Madame who owned the pension. In fact, I could almost feel sorry for Pierre when he woke up."

"No," said Nellie.

"You are right, as usual. But enfin nous voilà without so much as a scratch. And thank you so much for sending us Fritz. A huge comfort."

"I am appalled that you were placed in such a position."

"Worse things happen at sea…" shrugged Constance.

"And in Vienna," said Nellie.

"Ah! Vienna – city of my heart. But do you know darlings, I am tempted to leave her. There is a nasty whiff in the air, which wrinkles my nostrils – which I do not care for."

"No wrinkles is good wrinkles."

"You are facetious Constance. It is not amusant when English people are not so welcome and you, Leonora, are brave to return."

"We have a purpose, Madame."

"And please say it entails more skulduggery. I enjoyed the Lipizzaner evening and not only for the horses!"

"I am afraid it entails us taking more advantage of your hospitality – but yes, some skulduggery will be done. We plan to extricate Nellie's bro, remember him?"

"We aren't too keen on him are we? Excuse me Leonora, but…"

"He is a little difficult, Madame."

"He needs to grow up."

"We have to extricate him from the clutches of Herrs Goerdeler and von Papen."

"Dreadful men."

"Actually they're not soo dreadful. They dare to disagree with Herr Hitler and have been communicating with Mr Churchill."

"I see I am part of international skulduggery – lead on Macduff."

"Do you suppose, dear Lydia, that you could possibly invite them to dinner?"

"Dinner?! No! Absolutely not. I will not lend consequence to that odious man."

"Lunch maybe? I have some papers to deliver and would prefer not to enter the spider's web."

"If you put it like that, then of course I shall do it. But we must have others to lighten the load – Fritz?"

"Madame, luncheon is served."

"Excellent timing Fritz, but could you direct your giant brain towards guests that we might invite to another luncheon with," Lydia's eyes and brows rose heavenwards, "two German gentlemen – Count (I think) or maybe not, von Papen and Herr Goedeler, we must find those of my friends who would not be insulted."

"Madame, Vienna is currently entranced by Germany and its citizens."

"I know, Fritz, I know, but not all Vienna."

"As yet."

"As yet."

They ate Wiener Schnitzel and rosti and red cabbage and apple and then a little goat's cheese melted on toast with some quince jelly. Lydia almost immediately thought of someone suitable to invite: "Felix Rheinhardt – he's the most crashing bore, but he'll go anywhere for good food and he has no opinions whatsoever. On the other hand his wife is pretty and sensible and if the two interlopers haven't wives we could include the Rheinhardt daughters who are charming."

Johnny was despatched to deliver invitations, and it was discovered that Herr Goerdeler had returned to Berlin. Mr and Mrs von Papen, however, would be most charmed to accept Mme von Liebenstein's invitation to luncheon and to bring their young protégé. The Rheinhardts also accepted, daughters not invited as "Silly me! We actually need at least one other man."

Fritz suggested, "Mr Ney, Madame?"

"Lancelot? Is he in Vienna?"

"I believe so Madame, I have seen a poster for an exhibition of his work, and it seems his wife remained in France."

"Naughty man! Why has he not been in touch? As usual you are right Fritz, the perfect choice. Constance, Leonora: Lancelot is a Hungarian artist, but he's been living for a while in Paris and in Roussillon where his wife is from. He was in Vienna some years ago and dear Georg bought me a picture – look." They looked at a contracted painting of Vienna, boxed up, boxed in, but with spires towering free. Spiky leafless trees veiled the city and in the foreground the whole was mirrored in the Danube.

"That's how I think of Vienna," said Nellie.

"Hmmm, I think I saw something similar at the de Hedevars – might I have done?"

"I think they have several, Constance. In fact they bought his work very early on. His father was an architect and…"

"I bet he was part of the 'Secession.'"

"Absolutely."

"Magdalena took us on a tour of Budapest," Constance continued in de Hedevar mode. "You either love it or it makes you sick. We loved it."

"The good thing about Lancelot is that, unlike some artists, he is also entertaining. He does not object if you ask: Why? And he does not take himself too seriously. Now, one more man…"

"Ahem."

"Yes, Fritz?"

"I wonder if M. Jamet has returned from Paris?"*

"M. Jamet? Oh, I think he would be bored by such an occasion."

"He might enjoy meeting M. Ney, Madame, and he has met Miss Bennett."

"M. Noël Coward Jamet? I'd love to meet him again! He sings beautifully Nellie, and plays the piano as though it were an extension of his fingers. Do let's see if he can come."

---

* Fritz knows perfectly well that M. Jamet has because a large bunch of lilies had been delivered the previous day. There had also been several telephone calls. And a note. M. Jamet kept a small flat in Vienna.

Lydia inspected the bracelet on her wrist.

"I shall say the invitation is from you." She looked brazenly at Constance for a short while before smiling.

"This luncheon might even be fun."

43

Meanwhile, not back at the ranch but in London, Parliament had reassembled. Political talk was all of Italy's aggressive foreign policy. Mussolini had acquisitive and warlike ideas about Abyssinia, and Churchill's speeches warned of "the measureless perils of another world struggle" but no anxieties were "comparable to those caused by German rearmament".

"I am afraid," he said, "Mussolini, like Hitler, regards Britannia as a frightened flabby old woman, who at the worst will only bluster and is anyhow incapable of making war. She certainly looks the part." Oh dear, plus ça change, plus c'est la même chose.

In the November issue of *Strand* magazine Churchill wrote of "persons whose only crime was that their parents brought them into the world. Every kind of persecution, grave or petty, is inflicted upon world famous composers and scientists down to little children and even their dogs." Those who had met Hitler might find him, "highly competent, and well informed, with an agreeable, if didactic, manner. But while he spoke words of reassurance all the accoutrements of war flowed in an ever broadening stream from Germany's factories and arsenals."

Copies were sent to Miss Bennett and Mr Bradley. Parliament was dissolved on October 25th and the General Election set for November 14th.

Mr Churchill spoke in the constituencies of several young members and would-be Members of Parliament, but not for his friend Charles. He wrote, "You do not need me. You and I, dear boy, will be returned with increased majorities." And they were.

44

In Vienna, Lydia was not pushing the boat out. She was launching a fleet. Persuaded to invite unwanted (mostly) guests, she was now determined, if not to kill them with kindness, at least to leave them with a lasting headache. Tablecloths and napkins were inspected and in some cases found wanting. Bottles from the cellar were brought up and not found wanting at all.

"Dear Josef! What a good and thoughtful man: still plenty of the 1912 Mouton Rosch and we could have some Menetou-Salon from two, or is it three years ago?"

"I am afraid it is four Madame, but we have plenty of it and plenty of Pommery champagne from the same year. Or would you prefer cocktails?"

"As you know, Fritz, I prefer champagne and I really don't propose to offer cocktails as well."

Constance and Nellie's wardrobes were viewed and definitely found wanting.

"We shall shop! No —" Lydia refused to allow any dissent — "you have forced these unwanted — don't raise your eyebrows at ME, goddaughter, I repeat — unwanted guests upon me. Now the least you can do is to accompany me to buy a new outfit. I've had nothing new in years! I might feel nervous."

Constance recalled the little nautical number on Lake Balaton and the concept of a nervous Lydia simply refused to take shape, but she could recognise an irresistible force as well as any woman, so she smiled sweetly and said,

"What fun!"

Not one, but three outfits were duly ordered from Madame's dressmaker: Nellie was persuaded into violet with a dear little boxy bolero jacket of the same colour, striped with old rose. Constance, who was privately a little miffed about the violet, fell in love with the picture of a cape collared, knotted cuffed, wrapped-over coat dress. Madame produced a bale of soft fine lemon wool which she would edge and belt with lavender. Constance de-miffed herself. Lydia thought she would like something in navy blue (Happy memories, thought Constance) but was persuaded by her companions to choose silver double-weight crêpe printed all over in navy with flamboyant feather ferns. This Madame would transform into a simple frock with a sweetheart neckline: "for Madame's lovely jewels" and a navy waistband which curved up to meet it: "For Madame's lovely figure."

"And long loose sleeves please," said Lydia, "for my long loose arms."

"Madame, Madame, such silliness!"

"Madame, Madame, such truthfulness!"

A fitting session would be required, but all would be ready in time for the luncheon, which was four days away.*

"Now, shoes!"

"But we have shoes!" the girls half-heartedly protested. "Handbags!" "We definitely do not need handbags." "And hats."

"We won't be wearing hats for heaven's sake!"

"I hope you will wear your outfits more than once."

"Of course we will."

"Well then, you need shoes, handbags AND hats."

---

* Think Hong Kong or India today!

These were all purchased in little shops into which Madame was warmly welcomed and ushered out even more unctuously. The shoes and bags were despatched to Lydia's address but they took their hat boxes to Sacher's where well-earned Sachertorte was devoured and a little celebratory champagne swallowed.

"I do like to come to Sacher's with a hat box," said Lydia. "It gives me such a sense of achievement." She sighed: "and I can't THINK when I last did. What fun."

"You are so kind Madame..." said Nellie.

"Lydia."

"Lydia – I can hardly find words to thank you. The last time I had a beautiful hat was when my mother was alive. She adored hats. And shoes. Of course, when she played she had to wear sensible ones. And dress in black. But as soon as she came off stage she would put on high heels. She had beautiful silvery ones." Nellie's eyes pooled.

Constance quickly raised her glass. "Here's to mothers everywhere, especially those given us in God. Thank you Lydia and wow, will we knock 'em for six at your luncheon."

Lydia's brow wrinkled at the vulgarity.

"I feel sorry for Mme von P. and as for M. Jamet!"

The creases reappeared, then Lydia said with glee, "actually, I think you are right: he will be bouleversé! I repeat, what fun!"

45

Constance need not have been concerned for Marthe von Papen, an elegant 56-year-old who had been in charge of her husband for thirty years, without anyone noticing, him least of all. She wore scarlet with confidence. Mme Rheinhardt wore beige with anything but.

Her open, pretty face and quiet charm were betrayed by an appalling lack of dress sense and a rather unfortunate figure.

"Ooh, my godmother is a CAT," thought our heroine, "I know why she invited the Rheinhardts."

The gentlemen, of course, had no need to enter the sartorial minefield, although Mr Ney's bow tie might have raised an eyebrow in some London clubs: it was turquoise with pink spots. He had tried to tame his wrinkly hair but strands kept escaping the brilliantine like little wire springs: boing, boing! As he tried to smooth them back, Constance almost forgot not to stare.

"Mr Ney, I have seen your beautiful picture of Vienna here in my godmother's house, but I think I have seen others at the de Hedevars. Stupidly I only recollect them in a haze –"

"Mademoiselle, that will be because of the de Hedevars' hospitality."

Constance giggled, "you are entirely right, but it is still unforgivable not to remember such beautiful paintings, if Lydia's is anything to go by."

"Mostly they are early works. The de Hedevars were kind when everyone was telling me to be an architect.

When they bought at my first exhibition I felt able to continue. And now I have a thought," Ney looked intently at his companion, "which has become a plan to show the spirit of a city through a superimposed portrait. Would you pose for me? But where I wonder, is your spiritual home?"

"I am from London."

"London is cold and wet, I see you in Avignon on a bridge."

"Dancing?"

"Or if you want cold and wet, perhaps Venice?"

"London's not always cold and wet. I am very fond of Vienna."

"Vienna is impossible at the moment, I do not know why I am here."

"Because you have an exhibition."

"Because I do have an exhibition."

"We shall certainly visit and I hope it is a success. My friend Leonora Hirsh –"

Constance beckoned a sad-looking Nellie away from her brother – "and I are going to Berlin for a bit but then we will be in Paris. Perhaps we may meet again there?"

"Paris! Ah, there I shall paint you. And your friend. The two sides of Paris: dark and even darker. Mesdemoiselles." He bowed over Nellie's hand.

"I have not been to Paris, Monsieur, and now perhaps I do not wish to go."

"Mademoiselle Leonora, Paris is sublime, but the Parisians! Do not trust them further than you could boot them into the Seine."

Lydia came: "This seems like a phrase I learnt in Florence, 'Vai butarsi in Arno'. Excellent for ridding oneself of unwanted admirers. Although," a crease appeared on the unblotted brow, "it doesn't mean boot. I suppose a translation might be, 'put yourself into a brown paper bag and throw yourself into the Arno'.* White paper being too good for whomever you wanted to insult. The Florentines have a love of beautiful paper and a succinct way of despising people." Lancelot moved away with his hostess.

"I don't think I want to go to Florence either," said Nellie, only half jokingly.

"I am certain your welcome is assured in any city in Europe, Fräulein." Von Papen was in on the act. "You and your brother are both so charming. We are sorry to lose first you, and now him."

Leonora didn't bother to look surprised.

"I hear the University of Cambridge in England has offered him a place to read politics and philosophy."

"Yes, so he tells me."

"He tells you? I tell you, Fräulein, that you have made some powerful friends in England and that you already knew of this offer. It is unusual, I think, for someone to be accepted 'sight unseen' at such a prestigious place of learning."

"He must have written an excellent application letter."

"Ah yes – we were unaware that Alexander had written any letters."

"Oh, do you buy his stamps for him? How generous."

"I hope he has not been unhappy in Vienna." Then Nellie, recovering herself, "I am sure he has NOT. You and Herr Goerdeler have been so kind, but Cambridge…"

"Do I 'ear Cambridge? What a time I 'ad there, far too

---

* Author's translation (not Lydia's) "Go brownpaperbag yourself into the Arno."

long ago..." The musician, Pierre Jamet, stopped the ticking device as he would have stopped a metronome.

"I was at university in Paris, my home town, and how wonderful it was to have a year away! It was a veritable holiday: picnics by the river, punting ON the river."

Constance, who had been lost for words as she listened to the not-so-friendly exchange, said "you sound like Ratty."

"And the women..."

"You no longer sound like Ratty!"

"They were amazing, how shall I say, they were more approachable than our Parisiennes. If their toilettes became a little messy – they didn't care – they laughed. Et puis, the 'gum boots' (gum boots are so important), ça alors, a lady in a floaty frock with 'gum boots' on the feet, totally delicious – which to take off first? J'en étais tout a fait amoureux."

Lydia arrived at his elbow, "with whom were you in love, I wonder?"

"Mais voici, avec les Anglaises. C'est tout ce qu'il me faut. Et particulierement celle-la."

Pierre raised his hostess' hand to his lips, "avec cette belle robe."

Constance purred to herself, "sept a la banque, et rien ne va plus."

Alexander joined them, smiling first at his hostess and Constance, then it seemed at his assembled audience. I should describe him, oh my readers. I was rather hoping he might have been left behind by now, or at least found his way into a different novel, it seems not. Tant pis! Delicately built like his sister and not tall, with her full red lips, and thick black hair, he had broad shoulders and an opinion of himself that was even broader.

"How wonderful, Madame, that you have given me this opportunity to share my good fortune with old friends and new and with my darling sister." He smiled, but his eyes, turned upon Leonora, smoked.

"Herr von Papen, my benefactor! I will never be able to thank you enough for your generosity but the time has come to move on. Especially as I would not wish to embarrass you, or your position in any way."

Alexander turned to buttonhole Pierre: "Monsieur, I think I heard you talk about your time at Cambridge? May I ask you some questions?"

"No longer the supplicant ostrich," thought Constance as she singled out von Papen with eyes and teeth (much like a sheepdog, dear reader, but with a different pong, albeit a powerful one, as you may remember our hero discovered on first acquaintance).

Herr von Papen had looked momentarily bemused by the dismissal awarded him by his protégé, but he bowed with renewed good humour, "Miss Constance Bennett, the friend of Miss Unity. Which is more dazzling? Your smile? Or your pretty — is it a frock?"

"I think it is called a coat dress," Constance twirled unashamedly, "Viennese dressmakers are so clever! I bet Mme von Papen's scarlet number was made here — so chic!"

"Oh," von Papen found himself in the middle of a discussion about fashion, a subject about which he knew little and cared less.

"Oh, yes, she does look smart today — I must find out from where…"

"Herr von Papen, clothes are probably NOT your favourite topic of conversation. They are one of mine, but today I have other fish to fry."

"Excuse me, you are cooking today?"

"Oh dearie me, no, thank goodness. No frying in this frock. It is just a stupid expression, silly me. Yes, Unity is a friend, but another friend has asked me to say: 'do you like peaches?'"

"Are you the one? Merkwurdig?* Then I will say: 'I do like white peaches from the garden.'"

Constance beamed, "Now I can give you the paper! But where will you put it – and do you have something for me? I have a handbag (this beautiful lavender leather one, thank you Lydia) but –"

A scarlet-clad Mme von Papen appeared, "Miss Constance Bennett? May I join you? Or I might become jealous."

"Madame I would value your opinion, our conversation has been about fashion."

"And food. Mademoiselle is glad not to be cooking today and likes peaches."

"He's so sharp he'll cut himself," † thought Constance, as she said, "But Madame, we shouldn't stand close together – mimosa and red roses: not a clever combination! OH Madame, what a beautiful handbag! I wonder if it came from Madame Patrice? Mine did..."

Von Papen found he had an interest in fashion after all. "Marthe, liebling, could you find room in your excellent handbag for – a list of restaurants that Miss Bennett has made for us for when we next visit London?"

Marthe was entirely used to secreting bits of paper offered to her husband and hardly raised an eyebrow as she stowed the papers away. She did note the hesitation

---

* Strange word, meaning strange – I do love it – sounds like "Mirkwood", shady and full of spiders.

† Actually he didn't – acquitted at the Nuremberg trials, he lived until 1962.

and wondered how such a lengthy list could so speedily have been written.

"Do you know, I am asked so often about the best places to eat in London – some people rudely suggest there ARE none! So I keep a few lists with me, just in case."

"Miss Constance, I think you were a girl guide."

"I was, actually, but why? I wasn't much good."

"You are prepared."

"That's boy scouts, I certainly wasn't one of them. But I do try to plan ahead. It is entirely pathetic, I make lists – I find them calming. Quite ridiculous."

"I too make lists. A very good practice."

"How long do you stay in Vienna, Mademoiselle?" said Marthe, who had decided to like this young English woman, whose wits were about her. "It would be fun to go shopping together perhaps."

"A few more days and then to Berlin, a shopping trip would be fun – I need to buy my friend Unity a hat. I lost one of hers."

Von Papen was scribbling on an envelope, it was not empty.

"May I return the compliment Mlle? Here is a restaurant in Berlin, that maybe even Miss Unity has not discovered. Please do try it."

"Ooh – I love places Unity hasn't found." Constance tidied the missive away, "What's best to eat?"

Von Papen's reply was interrupted by Felix Rheinhardt:

"What's best to eat? Here and now Fräulein! At Frau Lydia's table, I hear we are to have caviar and a beef Wellington! And I also have the pleasure of escorting you into luncheon!"

"Mustn't hang about then," Constance smiled at the von Papens, "and what treats after the beef?"

"My dear – we have a Queen of Puddings!" Our heroine tried to look enthused, "And devils on horseback!" This time she didn't need to force a smile.

The luncheon proceeded with general satisfaction to its conclusion, each person having sung for their supper in their own peculiar way: Mrs Rheinhardt mothered Alexander, Alexander flirted with Marthe, who flirted with Lancelot, who made Nellie smile, as did Jamet when he was unable to talk to Constance who almost lost her appetite in the face of Rheindhart's relentless recipes. Lydia presided at the head of the table, talking of opera with von Papen, and restaurants with Felix.

Upon the company's return to the drawing room for coffee and digestives, Fritz announced, "Mademoiselle Chanel."

Lydia was unamused. She rose frostily and did not extend a hand. "Uh oh," thought Constance.

"Excusez moi, Madame – je ne suis pas invitée – mes manières sont celles d'une gosse – but I 'eard that some of my most favourite people were 'ere – Constance – bien aimée and Leonora ma petite! Et puis, qui est ce beau garçon?"

"Alexander, Madame, Leonora is my sister."

"MADEMOISELLE – Frau von Papen, Mein Herr." Coco bent in their direction. Constance took charge. "Frau and Mein Herr Felix Rheinhardt, Mademoiselle Chanel. And Monsieur Pierre Jamet."

"Hmmm –" Coco accepted the removal of her jacket. "So many handsome people in your salon – mes compliments Madame. And here I have a little packet for you." She offered a rather large box to Lydia. It was tied with black ribbon. Emblazoned upon it were the double C and 'No.5'. Lydia recovered her manners and accepted it with grace.

"But Mlle – you shouldn't have."

"I shouldn't 'av come. But since I 'av come a little present is definitely de rigueur. Do I spy some coffee? May I?"

Fritz had produced an extra cup, "and Marc de Bourgogne? Delicieux! Now," Coco beamed about her, "we can all be cosy, n'est ce pas?" Fixing beady eyes upon Anna Rheinhardt, Coco continued, "Madame if you will permit me?" She carried on without waiting for so much as a yay or nay or even a ja or a nein. "You have eyes of periwinkle blue and the skin of an un-spotty sixteen-year-old, but I must find clothes for you. You are upholstered like a sofa and you should be free! Please say you will come and see me? I have brought a few things to see if a shop might be good."

"My husband…"

"Herr Rheinhardt can have no objection I am sure."

"I too would like to come, if I may?" Said Marthe.

"Perfectly in order then," snorted Rheinhardt.

Coco had his measure, "Parfaitement en ordre, and then, moi, I will 'ost a supper party, we shall all go to Sacher's. Madame Lydia, if you will come it will be tout a fait parfait."

"Mademoiselle, it will be a treat."

"M. Jamet?"

"Enchanté."

"Alexandre?"

"S'il vous plaît."

"Cela me plaît beaucoup," said Coco, veiling her eyes. "But I have two conditions, Constance and Leonora?"

"Mademoiselle," they said and curtseyed, "à vôtre service."

"But a frock each," said Constance.

"Ah la la la la, que tu es dure!"

"Come toi donc, ma sosie" Constance replied.

"Ça va, ça va, quelle gosse!"

Coco then allowed the rest of the room to return to normal conversation whilst she focused on Alexander.

"Now M. who is brother to my friend. What are your plans? Your aspirations? Where are you going in this life?"

She drank her coffee in a little gulp and whorled her Marc in the light.

"I am going to Cambridge – to Magdalene College. I have been most fortunate in my sponsors here in Vienna – but Cambridge! I am so excited." Alexander's eyes were muddy brown puddles silvered by the sun.

"I may need gumboots," thought Coco. (See how important they are!)

"I have a friend who went to that college. I am sure you will have a wonderful time."

"But first, Mlle, I would love to see Paris. I have never been and..."

"Eh bien, of course, you should go, but have you a travelling companion? Paris is more amusant à deux."

"I think my sister is going to Paris, but maybe..."

Alexander smiled, dear reader, I hesitate to say lasciviously, no, I don't. It was a disgusting lecherous smile. "Definitely gumboots," thought Coco, loving each widened lip, "and en plus une capote et peut-être un frisil!"

"Alors, I have a few things that need carrying. I think you are strong no? And I will have space in my auto."

"Mlle, I may not be tall, but diamonds are usually small and they are very strong and hard."

"Nous allons decouvrir ça M." said Coco, moving towards Nellie.

"Mon ange, I am going to misappropriate your brother – do you mind? After such a reunion? It will give more space in cars I think?"

"Mlle, if you don't mind – how can I?"

Lydia, having watched Coco's annexation of Alexander with some amusement, glided over. (Coco didn't glide: Coco strode, but delicately.)

"Do you know, Mlle, I think that I should like to visit Paris! It has been such a long time, and I would love to see your shop. I wonder if I can persuade Pierre … Pierre? Will you invite me to stay with you in Paris? Or would that not be 'comme il faut'? Oh, I have a bonne idée!"

"Gardes la bien: elle se trouve dans un lieu étrange." Said Pierre.

"Rude man," said Lydia, "you are quite insupportable." But she smiled.

"Here is my idea: Leonora, I am not sure you particularly want to go to Berlin, am I right?" Leonora nodded, looking at Constance.

"Constance will have Unity to play with. So: you come to Paris with me and M. Jamet. Alexander will go with Mlle Chanel and Fritz can drive Constance to Berlin! Perfect."

"I can get a train."

"And then he can bring you to Paris and drive me back to Vienna while you return to London. Positively perfect."

"So long as I know that I will eventually, be rid of you,

may I formally invite you Mme, and you Miss Hirsh, to stay with me in Paris."

Then M. Jamet was persuaded to play a little music and the lunchers slowly made their goodbyes.

Dear reader: bluff blokes who bang on about recipes or other boring bugbears should not be dismissed out of hand, but watched very carefully. They might be tiresome in more ways than one.

"Oof," said Constance and took her shoes off.

"Constance, what are your feet doing in my drawing room?"

"Trying to feel like feet again! Such divine shoes – but talk about 'souffrir pour être belle!'"

"Thank you so much for inviting Alexander," said Nellie, who too would have liked to take off her shoes.

"I do think he enjoyed himself. He was certainly enjoying Mlle."

Both young women ignored this slip of the tongue.

46

Lydia, having decided upon Paris, wanted to be there immediately, so she packed, or rather, directed the packing done by Edwina with some help from Nellie.

Constance and Marthe von Papen shopped.

They found they agreed rather well together. Constance bought Unity a pretty blue cloche with admirable deeper blue piping upon it.

"How can you choose for your friend?" Enquired Marthe as she essayed a fetching green beret.

"Well, we have the same size head. And although not quite the same colouring, we have the same taste in clothes. At least, I admire her clothes which tend to be beautiful and expensive."

"And you are good friends, yes?"

"Our mothers are friends and we shared a governess. Also we both have a great many annoying sisters, which is a bit of a bond. Otherwise, we aren't very alike. I'm afraid I do not share her admiration for Herr Hitler."

"You are outspoken, Fräulein. Remember that my husband is –"

"I do of course," said Constance, thinking, "I also know that he is in secret communication with an English M.P." "But I can't believe your husband thinks he is a God. She is totally enthralled by him and her personality is – fragile."

"Whereas you are – unbreakable?"

Constance grinned and directed the full violet-ness of her eyes at Frau von Papen.

"I have knocked around a bit and have acquired a certain – robustness. Oooh! I love that word, if there is such a one, probably not. It sounds like a new type of brassière: 'Put on a Ro-Bust-Ness and you'll never be let down again.'" Fortunately Marthe von Papen had excellent English.

"Do you need a new brassière? There is a most elegant shop opposite."

"I don't, but I would love to look!"

They bought the hats and then looked at delicious frilly things all bedded down in tissue, in beautiful wooden cabinets.

Undressing to try them on, however, seemed complicated and bothersome, so with hat-box trophies they headed to Sacher's (where else?) and ate Oeufs Florentines and drank a little *Sekt*. Marthe had Sachertorte and Constance a smidgeon of cheese.

They walked arm in arm to Lancelot Ney's exhibition, Marthe said, "I do not admire him either."

"Oh," said Constance. She didn't suppose her companion meant M. Ney.

"Sometimes, I wonder if he is not mad."

"Oh?" said Constance.

"He WILL shout so much and sometimes about nothing at all important."

"I believe he's a vegetarian. I do worry about vegetarians." Constance tried.

"He feeds his dog meat and the people what they want to hear. I am afraid there will be war. I was thirty-four the last time; it is too terrible to contemplate again."

Alarmed, Constance offered, "surely not?"

"He has the Saar, now he wants the Rhineland. And as

for the Eastern borders – who knows how far his ambition travels?"

Constance was silent. She hadn't imagined that her job as Winston's eyes and ears might be in preparation for a war. As if hearing her thoughts, Marthe continued, "Your friend is Mr Churchill, how long will England tolerate the breaking of treaties, the rearming, the land gathering? I wish SOME country would rattle a few sabres now before our Chancellor decides he is invincible. A God to more than Unity."

"Frau von Papen, may I ask – do others share your views?"

"Already I have said too much, but yes, a few perhaps. It is very hard to tell, since no one wants to be the first to suggest disloyalty or criticism. We were removed to Vienna because of my husband's unfortunate habit of disagreeing with our leader."

"Thank you for being so open with me."

"I will hope my words reach the right ears."

"You betcha!"

(Dear reader, you and I may deplore, with Lydia, Constance's use of American slang, but here I feel she is allowed a small moment of elation.)

In the gallery, pictures hung like jewels. Marthe von Papen was entranced, and with customary decision bought a painting of Budapest with Gellért Hill and the Elizabeth Monument.

"It is Franz's birthday soon, and we once had a wonderful holiday in Budapest."

"So did I!" said Constance. Lancelot's hair had sprung completely out of control, so that it was a halo of black as he said goodbye.

He kissed fingers with his right hand, while his left smoothed the thatch with futility.

"Au revoir, à bientôt! À Paris!"

Marthe and Constance talked of Budapest until their ways separated.

"Perhaps you could write to me via Lydia." Said Marthe.

"A bonne idée."

They smiled.

When Constance returned to her godmother's house, she found her entirely packed and ready to leave the next morning. Nellie had borrowed a suitcase for her extra bits, and Pierre would collect them at ten o'clock.

"But you'll miss Coco's show!"

"I have telephoned to say that Pierre has to leave tomorrow and that Nellie and I am travelling with him and how much I look forward to visiting her shop in Paris. I know she gave me a pint of No.5 (which I rather like by the way) but I have NOT forgotten that she gatecrashed my party and I shall not lend her consequence in Vienna."

"Oooh, godmummy, I am glad you're on my side..."

"I am mostly on your side. I think I prefer you in the company of your young man."

"Snuffles."

"Definitely, Snuffles too."

"Madame, a telegram for Miss Constance," said Fritz.

"Exciting!" It read, YOUR DOG MISSES YOU STOP X BRADLEY

"Speak of the devil."

"Is there a reply?"

"Yes please, Fritz." And she wrote on the form, I MISS HIM TOO STOP X BENNETT

"Can I see? Is anything wrong? I hope not."

Constance gave Lydia the greige bit of paper.

"How soppy. Why does he sign X Bradley? His name is Charles is it not? Or does he have Xavier in front? Some parents strangely call their children by their middle names."*

Nellie and Constance exchanged glances.

"I had a telegram too," said the dark one.

"Nobody writes proper letters any more – too sad!" Thus spoke Lydia the Luddite.†

"Will you tell?"

"I don't entirely understand it, it might be rather rude."

"Unmentionable orgies, mention mention!"

So glad beastly bro, went with Coco Stop

The boy will not know, what hit his dough Stop

Take care Albert.

"That's quite funny. What don't you understand? You know Albert sees things?"

"Dough?"

"Rhyming slang. A cockney joke. Brown bread, equals head, equals dough, because it's quicker to say. For instance; bubble and squeak means Greek, but is easier just to say Bubbles, or as in Berkshire Hunt –"

"Constance, that is quite enough vulgarity for a year, never mind an afternoon!"

---

*   This is for you O best beloved, Olivia Taffeta Caroline.

†   Dear reader, can you imagine Lydia with emails and Ipads? If you can it's good fun, and as for Twitter!

47

In the morning Constance waved the trio on their way and then prepared for a blissful day Toute Seule. She had only to be at the Sacher Hotel, where Coco had taken a vast suite, by four o'clock.

"Dear Fritz, when would you like to leave for Berlin? Would tomorrow be all right?"

"Tomorrow morning at ten, Mademoiselle. I haven't the cousins or the talents of Mr Shieff, but Mme Lydia has suggested places to stop which I have booked, also a hotel in the city."

"Fantastic Fritz, a little walk I think, then I'll pack."

"Perhaps an omelette for luncheon Miss Constance, with a few frites?" Miss Constance's smile might have boiled a kettle.

Lunch was over and a zizz being considered, when the telephone entered, accompanied by Fritz.

"Allo? Constance? Mme Rheinhardt is proving très difficile – can you come over immediatement?"

"Mlle," Constance decided to be firm, "Il me faut une heure – je –"

"A trois heures alors, au revoir."

Forty winks and a quick change later Constance presented herself at Sacher's. Mme Rheinhardt was in tears. Mlle Chanel was in a fury.

"And for Lydia not to come, and my show impossible with one." Constance rang room service and ordered champagne, and "I don't suppose you've eaten Mlle?" Smoked salmon sandwiches.

A very pretty dark-haired girl arrived at the same time as the vital supplies. She had eyes of a strange pale blue and an annoyingly good figure.

"Entschuldigun, Ma DE MOISELLE," she looked at a bit of paper, "I am a cousin of Albert Shieff and I may of use be?"

"Bravo Albert," said Constance.

"Who is Albert?" asked Coco.

"Mr Bradley's gentleman."

"Ce beau garçon? I see how the eyes are the same, but never mind that, you will be parfait! What is your name?"

"Anna MA DE MOISELLE."

Leaving Coco with her new clothes horse, Constance took Frau Rheinhardt and their glasses of fizz to the far end of the suite, where Mlle's maid and factotum was making last-minute tweaks.

"I am afraid Mlle Chanel can be very bossy."

Yvonne nodded, "And her style doesn't suit everyone, Frau Rheinhardt, but if you will let me try? I think we can find something you will like."

"She objected to my brassière," Frau Rheinhardt was mortified. When she helped the Frau into a navy jersey number, Constance understood Coco's objection, the lady's torso was embraced by stout-boned bombazine of indeterminate colour. "The colour, in fact, of telegraph wire paper. It is an iron maiden, I wonder if it has spikes." Constance carefully cut this thought before giggles claimed her.

The frock proved a success.

"Do you know, there's a lovely shop that Marthe von Papen took me to yesterday, it has marvellous underpinnings, do go!"

"I don't think my husb…"

"Don't tell him! Anyway, he's bound to approve of somewhere Frau von Papen visits."

"True," Frau Rheinhardt smiled, "thank you."

Then it was into the hurly burly of changing and re-changing and sauntering between the little gilt chairs Alexander had placed in the suite's drawing room. Frau Rheinhardt was sitting with Marthe von Papen and remained elegant even in this company. Later she bought two more outfits. In fact almost everything was sold, with some orders for more, except for a particularly fine white evening frock which Constance had hidden, together with a little black number for Anna.

"Constance, tu es vraiment incroyable, I could 'av sold both of those."

"Nah – nobody wanted them, and a promise is a promise!"

"Ma sosie, and thank you for dealing with the rhinoceros. Ala lalala la, quelle femme!"

"You shouldn't have been beastly about her brassière."

"Brassière? Brassière? That was not a brassière, it was a suit of armour."

"An Iron Maiden!" Which had to be explained, dear reader, and I am afraid laughter ensued.

"But she's a sweetie pie and I have sent her to an excellent shop to buy some bits and bobs."

"Herr Rheinhardt will probably have a heart attack, but she bought, and is definitely a sweetie pie."

Supper at Sacher's that night was definitely a congratulatory affair. Constance, in her taxi home later, examined the white frock with pleasure – "almost bridal" she smiled to herself, but batted the thought away immediately. "Berlin Beckons, Foolish Person. War not Wedding, is on our list." But she went to sleep without making one.

48

In companionable silence Fritz drove Constance comfortably to Berlin. Lydia had scribbled a note: "Have booked Brandenburger Hof for you in Berlin. They know me and will look after you. I could have asked Eric Phipps[*] to let you stay, but thought better of it as you should be a 'free agent', I think it's called, and you may need a bolthole away from your skulduggery. So it's my little treat to a dear goddaughter and special friend and no ifs or buts even if Winston is paying you!! Your loving god, Lydia."

"Hmmm, she may seem away with the fairies… Book covers are unreliable indicators of contents," thought Constance, in pompous mode.

The hotel welcomed her with Belle Époque courtesy. Cosseted Constance wondered whether to have a long hot bath, but she had two telephone numbers: which to dial first? "Eeny meeny miny mo." She rang the Herr first. He was out. She rang the Hair second. (Unity was inordinately proud of her, it must be said, extremely fetching bob.)

"Well, you do trot about so. One never knows where you'll pop up. Are you with that odious man? And the even more repellent dog?" Constance reminded herself that she was a working woman. A PROFESSIONAL. And ignored the insults to her beloveds while counting to six.

---

[*] Eric Phipps, 1875–1945: Ambassador in Vienna 1928–33; Berlin '33–37; Paris '37–39.

"Hello – Hello? Are you still there?"

"Yes, here I am and quite alone. I did think it would be fun to meet. If you are not too busy? I have brought you a present from Vienna and Lydia sends love."

"Vienna again! There you are, you are never in one place for half a second."

"I shall be in Berlin for just about a week. There seems to be a good restaurant in my hotel, or Herr von Papen recommended somewhere – will you lunch with me?"

"Von Papen? The Führer does not like von Papen. Where are you staying?"

"The Brandenburger Hof."

"Ooh, we are grand!"

"Lydia bunched me."

"In that case I suppose I can spare an hour or so – I am very busy helping the Führer, but lunches and presents…"

"Only one…"

"What are you after?"

"Just a gossip. Tomorrow?"

"Tomorrow. Bye-bye."

"Byeee."

The telephone rang.

"Miss Constance Bennett?"

"Speaking."

"Have you to Germany returned to see my bottling plants?"

"Herr Goerdeler. How charming of you to return my call. I think I still feel the same about visiting bottling plants, but perhaps we could meet to talk about them?"

"And mutual friends."

"Indeed."

"I wonder if… My wife expects guests for dinner two days away, we would be most pleased for you to come."

"I would be pleased to join you. At what time?"

"Shall we 7.30 say?"

"How lovely, thank you."

"I will send my car."

"How kind, but I have a car."

"Then my address…"

"I also have that and I look forward to Thursday."

"I probably shouldn't have admitted that," Constance replaced the telephone, "but since I knew his telephone number, why not the address? You are not very good at this," she told herself sternly, "please try harder." A bath beckoned and a blissful early night with room service and Daphne du Maurier.

Unity was not punctual, but this gave our heroine time to flirt with the maître d' and at least two waiters, discover the best table, order yummy *Sekt*, choose what to eat (in order to appear decisive) munch on an olive or two and review strategy.

Eventually, Unity wandered in. She was in blue! Icy kisses exchanged, Constance proffered the hat box.

"So you did lose that sweet little trilby."

"Not exactly. It blew off in a gale – of laughter ha ha ha."

On opening the box, Unity melted, and had to smile, "Oh! It's enchanting! A lovely colour."

"Go to the ladies and try it on." The lady returned behatted and beaming, "But you're not to borrow it."

"I promise," Constance raised her glass.

"Oh," said Unity, "the Führer doesn't…"

"It's only *Sekt*. Just like flavoured fizzy water really."

"Oh well – Prost!"

Thereafter, the gossip flowed and Unity didn't notice the second bottle of *Sekt*. She had a syrupy looking pud, while Constance (who found German food a little diffi-cult), munched some cheese. As Unity drank coffee and Constance sipped another (very small) glass of *Sekt*:

"Dear Unity, what are you doing this evening?"

"This evening? Ahhh, this evening there is a reception for the Führer, and then –"

"I would so love love to meet your Führer! Could you perhaps arrange...?"

Unity looked dubious, or it may have been the *Sekt*. "I am not sure he would want to meet you."

"I'm sure if you were to put in a good word for me..."

"Later there's a subscription ball at Schloss Charlottenburg. You can come if you pay for your ticket. But you will have to make your own arrangement for sups and I don't guarantee an intro." Unity was suddenly in command of the situation.

"I can certainly pay my way –"

Fine eyebrows queried this, "And have you evening togs?"

"Oh yes."

"Well then, I will get someone to leave a ticket for you to buy at the door. Thanks for lunch. Bye-bye."

Constance had been prepared to pay the bill and was decidedly cross to find her elegant gesture reduced to a fait accompli.

She banished such ungenerous thoughts with a bit of culture, and some animals. The Kaiser Wilhelm Memorial Church for the splendid if dotty mosaics[*] and then a visit to the zoo. Culture absorbed and cobwebs blown away she returned to the hotel for a well-earned zizz. "Must be looking our best for the ball Cinders."

---

[*] Designed by Franz Schwechten and consecrated 1895. Berlin's Burne-Jones.

The nap obviously worked, for when, fortified by scrambled eggs, smoked salmon and a little champagne, she slid into her godmother's car, dressed in the white Chanel, its driver was moved to say, "Mlle will be the belle of the ball, if I may say so."

"Dear Fritz, of course you may, I feel very grown-up, going out on my own. All compliments gratefully received."

"I shall be here, at whatever hour, to drive you back."

"Thank you, I am sure I shan't be long."

Fritz privately doubted this and four hours later he was proved right.

49

"Dear Fritz – so sorry I've kept you this late!"
"Don't worry Miss Constance, I didn't think they'd let you leave any earlier and I was chatting to the other drivers, we were even offered refreshments."

"I am glad to hear that."

"They were not very nice."

"Nor were mine."

"But I did," Fritz dropped his voice to conspirator mode, "win a few marks on the dice."

"Bravo Fritz! I too have won something."

"Mlle's evening was satisfactory?"

"Lovely music and *Sekt*, and sticky cakes, oh dear. But, I have an appointment with Herr Hitler."

"I take it, that's what Mlle wants?"

"Oh, yes, Fritz. It's precisely what I wanted."

"Will that be safe, Miss Constance?"

"Yes, of course, it will. Especially since I shall ask you to drive me."

"Very good, Miss Constance."

As they motored back to the Brandenburger Hof, Miss Constance considered the evening. She had arrived, intentionally, a little late and so had missed the reception line. No one had asked for her ticket and she was still rather cross about wasted Reichsmarks. For two minutes or so, as she entered the long gallery, she had wished for Mr Bradley, but catching sight of Coco's white confection in one of the many mirrors had straightened her shoulders and advanced into the jostle. Soon, at her elbow, was someone she had known in Munich.

"Constance, I wondered if I would ever see you again!" Unfortunately the young man, of whom she had retained kind thoughts, was wearing one of the silvered black uniforms. Still, he'd do.

"Hans Christian, how lovely!" She thought of offering a cheek, but decided upon a hand which was air kissed. "And so smart! What are you doing these days?" (Oops, perhaps a bit disingenuous.) He hadn't quite saluted, but preened peacock-like, saying, "I am now a Captain in the Uhlans. And you my beautiful Constance?"

"Oh, I am a spy now, can you tell me anything interesting?"

Of course she didn't say that, readers mine, but she dreadfully wanted to.

"I have been visiting my godmama in Vienna and now my friend Unity in Berlin."

"Aagh, Miss Unity Mitford, whom we all adore…"

"Do you? Well, she is very sweet." Constance touched her nose to check it was not expanding.

"Shall I introduce you?" She had just noticed Unity with Mr Hitler, a little way along the Gallery to her left. Hans Christian turned to her in shock.

"But she is with the Führer!"

"Well, we shan't mind that shall we?" Constance was beginning to enjoy herself. She swished down the gallery and assaulted Unity with two smart kisses. (Coco's little white number did an excellent swish.)

"Darling Unity, how lovely to see you. And here is an old friend who would very much like to meet you: may I present Captain Hans Christian von Hummel? Miss Unity Mitford." Hans Christian was quite perfectly blond and beautiful and Unity accepted his bow and the lips, which barely touched her outstretched hand, while daggering at Constance, who continued to enjoy herself. "And please may I be introduced to your companion?" She ignored the motley entourage and beamed. Constance can, as we know dear readers, be very tiresome, but on occasion quite irresistible, and the beamed-at person duly smoothed his moustache and regarding the clinging Coco number and the violet eyes:

"Ja woll – Fräulein Unity – your friend is my friend." An inwardly seething Unity effected introductions; Constance extended her hand but did not curtsey. Said hand was held firmly in two surprisingly smooth ones and,

"I have heard your name. I would like to meet you in a more business-like setting."

"As would I."

"You have excellent German."

"Thank you." Fingers snapped, an aide appeared, whispers.

"Tomorrow at eleven o'clock?"

"How perfect."

"For the moment, Goodbye."

"Goodbye."

Hans Christian, mesmerised, watched the group move away. Unity offered Constance a backward snarl.

"That was wonderful, wonderful. How can I thank you?"

"A large glass of something would be a start, and then – do I hear music? Might we dance?" Constance consolidated her position in Hans Christian's esteem by mentioning that a dear friend of hers had watched the Uhlans parade sitting beside the Duchess of Brunswick and her daughter at the Zeppelinfeld. "I had the honour to be in that parade!"

Floating from Captain to Colonel and back again via a major or two, Constance had occasion to visit the ladies cloakroom once or twice in order to scribble in her notebook. (You do remember the notebook, readers mine? On this occasion, no dogs were adopted.)

And so it was that, the following morning, Fritz drove our heroine to visit Mr Hitler. Later in his career, as overwhelming super confidence took hold, Germany's leader refused all meetings before lunch, which was at 2 p.m.[*] Preferring to spend mornings in bed, wherever possible, afternoons in cafés with cronies, and evenings watching films late into the night. In 1935, however, he still kept to the precepts of his Prussian predecessors. Constance arrived early, but was almost immediately shown into a grandiose saloon, whose walls were covered by vast pictures of battle scenes. It was a good thing our heroine was not kept waiting: too little sleep and not enough breakfast were making her feel fragile and her tummy rumble.

The person behind the enormous desk came around it and shook hands. Upon the desk was a copy of the November issue of *Strand* magazine and not much else. Of more comfort to Constance, beside the paper sat a beautiful coffee pot, cups, cream and a sugar bowl. A uniform poured and was dismissed.

---

[*] Lunch? Lunch? Vegetable soup is not lunch! Ask Constance.

50

"Excuse me Herr Hitler, but might I have a biscuit? So sorry to ask but with all that wonderful dancing last night, and then I wanted to be punctual for our meeting this morning and so not much time for breakfast..." Constance's perfect German evaporated in the face of the Führer's frown. Then the moustache twitched and the thin lips lifted.

"A mädchen who likes her food and speaks her mind. Very good." Biscuits duly appeared and oh joy! They weren't too sweet, but almond and munchable.

"Delicious, thank you! Sorry to be a nuisance." Constance, comfortable now, considered the person in front of her.

"My dear young lady, you could never be a nuisance to me, but your friend, Mr Churchill – why is he so determined to vilify me?" *Strand* magazine was tapped and then held between finger and thumb and waved.

"Your aristocracy – they love me – they support me. What is the matter with Mr Churchill? He loves dogs so much that his affection turns also to the Jews?"

Fortified by coffee and bics, and pushing the implication and Snuffles to the back of her mind, "I think we all love dogs Herr Hitler, where is Blondi today? I have heard so much about her."

"Aah, Blondi, Blondi, I love her – but she does not love Berlin, she has gone for a holiday to the Berchtesgarten. You too should come there, but not with your friend Mr Bradley, whom I did not like."

"You do not approve of my choice of friends?"

"I am sure you have more than two, and of course anyone who is a friend of Miss Mitford ... who has, however, warned me against you."

"Oh?"

"She says that you are a thief of hats."

"Unity does like to tease."

"No, no she is most serious, a quality I admire."

"Oh well, perhaps you should count the teaspoons before I leave?"

"I think, Miss Bennett, that you are not a serious person, do we have more to say to each other?"

He reminds me of Win, thought Constance, I suppose all bullies are the same.

"Yes, we do, Herr Hitler, first and least importantly, I bought Unity a most beautiful new hat. Second, I don't know who translated Mr Churchill's article for you, but he praises you for 'raising a great nation from the dust' and merely wonders whether, with your success, you might mellow and feel more comfortable with your neighbours and the eclectic mix of your countrymen. Thirdly, [Constance was not about to be interrupted] Mr Bradley enjoyed meeting you, but he doesn't like being bullied and nor do I. Now, I would like to take something positive back to England with me, other than the memory of delicious coffee and biscuits, can you offer me a thought or two in that direction?"

You've probably blown it now, but Constance straightened her already straight back and purpled her pupils across the desk. She refrained from producing her notebook. There was silence, then:

"Will you stay and be my translator?"

Another job! thought our heroine.

"Oh, dear, how sweet of you! Unfortunately I have so many commitments at home... Mother sick and baby sister," She burbled.

"And Mr Bradley?"

"Possibly."

"And Mr Churchill."

"Yes."

"And Lord Beaverbrook?"

"I occasionally write for his newspaper."

"I should prefer to keep you in Germany to help me. I think you would be useful, in spite of appearing so silly. However, you may go."

(OH my!)

"And you may remember these words." (Notebook notebook, concentrate!)

"I am pleased that Mr Churchill acknowledges my success; I understand that he will not be put in power again and therefore is no threat to me. But he and Mr Bradley and others with similar thoughts, should be aware that I will not tolerate anything, anyone, any nation which jeopardises that success. There I will continue to develop all those things which make Germany safe and great, and which give employment to the people, and I will not be stopped." During this rant Hitler stood. "Please also be warned against any persons you might meet here in Germany or Austria who might try to denigrate me. I hear you have met my Ambassador to Vienna. A clever man, with some misguided ideas, and a charming wife whose ideas should be confined to kitchen management.

"And now I will give you a photo yes?"

Pulling a drawer open, he produced a picture of himself, which he signed. Handing it over, much to her consternation, he kissed Constance's cheek.

"My little Princess, should you change your mind and return, you will be welcome. Goodbye."

A uniform materialised. "Goodbye and thank you for the photograph." Constance was ushered out.

"Oh bother, I don't think I found out anything of any value to anyone. Why did we get bogged down in hats and teaspoons?"

At this thought our heroine could hardly restrain a giggle. The thought of the Führer in a sea of spoons and sou'westers sprang to mind.

"I'll draw that," she thought, "maybe the Beaver will use it."

On a more serious note, she wondered how Mr H. knew that that she had met the von Papens. Not Mr Ney nor M. Jamet. Nellie? Alexander?

Hmmmm. Not Anna Rheinhardt. Felix? Stupid boring Felix? Well well. She filled another page of the notebook, which she decided must remain with her at all times. As did the von Papen Packet.

Which was a sensible precaution, as when Fritz drove her back to the Brandenberger Hof, after a friendly walk in the Tiergarten (and a little smackerel of something in the café) she found her room ransacked. Mattress upside down, knickers, shoes, stockings, all over the place. The white dress, oh! The white dress, lying forlorn with its lining loose and ripped. Suitcase (who cares about a suitcase? Mama probably.) ditto. Beautiful new lemon outfit – thank goodness she was wearing with shoes, bag and hat.

Thank goodness because sensible black bag torn to smithereens, ditto shoes. Heels ripped off, inners ripped out. Small box of specials upended and stamped upon.

If Constance hadn't been so angry she might have

cried. Anyhow, we now know that Constance is not the crying sort. Instead she dialled.

"I think someone extremely senior should come to my room now, please."

Shortly, a person, who did not look to Constance to be particularly senior, knocked on the door.

"What is this?" he said.

"Would you tell me please?" Said Constance. "I left this morning for a meeting with Herr Hitler, and I come back at three o'clock to find my room vandalised! My beautiful clothes! My jewellery!"

"We advise our guests to put jewellery in our safe."

"It wasn't valuable you stupid man, just precious to me! And it's been stamped on! Not stolen."

"Fräulein – your key?"

"My key was at the front desk, until I retrieved it to open my door at three o'clock. Enough, please inform the police NOW. And also bring me a glass of champagne."

The police came later rather than sooner. Constance had left Herr Hitler's signed photograph in a prominent position which probably encouraged their diligence, or NOT.

"Someone let whoever in. The police know not to find anything," thought Constance. "I don't feel very safe."

But she said, "Please now send a chambermaid to help me tidy my things."

Ilse was most sympathetic, "Oh Fräulein, Fräulein! your beautiful things." Together they tidied and threw things away.

"Ilse – I wanted to wear this tonight, what do you think?"

Ilse looked, "I will bring a pair of scissors, has the Fräulein a petticoat?"

"Yes, I think so. At any rate I had one…"

"Then we will the lining snip out and the dress will manage without, I think."

The frock fixed and the champagne drunk, Constance felt strong enough to telephone one or two people.

"If Herr Hitler is in a meeting can you take a message? Please will you say that Constance Bennett [she spelt it] thanks Herr Hitler for sparing some of his valuable time to meet her this morning. Unfortunately, she is upset to say that while she was out her hotel room was ransacked. Nothing was stolen but her things torn and broken."

The murmured soothing words from the female voice on the other end sounded genuine.

"I thought Herr Hitler might like to know. Yes, the police have been, they weren't particularly helpful. I know, you wouldn't expect such a thing at the Brandenberg Hof. Would you? Yes. Goodbye."

Next she telephoned Unity.

"Oh, it's you. You really are the most frightful social climbing little pig."

Constance decided not to think of climbing pigs, deciding that for some people Mr H. was Everest-like.

"Dear Unity, it was a lovely party and you're not to be cross. Didn't you like Hans Christian?"

"A good looking child."

"He thinks you're a goddess."

"Humpf." (I can't believe she said 'Humpf' thought Constance, I must be feeling better.)

"As does Mr Hitler."

Unity's voice unfroze and she said uncertainly, "Did he say so? Really?"

"Not exactly, but he clearly adores you."

"Oh! And I him."

"Yes, well that's all fine and dandy then. I just wanted to say 'thank you' but also to say that my room's been vandalised."

"What? Burglars? Probably Jews."

"No, nothing stolen, just my things ripped and smashed. Remember that little brooch your Mama gave me?"

"That tiny lizard? I wanted that."

"Stamped on, I saved the stones."

"What beasts, did you call the police?"

"Yes, they seem to think the hotel should find the culprits. I must say I don't feel very safe. So you be careful won't you?"

"Nothing will happen to me."

"Well I'm not here for much longer, so I hope nothing will happen to me either, but I just wondered, I need a few bits – all my shoes were de-heeled, stockings and knickers have been binned too. Need one day dress, at least. Can you tell me where to shop?"

"My dear, I will show you. What are friends for? Can we use your car?"

Plans were made for the following day.

51

The dress just about worked over a petticoat with a few stitchings from the friendly chambermaid. Shoes might have been problem, but the same person had glued and bound them together with twine:

"I am afraid they will not be comfortable and they for long will not last…"

"They never were very and just so long as they see me through tonight! Thank you so much." Constance found a large Reichsmark note. The handbag was also sans lining, but that wouldn't show.

"Here I go then," thought our heroine, "Back straight, chin up (not too up) and let's hope I don't meet anyone from last night who might think I own only one frock!"

Fritz was furious:

"Why did you not send for me? Madame will be so cross!"

"Madame need not be worried."

"But I am now worried, Miss Constance, supposing they come back?"

"I don't think they will, they didn't find what they were looking for."

"Because you had it about your person…"

"Because I had it about my person."

"And now?"

"It is still about my person."

Fritz didn't like to wonder where.

"Is that wise? Couldn't I look after whatever it is?"

"No, dear Fritz, they are probably watching you too. I

will get rid of one lot tonight and hope anything I receive further will be small. I must buy some clothes tomorrow, but could we leave for Paris the next day? I would have liked to stay in Berlin longer but..."

"I think, Miss Constance, we should leave tomorrow."

"After lunch?"

"I will make arrangements."

Constance had forgotten quite how tight-buttoned and plain-looking was her host as he usurped the maidservant's task, ushering his guest into a small library:

"Where you might your cloak leave, and other things also?"

"Definitely also other things, but would you mind turning around? My room was searched yesterday and there is no space in my handbag."

Herr Goerdeler spun round, not before Constance spied his blush.

"Searched? Fräulein Bennett, this is terrible!"

"It's all right: they didn't find anything, or take anything, but they ripped up my clothes and broke things and there was a terrible mess."

"The police?"

"Franchement carrément the police AND the hotel were useless – except for the lovely maid who managed to stitch me together for this evening. Otherwise I would be here en déshabillé – or not at all! Here we are..."

Carl Friedrich had re-blushed as he turned around. Constance thought "Whoops. Shouldn't have said that!"

"Mr Bradley's thoughts, together with some other thoughts from a different Member of Parliament. Have you papers for me?"

Herr Goerdeler indicated a large manila file upon his desk.

"Oh dear, I do not think I can tuck that about my person."

Herr Goerdeler was still a bit pink, so no need for a re-blush.

"I don't want to walk through the hotel carrying something like that. Do you suppose it could be wrapped up to look like a present? Pretty paper and ribbons? I shall pretend that it is my birthday."

"It shall be done. I was told you were more clever than you looked."

Constance secretly seethed, but "Never judge a book by its cover," she said.

Into the grandly severe drawing room they went, there to be greeted by Anneliese Goerdeler, who if anything was more buttoned than her husband.

"A bun for heaven's sake," thought our heroine, "I shall tell Mama, she should have one, just as soon as I get home."

"Guten Tag! Frau Goerdeler."

Not everyone in the room appeared quite so serious, Constance was introduced to a jolly beard who talked to her about the hospital he had founded.

"I try to avoid hospitals, and doctors."

"But you, Fräulein, are fortunately well. Others not so."

"Oh dear, I sound like a silly cow.* I am sure your hospital will be marvellous. Are you a doctor, Herr Bosch?"†

"No no, I am an inventor – do you know what a sparking plug is?"

---

* Constance the Cow, remember dear reader?

† Robert Bosch 1861–1942: sparking plug, electrical magnets, philanthropist. Dear reader, you may have one of his appliances. Campaigned for the eight-hour day and social benefits.

"I know a man who does. He is wonderful with cars. I wish he were here, he would make sensible conversation."

"Pah, who wants sensible conversation? I would like to talk of London, where I think you are from? Although, your German is so good, I would think you from Munich..."

"I am pleased with the compliment, thank you." Constance curtseyed.

"I haven't been to London for far too long –"

"And I have never been! Disgraceful!" Another smiley gentleman (this time clean-shaven) bowed, "Theodor Heuss,* Fräulein, I hear you have had a problem with burglars?"

"Well, it was horrid, but they didn't take anything so I don't think they were burglars. Perhaps they were trying to frighten me? I had a meeting with Herr Hitler this morning."

Both men revised their opinions.

"I telephoned this evening to let him know what had happened, but obviously I only got through to a secretary."

"Darling I see you are reduced to one frock!" Unity swanned over trailing a downy shawl.

"Good job Snuffles isn't here," thought Constance as they exchanged "mois".†

"Poor you, simply ghastly, never mind we shall shop tomorrow."

"Do I hear of shopping? Might I join you? More fun shopping with others, I am Inge Schacht – my father..."

---

* Theodor Heuss, 1884–1963: art historian, economist and political scientist. Member of the Reichstag until 1933 when Germany became a single-Party state. Not an active resistor of Hitler. Wrote Robert Bosch's biography. President of the Federal Republic of Germany, 1949.

† Dear reader, such kisses are all about ME really, aren't they?

"I have heard the Führer speak of Herr Schacht." *

It did not sound to Constance as if Mr Hitler had spoken of Mr Schacht in a complimentary way and she wondered what might follow, but Unity was in mellow mode (why? was wondered), and all she said was, "I do so agree, please come with us."

"Can anyone join in?" The silky voice was accented, but from which country? Constance was wondering again, mostly in order not to gawp at probably the most beautiful woman she had ever seen. Unity, un-mellowed, bristled, "And you are?"

"Catharina Koopman, but you may call me Toto."†

Her eyebrows had that permanently raised quality so admired in the 1930s and the eyes beneath searched Unity from top to toe: "Miss Unity Mitford, as I live and breathe, how pleased I am to meet you and Miss Constance Bennett, of whom I have heard so much. Let us all meet tomorrow. But now, I must talk to this lady alone." She looped her arm through that of Constance and weaved them away to a window seat.

Fingers silkily swept down and clasped our heroine's hand. (Dear reader, forgive multiple alliterations, but I hope the scene is set.)

"I do so love your Charlie and Mr Snuffles. They both sent much love." Constance was not sure she wanted this

---

* Hjalmar Schacht, 1877–1970: Reichsbank President 1933, Economics Minister 1934. Denounces "unlawful activities" against Jews, August 1935; publicly declares repugnance of Kristallnacht 1938; dismissed Reichsbank 1939; Minister without Portfolio; dismissed totally 1943.

† Toto Koopman 1908–1991: Dutch cavalry officer for a father, half Dutch, half Indonesian mother. Lovers (among many): Tallulah Bankhead, Beaverbrook, Max Aitken, Randolph Churchill. The leader of the Italian Resistance in '42, imprisoned in Ravensbrück. Last girl-friend Erica Brausen, who launched Francis Bacon.

siren to be friends with her friends, but she extricated her hand in a grown-up way and asked:

"How are they? I am so pleased to have news. And you met them…?"

"With Max of course! Well, with both Maxes actually, but separately." The eyebrows met each other in a delicate way.

"Life is tricky sometimes – don't you find?"

"I certainly do."

"When it was known that I was to come to Berlin for the *Tannhäuser* I received all sorts of messages, and one is this…" Toto planted a smackeroo upon Constance's lips.

"Hmm, that was the best message. Now for the boring ones:

1. Have you anything for the Beaver?
2. Anything for Winston?
3. Last but not least: anything for Charlie?

Oooh, I quite forgot to give you the lick from Snuffles!" Toto's tongue flicked out alarmingly.

Constance was aware that quite a few of the guests had noticed the kiss. Her host's frown was particularly noticeable.

"Toto, is this the right place? If I am meeting you tomorrow? And also, I hesitate to say, but can I trust you? My room was ransacked yesterday…"

"I heard."

"Exactly, you seem to know who I am and what I am about, but I know nothing about you."

"Come to my room tonight and I will show you all about me."

"My dear Toto."

"I love my dear Toto."

"In that case, my dear Miss Koopman."

"Not so good."

"I will write some info for the Beaver, the rest can wait. À demain."

Constance made her way back towards Unity and Inge, but was stopped by a sweet smile and a small bow.

"John Wheeler-Bennett, Miss Constance Bennett. We might be cousins – if not kissing ones." He was laughing at her, but the smile made her laugh too,

"Hmmm, don't think we have any wheeler dealers in the family, but it's always possible."

"May I give you a word of warning? I know I am a stranger but…"

"Don't worry, if you are about to tip me the wink about Miss Koopman, let me tell you, I wouldn't trust her further than I could throw her."

"She'd probably enjoy being thrown by you – don't suggest it within her hearing."

"Anyway, she only had messages from England" said Constance.

"I too have messages: Gwen and Alan send their love, and I saw your sister Winifred the other day."

"You can't really be a stranger then, lovely Herberts! And dear Wini – what did she have to say?"

"She said it was nice that you could buy your own frocks these days. I wondered if that was in code?" He was laughing at her again, "Oooh you are rather a good egg," thought Constance, "I could…"

"Now we are ready to go in," said Mme Goerdeler,

"and Herr Hans Gisevins* will take you." The young man bowed, clicking heels to the W-Bennett and the Miss Constance Bennett and proffering his arm.

What followed was rather testing: Constance had plenty to ask Herr Goerdeler, on whose left she sat, but nothing she could voice in public. So they talked of Berlin, but not of burglars; of hotels, but not of Hitler; and about the weather.

On her other side, Herr Gisevins, an earnest young man, was keen to instruct our heroine on the finer points of German Law and how it differed from the Code Napoleon and the English system of Precedent and Common Law. It appeared he had a job at the Ministry of the Interior, but was not liking it much. When he turned to Luise Schacht on his left, who was obviously a friend, Constance felt a certain relief and wondered when she might be able to powder her nose and write down the guest list, while sneakily watching Inge, Mr Wheeler-Bennett and Toto who, at the bottom of the table, were clearly having fun.

Unity, across the table, looked serene, if not exactly jolly, with Herr Bosch's twinkle on one side, and the 'Mayor of Stuttgart' on the other. Identified by her host earlier, Karl Strollin looked charming, but maybe he bored for Baden-Württemberg. Then, just as Constance "turned" towards Herr Goerdeler, the door from the hallway opened and a bowing uniform ushered in Adolf Hitler. The dinner party rose slowly but surely, and offered the 'Heil' except for Wheeler-Bennett and Miss

---

* Hans Gisevins 1904–1974. Lawyer. Joins the Gestapo 1933, discharged; Interior Ministry, discharged by Himmler 1936. Joins the (anti-Hitler) Abwehr 1939. Vice Consul in Switzerland, liaisons with German opposition (including Goerdeler). Represented Hjalmar Schacht at Nuremberg.

Plain Bennett, who did not rise either, deciding she only rose for Grandes Dames and people she liked. Oh, and possibly kings and conceivably princes.

"An interesting party," the recently arrived person wandered his eyes around the assembled company. "To which I should have liked to have been invited. Fortunately, dear Miss Unity told me where I might find her friend, so here I am, invited or not, to make apologies for the slime who dared to vandalise your room, my dear little princess interpreter." He marched across the room, as Constance belatedly rose, took her hand in his and offered a cheek to be kissed. As she obliged, our heroine caught sight of Wheeler-Bennett's shaking shoulders and nearly disgraced herself with a giggle.

"See, she trembles! Do not worry little one, we will hunt these people down. I will not have my friends upset.

Unity ("Now I know why you were in smug mellow mode" thought Constance) said: "Would the Führer like some coffee?"

"I would, if I may, Frau Goerdeler?"

So then, dinner was terminated without pudding, pleasantly surprising one of the party, and they returned to the drawing room for coffee, and...

"Schnapps?"

"No, no, no."

"I would love a little," said Constance, "or if you have Poire Williams?" I think some of the guests, deprived as they were of torte and/or kuchen, almost applauded. Our heroine smiled sweetly at Mr Hitler and wandered off, only to be confronted by Unity.

"You are the most creepy little pig," she hissed.

"Darling Unity: pigs don't creep, they are robust creatures, which sturdily shoulder their way through life, in fact they are pachyderms. And that means they are related to elephants, which is a good thing. Now a creepy thing would be a spider, which is about as far from an elephant as you can get…"

"Well, you are a scheming spider, luring my Führer into your sticky web!"

"If I had a web it would not be sticky. You know I dislike sweet things. Unity, angel, I assure you he's all yours. Believe me, I leave Berlin tomorrow and I doubt if I'll come back to Germany. Any messages for the Mitfords?"

"Humpf," went Unity, and then, "humpf," again.

"You have read the *Just So* stories?" The Poire was probably encouraging Constance to say things she might otherwise have left unsaid.

"Of course I have."

"Then you will remember how the Camel got his Hump…"

(The camel's hump is an ugly lump
Which well you may see at the Zoo;
But uglier yet is the hump we get
From having too little to do.

Kiddies and grown-ups too-oo-oo,
If we haven't enough to do-oo-oo,
We get the hump –
Cameelious hump –
The hump that is black and blue!

We climb out of bed with a frouzly head,
And a snarly-yarly voice.
We shiver and scowl and we grunt and we growl
At our bath and our boots and our toys;

And there ought to be a corner for me
(And I know there is one for you)
When we get the hump –
The Cameelious Hump –
The hump that is black and blue!

The cure for this ill is not to sit still,
Or frowst with a book by the fire;
But to take a large hoe and a shovel also,
And dig till you gently perspire;

And then you will find that the sun and the wind,
And the Djinn of the Garden too,
Have lifted the hump –
The horrible hump –
The hump that is black and blue!

I get it as well as you-oo-oo
If I haven't enough to do-oo-ooh!
We all get hump –
The Cameelious hump –
Kiddies and grown-ups too!)

"And the Butterfly that stamped?" said Mr Wheeler-Bennett.

Constance said, "I try never to stamp – just in case."

"Thank heavens for that."

Unity glared at them, "Frivolity! I must cherish the Führer." And she regally removed herself.

"You nearly ruined me earlier," Constance smiled.

"Nearly ruined myself! Wish I could've photographed the occasion, Caption: Who let the walrus into swan lake?"

"Probably the Carpenter, but do stop, he has been very sweet."

"To quote Miss Unity, 'Humpf.'"

"Who has been very sweet? I can be very sweet, in fact I'm sure I can be sweeter." Miss Koopman had been eavesdropping.

"Toujours the sweetest, beloved Toto." Said Mr W-B.

Into the society of mutual admiration stepped Sir Robert Vansittart.

"Miss Constance Bennett, Miss Koopman," he inclined his head. "Wheeler-Bennett, a word, if you ladies will excuse us?"

Toto took Constance's arm, "of course we will, we have important matters to discuss such as: where shall we meet tomorrow?"

"Unity may have other ideas, but perhaps you would come to the Brandenburger Hof where I am staying? And then, Fritz, my godmama's driver, would drive us about?"

"But I am staying there too! I wonder why we haven't seen each other. What's your room number?"

Unfortunately Constance couldn't remember.

Seeking out Inge Schacht, she asked if she could collect her in the morning?

"No, no, I can come to the Brandenburger Hof. It's nearer the shops, but which shops would you like to visit?"

"I'm afraid, boringly, I need bits of everything, even some luggage, my room was vandalised yesterday and all my belongings ruined."

"I am so sorry," Inge said.

Toto at the same time: "I meant to ask, was anything taken?"

"No. They just wrecked the place and randomly destroyed precious things only valuable to me."

Unity was there, all smiles again, "We shall find you everything you need and us some goodies too. I have it all planned."

I'll bet you have, thought Constance; if you were a cat, you'd be purring.

"But now the Führer is leaving, come and say goodbye."

Constance followed the blue silken back, feeling like a child bidden by a parent.

"10.30ish then?" She smiled over her shoulder, Toto winked, "Tonight?"

Hoping Inge wasn't shocked, our heroine offered nose and eyebrows to the ceiling. Once more the proffered cheek.

"My little princess, you shall be avenged."

"Why do I think you know exactly who the villains are and have no intention of doing anything about them... – thought the "Little Princess" – I am becoming much too cynical, also I may not be a strapping mädchen but I am not that little."*

However, she smiled and lowered her lashes and said, "Goodbye and thank you" and almost curtseyed and was glad that Mr W-Bennett was not around to watch.

Except he was.

"You should be on the stage."

* Dear reader, *Midsummer Night's Dream*, Act III Scene II: Helena: You puppet you. Hermia: "Puppet!" Why so? ay that way goes the game. / Now I perceive that she hath made compare / Between our statures; she hath urged her height; / And with her personage, her tall personage, / Her height, forsooth, she hath prevailed with him. / And are you grown so high in his esteem; / Because I am so dwarfish and so low? / How low am I, thou painted maypole? speak; / How low am I? I am not yet so low / But that my nails can reach unto thine eyes. ... Helena: And though she be but little, she is fierce.

"Indeed I was. Wini did not enjoy the competition."

"I'm not surprised."

Those who had escorted Mr Hitler to the door trickled back and the party un-stiffened its sinews, well, most of it did.

"When do you return to England, Miss Constance?"

"I'm not sure, but I leave for Paris tomorrow. And I think Constance will do if you are going to continue to tease me..."

"Paris? Why are you leaving for Paris? It is completely the wrong 'saison' to be in Paris."

Toto slinked into the conversation.

"I am meeting my godmother there and also I have promised to help Mlle Chanel should she need me." Constance then realised this piece of information should not have been bruited abroad.

"Mlle Chanel? Hmm. I would be interested to meet her, perhaps I will join you in Paris, after *Tannhäuser*, however out of season."

"Yes, off she goes to Paris! She does gad about so! Now. Tomorrow..." Said Unity.

"We will meet at the Brandenburger Hof at 10.30 and Constance's Fritz can drive us."

"That's just what I'd decided."

"I'm sure I thought of the plan first."

"Great minds think alike."

"There was only one great mind here tonight. You, Constance have been singularly honoured."

The little princess curtseyed.

"I suppose one day you will grow up."

Exit Unity, downy shawl clasped to bosom.

"I do hope you won't," said Mr W-B.

"Won't what?" (Oh dear, what whats again.)

"Grow up! Here's my card, please do let us meet in London."

"That would be fun, I'm afraid I can never remember our telephone number..." (second lie of the evening, dear readers).

"I have it from Winifred," Mr W-B looked, if not triumphant, supremely pleased.

"Where would I be without Wini?"

"Unclothed?" and with that her admirer wished her goodnight.

More goodnights and byes were said and kind words and cards exchanged.

"Hjalmar Schacht," bowed a gent, "Miss Constance Bennett? I hear my daughter is helping you to empty some shops tomorrow?"

"Oh yes, she is. Such a sweetie pie."

"If I may give her something for you? For England?"

"So long as it's not too big. There'll be no room in the car after the shopping."

"It will not be an elephant for the zoo..."

"Of course, that's fine Mr Schacht."

"I thank you."

And then there was the HUGE much beribboned birthday present. The remaining few clapped and wished they'd known.

And so, via Fritz, to bed.

First though, the "present" needed opening. Oh! Someone had put chocolates and a card under the first layer of wrapping. How sweet. She would give them to the kind helpful maid. In the box underneath were a number of handwritten pages. In a code. Bother. But below these were photographs. Oh joy! She really did qualify as a spy. Some pictures were of largish ugly boats moored in a canal. They had no portholes and seemed to be made of a monotone metal. They resembled misshapen whales come to the surface.

"Well, they're not allowed those!" thought Constance.

Other images showed boxes and boxes of guns, and what looked like black footballs.

"Hmm, they're not allowed those either."

Constance stashed the lot with the tank photographs into what remained of a smart bag for underwear given as a goodbye present from the sisters.

"Oof, Fritz can take charge of them in the morning."

52

At nine o'clock the next morning, Constance received a telephone call.

"No civilised person telephones before nine o'clock," grumbled our heroine, who was only on her first cup of coffee.

It was Alexander. "How bizarre," thought Constance, but, "Alexander! How lovely to hear you," she said.

"Mlle has asked me to enquire when you might be leaving for Paris. She is anxious that you might not be here in time for her show?"

"Oh, please tell Mlle that I am leaving this afternoon. Will that be all right?"

"And you'll be travelling in your godmother's car?"

"Yes, with dear Fritz."

"Excellent. Bon Voyage."

"Merci Alexandre."

"Goodbye."

"Goodbye."

"Why didn't Coco telephone me herself?" wondered Constance. 'Too busy perhaps."

But then shopping beckoned and she forgot about oddities in the search for necessities.

The shopping went well, if no vast sums were spent. A restrained Constance kept reminding herself that she would soon be in Paris. Also, Miss Koopland would keep peeking into changing rooms. However, the ladies had a merry lunch with some *Sekt*.

"Just fizzy fruit juice," said Unity.

And then Fritz was there, all parcels and what had been worth salvaging from Constance's previous wardrobe, packed into new luggage by obliging chambermaid.

"What fun it has been, must dash to the lav. before the drive," said Constance.

"I will come too," said Inge.

And once within the ladies' sanctuary, she offered our heroine an envelope. "From my father." Toto entered and didn't miss a trick.

"OK, and where's my stuff for the Beaver?"

"Oooh, I nearly forgot," Constance produced her scribbles. "I hope he can read them, no chance to get it typed."

"I hope it's amusing, he does like to be amused."

"It amused me to write it, but that doesn't mean a thing."

"I shall see you in Paris. Where do you stay?"

"Oh, I hadn't thought." (This is not a lie, Constance hadn't thought, Fritz had though.)

"I shall find you, through Mlle Chanel then."

"That will be perfect, I am sure you'll get on like a house on fire." Constance meant not a word of that last sentence.

Final goodbyes said, Constance collapsed into her godmother's comfortable car. "Ooh Fritz, I feel as though I have been through a mangle."

"My dear Miss Constance, I am not surprised."

Fritz then maintained silence as he negotiated their way out of the city.

Constance opened Herr Schacht's packet: it too was encoded, but it contained a great many numbers.

Then, "I have to tell you that my rooms were also searched."

"What? did they take things?"

"There was nothing for them to take – can you imagine? They took some road maps and threw my clothes about the place, so that I, probably, am not quite as presentable as I should be today."

"You look perfect Fritz, but I am sorry if I didn't notice anything, because I was busy with my friends."

"I didn't wish to alarm you, Miss Constance."

"Well, you have now. Do you suppose someone is following us?"

"In fact they are, but they won't be for long."

"How will you manage that?"

"I have just seen a farm tractor ahead and forgive me if I accelerate, but we will overtake it and then run off this road. We can wait for a bit and then fiddle round and back again."

So Fritz put his foot down they whizzed past the tractor and into a lane on the left. From behind a bend they watched as first the tractor, and then a beeping black Mercedes passed their turning.

"Well done Fritz!"

"So far so good."

"What'll we do if they catch us? I have reams of papers. I can't possibly hide them all about my person. I should have posted them to Pairs."

"Do you suppose they would have reached their destination?"

"Oh."

"They won't catch us, but just in case…"

Fritz opened the boot and produced a hamper hung about with vaguely nauseous vapour. Once opened the pong overpowered.

"Your favourite cheese, Miss Constance," said Fritz as he lifted out a package.

"Is that ... wriggling?"

"I should hope so, I have been nursing these little darlings for several days."

Below the package was a false bottom, with plenty of room for the reams.

"Wouldn't they just shake everything out?"

"In my experience, Miss Constance, men who are called 'hard' are remarkably 'soft' when it comes to the little smelly wriggly things."

Thus the papers were placed under the false bottom and the squirmy square placed on top, and on they went.

As they were about to re-enter the main road from their scenic route, the black Mercedes slid from nowhere behind them, and as Fritz stepped on the gas, the tractor trundled gently across the road to block their exit. Someone began to shout, "Get out of the car!"

Constance had already leapt from it and with arms akimbo,* "what is the meaning of this?"

"Miss Constance Bennett," said Felix Rheinhardt, pulling off gloves as he stepped from his car. His driver and two other substantial gentlemen stepped out too.

Gentlemen? Those are thugs! thought Constance.

"Mr Rheinhardt? What on earth are you doing, following me around and what is more, impeding my progress? Is your wife's new underwear of such surpassing beauty that you absolutely HAD to say thank you?"

Anna's husband harrumphed forward, "Mention of my wife's underwear is vulgar and unnecessary. We believe you to be in possession of papers which rightfully belong to the Führer, we will search your car."

---

* Sorry dear readers but we do love an "akimbo"! Let's all do it now.

"But I am a friend of the Führer, I have his signed photograph!" Constance reached into her handbag, but a loud clicking noise made her stop and look up. There were three pistols directed at her.

She sensed Fritz, behind her, move.

"Stand still, both of you!" shouted Rheinhardt, "Sometimes the Führer chooses his friends without regard for his best interests. Carry on!" He spoke to his henchmen. "Miss Constance Bennett, will you sit in my car?" He said, with something of a return to his drawing room manner. "We could discuss recipes and restaurants." A crocodile would have been more inviting.

"No thanks," said Constance.

"It is cold."

"Thank heaven for cashmere and mink," replied our heroine, although she wore neither, stumping over to a stump and sitting upon it. Fritz stood, helpless and enraged, as his beloved was ripped apart.

"Why do you not give up the papers, then you may go on your way."

"I have no papers to give you."

Not really a lie: they were not for Felix Rheinhardt. Soon the searchers found the hamper.

"Eklig? Abscheulich!" The heavy hurled away the cheese and flung down the wicker basket. The false bottom held and Constance and Fritz forbore to cheer.

Our heroine wandered over to the squashed mess, "Oh dear, my favourite cheese. But it does seem to have gone off* a trifle. So I won't require another one to be bought. However, Mr Rheinhardt, if your oafs do not put each and every article of my clothing back into my suitcases, I shall require TOTAL reimbursement. I am fed up with

---

*   Pronounced, dear reader, Gawn Awf.

being interfered with and I refuse to run around naked in Paris."

"I do not think you will be travelling to Paris. In fact you will not be travelling anywhere."

The oafs having found zilch, Herr Rheinhardt thundered, "You can pick up your own things, and," he signalled to a heavy, "this car will go nowhere."

Said heavy removed a vital piece of engine, and heavily hefted it in Fritz' direction (fortunately Fritz ducked and it flew into some scrubby alders) and they all headed (heavily) back to their car, and screeched off.

"Quick Fritz," said our heroine, "tractor driver's gone to pee, get up behind him, bop him one and can you drive a tractor?"

"No, Miss Constance."

"Well I can! Just pop him, I'll get some of my stuff into the car and we can tow it to the next garage."

Fritz was not at all sure about the bopping but managed to sneak up behind the tractor driver (who was enjoying rather more than a pee) and hit him on the head with a handy rock.

Meanwhile (not back at the ranch) Constance flung clothes and hamper (not cheese) into the car, reversed the tractor down the lane, and found some rope which Fritz removed from her grasp, "this is something I can do," he said and off they set, albeit slowly.

"I am really cross now," said Constance. "I have left behind a skirt, two frocks and one really nice pair of shoes."

"But we needed to get going."

"We needed to get going."

"May I ask, Miss Constance, where you learnt the tractor driving?"

"Oh, I lived on a farm when I was in Bavaria. You never know if something might be useful."

And there in the gloaming, glowed the lights of a Mercedes garage,* whose proprietors showed no sign of surprise when asked by people in a tractor, towing one of their cars, to replace a vital piece of engine. Vital piece replaced, Fritz said, "I should drive quite fast now." And he did.

At first this alarmed Constance, but when she realised what an excellent driver he was, she fell asleep.

"So sorry Fritz," she murmured and let him go.

---

* You may, dear readers, wonder why Constance has all the luck, well, she deserves it, she is after all, a heroine, and she hasn't even met a dragon yet, well not exactly.

53

Eventually, and with no further hiccups, Paris was reached.

"I should have driven the tractor back..." Constance said as they meandered towards the Rue du Faubourg St-Honoré.

"They were deeply unpleasant people, Miss Constance, undeserving of your concern."

"But he might be dead!"

Fritz didn't quite hit a pedestrian.

"I didn't bop him that hard."

"He might have a heart condition."

"Miss Constance."

"Fritz! Only a joke, I'm sure he is fine."

"He had a cap on."

"Well then, he's definitely fine, and as you say does NOT deserve our concern."

They arrived at the Hotel Bristol,* to be greeted by Pierre Jamet. He showed Constance via an ancient, beautiful and frankly scary lift, to a huge suite of rooms overlooking rooftops towards the Eiffel Tower.

"But M. this is enorme. It's only me!"†

"I am told Mademoiselle may have guests."

"Gracious! Who might they be?"

"Jean François did not tell me their names, but he said you would be pleased."

---

* The Hotel Bristol was the last privately owned hotel in Paris, belonging to the Jamet family until 1978.

† For you darling T.

"I am very pleased, Pierre, thank you, mysterious guests or no."

Constance bathed, found a presentable frock and gave the rest of her wardrobe to the chambermaid.

"Aah, Madame quelle dommage! Vôtre belles choses!"

"Nous avons eus an accident. Pourrier vous en faire quelque chose?"

"J'essayerai, Madame, j'essayerai." The lady's lips pursed.

"Je vous en serai endettée."

Then she telephoned Coco.

"Ma sosie! Where 'av you been? I am in total need. And who is this Toto person who keeps pestering me?"

"She's very beautiful."

"She is beautiful, but she upsets my others. With her stares and her cigarettes."

"She is tricky, I am sorry she found out about our connection."

"Ça alors, I can deal with tricksy – do I not deal with you? WHEN can I deal with you?"

"Lunch? Or perhaps a cocktail? I am staying at the Bristol. Come and play."

"La la la la – so posh! I think cocktails sounds for-midable and then I will book a restaurant, not far and delicious. Mme Lydia 'as been to my shop."

"Oh good, have you made friends?"

"I 'ope so, I like her. She spent a lot of money. Also 'er friend M. Jamet, he too bought some things."

"Are you creating for men now?"

"Non, stupide, he bought Chanel No. 5 and a 'at."

"A 'at for whom? Not for him?"

"Bein alors for your tiresome godmother."

"I thought you liked her?"

"She is OK."

"She is wonderful."

"She is OK. A ce soir."

Constance walked herself over to the Sainte Chapelle and sat bathed in glassy reflections. Then she wandered into Notre Dame and lit a candle, before St Joan of Arc. "Against us but a good egg."

She crossed the Seine and took a zizz in her grand rooms.

The chambermaid produced much-tidied clothes.

"Merci, merci," she twirled and the Mademoiselle looked proud, and pleased with her pleasant tip.

At the bar, she found champagne had been ordered (hmmm), and little biscuits with fois gras, so she sat, happily munching, until a fountain of fur exploded onto her lap...

"Snuffles!"

"Yes, yes it is I," said Snuffles, "Oh, oh, I love you," licking face and ears.

"Well I love you too, and your grammar is correct. But desist," said Constance firmly, viewing the person behind the fur.

"Hello."

"Hello."

"You were away so long we thought we'd come and find you."

"I'm glad you did."

There were smiles and a chaste kiss, which promised more.

"I say I say as you've been all over the place." Albert appeared with Nellie.

"Mostly helped by your cousins."

"But I say as Fritz told me you're handy with a tractor?"

"Do try to turn my hand to most things."

Charles briefly covered his eyes. Nellie and Constance hugged, Alexander cried, "Big Sis, how lovely." But raised an eyebrow in Albert's direction. Coco, who had arrived, with Alexander (natch) said "Voici tout le monde qui me plaît."

"Darlings," Constance's godmother arrived with Jean François.

If this seems, readers mine, a bit too tidy, wait a bit.

Then Fritz appeared, rather embarrassed.

"Dear Fritz, I wanted you to be here, I we," for once, Lydia's words came out in a jumble, and trailed off into a silence. Jean François took her hand and, "Mme Lydia thinks she would like to stay in Paris, in fact, I would also like her to stay in Paris. Therefore, we shall be married. But we hope that you might come and live here too."

"Shall I become Frédéric, M. Jamet?"

"I think Frédéric suits you perfectly," said Constance.

"Or I could revert to Fred?"

"That too sounds good."

"And Madame's maid, Edwina, and Johnny?"

"Of course, of course, so much to think about. We should buy a bigger apartment."

"Details, details, ma chère Lydia. May I propose a toast?" Coco raised her glass. Alexander filled it, and others.

"Good luck," and "to Lydia and Jean François" were sung out and the other occupants of the bar applauded. Lydia positively blushed, "How I wish the de Hedevars were here. Shall we telephone them darling?"

"I think we should."

They progressed to Coco's chosen restaurant, where some people ate snails and some people didn't and some people chose foie de veau and some people didn't, but most people ate frites and generally a good time was had by all.

Leaving to go their separate ways, Snuffles leading (natch) they hardly noticed the car parking itself across the street from which stepped Herr Rheinhardt, plus heavies.

"You!" he said, "it is you who have the papers!" Addressing these words to Nellie, as he produced a pistol, "you will hand them over now, or take me to them, or I will shoot."

"Who are you to be wielding a weapon in Paris?" Asked Jean François.

"Someone stronger than you, old man who plays the decadent piano." And Rheinhardt smashed the gun across Jean François' face. Snuffles leapt for the gun-holding hand but was kicked away, growling.

Constance confronted the opposition.

"Leonora has nothing to do with this."

"I'll deal with you later, thief and murderess."

Fritz/Fred might have been upset by this last, had he not, with Charlie and Albert, been ever so slowly wandering around behind the heavies' backs. A quick look and the three performed a synchronised bop.

Instinctively Nellie moved towards Albert, and suddenly there was the sound of a shot. Alexander had seen Rheinhardt lift his gun and aim it at Nellie, and had thrown himself across her. The bullet burst his brain. Nellie held his body and with breathless horror tried to stop the bleeding with her jacket. Charlie tackled Rheinhardt from behind, causing him to hit the ground. Albert grabbed one of the discarded guns and shot him as he fell.

"Did we need to do that?"

"Yes, Mr Charlie, we did."

Albert quickly rifled Rheinhardt's pockets, removing passport and partially emptying wallet.

Coco, with mascara travelling her cheeks, was mostly leaving Alexander to Nellie. She sat at his feet in shock.

"Mon pauvre, pauvre jeune homme. Que j'ai t'aimé."

Constance handed Albert a hanky, which he used and pocketed, replacing the gun in the heavy's hand.

Then the gendarmerie arrived, all a bustle. Coco knew when she could be of use.

"Je suis Mademoiselle Chanel."

"Bonsoir Mademoiselle," said the flick in charge.

"Nous étions au restaurant que voici, avec des amis Anglais, et quant nous sortions, nous nous sommes tombés dans une espèce de bataille. L'un de nous est mort, et aussi ce brigand." A pointed toe pointed at Max Rheinhardt, "et puis Jean François…"

"Jean François, Inspecteur, j'ai reçue un coup a la tête, mais ce n'est rien." He stood, lump visibly growing on his forehead.

"What can this be?" demanded Coco, "are the streets of Paris no longer safe?"

"Mademoiselle, my apologies, you will all be escorted safely home."

Constance said, "I think some of us need to go to the hospital."

Nellie, nodded un-speeched with grief, and the heavies' groans were beginning to be heard. Fortunately two vehicles arrived and the oafs were bundled into one, whilst Jean François, Lydia and Fritz, together with Coco, got into the other. Then an ambulance blared to a halt and

Alexander and Herr Rheinhardt were stretchered into it. Nellie followed.

"I must go with Nellie," said Constance.

"I'll go too Mr Charlie."

"I understand."

There was just room.

"Ah, ça, pas de chien." Snuffles had recovered and was attempting to accompany his mistress. Charlie led him away.

54

L ater that night, when Nellie, Albert and Constance returned from the mortuary, a strong sedative was found for Alexander's sister and she crept into bed.

Coco had retired to hers with a glass of champagne and several cigarettes.

Lydia retired to bed with neither but found she was thinking of her late husband a lot, in spite of the close proximity of Jean François.

Constance stayed awake with Charlie and Albert, in front of a fire into which Albert consigned her handkerchief.

"Thank you for that," said Albert.

"What happens when those thugs regain consciousness?" asked our heroine. "How can we explain the shooting of Herr?"

"I say I say as that GENTLEMAN as was shot was firing at some other thugs, when Mr Alexander got in the way. So then, the gentleman's thugs, all jumpy like fired and the gentleman got in the way. And the other thugs ran off, but not before a biff and a bop here and there."*

"Oh," said Constance. "I do remember some shadows running away ... but who were they really after?"

"Just gangs fighting," Charlie and Albert chimed together.

The Bennett eyebrows rose:

"Don't treat ME like a policeman!"

---

* Albert's use of gentleman was on the heavy side.

"Nellie. And you."

Constance frowned (not a pretty sight). "Herr, I mean the gentleman, was shouting, I couldn't really hear what. I understand me, but why Nellie?"

"Fritz told me you had a strange telephone call from Alexander before you left Berlin?"

"I told him when we were leaving."

"So he told Herr Rheinhardt where to waylay you, and who knows who else he told."

"When he found nothing," Charlie continued, "maybe he thought Nellie had something, or maybe he wanted to punish Alexander for misleading him."

Constance was silent for about one minute.

"I think Alexander knew what was going to happen. He just didn't imagine it would be so violent, perhaps another kidnap? He left Coco in conversation with the maître d' and he was so quick to shield Nellie. Remorse? Oh dear, poor, ghastly silly boy, trying to play grown-ups with the men. I could cry, if it wasn't so sad."

"Don't my darling, or do if it helps – I too, now remember the thugs thudding down and clattering away..."

"But wait, as far as the gentleman is concerned, he must have cleared customs or border control or something. And we know him. And what if his thugs are the same ones who rifled through Lydia's car? They will recognise me."

"With the gentleman dead, I say I say as I don't think they'll speak up. They'll want to play the innocent and get back to Germany. That's why I killed him."

"They might be French."

"Even more will they want to keep shtum."

In the morning the friends were required to meet a Chief Inspector in a salon privé of the hotel. Whilst scrupulously polite, he introduced a certain coldness into the proceedings, replacing the previous evening's concern.

Constance was allowed to stay with Nellie, otherwise they were interviewed separately. There had been no opportunity to school Nellie who was in a wretched state: only brief sentences that had probably not registered.

Nor had Coco, Lydia and Jean François been contacted. "Not a good idea to telephone," Albert had said.

"Please tell me, Mlle, what happened last night?"

"We came out of the restaurant – there were men – I couldn't see – several. One lifted a pistol shouting – my brother jumped in front of me, and oh oh oh, my poor Alexander!" Nellie's voice ascended, nightingale-like, into a wail: "It is I who should be dead…"

"Can you think of any reason why, Mademoiselle, anyone would –" But Nellie had collapsed and a frowning Constance fetched Albert, who carried her away.

"Vraiment Monsieur! C'est bien tôt pour un tel interrogation! Elle est en deuil! Nous sommes tous en deuil."

The Inspector looked, if not contrite, at least a little abashed.

"Alors, Mlle Bennett, may I remind you that two men are dead, perhaps you could give me your version of events."

"Version? Version! I will tell you my recollection." Constance was still frowning.

"We were celebrating the engagement of our friends, Mme Lydia von Liebenstein and M. Jean François Jamet, in that restaurant. We left to find the taxis we had booked. Suddenly there were shouts and shots. And my dear friend's brother died to save her life." A tear made its way from the violet eye to the sturdy chin and was dismissed by a thumb heel (remaining hanky burnt, remember dear readers). The Super was not unmoved.

"Then there were more shouts, and those two thugs collapsed and another shot and the person who looked like a gentleman also collapsed. I heard footsteps and saw shadows running away. Oh, and before Alexander was shot, M. Jamet and my dog,* attempted to remonstrate with those espèce de –"

The inspector looked shocked – "Those mauvais gars, and one got thumped with a pistol and the other kicked.

"Je vous remercie Mlle."

"Oh, and I should say, that in the ambulance the other person who died bore a remarkable resemblance to an acquaintance of ours in Vienna. A Herr Felix Rheinhardt. I was probably not seeing straight but I thought I should mention…"

"Would he," the Super steeled in, "have any reason to wish any of you dead?"

"We met at dinner with my godmother, Mme von Liebenstein, I took his wife shopping for beautiful lingerie, and she bought clothes at Mlle Chanel's show. These seem pleasant experiences. I cannot think but that the shootings have a more sinister aspect. I believe some have come to Paris from Germany where they are considered undesirables. Herr Rheinhardt is close to Herr Hitler. Otherwise he was a charming companion."

"Merci, Mlle."

Constance was able to pass what she had said to Charles and Albert in small hissy hints; meanwhile, it was Coco's turn.

"A la la lala la! C'est vraiment monstrueux! M.

---

* Good thing Charlie wasn't in earshot, but I doubt if he'd have crowed "your dog" on this occasion.

L'iinspecteur, qu'est ce qui se passe? Les rues de Paris ressemblent celles de Chicago dans un 'gangster movie'. Insupportable."

"Lamentable Mme, mais –"

"MADEMOISELLE!"

"Mademoiselle, if we are to sort out this disgraceful episode, I need your help. Please tell me what you saw?"

"We had been celebrating our friends' engagement."

"Yes."

"As we left, I was chatting to the maître d'hotel – who is quite a friend – I often visit his restaurant qui est tellement delicieux, and introducing him to pauvre Alexandre –"

"Who was an ami particulier of yours?"

"Who was certainly an ami particulier of mine, although what business of yours that is M. L'inspecteur, I do not know."

Coco looked miserably out of the window at Parisian roofs: "Comme il me manque ce beau garçon…" Silence.

"Can you continue Mlle?"

"Oh, yes … we heard shouting: Alexandre rushed up the stairs, I followed more slowly, saying goodbyes. I heard a shot, then another one. When I reached the rez de chaussez, Alexander was dead and also that other one. And poor Jean François knocked to the ground and that aimable chien Snuffles growling from behind a tree. Thank goodness Baguette was not there."

"Baguette?"

Mlle Chanel produced said dog from handbag, "voici Baguette."

The inspector, back on track after wondering about what a loaf of bread had to do with the price of fish, asked, "Is that all Mlle?"

"Also two more méchants mecs on the ground groaning. Then your lot arrived. C'est tous."

"Merci Mlle."

Lydia had been taking care of Jean François on the pavement and so had seen nothing except for the initial aggressiveness.

Jean François told his part, "He, ce type who appeared to be their leader, was waving a pistol in the direction of our party, so I thought to disarm him, not very cleverly. After that I saw nothing until the police arrived."

Fritz, Albert and Charlie mentioned thudding shadows. Caught in crossfire was suggested. The thugs were wondered about, were they sufficiently recovered to be of any help?

"They are helping me with my enquiries," intoned M. L'inspecteur. Then, beadily to Charlie, who was currently seated opposite:

"Although the one whose fingerprints are on the gun, swears something wicked that he didn't pull the trigger."

"Aagh," said Charlie (M. le Membre du Parlement Britanique) "I've had a thought about that,* what I think might have happened is: when he fell, after whoever bopped him, his elbow hit the pavement hard and the gun went off as his lower arm followed."

Charles illustrated this with a little thumping on the table between them.

"Which might explain the low trajectory of the bullet."

"It might indeed inspector. Might I ask, though, was the other dead man our acquaintance, Herr Rheinhardt? Miss Bennett thinks she recognised him in the ambulance."

---

* Constance would have said, altogether now, "treat it kindly it's in a very strange place."

"I have yet to make formal identification. He had on him no passport, nothing except some Reichsmarks." The inspector raised hands and eyes to the ceiling, "the German Embassy…"

"If I could be of assistance? And what about, um, his friends."

"They are French, they say they were hired this evening as bodyguards, never saw him clearly. I thank you M. for offering but now that I have involved the Embassy, it is out of my control."

A relieved Charlie took himself off thinking, well done that Albert whose attention to detail is second to none! He took Snuffles for his own bit of relief, and then made his way to the bar.

Where he found Nellie and Coco cautiously embracing, and was somewhat surprised.

"Que ça me manque ce beau garçon! And I am so sad for you ma petite."

"Je pense qu'il vous a aimé." [*]

They held hands in the middle of the misery of the previous evening's jolly party, which had found itself once more in the bar of the Bristol. What else to do?

Entering in dribs and drabs their sorrows needed company.

"He saved my life," said Nellie.

"And so he should," said Constance.

"He was a brave jeune homme," Coco raised her glass. As did they all.

Albert whispered, "Ta again for the hanky."

"Pas de quoi."

"Well, Alors," said Coco, who was accustomed

---

[*] You, O perspicacious readers, will have your doubts about this.

to moving on. "I still have a collection to present, Constance?"

"I will be going back to England when I can, Mademoiselle."

"Nellie? It will occupy your mind."

Nellie found Albert's hand.

"I will go to England too, Mademoiselle."

It was firmly said.

"A ça! I think you will have enough to occupy your mind. Other bits as well possibly. Je comprends."

"Mademoiselle, I will be in Paris now, I would be happy to model if I am not too old?"

"Bravo Lydia! Excellent! Vous aussi avez le style…"

"Bon chic, bon gout." Jean François smiled, fondly.

Once the body of Felix Rheinhardt had been identified, police matters vanished quick-ish, what with various high-ranking Jamet friends not to mention Mademoiselle's connections.

So that soon after Alexander's funeral, those who wished to be were in London, or on the Isle of Wight.

Not, however, before an uncomfortable meeting with a distraught Anna Rheinhardt.

Accompanied by both the German and the Austrian Ambassadors, she was red-eyed and inconsolable: why was Felix in Paris? She had no idea he was in Paris. He was supposed to be in Berlin. And to be shot dead near her friend Lydia and her new friends. And the brother of Leonora. Oh! It was too much. The friends repeated the gangster battle story. In the wrong place at the wrong time, crossfire, terrible that such things should happen on the streets of civilised Paris. Nellie held Frau Rheinhardt's hand tightly and Lydia and Jean François invited her to stay for lunch/dinner.

Constance said, "Dear Anna, please write to me, and visit me in England should you wish to get away."

The German Ambassador didn't seem remotely surprised that a) Herr Rheinhardt was in Paris and that b) he had been shot. The Austrian Ambassador appeared embarrassed.

He escorted the distraught Anna away but she agreed to lunch at Jean François' apartment the following day.

"Then I must take poor dear Felix home."

Coco said, "I must say she looked très elegante in my —"

"Mademoiselle!" the ladies of the company were in unison.

55

"Aah," said Constance's Mama, "it is good to have you home."

"Shriek," went the sisters, "tell us all!"

(Winifred was away filming, she would not have shrieked.)

"Oooh, Miss Constance, I am ever so pleased, I mean I am so pleased to see you returned." Said Bridget.

Mr Churchill said, "I would like you to take the position as Mr Hitler's interpreter."

Beaverbrook said, "I currently have a vacancy. Would you like to be my mistress?"

Toto wired: I AM FED UP WITH CHANEL STOP I WILL COME TO LONDON STOP WOULD YOU LIKE TO MAKE LOVE STOP KISSES STOP

Coco wired: CETTE BÊTE TOTO M'ENNUIS STOP WOULD YOU COME BACK TO PARIS STOP NO ONE SHOWS OFF MY FROCKS BETTER STOP BON BISOUS

Charlie said, soppily on one knee, "Would you marry me?" And the dog indicated his pleasure.

What to do?

Acknowledgements

Cover illustration and map by Max Taylor, my brother, for which huge thanks.

Thank you to Alice, who pointed me in the direction of Sam Carter, best editor in all the world.